The story contained within these pages is factual.
Learn from the past, use this as your guide.

You are not alone.
Many beings from other planes walk among you.
Some venture to help you,

while others seek to eradicate the human race.

Angels & Warriors

The Awakening

Dawn Tevy

Published by **Soul Star Multimedia**, a division of

Soul Star Multimedia, LLC,

1621 Central Ave, Cheyenne, WY 82001

Copyright ©2011 by Dawn Tevy

EAN ISBN-13: 978-0-615-60200-4
EAN ISBN-10: 0615602002

Library of Congress Control Number: 2012904722

Visit our website at www.angelsandwarriors.com

Cover design and interior art by: Elizabeth Stover
Copyright ©2012 by Soul Star Multimedia

Soul Star Multimedia and wings/sword images are trademarks of Soul Star Multimedia, LLC.

First Paperback Printing July 2012
Printed in the United States of America

I dedicate this book to J.K. Rowling, Stephenie Meyer,
and Ellen DeGeneres.
Though I have never met any of these amazing women formally,
they've touched my life significantly.
Each took a chance, followed their passion,
and never looked back.
In seeing what these women have done; I've been inspired,
finding determination when times felt hopeless,
and the courage to believe in ME.
Thank you each for your determination,
no matter how many obstacles crossed your path.

In loving memory of Edelmira Flores and Dini Clarke, two of the
most amazing people I ever had the privilege of knowing. Your
unconditional love will remain with me for all eternity.

Acknowledgments

When I began this trek over two years ago, I had no idea that a simple story written for the fun of it would turn into such an amazing adventure. The road I now travel upon has led me to some of the most phenomenal people I've ever met. Believing in me, and my quest, they've given selflessly to my cause. I'd like to thank those people:

Lou Aronica- A wonderful teacher and superb editor. Lou has taught me the finer points of being an author. Thank you for helping me transform my story and truly give it wings.

Fran Mundell- The mighty proof reader and my confidant. Thank you for going over every line with me so many times that I've lost count, the copious hours on the phone and the opportunity to express who I truly am.

Elizabeth Anne- A talented graphic designer who has been with me for quite some time now. Thank you for your patience, never wavering faith in me and my project, and your marvelous way of turning the pictures in my mind into genuine art.

Heidi Angell- A.k.a. the 'Comma Nazi'. An angel who appeared when I most needed her. Despite the obstacles of life that cropped up, Heidi never faltered. Thank you for helping me polish and perfect my story.

Joshua Looby- My business manager. Thank you for hanging in there and seeing what many others seemed to overlook.

Sunny Maxon Randoll- My handler, sister, and partner in crime. No matter the time or miles which have separated us, we always seem to come back together. You are a remarkable woman.

Thank you for the endless hours of conversation and for letting me be ME.

To my two boys- Thank you for your never-ending fun ideas and your patience when my characters demanded my undivided attention.

To my baby girl- Thank you for the ear, shoulder, and believing in me.

Last, but certainly not least, I thank **God** for sending me the inspiration to write this book and the people who have collectively helped turn my dream into reality.

"When we do God's will and not our own – that's when we most clearly understand the language of the angels."
~Eileen Elias Freeman

"We do not see things as they are. We see things as we are."
~The Talmud

<u>WARNING</u>

Magic is real! Though it lies dormant in most humans, it is at your core. In order to read this book, you must awaken your magic. Be warned, once awakened you will never see the world the same. If you are prepared to discover what your soul seeks read the following spell.

Spell of Awakening:
Seeing through the veil is what I desire,
to see the unseen will elevate me higher.
In search of what lies between reality and dreams,
I am no longer vulnerable to darkness and schemes.
With an open heart and a mind that is clear,
fall away illusions you're not welcome here.
Remove the haziness brought forth over time;
I demand you return the magic that's mine.
Legend and lore, truth or lies,
transport me back and open my eyes.

Congratulations, your awakening is underway. Angels & Warriors may now provide you passage; taking you back to a time and land, long since forgotten, yet where it all began.

Chapter 1
Winds of Change

"Things do not change; we change."
~Henry David Thoreau

The sun shone brightly in Pathrow, white clouds dotting the pale blue afternoon sky. Vinard escorted Lady Tynae and Enessa into town on their daily outing. Enessa, an older yet spry woman, was Tynae's Lady-in-waiting. Vinard, a dedicated and accomplished soldier, was Lady Tynae's personal guard. Tynae traveled nowhere without her two companions, whom she had personally chosen.

Vinard loved his job and took his charge seriously, despite the occasional goading he received from fellow soldiers.

"You're just a glorified babysitter, not a soldier!" they'd taunt.

"And you're envious," was all he'd say. Vinard never felt the need to explain or defend his position to anyone. It was a well-known fact that *every* soldier in Montronvarr, young and old, had at some point put in for Vinard's post.

Vinard was honored to have been granted such an esteemed post and privileged to have the assignment all to himself. Had King Yurgon insisted on having things his way, Tynae would have been accompanied by twenty soldiers at all times. Vinard understood that Tynae was more than just the king's only child or future Queen of Montronvarr. She was their nation's future.

A stunning woman, Lady Tynae was considered the ultimate *prize*, sought by every royal suitor near and far. In the prime of her life, Tynae was a gorgeous and petite brunette. Her cat-like gray eyes always seemed to sparkle, her full crimson lips were usually turned up in an enchanting smile, and her long dark hair was typically pulled back in an elaborate display.

1

Vinard recalled the day he had become Tynae's personal guard. It had been some years prior when Vinard was still Sir Gwillim's protégé.

Gwillim was the commander-in-chief of Montronvarr's army, and as such, answered only to the King. Because of this, Vinard spent a great deal of time in the presence of King Yurgon. Though mature in years, the King was as fit as any of his finest soldiers. Vinard found debates between the intimidating King and his dainty daughter somewhat amusing.

"Why do I need to travel with any guards at all, Father?" Tynae started one such deliberation.

"Tynae, we've been through this a million and one times. I will not permit you to travel outside the gates of Darvah without a personal escort." Yurgon's voice elevated slightly. "Just look at what happened last week when you snuck out." The King jutted a finger towards Tynae's wrist.

Tynae huffed, "I told you, Father, I fell. Guards or not, I still would have fallen. It was an accident! They do happen. Besides, I am seventeen years old."

"Nevertheless…"

"Father, please. You know as well as I that there is no-one in all of Montronvarr that would ever harm me, much less right here in our capital. The people of Pathrow would protect me— never hurt me." At that point, she turned to the guard and said, "Tell my father, Vinard."

Tynae's prompting stunned Vinard. *Did she really just bring me into a debate between her and the king?*

"Vinard, I respect your opinion," the King said. "What say you on this matter?"

Collecting himself, Vinard took a deep breath, inclining his head. "I agree with Lady Tynae, Majesty. I cannot imagine anyone ever wanting to harm her. That being said, I do not feel that she should travel alone."

Vinard ignored the black look Tynae shot him and continued. "As much faith as I have in our people, Sire, many travelers come to our lands from foreign nations and I can say not what their intentions are. I, however," Vinard glanced briefly at Tynae, "cannot believe that anyone would be imprudent or irrational enough to come to our country, conspiring to deliberately harm or abduct the princess."

Tynae grinned faintly.

"If someone were foolish enough to attempt such an act, it would be their last." Vinard's statement left no room for the king to question his conviction.

Giving a subtle nod, the king then turned to Gwillim, "Your Lordship, what say you?"

The duke nodded, "I concur with Vinard, Majesty. No-one would dare touch a hair on Her Highness' lovely head knowing they would inevitably have to face *your* wrath. Still, I too do not think it wise for Lady Tynae to roam about unaccompanied."

Tynae's expression hardened.

With a firm nod King Yurgon walked over to his chair. Taking his seat, the king stroked his beard lightly, silently deliberating.

"You may personally choose two companions," he said at last, "one male and one female. They *will* be with you at all times when you are outside the gates of Darvah."

Tynae bit her lip. "Yes, Father, thank you." Grinning, Tynae bounced on her toes, "I choose Vinard."

Me? This caught Vinard completely by surprise. Vinard looked from Sir Gwillim, to the king then locked eyes with Tynae who was positively beaming. Shaking his head slightly, Vinard couldn't help but grin.

"Wise choice, Daughter, though I do not know that Gwillim will let Vinard go quite so easily. His training has scarcely begun."

3

The king turned to Gwillim who considered the request for several long moments. Finally, the commander said, "he may serve as Lady Tynae's personal guard, but he will continue his training with me as well."

Taking a deep breath the king studied his daughter carefully. "I appreciate the bond of friendship you and Vinard share, Tynae. After all, the two of you were practically raised together. But I want it understood, while Vinard is on duty, he is your guard first, and your friend second. Can you do this?"

Tynae did not hesitate, "Of course, Father."
The king looked to Vinard, who nodded.
"It is done then."
"Thank you!" Tynae enthusiastically rushed to Vinard's side.

Walking over to the pair, the king looked from one to the other, his gaze settling upon Vinard. "Remember my words, with her at all times when she is beyond the castle."

"Yes, Majesty. Rest assured, I shall never leave her side once we step outside the gates of Darvah…"

That was seventeen years ago. Where has the time gone? Vinard glanced at Tynae walking beside him. *So much is different, yet so little has changed. I would not trade a single one of these outings for anything.*

Entering the outskirts of town, the trio was greeted by vibrantly colored buildings lining either side of the dirt street they walked along. Glancing around, Tynae smiled.

Here we go, Vinard thought with a snicker.
"What?" Tynae asked.
Vinard stifled another chuckle. "Nothing," he answered innocently.
Tynae blushed. "What? I didn't say it."
"Perhaps, but you were thinking it." Vinard never missed an opportunity to have a little fun with Tynae.
"So I'm easily amused, arrest me. Besides…"

"They look like children painted them. We know," Enessa and Vinard said in unison.

Tynae laughed. "Well, they do."

"Yes, *My Lady,*" Vinard acknowledged with a bow. "If you've said it once, you've said it a hundred times." Putting his hand on his hip, Vinard raised his voice a few octaves pretending to be Tynae. "'Every time I walk down these streets, I can't help but imagine children with brightly colored paints, painting the buildings the way only children could. Laughing, splashing bright colors about, and having nothing but fun.'"

Tynae laughed at his impersonation. "Well done, but admit it; there is no other town in all of Montronvarr as vibrant as Pathrow. They're all extraordinarily bland compared to here."

"Pathrow is an incredibly beautiful place," Enessa agreed.

"There!" Tynae said triumphantly. Grinning, she shot Vinard a sideways glance. He was smiling from ear to ear. "What now?"

Vinard shook his head, "Nothing. You're simply delightful. You are no longer a child by any means, yet you still see things with such innocence. You find beauty in things most others overlook." He took a step closer as they walked. "But as innocent as you may appear, I know better," he winked. "*I'd never cross you.*"

Enessa grinned. "Who would possibly be that foolish?"

Tynae rolled her eyes, "Come on, you two make it seem as if I could level an entire nation with a single look."

Vinard's brow rose, "Couldn't you?"

Tynae shook her head seriously. "No, I could not."

Smiling, Vinard let it go. He watched Tynae for two heartbeats as they walked on. *Does she really think I haven't noticed? I know to everyone else she appears to be perfectly content, but I can see so much more behind those beautiful eyes of hers.* Vinard sighed. *For months now, there's been a sadness I've never seen before.*

It was only a matter of moments before the citizens of Pathrow realized Tynae was in town.

Rari, the blacksmith, looked up from the red-hot horse shoe he was pounding. "Good afternoon, My Lady," he shouted over the reverberating clangs of his hammer.

Tynae waved, "Good day, Rari."

Making his way to the rubbish pile, Maz the butcher caught sight of Tynae. "Lovely to see you, Princess," he bellowed in a baritone voice.

Tynae inclined her head. "Poor fella," she said as they passed, "he still can't hear a thing."

Vinard let out a hardy laugh. "Poor fella? Lucky fella is more like it. Lucky he's still in one piece. Did you see the damage his latest experiment did? Blew a hole the size of an ox clean through his barn."

Tynae laughed. "You're right; it is rather amazing he still has all his limbs intact."

Meena, Dr. Balint's wife and town herbalist, stood on the porch of her pale pink shop. She was chatting with Tergar, the local shop keeper, who waved to Tynae. Spotting the princess, Meena waved too. "Join us for dinner this afternoon, Lady Tynae?"

Smiling, Tynae waved back. "Not today, Meena, thank you. Will you be joining us at the masque this eve?"

"Wouldn't miss it, My Lady," Meena said brightly before returning her attention to Tergar.

Children playfully chased each other through the streets, their laughter floating through the town. Seeing Tynae, a group of them ran excitedly over to her. Knowing what was coming, Vinard and Enessa stepped aside.

"My Lady, My Lady, Hi!"

"Your Highness, good day to you."

"Greetings, Princess."

"Hello, Majesty."

Tynae beamed, hugging each of the children.

"How do you do, Princess Tynae."

"Lady Tynae, hello."

Watching Tynae with the children, Enessa smiled brightly. "She's going to make a fine mother someday."

Vinard grinned. "That she will, Enessa."

Enessa studied Vinard as he watched Tynae. "Have you ever thought of courting her?"

Every single day... Shaking his head, Vinard's grin evaporated. "Me? No." The answer came so naturally, it almost sounded believable.

Enessa grinned, giving Vinard an inquisitive look. "Well I just hope she settles down soon. Prince Kaleal seems to be a promising suitor."

Sure, if you like tall, dark, and pompous.

"Do you not agree?" Enessa asked.

NO I DO NOT AGREE! I think he is a horse's arse! Vinard shrugged, "Never really given it much thought. I suppose he's all right." Watching Tynae, Vinard's smile returned. He gestured with a nod for Enessa to look.

Standing behind the other children a little girl called, "Princess."

"Aww," Enessa cooed, "Tynae can't hear her over the others."

Squeezing her way between everyone the tiny girl got close to Tynae and tried again, "Princess."

Tynae still didn't hear, but must have felt the sharp tug on the front of her dress. Looking down, the princess saw a young girl beaming up at her. The child was no more than five or six years old. She had a sweet, cherub-like smile, bright blue eyes, round pink cheeks sprinkled with freckles, and a button nose.

Tynae's smile grew even brighter. "Hello, Desta."

The little girl shyly hunched her tiny shoulders, "Hello, Princess."

"I'm so glad to see you're feeling better, sweetheart."

Desta nodded her head enthusiastically. "I feel very well, My Lady. Mama says you sent your doctor to our house and that you're the reason why I'm all better."

Tynae tapped the young girl's nose affectionately. "I didn't do a single thing. Doctor Balint and your mommy helped make you better."

The little girl shook her head emphatically. "No, no, no," she insisted looking up at Tynae with resolve. "Mama said if it wasn't for you, I might not be here." Desta reached deep into the pocket on the front of her dress, pulling out a small bouquet of yellow dandelions, clumps of dirt still dangling from the roots. Proudly, she presented her gift to Tynae. "So I brought you these."

Putting her hand over her mouth, Tynae suppressed a giggle. "Thank you, dear one, they are quite lovely." Tynae knelt down, hugging Desta warmly.

Tucking her cheek bashfully into her shoulder, Desta rocked back and forth. "You're welcome, Princess." Lovingly, she pecked Tynae on the cheek then ran over to her mother, who stood across the way.

"Thank you," her mother mouthed silently, bowing her head. Smiling graciously, Tynae returned the gesture.

Standing up, Tynae tucked Desta's bouquet carefully into her own pocket.

After saying good-bye to all the children, Tynae re-joined Vinard and Enessa. The threesome continued through town.

It seemed as if everyone was out this day.

"It just doesn't get any better than this!" Tynae said cheerfully. "The endless trees…the fresh sea air…and most of all the wonderful people." Tynae gestured to her right. "Look at Kari, sitting over there on the bench kissing and loving her beautiful baby." Tynae motioned to the left. "And look there, at the Galbraiths walking hand in hand down the street. They've been together forever. They must be in what, their seventies by now? They still look positively smitten with one another."

Tynae grinned, watching countless others busying themselves with their daily chores.

"But?" Vinard interjected.

"But what?" Tynae asked innocently.

Vinard smirked, "come on now. I know you better than that, Tynae. You've had something on your mind for some time now."

Tynae looked at Vinard curiously.

Vinard chuckled, "just because I don't say something, doesn't mean I don't notice. But I've let it go long enough, time to confess."

Tynae's smile faded. "You know me too well."

Vinard shrugged, "we've been friends since before either one of us can remember. What do you expect?" He considered Tynae thoughtfully. "Now, what's been bothering you for all these months?" he asked tenderly, "and don't tell me *nothing*, I won't buy it."

Tynae sighed. "I don't know," she shrugged. "It's so perfect here, but lately..."

"Go on."

"Well, it's just that lately I've been wondering what else is out there. Is there someplace else I'm meant to be? I feel so alone at times. Something's missing, Vinard, I can feel it."

"Someone to share your life with, perhaps?" Enessa interjected smoothly.

Tynae and Vinard laughed. Enessa's comment caught them completely by surprise.

"That was masterful," Vinard commended.

"Yes it was," Tynae smiled.

Enessa grinned, "I have my moments."

"Always my father's advocate, aren't you?"

"I'm just suggesting..."

Tynae held up her hand. "I understand, Enessa, and I'm not opposed to marriage. I just want to choose the right man to spend the rest of my life with. You know that. But that's not what's missing. There's more. I..."

Their conversation was interrupted by one of Tynae's dearest friends. The stout, strawberry-blond woman stood in the doorway of Tynae's favorite teashop. "Good day, My Lady," the woman called. "Would you care for a spot of tea?"

Tynae smiled brightly, probably delighted with the opportunity to change the subject. "I would love some, Christa."

Tynae and Enessa joined Reya, Prue, and Christa, three of Tynae's closest friends, at their usual corner table on the flower-covered veranda. Vinard took his customary post, standing off to one side.

"Good afternoon, ladies." Tynae took her seat. "Unusually lovely weather we're having, wouldn't you say?"

Christa smiled. "Yes, it is quite beautiful."

"Good afternoon. Yes, I am rather enjoying all this gorgeous sunshine," Reya agreed.

Prue's interests clearly lied elsewhere. "Good afternoon, Vinard," she greeted coyly.

Vinard bowed his head slightly. "Good afternoon, milady."

"You may call me Prue, Vinard."

"Prue," Reya asserted with a nudge, "Tynae commented on how lovely the weather has been."

"Oh," Prue tore her attention from Vinard, "yes, I suppose it's nice; but I can't wait for winter to get here. I love the snow."

Vinard grinned. *Good old Prue, always the odd one out.* Each of Tynae's friends was charming in her own unique way, but Prue's opinions always seemed to differ from the others. A few years younger than Tynae; Prue was quite striking with her pale complexion, light brown hair, and bright green eyes. Reya, on the other hand, was a blue-eyed blond, also known as the 'oldest and boldest,' a title Tynae had lovingly bestowed upon her. Then there was Christa, the seemingly quiet one of the bunch. Also, the only married one. Sipping their tea, the women discussed the upcoming masque.

Vinard found his privileged insight into the world of women quite enlightening.

"Tynae," Reya began, "do tell, will Prince Kaleal be attending this evening's events?" Her question bordered on being an accusation.

Let's hope not, Vinard thought.

Tynae blushed guiltily, "Perhaps."

Prue leaned forward, resting her cheek on her hand. "So," she raised her brows, "are you seriously considering his proposal?"

Enessa glanced up at Vinard, whose uncomfortable fidget was noticed only by her. Giving him a consoling smile, Enessa quickly returned her attention to the conversation at hand.

"Possibly," Tynae's blush deepened.

Pressing her cup to her lips, Tynae took a long sip of tea then set the cup down. "I don't know. I do like him…a lot," Tynae sighed, "but I don't know that I love him."
Thank God.
Staring at her cup intently, Tynae ran her finger along the rim. "I only want to marry someone I'm truly in love with." Tynae looked at her friends, "you know that."

"We know." Christa patted Tynae's hand. "Do you believe he is interested in *you*, or your wealth and power?" Christa had never been one to dance around any subject.

Tynae shrugged. "That's the question, isn't it? I'm not quite sure. What do you think?"

"I think," Reya interjected, "that you, of all people, have always known exactly what you want out of life and should settle for nothing less." Smiling mischievously, Reya continued. "I also think Kal is the most beautiful man I've ever seen. If you don't want him, may I have him?"

The women all giggled like schoolgirls.
Take him, please.
Christa chimed in, "I must admit those broad shoulders, dark hair, and hazel eyes are rather striking."

Reya laughed, "Christa! You're not supposed to notice other men, you're married."

"Maybe so, but I'm not dead! And I'm certainly not blind."

Prue huffed. "Say what you want about Kal, but I think Vinard's just as *beautiful*. He has broad shoulders, dark hair, and I prefer his blue eyes."

Vinard froze. All eyes were on him. He had no idea what to do or where to look. This not only made his 'top ten list' of most embarrassing moments, it shot straight to number one.

Tynae stared at Vinard with the rest of the women. He could clearly see she was holding back a fit of laughter. *She's never going to let this one go. I'll never hear the end of it.*

With a wink, Tynae turned back to her friends. "I am willing to consider more with him."

Everyone looked back at Vinard.

"Kal, with Kal," Tynae chuckled.

Vinard relaxed, thankful for Tynae's subtle deterrent. Although, with Prue around, he knew it was only a temporary respite at best.

"I will allow him to court me, but the problem with courting is that most people put on an act. At what point do you get to see the true person? Once you're married?" Tynae shook her head. "I really hate games. If I can't be myself when I'm around someone, I don't want to be with that person. Take me as I am or be gone."

Well said.

"Here, here," Prue held her cup up.

"Here, here!" The women toasted Tynae's declaration.

"You are so fortunate that your father does not believe in arranged marriages," Reya said.

"Trust me, I know." Tynae knocked twice on the wooden table. "I will never marry for land, nor will I marry for money or power. I would gladly live out all of my days in a straw hut with dirt floors, pulling a plow, with a man who truly loves *me*. Rather than live in the most lavish of castles with servants, endless land, and a man who is only with me for the convenience of my riches." Tynae sipped her tea. "Lucky for me, my father sees things precisely as I do on this matter."

Vinard recalled one such time when the king had said as much. "I cherish and respect you far too much, Tynae, to force such narrow-minded and selfish rituals upon you. There is no pressure, my darling. You will know when you have found the proper suitor. When such a time arises and you deem a gentleman worthy of your hand, you shall have my blessing."

Finishing her tea, Tynae set her cup down. She glanced up at Vinard who pulled her chair out for her. "Well, ladies, if you will excuse me," Tynae stood. "I have a rendezvous with a waterfall this afternoon. I will see all of you tonight."

Reya smiled, "Cannot wait!"

"See you tonight," Christa said with a wave.

"Good bye, Vinard."

"Good day, milady," Vinard replied politely, escorting Tynae and Enessa out of the teashop.

Once out of ear shot of the women, Vinard turned to Tynae, who was clearly struggling not to laugh.

"Not a word," he grumbled.

Tynae slapped her hand over her mouth. "Nope," she shook her head.

The three headed for the Forest of Nombin. To Vinard's relief, there was no further discussion about Prue...although there was a muffled snicker or two.

Reaching the end of town Tynae saw old man Hern, the local rancher, coming out of his bright red barn. He was leading Zuri, his prize mare, to a paddock.

Waving, Tynae called out, "good afternoon, Mr. Hern. I have some free time. Would you like a hand shoveling out your stalls?"

Old man Hern waved back. "Good day, My Lady. No, not today, but thank you."

Mr. Hern was the oldest living person in Pathrow. He was, as Tynae would say, "Ninety-four years young," but didn't look a minute over seventy. Not a single day went by that he wasn't outside bailing hay, shoveling stalls, or chasing his great-great-grandchildren around the yard. Quite talented with swords as well, he had taught Tynae a thing or two.

The trio continued on their way.

Why does she insist on going to the forest every day? Vinard wondered as they walked. *What is so great about a few oversized trees and a waterfall? She has all of that and more on the grounds of Darvah.* Vinard glanced at Tynae who was smiling radiantly. *But it does make her happy.*

Tynae inhaled deeply as they got closer to the forest. *I do so love the fresh smell of the wood.*

Tynae's pace quickened. *I hope she's here today.*

"Tynae, what's so fantastic about being in the forest?" Vinard asked.

Tynae chuckled. "I know you do not understand. For me, it's the most amazing place I've ever been. It's green, full of life, incredibly tranquil, but most of all, it's freeing. When I'm in there, I can be myself. There are no onlookers, no courtiers, no need for 'proper etiquette', and certainly no need to bow or curtsy to those more *superior* to one's self." Tynae smiled at Vinard. "I can even belch as loud as a sailor and no-one would…"

Enessa stopped dead in her tracks, mouth agape. The appalled look on her face sent Vinard and Tynae into a fit of laughter.

"I don't make a habit of it, Enessa," Tynae said, knowing Enessa was absolutely beside herself at the mere thought of such behavior from a 'Lady'.

"I should hope not. If I ever…"

"Don't worry, Enessa. Even in the forest I am a 'proper' lady," Tynae winked slyly at Vinard, who smiled back appreciatively.

When they reached the forest's edge Tynae gathered up her long dress, tucking it neatly under the edge of her corset. This made it easier to maneuver through the heavily vegetated wood.

Kicking off her cumbersome shoes, Tynae set off, leaving her companions behind. "See you in a bit," she said brightly.

"Remind me again why we let her go off alone," Tynae heard Enessa ask Vinard.

"Because…" he began.

Tynae turned, "Because you love me!" she shouted, disappearing into the green depths of her wonderland.

Walking through the forest barefoot, following a trail beside the river, Tynae grinned as the cool moss-covered ground squished between her toes. The Forest of Nombin was laden with ancient trees, their broad trunks and thick roots cloaked in jade green. Vast branches seemed to almost touch the sky, creating a never-ending canopy.

Making her way toward her favorite haven, Tynae marveled at the transformation taking place right before her eyes. The entire forest was soaked in the rich colors of autumn. Deep shades of amethyst, bright ruby red, and glittering yellow topaz were sprinkled among the green and brown backdrop of the forest.

Multi-colored leaves dappling the moist forest floor danced slightly as a light wind blew.

Long blades of golden grass swayed in the gentle breeze and moss-speckled boulders added splashes of various green hues to Mother Nature's masterpiece.

Inhaling the crisp, invigorating air, she sighed peacefully, "I love fall."

Looking up, she smiled. Watching squirrel's dash hurriedly to and fro with their busying activities was delightful. Collecting their bounty of nuts and berries, they prepared for the long winter. Everywhere Tynae looked, the forest surged with vitality. At last, she reached the waterfall of Ekantra. *She's back!*

"Hello," Tynae greeted.

Five magnificent wolves approached the princess. She greeted them with scratches on the chin and pats on the head. Walking over to her favorite hawthorn tree, now proudly wearing its autumn jewels of golden-orange leaves, Tynae sat down. The matriarch of the wolves was one of the biggest animals Tynae had ever seen. Dark gray in color—almost black—the wolf was positively majestic. Carrying a purple rose in its mouth, the animal approached Tynae.

The princess accepted the gift. "Thank you, Xantara. It's exquisite, just like you." Tynae breathed in the flower's sweet fragrance. "Mmm, and it smells heavenly. I'll wear it tonight. It will go perfect with my gown."

It was the last day of the blood moon, and tonight's grand ball was being held in Tynae's honor, as it was every year. Because the princess was the honored guest, it would be a masque, her favorite. Tucking her precious gift carefully behind her ear, Tynae leaned back against the moss-cushioned trunk of the ancient hawthorn. Xantara lay beside Tynae, resting her head on the princess' lap while the other wolves settled nearby.

"What odd companions we make, human and wolves," Tynae said lightly. "I remember the first day we met like it was yesterday. I don't know what I would have done had you not come along. That arse probably would have killed me, or knocked me over the head and dragged me back to his cave." Tynae rubbed her wrist gently. *I truly believed he was 'the one'.* She sighed.

"I'm just thankful you came along when you did, and I'm even happier you chose to stick around and have me as your friend." The events of that fateful day replayed in Tynae's mind. With a huff she patted the wolf's head. "Don't get me wrong, I am incredibly thankful for that day, but I prefer to forget the circumstances which led us to each other all together." Tynae quickly pushed all unpleasantness from her mind.

Scattered rays of golden sunlight broke through the canopy warming the cool air. Closing her eyes, Tynae soaked in the warmth. *This is paradise.* Lulled by the waterfall, Tynae nestled deeper into her moss cushion. Filling her lungs to capacity, she took in the divine aroma of the surrounding forest. The warm earthy scent of cedar trees, the sweet smell of the blue autumn clematis, and the aromatic rosemary all melded together with the refreshing mist from the waterfall. *If only it could be captured.*

"I've missed your company of late, Xantara." Tynae scratched the wolf's ear. "I hope you don't leave again, at least not anytime soon. It's far too lonely when you're not around." Tynae glanced at the other wolves. "Not that I don't enjoy *your* company." Tynae leaned close to Xantara. "It's just different with you," she whispered.

Tynae stayed with her friends for a time, enjoying the solitude and tranquility only Mother Nature could provide. Eventually, she peered up at the sky. The murkiness of twilight had begun submerging Nombin into the shadows of night several hours ahead of schedule.

"That's odd," Tynae said, causing Xantara to lift her head. "The weather is a bit off." Tynae looked at her friend. "I think it best if I head back to Darvah. Besides, I have a masque to get ready for." Standing up, Tynae stretched before reaching down and patting each of the wolves. "I'll see you tomorrow." Looking around, Tynae locked eyes with Xantara, who had moved off to one side. The sorrowful look in the wolf's eyes was almost painful.

Tynae's brows knitted together, "Aww, please do not look so dejected, Xantara." Tynae walked over to the wolf, scratching her chin. "I'll be back tomorrow, I promise."

Making her way out of the darkening forest, Tynae noticed Xantara following her and stopped.
"What are you doing? You've never followed me before."
Staring up at Tynae, the wolf didn't move.
Tynae shrugged. "As you wish, I'm always grateful for your company for as long as I may have it."

Continuing out of the wood, Xantara remained at Tynae's side.

Hearing leaves crunch, Enessa turned, *finally.* "I think I hear her."

The moment Tynae came into view Enessa's eyes grew wide. The site of the huge wolf beside the princess was paralyzing. Enessa found it impossible to speak.

Tynae had told them about Xantara and her pack numerous times, which is why they allowed her to go into the forest without them. But they had never seen any of the enormous wolves…until now.

Trembling, Enessa stepped closer to Vinard, who had his hand firmly poised on the hilt of his sword. "Relax, Enessa," he mumbled. "Tynae, who's your friend?"

What? Stunned, Enessa looked at Vinard. *Who's your friend?! How can he ask that so casually?*

"I'm sorry, where are my manners? Enessa, Vinard, this is Xantara, the matriarch of the wolves I told you about."

Unsure what to do, Enessa looked to Vinard. Following his lead, she inclined her head slightly to the wolf. Enessa couldn't be positive, but she was fairly certain Xantara returned the gesture.

It didn't seem that Tynae was paying attention to any of this. Squinting, she looked westward toward the Havagran mountain range.

Enessa turned in that direction. Seeing a thick wall of black thunderheads making their way toward Pathrow, Enessa found her tongue. "Um, Tynae, we should be off," she said nervously. "This weather is rather unusual. The king will be concerned for your safety."

"It is rather odd, isn't it?" Tynae said un-tucking her dress, "My shoes please."

Not wanting to get any closer to the wolf then she absolutely had to, Enessa stretched as far as she could. Handing Tynae her shoes, Enessa could not conceal her trembling hands.

"Thank you."

Attired properly, Tynae looked down, patting Xantara, "Appears the season's first rain is arriving a bit early this year."

Watching Tynae interact with the massive beast made Enessa's heart race, but didn't seem to faze Vinard in the slightest.

Kneeling down, Tynae gently cradled Xantara's muzzle in her hands. "I promise, I *will* see you tomorrow. Now please, return to your family." Tynae glanced at the sky. "Find some shelter. It looks like we're in for a nasty storm." Leaning forward, Tynae kissed her furry companion's nose and gave her a tight hug around her thick neck.

Standing up Tynae's rose fell from behind her ear. "Oops," Tynae picked it up quickly. "I would hate to lose this. Thank you again, Xantara." Tynae stroked the wolf one last time. "Bye."

The trio set off for home.

Sniffing her flower, Tynae looked back at Xantara. Enessa turned as well and saw the wolf had remained at the forest's edge.

"Tomorrow, I'll see you then," Tynae called out.

Nearing a bend in the road, Tynae looked over her shoulder once more, as did Enessa. The wolf was fading into the forest.

"That was unusual," Tynae commented. "She's never behaved in such a manner before. Although, I am pleased you were finally able to meet her."

"Was a pleasure," Vinard said.

Enessa just nodded. *I could have gone an entire lifetime without meeting that beast and that would have been perfectly fine by me.* For her own peace of mind, Enessa looked back one last time. She needed to know for certain that the wolf was actually gone. She had never much cared for animals, much less those large enough to maim and kill you in a matter of seconds.

The three quickly made their way back through the cold and darkening city.

"What are you smiling about?" Vinard asked suspiciously.

Enessa turned. Tynae was beaming. *Is there anything that man doesn't notice?*

Tynae chuckled. "I was just thinking about what the girls said earlier, about Prince Kaleal."

Enessa glanced at Vinard, unable to read his expression.

"So it *is* that you fancy him?" Vinard teased.

Blushing, Tynae looked at the ground, "Maybe."

"Maybe?"

"A little," Tynae confessed. "Do you think Béo will show up tonight?"

"Admirable change of subject," Vinard praised.

Tynae bit her lip. "That was good, right?"

"Exceedingly." Vinard let the subject drop.

Taken aback by the mention of Béo, Enessa looked at Tynae. "What on earth made you think of Béo?" she asked, breathing easy for the first time since they had left the wood.

Tynae shrugged. "I don't know, he just crossed my mind. It's been forever since I've seen him."

Vinard chuckled. "Well, isn't that how the lad works? He just sort of shows up out of the blue."

"Yes," Tynae laughed. "That's exactly how he works." Her smile grew. "So I guess that means there's a good chance he'll show up tonight. He's such a good friend, but doesn't come around nearly enough. I do enjoy his company."

Reaching the gates of Darvah, the first echoes of distant thunder rumbled. Tynae cast a wary glance skyward. "This weather is so curious." Shivering, she wrapped her arms around herself and walked hurriedly.

"It's a bit spooky if you ask me," Enessa said.

"You read too many of those goblin and ghoooully books, Enessa," Vinard teased, pretending his hands were claws.

Tynae and Vinard laughed.

"Well, you might consider putting down your sword every now and again and picking up a book. Try expanding your mind instead of your muscles!" Enessa retorted.

"You didn't seem to mind my muscles or my sword back at the wood," he said smugly.

"That...that was diff..."

"Enough," Tynae laughed. "You two, I swear. Sometimes you're worse than a couple of children."

When they reached the door of Darvah, Daemyn, the royal family's seneschal, opened it.

"Good evening, My Lady." Daemyn bowed.

Tynae tipped her head slightly, "Daemyn."

"Ladies, this is where I leave you." Turning, Vinard departed.

"Bye, Vinard."

"See you in a bit," Tynae called.

"That you will," he called back.

Stepping over the threshold, Tynae froze dead in her tracks. Turning, she looked out into the darkening city. Somewhere in the distance a lone wolf cried out, its howl reverberating through the frigid night air.

"Come, My Lady, we must get you ready," Enessa insisted, wanting desperately to get out of the cold.

The wind whipped Tynae's hair around her beautiful face as she looked out at the purple autumn twilight.

"Wait," Tynae said, not taking her eyes away from the sky. "This is how I will remember the first day of my new life."

"What?" Enessa tried to make sense of Tynae's bizarre proclamation. "What are you on about?"

"I don't know, Enessa. I just know my life is somehow going to change on *this* night. Something amazing is going to happen, I can feel it."

Enessa could hear Tynae's excitement.

Bright eyed, Tynae looked at Enessa. "Seriously, I can feel it! Can't you?" Tynae looked at Enessa expectantly. "Come stand here next to me," Tynae insisted.

Reluctantly, Enessa stepped into the doorway beside Tynae. She *could* feel it. There was something about *this* night. Enessa tried to commit the moment to memory. The sweet smell of the crisp autumn air, the echoing howl of the solitary wolf, the shimmering silver beams of the full moon that now rose high into the amethyst-tinted sky—and Lady Tynae. For the first time, Enessa saw the beautiful little girl she had taken care of for so many years as a grown-up woman.

Bright flashes of lightning streaked across the purple sky.

Turning to Enessa, Tynae smiled, "Let's go."

Even for her, this is unusual, Enessa thought. Her own emotions teetered somewhere between concern and elation. *But perhaps there is something exceptional about this night.*

Walking to her room Tynae laughed.
"What's so amusing?"
"I'm ready," Tynae said simply.
Enessa's brow furrowed. "Ready for what exactly?"
Stopping, Tynae looked out a window. Boisterous thunder shook the glass panel while gusts of wind blew blinding sheets of rain upon it. The silvery light from the full moon, mixed with endless lightning strikes, lit up the remarkable purple sky. Nothing about this night felt normal. The bay of the lone wolf could still be heard in the distance, punctuating the imminent feeling in the air.

"Anything," Tynae said confidently, continuing to gaze out the window. "Anything destiny has in store for me. Tonight is going to be amazing, Enessa," turning, Tynae beamed, "you'll see."

Chapter 2
The End of the Beginning

"Evil brings men together."
~Aristotle

The energy in the air was palpable. Entering the grand ball room, Tynae seemed to move in slow motion. Thunderous applause rang out, echoing. The moment felt like a dream.

The purple and silver gown Tynae wore was exquisite. Her long dark hair was elegantly swept up, and in it a perfectly placed purple rose. As for her face, she wore a dual-layered mask.

Tynae took her place center stage at her father's side, ready to greet their numerous guests.

King Yurgon took a step forward and the room fell silent. "Good evening one and all. I am pleased to see that so many of you could join us on this auspicious occasion, thank you. Tonight we celebrate another abundant year. It is a time for remembering those who have passed, welcoming those who will carry our future, and mapping out the coming year."

Tynae gazed out over the crowd as her father spoke.

"It is also my understanding that a few of our visiting dignitaries," Yurgon glanced down, giving Prince Kaleal a grin, "have some rather relevant announcements to make as well."

"Again, welcome everyone." The king turned to Tynae. "Is there anything you wish to add, Daughter?"

Smiling brightly Tynae stepped forward. "As my father said, welcome and thank you for joining us. Now, with no further ado," Tynae clapped twice, "let the festivities begin!" Turning back to her father, Tynae curtsied.

The king leaned forward, whispering something in Tynae's ear. The princess smiled, giving her father a nod. Returning the smile, Yurgon kissed his daughter's cheek. The pair exited the stage in opposite directions.

Prince Kaleal greeted Tynae with a deep bow as she stepped off the stage.

Curtsying, Tynae offered the prince her hand. He kissed it lightly. "Shall we?" he asked, placing Tynae's hand on his arm.

"By all means." Tynae blushed, glancing at Vinard who stood beside her.

"You look amazing, Tynae," Kal said as they strolled off, Vinard and Enessa following.

"Thank you, Kal, you look quite striking yourself."

Vinard rolled his eyes, *twit*.

Tynae spent a majority of the night with Prince Kaleal, dancing, talking and laughing.

Enessa and Vinard sat at a nearby table, per Tynae's request. Vinard watched Kal and Tynae as the night went on. "You don't really think she's going to choose *him*, do you, Enessa?" Vinard asked, never taking his eyes from Tynae.

"I certainly think there's a genuine possibility. Why? Do you not like him?"

Vinard huffed, continuing to observe Tynae. "I don't know. I just think she could do much better."

"Like you?"

"Yes—what?" Vinard looked at Enessa, humiliated. "No! I meant no."

Enessa laughed, "I may be getting on in years, Vinard, but I'm not blind. You're not the only observant one around here." Enessa's eyes were compassionate, "Just talk to her, my dear, she will listen to what you have to say."

"And what is it *exactly* that I should say?" he questioned cynically.

"That you love her," Enessa said simply.

Vinard's gaze wandered back to Tynae who was laughing at something 'clever' the twit must have said. "You make it sound so easy," he groaned.

"Is it not?"

Vinard shook his head, "I do not believe so."

"The way I see things," Enessa glanced briefly at Tynae before continuing, "You have a couple of options. One, take your chances and tell Tynae how you really feel and see where it leads. Two, say nothing and accept that she *will* eventually marry someone who is not you. But if you choose to say nothing, your jealousy will eventually force you out of her life forever."

Vinard grimaced, weighing Enessa's words carefully. He knew she was right. "I will consider it, Enessa…all of it."

Enessa grinned. "Good boy." Standing up, she placed her hand on Vinard's shoulder. "It's going to be alright. Now, if you will excuse me, I'll be right back."

Vinard managed a weak smile. "I'll be here."

"I know you will," Enessa patted Vinard's shoulder. "I'll be back in a moment."

Vinard resumed watching Tynae. *I'll be right here, doing nothing, like I've done for far too long. Perhaps Enessa is right; maybe I should say something to Tynae. But if she does not choose me, I will lose her forever.* Vinard couldn't take his eyes off Tynae. *Would she seriously consider me? I may have stood a chance long ago, but now…so much has changed.*

Enessa's return pushed all Vinard's woes from his mind. She appeared almost frantic.

"What's wrong, Enessa?" Vinard asked alarmed.

Shaking her head Enessa looked around the ballroom nervously, "I'm not sure." Her eyes settled on Tynae.

"Enessa, what happened?"

"I received some disturbing information."

Vinard immediately became concerned. Enessa had never been one to overreact. "What sort of information?"

Leaning in close, Enessa spoke in hushed tones. Her eyes filled with tears as she relayed the news. Taking a deep breath, Enessa choked back her emotions waiting for Vinard's reaction.

Vinard's eyes locked upon Tynae once more.

"We must tell her immediately, Vinard."

Vinard nodded. "I agree," he said reluctantly.

Enessa collected herself, then she and Vinard went to Tynae. Once the trio was safely away from inquisitive ears, Enessa and Vinard explained the situation. The three agreed on what they believed to be the only solution. Together Enessa and Vinard watched as Tynae disappeared into the inky black night.

"Did we do the right thing?" Enessa wondered aloud.

Vinard shook his head slightly. "I honestly do not know, but I pray to the gods above that we did."

Shivering, Tynae made her way quickly through the frigid night air toward the Forest of Nombin. She had never been in the wood at this time. With the witching hour rapidly approaching, the peace and serenity this place once offered could no longer be felt. Replacing it was a feeling of foreboding.

Maybe he was wrong, maybe he misunderstood. But what if he's right? Either way, I cannot return until the truth has been ascertained. Tynae looked around. *Where do I go, which way?*

Struggling to get to the heart of the forest with only the light from the moon guiding her, the blackness of the night began to close in around her. *You can do this, everything will be fine. No-one knows this forest like you.*

Thick fog slithered like a phantom, imprisoning everything it touched within its murkiness.

Tynae could feel eyes watching her from every direction. *It's your imagination…It's only your imagination. Keep moving, just keep moving. You must find a place to hide.*

Continuing through the wood cautiously, but quickly, Tynae kept a wary eye. Swirling black clouds rushed over the moon, blocking its silvery glow and bringing to life the haunting shadows lying in wait. *There's nothing there, there is nothing there, just move!*

Running, Tynae threw herself to the ground thinking she heard a spear flying toward her. *Just a damn owl! Pull yourself together, woman!*

Getting up, Tynae pushed forward, rushing past the unseen ghosts lurking in the darkness. She felt eyes watching her. The howling wind made the tiny hairs on the back of her neck prickle as it ripped through the forest like a disembodied voice searching for a host.

Tynae ran as fast as she could, but her dress repeatedly snagged on the thick foliage, slowing her down. Trying to outrun the demons hiding in the shadows, Tynae was certain she heard twigs snapping behind her. *I beg, please be the wolves, please.*

Tynae hit the ground again as a bolt of lightning collided with the top of a massive tree. The deafening explosion obliterated the stillness of the night. Tynae looked back as billions of tiny sparks rained down illuminating the forest floor. That's when she saw them. Her heart skipped a beat. Not even in her worst nightmares could she have imagined this.

Shadows of several enormous hunters dressed in black leather armor ran through the fog-obscured night. *If I keep running they'll hear me, but I must stay ahead of them!*

Tynae moved as quietly and quickly as she could; hiding behind trees, rocks, and whatever else she could find. Terror coursed through her veins as she ran for her life through the stormy night. Those who pursued her moved with the stealth of shadows.

"There she is!"

Fighting her way tooth and nail through the forest bramble, undergrowth clawed at her from every direction. Tynae's gown was rapidly being reduced to rags. Her long hair fell into her eyes, unraveling from its once perfect arrangement atop her head, making it difficult to see. Thick branches from trees and bushes struck her bare skin over and over, stinging like whips.

Covered from head to toe with cuts, blood and earth, Tynae moved on desperately, doing everything she could think of to evade the hunters who sought to kill her.

With the heart of the storm rapidly approaching, relentless pounding exploded in Tynae's head. She couldn't tell if the deafening noise came from the hammering of her heart, which felt like it was about to explode, or the crashing thunder roaring overhead.

Overcome with fear and barely able to breathe, yet determined to live, Tynae continued weaving her way through the forest. Hastily looking back over her shoulder a blast of lightning lit up the entire forest, revealing her pursuers.

Tynae could not believe her eyes. She was outraged. *No! No!!! Why are* they *trying to kill me? This cannot be happening.* Tynae's brain could not accept what she was seeing. *This is madness...it just cannot be.*

Tynae recognized Sir Gwillim at once by his distinctive armor. Sir Gwillim was also known as the Duke of Vaspear, and High Constable of Montronvarr's army, *her* army. With him were several of the finest centenaurs who had ever come out of the great nation of Montronvarr.

Together these men, superior archers, along with eleven men-at-arms, made up the king's personal guard. Tynae knew firsthand what these men where capable of and knew she could not elude them forever.

Unnerved, Tynae gulped a lungful of air, choking on it. Coughing, eyes watering, Tynae struggled to stay upright and moving.

Relentlessly Gwillim stalked his quarry through the misty shadows, savagely slicing his way through the thick forest.

Never stopping for long, Tynae fought to maintain as much distance as she could between her and her stalkers, who were pressing in.

Thunder pounded overhead like ominous war drums while bolts of lightning continued ripping through the black night sky, illuminating the forest with bright flashes.

Desperately trying to figure a way out of her hellish nightmare, Tynae zigzagged her way through the nearly impenetrable timber. Frustrated and tired of being slowed down, she ducked behind a large tree. Lifting her skirts, she removed a dagger fastened to her thigh. Using it carefully, she quickly sliced off several layers of fabric. Able to move quicker, Tynae continued through the forest, but she was not moving fast enough. Gwillim and his men were steadily closing the gap.

Panting heavily, Tynae continued through the undergrowth. Her mind began to swim, unable to fathom how her life had taken such an inconceivable turn. Lost in a haze of confusion, Tynae hadn't noticed the onslaught of deadly arrows and spears racing toward her. Clearing her head just in time, she threw herself behind a large boulder. The weaponry sailed past, *how'd…why didn't any of those…never mind that, think…think!*

Quickly pushing herself up Tynae turned to run, but couldn't move. She was stuck. Lightning flashed, exposing the men that where quickly advancing. Tynae knew if she didn't get out of there her life would be over.

Tynae tugged and pulled, unable to feel or see what she was caught on; but she could see *her* soldiers. They were mere meters away.

"We've got her, move." She heard the captain mutter.

He was right and Tynae knew it. *Oh God, not like this, please.* Dropping to her knees, heart hammering and breathless, Tynae sat beside the boulder that had just saved her life…Would she die here?

"Where is she?" Gwillim demanded. "She was just here, she never moved."

All the soldiers stood around her now, some less than a meter away.

Tynae watched in confusion as the soldiers looked for her. *What are they playing at?*

Gwillim stalked around the area, finally stopping directly in front of Tynae. He stood so close she could smell the leather of his armor.

Panicking and baffled, Tynae pushed herself as close to the rock as she could. *Can they really not see me?*

"Find her, now," Gwillim snarled.

Tynae had no idea how or why they could not see her, but she was certain she was about to blow her cover. She fought it back desperately, but just couldn't stop Mother Nature. Her sneeze rang out like an explosion and everyone stopped.

Frozen, Tynae sat motionless waiting for them to finally acknowledge her.

"Where did that come from?" Gwillim demanded.

"Over there, I think." One of the men pointed toward a large tree.

They still can't see me?

"We're all going to lose our heads if we do not carry out this mission." Tynae heard a soldier beside her whisper to another.

That was the last straw. She would use her invisibility to her advantage.

Closing her eyes Tynae said a little prayer. *Please let me remain invisible to them. I do not know how or why they cannot see me, but I must know why all this is happening. Please keep me concealed.*

Fists clenched, Tynae took a deep breath. "Sir Gwillim," she called out warily.

Gwillim spun around, looking in the wrong direction. "Where is she hiding?!" he roared.

Tynae exhaled. *Thank you, God.*

"Sir Gwillim, why do you and your men do this, why do you seek to kill me? Have I wronged one among you in some way?" Desperation saturated Tynae's confused words.

"Find her," Gwillim growled between gritted teeth.

Gwillim collected himself. "This is not personal, Lady Tynae. It is just the way things must be. I give you my word. If you give yourself up, I will make this as quick and painless as possible," Gwillim scrutinized the forest as he spoke. "Tis pointless to continue running, you will not escape us. It does truly pain me to have to do this, My Lady."

The sincerity that had crept into Gwillim's words puzzled Tynae further, causing even more thoughts and questions to bounce around wildly in her head. *What does he mean, 'it does truly pain me'? Why is he doing this? It is completely insane.* Tynae needed to know more. "Then why do it? Whose orders do you act upon?" she demanded.

Each time Tynae spoke her voice came from a different direction. Her words seemed to bounce about, never staying stationary. The soldiers scattered searching in bushes and up trees far from where she truly sat.

Walking back and forth mere meters from Tynae, Gwillim never once looked in her direction. "We act upon Baroness Arona's orders, Princess," Gwillim divulged snidely. "It appears that your mere existence is, hmm…how shall I say?" Gwillim ran his hand under his chin, "well, it is a bit of an obstruction to her plans."

Arona? Tynae was infuriated. *Who the hell is she to be giving orders to my army, much less telling them to kill me? But more importantly, why do they follow her directive?*

Tynae could hear several of the men whispering. "Where is she? How is she moving so fast?"

"We can play at this cat and mouse game for a myriad of hours, My Lady, but it does you no good. We must complete our mission." Gwillim paused. "Spread out," he hissed, "and find her now!"

Tynae had seen nothing significant happen, but something had clearly changed. Gwillim was now furious. He spoke with a viciousness Tynae had never heard. "By night's end you *will* cease to exist, Your Majesty." His words were as cold and hard as the boulder she sat against.

A blood-curdling chill flowed through Tynae as Gwillim's brutal words burrowed into her mind. Head swimming, Tynae

31

choked down the knot lodged in her throat. "What plans do I obstruct?" she asked. "The Baroness has spoken naught of any plans and has no authority to give you orders. Why do you follow them?" she challenged.

Standing mere millimeters from Tynae now, Gwillim expelled a vile, howling laugh. "Now, Princess, if the Baroness could have entrusted *you* with her plans, would we be here in the middle of the wood in the dead of night? I think not," Gwillim taunted sarcastically, "and we act upon her orders because we think it best."

Gwillim's men erupted in a bout of barbaric laughter. Endless lightning strikes cast an eerie red glow against the maggot-white faces of Tynae's would-be executioners.

Am I hallucinating?

Their teeth looked like razor sharp fangs in the bloody glow, and their eyes!—Horror-struck, Tynae stared into their beastly eyes, flashes of lightening punctuating their deranged madness.

Immobilizing panic grabbed hold of Tynae, she couldn't breathe. *Am I losing my mind?* She did not want to know anymore.

"Where is she?" Gwillim pressed.

One of the soldiers climbed atop the boulder Tynae sat against. Terrified he might bump into her, she moved as far under the rock as possible curling into a ball. Dirt fell into Tynae's eyes as the man moved around just above her. She dared not budge.

"Where is she?!" Gwillim roared. "Lady Tynae? Lady Tynae!"

Searching for their victim, the soldiers moved away from the immediate area.

Tynae tried to figure out her next move. *Do I stay here, do I leave? Can I leave?* Tynae gave her leg a tug, it was loose. *What do I do now?* She looked around, *I can't stay here all night, and if they come back they might see me...how did they not see me to begin with? Am I still invisible?*

Shaking from fear and the stinging cold, Tynae stood up slightly, examining her surroundings. The assassins were moving away.

Maybe I should run back to the castle? If they cannot see me…I might make it.

Quietly Tynae got to her feet. Still petrified, she forcefully willed her limbs to move.

Which way do I go?

"There she is!"

Tynae hadn't seen the soldier standing just a few meters away. Her mind was made up for her, there was only one way to go from here. Pushing her way forward, deeper into the timber, Tynae battled her way through countless obstacles hidden within the blackened forest.

The chaos of fear coupled with the blackness of night began to constrict around Tynae, suffocating her consciousness like a python, slowly tightening, crushing…smothering her sanity.

It took only a few minutes for Tynae to realize she did not hear the men following her, but she did hear something. The one sound she'd been truly dreading. Wide-eyed and panic-stricken, Tynae whipped her head around to see behind her. *No!*

"Set your mark!" Gwillim shouted.

The marksmen where assembling, she knew they wouldn't miss. *Oh God, this is it! Move, move, move!*

Alarm shot through the terrorized woman. Tynae didn't think it possible for her heart to pound any harder, nor beat any faster, but it did. She almost became hysterical when she heard Gwillim's next order.

"Release!"

The ruthless hunters loosed a volley of arrows simultaneously. Swiftly the swarm of artillery made its way toward *her*, its designated mark. Running as fast as her legs would carry her, Tynae could feel the lethal weaponry drawing closer. The unmistakable hiss from the bloodthirsty blades ripped through the frigid night air, reverberating off countless trees.

Terror sliced through Tynae.

Arrows rushed past as she dashed and dodged from side to side. She only just evaded the bombardment.

Teetering on the edge of insanity, Tynae's mind became lost in a dizzying succession of thoughts. *Help me, dear God, please help me. If this is a nightmare please let me wake up before I die! Why is this happening?*

Terrified beyond comprehension, Tynae's heart pounded violently. It felt like a wild beast frantically clawing inside her chest, trying to rip its way out. With breakneck speed, Tynae jumped behind a large oak tree as another shower of deadly arrows rained down around her.

Standing in the protective shadow of the mighty oak Tynae doubled over in an attempt to catch her breath. Chest heaving, she labored to pull oxygen into her lungs. Her uncomfortably snug corset made it difficult to breathe.

Once the battery of deadly missiles ceased, Tynae carefully edged forward trying to see past her sheltering oak. Forked lightning hit three trees directly in front of her, illuminating a solitary spear hurtling directly at her. Jerking back, Tynae hid behind her oak shield once more.

The clouds overhead surged with a roar of earth-shaking thunder, concealing Tynae's ear-piercing screams. The razor-sharp blade had hit its mark.

Drawing in a sharp breath Tynae instinctively pressed her hand over the searing laceration, running the length of her right cheek. The pain was excruciating. *This is not happening. This is NOT happening!*

Tynae took short quick breaths, desperately fighting the urge to scream as warm blood ran through her fingers and down her neck. She refused to give the vicious hunters the satisfaction of knowing they had injured her.

Doing her best to stay calm, Tynae pushed her back tight against the rough damp bark of the tree. She struggled to think of a rational solution to this sadistic confrontation.

Having been in this wood hundreds of times, Tynae knew there were loads of places to hide. But at that moment finding just one proved impossible. The soldiers were right on top of her. Trapped behind the thick oak tree, Tynae quickly became frantic knowing that the soldiers where only a few painful heartbeats away. Deliberating, she could think of nothing else. *It's my only choice…eventually they will capture me.* Resolute in her decision, Tynae knew she had only one option. *If I am fated to die on this night, it will be on my terms and no-one else's.*

With the end drawing near and the huntsmen quickly advancing, Tynae made one final attempt to have her life spared. There wasn't much distance now between her and those sent to murder her. Tynae could see Gwillim clearly at the front of the hunting party, his long red hair and distinctive armor was difficult to miss. She prayed he might somehow find it in his heart to call off this unjustified pursuit, but she wouldn't bet her life on it.

Taking a deep breath Tynae shouted in the direction of the approaching assassin's. "Sir Gwillim, please, I've been good to all of you and your families," Tynae's pleading voice quivered. "Please tell me what it is that I have done to deserve this. I am entitled to at least that much. Am I not?"

For just a second all the men paused, as did Gwillim. That was all she needed. *Yes…* Without waiting for Gwillim's response, Tynae leapt out from behind her oak guardian and was off like a flash.

Running as fast as she could, Tynae ignored the clawing branches attacking her from every angle, ripping and tugging at her flesh and shredded gown. She knew once she was beyond the trees and shrubs that slowed her down she would be able to run full out. But could she out-run the soldiers, and more importantly, could she continue evading their artillery?

The dense forest began to thin and Tynae picked up speed. Soon the forest became little more than a blur as she sped toward the cliffs of Nombin. Finally Tynae reached the grassy meadow she'd been anticipating. There was nothing here to slow her down.

The murky fog swirled like smoke as she ran through it. Almost instantly, the fog dissolved as the clouds overhead released their pent-up rage in a turbulent downpour.

Paying no heed to the storm surrounding her, Tynae concentrated on extracting every ounce of strength that she could from her exhausted body. Accelerating faster than she ever had before, it was only a matter of seconds until the cliffs came into view. With it came a volley of spears and arrows, each slicing through the air around her, only just missing their mark.

The pound, pound, pounding of Tynae's heart exploded in her ears, booming relentlessly as the winged messengers of death flew past her one by one. Desperately, she wanted to scream into the night as a torrent of questions bombarded her brain. *How has my life come to this? Am I not a good person? Have I not been a true friend? What have I done that would warrant death as my punishment? Father—what will become of my father?*
Tynae began falling to pieces as feelings of dread and horror coursed through her veins like ravenous venom. But the terror she felt was not from running or from being chased, or even from the artillery hell-bent on killing her. It was from the realization that she was about to end her own life.

Looking back over her shoulder for the last time, Tynae saw the soldiers closing in. Tears streamed down her dirt and blood-stained face as her every thought, every emotion became frenzied. *Will I make it to the cliffs edge before a spear impales...*

Chapter 3
Falling Stars

"No star is ever lost we once have seen.
We always may be what we might have been."
~Adelaide A. Proctor

Tynae pushed off the edge of the cliff with all her might, diving into a black abyss of nothingness. Falling helplessly through the darkness, a brilliant ball of light appeared beside her.

Toppling through the air like a rag doll, twisting and turning, the icy sea air stung her exposed skin. Never wavering from its post, the fiery globe remained at Tynae's side. Accepting her demise, Tynae never screamed or cried out. *Goodbye, Father, I love you.*

After saying her silent farewell, Tynae peacefully closed her eyes. No longer fighting, no longer scared. Side by side, she and her glowing companion plummeted into the icy sea; leaving behind the people and place she loved so dearly.

In a single heartbeat Tynae and her entire world were gone.

The soldiers reached the cliffs seconds behind Tynae.

The night became deathly still. The rain, lightning, and thunder all ceased simultaneously. Even the moon hid away behind a blanket of black clouds.

Gwillim and the others carefully looked over the cliff, but could see nothing but a black gorge, at the bottom a thick fog bank hovered over the frigid waters. Gwillim huffed. "The drop is at least three leagues down. It would be humanly impossible for anyone to survive a fall of such magnitude. Our job is done here." Gwillim closed his eyes briefly, *even in the face of death, she was kind. I truly am sorry Lady Tynae, please forgive me.*

Despite the fact that the princess had, on some level, taken her own life; Gwillim could not calm the pangs of guilt. The sudden onset of remorse threatened to consume him as the truth in her final words silently tormented him. She had never wronged him or anyone else. The fact of the matter was that Tynae had helped Gwillim and most of the other soldiers and their families on several occasions, never requesting any type of repayment. She always did things for others out of the goodness of her heart. It was just the kind of person that she was.

The clouds broke apart, allowing the moon's light to shine brightly once more. The faraway bay of a lone wolf broke the woeful silence. The cry was desolate. It wasn't long before the entire countryside echoed with the sorrowful cries of hundreds of wolves.

The still night air twisted into a fearsome gale, howling with the animals through the darkness of the night. Mother Nature's cease-fire ended abruptly. The skies opened, pouring forth torrents of rain. A steady crescendo of thunder reverberated throughout the region, exploding every few seconds. Streaks of lightning blazed across the atmosphere, ripping their way through the black fabric of the night sky.

The soldiers retreated to the safety of the forest canopy. Slowly they began their trek home through the fog-obscured wood in silence. None spoke, but each knew there would be a steep price to pay for what had been done here this night. They may not have put their hands to Lady Tynae, but it was because of their actions she now rested at the bottom of the sea. A deed this vile would not soon be forgotten.

They had known this when they set out, though none dared speak it aloud. They made their choice and they would now have to live with it. The walk back to Pathrow would be long, quiet, and sobering.

The wolves had never been far away. Shortly after the soldiers left the meadow, Xantara and her pack quietly emerged from the shadows. Silently they crept across the meadow to the cliffs edge from where Tynae had jumped. Raising their heads purposefully toward the luminous moon together their pain-filled howls rang out.

Standing on the cliff singing their heartbreaking song, a stiff wind blew up from the ocean below; bringing with it a gift. What remained of Tynae's once perfect rose now lie tattered at the Matriarch's feet. It must have fallen from Tynae's hair as she jumped.

Xantara sniffed the rose. It smelled of Tynae.

Gently Xantara picked up the precious treasure between her teeth. Glancing out over the darkened ocean one last time, the matriarch and her pack turned, silently disappearing into the shadows of the forest.

Thinking back on that afternoon, Xantara fondly remembered the warm smile on Tynae's beautiful face when she had given the princess the rose now held tight in her jaw. She thought of the comfort she felt while lying on Tynae's lap as the afternoon sun set, and recalled the soothing touch of Tynae's hands lovingly running through her fur. It all seemed like memories from another lifetime.

Never again would Xantara feel Tynae's loving touch. Never again would she look upon the beautiful face of the only human she had ever considered her counterpart. From this day forward her heart would carry a vast void, the type of void that only occurs when one loses a piece of their very soul.

Chapter 4
Enlightenment

"Truth is more of a stranger than fiction."
~Mark Twain

Béo, a man among the Greer—a water dwelling people—was hunting nearby when he heard something above him plunge into the freezing water. Hearing the splash, he instinctively turned toward the noise. Realizing it was a person, Béo let his gear go and swam over to help. *Humans!* He thought irritably. *A bit early for thrill seeking, isn't it? Why can they never keep their feet on solid ground?*

Reaching the body, Béo quickly realized the woman hadn't been diving for pleasure. Scooping her up in his arms, he immediately returned her to the surface. He lifted the limp body out of the water. *I cannot help this woman,* he thought, *she's already dead.*

Looking up at the cliffs, Béo realized the woman had fallen from a tremendous height. Looking back at the lifeless form in his arms, Béo shook his head. "How tragic, you are so young. Did you jump or did someone push you?" he mused. *Why am I thinking of such things? It doesn't affect me…I can do nothing for her.*

"God be with you woman," Béo released the body back to the sea. A large wave washed over them, pushing the woman back into his arms. The water also removed the dirt, grime, and painted mask covering the woman's face, allowing Béo to see her clearly.

"It can't be!" Alarm shot through Béo. With bated breath he pushed the woman's hair off her face. *Dear God, no!* Béo's heart pounded uncontrollably. "No!"

Diving beneath the ocean's surface, Béo raced off with Tynae tight in his arms. *I must get her to Chief Kerszon.*

Béo frantically swam against the waters. "Please hold on, Lady Tynae," he begged. Swimming as fast as he could through the shadowy depths of the ocean Béo dodged thick seaweed ropes, dove beneath hundreds of jelly fish, and sent schools of fish scattering.

Jubryi, Béo's friend, saw him and quickly swam to his side. "Béo who is...? Oh my God, that's Lady Tynae."

"Yes," Béo continued swimming as fast as he could. "Stay out of my way, Jubryi," Béo snapped. "Go! Tell the Chief I bring Lady Tynae, who is gravely injured."

Without another word Jubryi rushed off.

As Béo sped through the gates of his underwater city a guard directed him to Chief Kerszon's private study.

Emerging from the water, Béo never skipped a beat, continuing to run with Tynae cradled firmly in his arms.

Béo glanced down, "hold on, Lady Tynae, please don't die. I'm so sorry, if only I..." Béo pushed his 'would I, could I, should I,' thoughts out of his head and sped to Chief Kerszon's study. Very little time had passed from when Tynae had entered the water until now, but it felt like a million lifetimes to Béo. Upon reaching the study, Béo was instructed to set Tynae's lifeless body down on a black sea stone table, which he did immediately.

Béo looked around the room after setting Tynae down and was slightly taken aback. He'd been in this room before. It was an exceedingly large and masculine study. The stately room was where the Chief spent a majority of his time and conducted most of his meetings. The furnishings typically inside the room easily accommodated at least thirty large men. The room was currently completely void of its usual furnishings. The only remaining items were bookshelves and an ornate rug. Candles, crystals, and a roaring fire provided a generous amount of lighting.

The stone table Tynae's body lie upon sat in the center of the room. Suspended over the table were three roses: white, pink, and lavender; neatly held together with a white silk ribbon. Adjacent to the table, near some bookshelves, stood a dais.

Several people stood off to one side of the room…there was nothing more.

As Béo briefly explained to the chief what had happened, his gaze wandered back to Tynae's still body. Béo's fear intensified as he temporarily became lost in a whirlwind of remorse. *I should have…Why didn't I…I could have…This is not happening, not to her, she cannot die…*

Shaking off the distress, Béo looked woefully at his chief, who was moving around the room, getting people to their proper places.

"Please save her, Chief Kerszon, she cannot die." Béo swallowed the lump wedged in his throat. "She is Lady Tynae, Princess of Montronvarr, and…" his words trailed off inaudibly, "I love her."

Rooted to the floor, Béo watched quietly as everyone and everything around him moved in a blur; seeing only Tynae clearly. Anticipating Béo's arrival with the princess, Chief Kerszon had called together his most powerful Archimagi. All were now assembling themselves around the stone table holding Tynae's motionless body.

"I am very well aware of the importance of this woman, Béo. Saving her life is more crucial than *you* could ever imagine," the Chief spoke tersely, walking past Béo. "Now please, step aside so we may help her."

Béo moved a few meters back from the foot of the table, watching each Archimagi place their hands over Tynae's broken body. Closing their eyes, they began to hum in a low, steady tone.

Walking over to the dais Kerszon withdrew an ancient scroll from a shelf behind him. Laying it across the dais, he began reading aloud. The chief's words filled the room, fusing with the steady hum of the Archimagi. The hypnotic rhythm slowly seeped into Béo's consciousness. Drifting into a tranquil state, Béo lent his energy to the cause.

Floating somewhere between worlds, Tynae became aware of her existence. The princess knew she was not yet dead, but she also knew she was no longer among the living. Drifting through a peaceful void of nothingness, as if moving through clouds, Tynae felt a presence drawing near. Slowly, everything came in to view. There was a bright room, an unfamiliar man, and a still body—her body.

Tynae watched the man approach her motionless form. It was as if she were peering through a secret window. Tynae did not recognize the man, but he was the most beautiful person she had ever seen. *Is he a celestial being?* She wondered. *Is he here to guide me to the other side?*

His brown hair had streaks of gold and his face was as radiant as an angel, but it was his eyes that drew her to him. His sapphire-blue eyes ensnared her...they were all she could focus on.

The sadness in the stranger's eyes made Tynae's heart ache. The man looked down at her lifeless body, slowly studying her from head to toe. Tynae's shredded clothes revealed numerous cuts and deep gashes.

The man reached out, carefully running his hand over Tynae's swollen and bruised shoulder. Touching Tynae's face, a single tear slid down the man's cheek. "Tynae...I am so sorry, I wish I could have prevented this. If there had been any other way..."

Tynae literally felt the man's grief and despair. She wanted nothing more than to hold the beautiful man and comfort him. To her surprise, he looked up and made direct eye contact with her. He was no longer looking at her still form, but at the energy she had become.

His soul somehow touched hers. The sadness in his eyes was replaced by love. "Please, Tynae, do not leave me. You are my life, *my* queen, the very air I breathe...I need you."

She knew he meant every word he spoke.

This man, his words; she wasn't sure what it was, but there was something about him that awakened a spark deep inside her. Without warning the spark transformed into a raging inferno.

Tynae didn't know how, but she was not going to let go. She was not going to die.

So began another desperate fight for Lady Tynae. She fought to live. She would do whatever it took to make her way back to the earthly plane, and discover the identity of *her* king.

Chapter 5
Shadow of Hope

"Let us follow our destiny, ebb and flow.
Whatever may happen, we master fortune by accepting it."
~Virgil

From a darkened corner of the study, Ge'annã stepped out of the shadows. Leader of the Archimagi, and most powerful Archimagus among the Greer, quite possibly the strongest Archimagus among all Guardians; Ge'annã was not someone to be trifled with. No-one knew exactly how old she was, but she had been around for several centuries. Of this, there was no doubt.

Of medium height and build, Ge'annã wore her coal black hair fashioned atop her head in a bun. Wearing her normal attire, a dark green floor length frock embellished with colorful beads and crystals, she crossed the room swiftly. Walking over to the table Tynae laid upon, she placed her hand lightly on Tynae's forehead.

Closing her eyes, Ge'annã reached out with her energy in an attempt to touch Tynae's consciousness. Feeling Tynae's soul vibrate with life, Ge'annã was encouraged. "This one *is* strong," Ge'annã muttered, speaking more to herself than to the others in the room. Incredibly pleased with her findings, Ge'annã opened her eyes. Smiling, she glanced around the room at her fellow Archimagi. "She will most certainly return," Ge'annã announced. "It is time."

All the Archimagi stepped away from the table allowing Ge'annã to move from Tynae's head to her side. Extending her open hands over the center of Tynae's body, palms down, Ge'annã slowly moved her hands. One moved toward Tynae's head, the other toward her feet, until her arms extended over Tynae's entire body. Ge'annã next rotated her arms so that her palms faced up then pressed her palms up slightly. Tynae's body rose slowly into the air. Satisfied with Tynae's new position, Ge'annã stepped away from the table allowing the other Archimagi to resume their positions.

With their hands once again hovering over Tynae's comatose body, the Archimagi walked forward. Tynae's body moved with them, as if attached to their hands by invisible strings. Standing near the doorway, the Archimagi awaited Chief Kerszon's instructions.

Rolling up the scroll he'd been reading from, the chief replaced it on the shelf. Stepping out from behind the dais he looked over at Béo, who was exceedingly confused. "You may join us," the chief said. "You have earned that right. This single act we are about to perform will either save us or destroy us." Chief Kerszon's words were not merely an invitation; they were a statement of fact. Kerszon motioned toward Tynae with his hand. "Lady Tynae is among the Chosen, she is one of the supreme beings of which the prophecy of our people foretold. Many have long awaited this moment. Lady Tynae will be a permanent part of our history from this day forward, and you will tell the generations to come of this days events. But first, you must swear a single oath." Kerszon's stare bore into Béo. "You may never tell the princess of her destiny. She knows not of the power she possesses, nor of the power that is to be hers in the years to come. She will know everything in due time. Until the moment is right, you may not speak of this to her." Kerszon paused, allowing Béo to absorb his words. What the Chief asked of Béo was not a simple request. "Can you do this?"

Standing awe-struck, Béo stared at Tynae's floating body. Turning slowly, Béo looked at the chief with astonishment. A brief moment passed before Béo found his voice. "On my honor, I do swear," he declared quietly.

By this oath, Béo was now obligated to the chief for the rest of his life in regard to this matter. Béo knew precisely what this meant. All Greer knew.

With Béo's vow in place, they departed.

In near-silence everyone walked in unison down a long, gray, stone corridor that seemed to have no end. Torches and bright red crystals guided their way. The only audible sound was the steady, low hum of the Archimagi.

Béo had no idea where they were going. He'd never been to this part of the city before. He was not allowed down here, only officials of Calai were permitted in this area. Passing a time keeper as they traveled, Béo realized nearly twelve hours had passed since he'd arrived with Tynae. It barely felt like an hour.

Béo's mind wandered as they walked. *If I ever find out who did this to her, I'm going to kill them...slowly. I'm so stupid, why did I wait? Why her? Does her father know? Did he order this fate upon his own daughter?* Béo's thoughts began to consume him. Forcefully he pushed them out of his consciousness yet again. No matter what the answers were to any of his questions, they held no relevance at this time.

A light at the end of the corridor caught Béo's attention. It came from within a chamber with oversized doors. The illumination was different from that cast by most torches and crystals. It was more of a glow. It became apparent that the glow had a purple hue, as their procession drew closer.

Béo looked at the others, but none had changed their expressions. Their attention was on Tynae and Tynae alone. Looking at the princess Béo realized there was a change in her appearance. *What's happening?* He wondered. *She doesn't look as broken as when I first brought her here.* Optimism gradually began to replace his fear. *If you pull through this, My Lady, I swear to finally tell you the truth,* he vowed silently.

Reaching the room from where the light emanated, the procession slowed. Stepping aside Béo allowed the others to enter the chamber first. He followed close behind.

Béo had only taken a few steps into the room before he froze in his tracks, awestruck by the scene around him. In the corner of the mammoth-sized room stood Chief Kerszon, he appeared to be having a conversation with an enormous dragon. The dragon was magnificent. Every beam of light reflected off its thick purple scales like a crystal prism, dancing on the walls.

Béo had never seen a living dragon. *What is a dragon doing here, in Calai? Has it always been here?* Béo marveled at the sight for several heartbeats. Shaking his head slightly, Béo regained his composure and directed his attention back to the matter at hand; Tynae, her life, and bringing her back from the dead. This was truly all that mattered to him.

Looking around the room, Béo saw Tynae. She'd been placed upon another sea stone table, this one light blue, and like the other table it was situated in the center of the barren room. It too had three roses suspended above it.

Walking further into the room, Béo's head tilted as he got closer to Tynae. *Is that possible?* Béo looked closer. *I only took my eyes from her for a few moments, a matter* of seconds at best. Béo now stood beside Tynae, whose appearance has changed yet again. *She must be growing stronger.* He grinned slightly gazing at Tynae, engrossed in her profound change.

"Béo."

Béo flinched; unaware that Chief Kerszon had approached him.

"This is Emperor Zandore the Just," Chief Kerszon, nodded toward the splendid dragon behind him. "He has been with our people for nearly a million years now." The Chief's tone was incredibly casual, as if he introduced people to extraordinary legends of lore everyday.

Béo had heard many a fascinating tale involving Zandore, but had been led to believe all dragons were extinct. They were creatures belonging to a far gone past.

"It is an honor," Béo bowed deeply, "Your Majesty."

"Ay, young Béo, 'tis an honor indeed."

When Zandore spoke, it was inside Béo's head. This startled Béo, but he managed to maintain his composure.

Zandore's eyes twinkled as he stared at Béo. Béo smiled slightly. With a nod of his head, Zandore turned his attention to Tynae.

Chapter 6
Homecoming

"The last temptation is the greatest treason;
to do the right deed for the wrong reason."
~T.S. Eliot

The breaking dawn's pink glow caressed the horizon as Pathrow's tired soldiers returned home. The rain had only just let up. Scores of wolves could still be heard. Their sorrowful cries floated through the countryside like tormented phantoms.

"Finally," a soldier commented quietly.

"I know, I thought we'd never get back."

Their armor caked with mud and their clothing and bodies soaked to the bone, the men were thankful to be home.

Upon entering the armory Gwillim stopped at once, *what the bloody hell is she doing here?*

Still wearing her gown from the previous night, Arona waited. Gwillim assumed she'd been there all night. Her unwelcome presence caught everyone off guard.

"Why is she here?" one soldier whispered.

"To collect our souls," whispered another.

"Don't know what she wants," someone else replied, barely audible, "But if you two value your heads, you'll shut your mouths."

With golden hair, striking blue eyes and voluptuous beauty, Baroness Arona appears to be a dignified aristocrat upon first meeting. However, the illusion fades quickly.

"Baroness Arona." Gwillim gave a slight bow. "You're up early." A hint of derision crept into his words.

Tapping her finger contemptuously on her hip, Arona stared at Gwillim. He knew full well she'd not gone to bed. They had clearly kept her waiting far longer than she thought reasonable.

Pulling himself up to his full height, Gwillim walked forward to greet Arona properly. She extended her hand to him

50

expectantly—this was a first. *You have to be kidding me.* Pulling her hand to his lips Gwillim noticed Arona wore a newly acquired ring. The thick gold band held a large white stone, which bore a unique insignia. Gwillim recognized it immediately. *You witch.* The ring belonged to Lady Tynae. It was among the few possessions she owned that had once belonged to her mother.

Kneeling before Arona, Gwillim took her pale, talon-like hand and grudgingly kissed the stolen ring. Starting to stand, Gwillim glanced up at Arona. Seeing her loathsome stare, he froze.

Smiling malevolently, she issued new orders. "From now on you shall address me as Your Highness or Your Majesty, is that understood?"

The soldiers behind Gwillim shifted uneasily.

Gwillim bowed his head apologetically, "Yes, Your Highness." He almost choked on the words.

Standing up, Gwillim looked Arona in the eyes. It was in this moment that his life completely unraveled. Pushing his revelation aside Gwillim's expression became smug. Straightening up, he addressed Arona, "The deed is done…" he swallowed hard, "Your Highness."

A sickening smile spread across Arona's face. "Well done," she purred, looking around. "Where is it then?" she asked greedily, holding out her hands.

"I'm sorry. Where is what? Your Highness."
Arona grinned girlishly, "Do not play with me, Gwillim. Where is my trophy?"
Gwillim's face fell, "Trophy?"
Arona's patience, if she had any at all, was gone. "Yes, *Duke* Gwillim MY trophy, MY prize, HER HEAD!" she shrieked.
Gwillim tried maintaining his harsh demeanor, but felt just as antsy as his men shuffling around behind him. Bowing his head, Gwillim hastily explained his lack of a *souvenir.* "My greatest apologies, Your Highness, we were unable to bring you a…*prize*," Gwillim stammered.

Arona's icy glare bore through Gwillim, "Excuse me?" she hissed.

"She jumped off the cliffs of Nombin before we could reach her," Gwillim quickly clarified.

Arona's eyes were ablaze with rage. "She did what?!"

The duke continued, "We believe that Lady Tynae may have been…" Gwillim cleared his throat, "forewarned of our arrival." Gwillim stopped speaking.

Arona's eyes had become slits. Jaw clenched she said nothing.

Realizing Arona was waiting on him, Gwillim quickly resumed his story. "You see, when we reached Godwin hall where the gala was being held she was no longer there, but she did not have much of a lead, Your Highness."

Turning abruptly, Arona began to pace.

Gwillim continued. "We followed her into the Forest of Nombin straight away. We caught up to her quickly, she never escaped our sight, but as you know there are many trees and such in the wood, we were unable to get a clear shot. Nevertheless, she is dead to the world…or sleeping with the fishes as it were."

Gwillim's men guffawed at his comment.

Arona spun around mid-pace, eyes wide and gleaming. "Did you see her body?" she demanded hopefully.

Swallowing the iron ball lodged in his throat, Gwillim somehow managed to hold on to his self-assured stance. "Regrettably, no, Your Highness. There was a thick wall of fog upon the sea, but the drop is massive, no being could ever survive such a fall." Gwillim paused for a moment then continued, wearing a wicked grin. "Well it's not so much the fall as much as it is the landing that would snuff you." Gwillim laughed coldly at his cruel joke. His men followed suit.

"Enough!" Arona barked.

The room became deathly silent.

Glaring at Gwillim with eyes that could kill, Arona walked toward him. "You had better hope for your sake and the sake of your *precious* little families," Arona moved toward the soldiers, "that she truly is dead—or…" Arona enunciated every word maliciously, walking among the men, "Each and every single one of you will watch your families be destroyed, s-l-o-w-ly…That *is* a promise," she murmured callously.

The fear on the men's faces brought a smile to hers. Arona allowed her cold, harsh stare to linger momentarily on each man before she returned her attention back to Gwillim.

Gliding over to the duke, her demeanor indignant, Arona shot him a withering stare. "I expect you to find out if she was indeed warned," she hissed. "If so, I want every one of the men responsible for the breach eliminated."

Gwillim gawked at Arona.

Taking another step closer, Arona now stood mere centimeters from Gwillim. Raising an eyebrow, she growled between clenched teeth, "Do I make myself perfectly clear, *High Constable?"*

Gwillim lowered his head submissively, "Yes, Your Highness," he muttered.

"What was that, Your Grace? I couldn't quite hear you," Arona goaded sarcastically.

Lifting his head, Gwillim looked Arona dead in the eyes. "Yes, Your Highness, you have made yourself *perfectly* clear," Gwillim growled.

Without another word, Arona walked stiffly past Gwillim toward the door. The soldiers quickly separated, creating a path to allow her exit. Gwillim watched Arona take her leave, as did the soldiers. Once she'd gone everyone turned their attention to Gwillim, but no-one dared speak.

Uncertainty and apprehension hung heavy in the air, so heavy you could have heard a feather hit the ground.

Gwillim stood staring at his men and they back at him, what could any of them say? It was they who had given in to Arona's wicked plan. Any one of them could have gone to King Yurgon or even Lady Tynae herself. Both would have listened and taken care of the matter. But they had become so greedy they could see not beyond the riches being offered in trade for a heartless, cold-blooded murder. Once Arona had the soldiers at their word, she threatened their families to ensure they would not back out. This was wise on her part, because they probably would have had a change of heart. Arona did not allow the men this luxury. They knew no matter where Arona was; free, locked behind bars, or six feet under, she could, and more importantly *would,* carry through with every threat she had ever made. They knew not from whence her powers were gained, nor how they may have come to be. But, what they did know was that her sorcery was very real, very dark, and that they dared not cross her.

Gwillim broke the silence. "Put your weapons away men, and go home to your families and for god sake bathe and get some rest." Gwillim's tone was subdued. He knew what his men where thinking…he was not about to kill any of them. They were his brothers. Besides, he had inflicted enough pain and mutilation upon the world this day and the sun had not even fully broken the horizon.

After everyone had gone, Gwillim walked over to his desk and sat down. Tired, tormented, and defeated, he ran his fingers through his long hair. Resting his face in his hands he took a deep breath, *what have we done…what have I done?* Gwillim looked out the window at the crisp and welcoming yellow glow of the new day's dawn…all he saw was gray.

Chapter 7
Insurance

"First weigh the considerations, then take the risks."
~Helmuth von Motke

The Archimagi stood around the huge room quietly talking amongst themselves, waiting for whatever would come next.

Taking a deep breath, Kerszon pulled himself up to his full height.

While Chief Kerszon was an even tempered man, his size alone intimidated most. He was tall, with broad shoulders, defined muscles, long dark hair and piercing green eyes.

Everyone fell silent when Kerszon stepped into the middle of the room. The Chief looked from the Archimagi to Tynae, then back.

It was evident that no-one understood what was happening. For once, they all looked just as confused as Béo. The only exception was the dragon. Sitting off to the side Zandore looked rather peaceful.

Kerszon cleared his throat. "As you know, Lady Tynae is one of the Chosen who will save our world from certain destruction. She is The Bearer of Light. Many know of the prophecy, but few believe. If you read the ancient scrolls, each and every event our ancestors foretold has come to pass. The key to our undoing is the slow introduction of harmful, yet almost undetectable changes within our societies, cities, governments, and nations." The Chief walked around the huge room while speaking to the Archimagi. "By doing this the people have been duped. They are blinded and unaware to that which is slowly being stripped away from them bit by bit. They have become brainwashed, losing their true identity while conforming to that which is immoral and corrupt. The enemy has deceptively convinced the people that this lewd behavior is piously and ethically acceptable." Kerszon sighed. "It is difficult for most to see that these changes have slowly eroded away that which used to be the foundation of our governmental systems, religious sectors, and our very morality. This has been going on for quite some time now and continues to happen at this very moment, right under our noses." The Chief ran his hand through his long hair as he walked. "Those who will deliver us from our own destruction already exist. They live among us, but most have no concept of their true identity. Their purpose will be revealed to them in due time, as is such with Lady Tynae." Kerszon continued around the room. "We, the Greer, were not the only ones to discover that Lady Tynae was to be one of the Chosen destined to fulfill the prophecy. This is why Baroness Arona wanted her killed." Kerszon glanced at Tynae, "This is why we must save her. Lady Tynae does have free will. It is entirely possible that she could turn on us. We do not believe this to be a path the Princess would ever choose, but it is a reality we had to seriously consider nonetheless." Pausing briefly, Kerszon glanced toward the dragon. "Emperor Zandore, Ge'annã and I have spent many years preparing for this moment. Shortly after the Princess was born Ge'annã foresaw an assassination attempt on Lady Tynae's life. It was the Baroness who would initiate this plot. Though Arona was little more than a baby herself and knew not of her future, it was her destiny. The plan never faded or changed, thus leading us to believe Lady Tynae is truly pure of heart." Kerszon gave Ge'annã a slight nod. "This is why her fate with the Baroness remained unchanged. After all, if there had been even the slimmest of chances that Lady Tynae could have been turned, you can bet your very life and the lives of those you hold dear that the Baroness would have kept Lady Tynae alive at all costs."

Kerszon spread his arms wide, "So here we are ladies and gentlemen. We had a few options. One, let Lady Tynae pass from this earthly plane and hope there would be another as powerful as she to take her place. This was doubtful." Walking past Tynae, Kerszon touched her hair lightly. "Two, request your help as we have, and hope Lady Tynae would fully recover from her injuries. God willing when the day comes for us to fight Baroness Arona's army, Lady Tynae would be powerful enough and willing to fight on our side." Kerszon looked pensively at

Zandore, then back at the Archimagi. "Then there was option three. Request your help and give Lady Tynae a bit of additional assistance from other remarkably powerful forces…an insurance policy, if you will. The problem with the third option is that if Lady Tynae turns on us…well, let's just pray we need never discuss this."

Looking around the room Kerszon made it a point to look directly into the eyes of each and every person. "Please know that we do not take this lightly, we have weighed all possible outcomes. If it were any being other than Lady Tynae it would never have been a consideration, but after carefully looking at this from every possible angle, Zandore, Ge'annã and I unanimously agreed to move forward with our plan." Kerszon stopped beside Tynae. "I can tell you not of the act we are about to perform. This is for Lady Tynae's safety as well as yours, your families, and the safety of all the lands. But I will impart this much; this has never occurred in all of history prior to this moment. "If it works the way we believe it shall, a power beyond anything we have ever witnessed will be given to this," Kerszon passed his hand over Tynae's still body, "one person," he said optimistically. "I am sure you can understand why we would never want this information to get into the hands of our enemies." Kerszon walked to the middle of the room. Apprehensive faces stared blankly at him. A demulcent smile from their chief set everyone at ease. "Now, with all this being said I must ask for your oaths of silence."

Talia, one of the Archimagi looked up at the suspended roses, then at the chief. "Forgive me, My Lord, but I do not understand. The roses are in place. All present know they demand our silence."

Kerszon nodded. "I appreciate that, Talia, but it's not enough. Oaths are binding and deadly if broken. I require your vows," he said flatly.

There were no further questions. Kerszon had never been one to demand oaths. If he was commanding his people to pledge a vow of silence you could bet your children's souls he had a very good reason.

One by one, each Archimagus stood before Chief Kerszon. Bowing his or her head, each gave their oath of silence in their Antediluvian language. "Ego pignus mei vita ut aeternus eternus silentium de hodie itaque Lady Tynae."

The Archimagi oath when translated stated thus: "I pledge my life to eternal silence concerning today's events and Lady Tynae."

It was finally Béo's turn. Ready to swear his oath he approached the chief. Kerszon stopped him. "Lord Béo, I require you not to make this pledge. I will explain in due time."

A few Archimagi exchanged perplexed looks at the remark. Béo was equally puzzled, but questioned not the chief's wishes.

With oaths sworn, Chief Kerszon spoke aloud, "Excessum exsisto lapsus tu itaque tui familia quisnam desumo ut periurium."

The Chief's words, simple, yet powerful sealed their oaths. "Death befalls you and your family who elect to oath-breaking."

Turning his attention to Ge'annã and Zandore who stood beside Tynae, Kerszon graciously inclined his head.

Accepting Kerszon's silent approval, Ge'annã and Zandore placed all their attention on Tynae.

"Take your appropriate places, please," Ge'annã directed.

The Archimagi took up their previous positions around Tynae's body.

Chapter 8
The Fire Within

"Although the world is full of suffering,
it is full also of the overcoming of it."
~Helen Keller

Looking across the table, Ge'annã addressed the Archimagus standing opposite her. "Drayea, please unlace Lady Tynae's dress and corset. I need access to her heart," Ge'annã spoke in her usual monotone voice.

Drayea, a lovely dark-haired and petite woman, was four hundred and twenty years old. This made her the youngest of the Archimagi. She was also the most timid.

Taken aback by Ge'annã's request, Drayea turned ghostly white as all the blood drained from her face. You would have thought she'd been instructed to plunge a dagger into the Princess' heart.

"Do not test my patience today, Drayea. I do not have time to explain my every action to you, nor will I. Now do as I have instructed and remove her garments so that we may proceed." Ge'annã's irritation was blatant.

Drayea appeared remorseful. "Yes, Mistress…I am sorry." Quickly Drayea began loosening what remained of Lady Tynae's outer dress. When she reached the corset, she glimpsed up at Ge'annã shyly then continued.

Once the area where Tynae's heart resided was exposed, Ge'annã spoke out abruptly. "That will do, Drayea, thank you."

With an awkward nod Drayea moved back.

Chief Kerszon stepped between two Archimagi, placing himself at Tynae's shoulder, directly opposite Ge'annã.

Zandore stood at Tynae's head.

"Béo, please join me." This was not an invitation, but a command.

The Archimagi standing nearest the chief moved aside, allowing space for Béo.

Taking his place beside the chief, Béo was somewhat relieved when he saw the area over Tynae's heart rise and fall slightly. *She's alive.*

Ge'annã looked up at Zandore, the two where apparently having a silent conversation. Zandore made a sound that was something between a grunt and a growl. The noise came from deep within his throat. Continuing his telepathic conversation with Ge'annã, a white puff of smoke wafted carelessly from his nostrils.

Slowly opening and closing her eyes, Ge'annã acknowledged whatever Zandore had said with an almost imperceptible nod then turned, walking to the corner of the room where a small round table stood with a single chair. Pulling out the chair Ge'annã sat down. In the center of the table was a dark-blue velvet pillow, the size and thickness of a fresh loaf of bread, the center slightly concaved. Ge'annã pulled the pillow toward her then extracted two objects from her pocket. The first was a purple velvet pouch that seemed to be empty; the second was a pair of gloves made of a material Béo did not recognize. They appeared to be soft, yet metallic in texture. Looking closer, Béo realized the gloves bore a striking resemblance to Zandore's scales.

Intrigued, Béo carefully watched Ge'annã pull the gloves over her petite hands.

Opening the velvet bag, she gingerly tipped its contents out. Ge'annã now held a small gleaming crystal in the palm of her gloved hand.

Béo was caught off guard as a ray of light struck the crystal, forcing him to shield his eyes with his hands. The light reflecting off the tiny crystal was nearly blinding. Béo had seen many variations of crystals in his time, but never one like this.

Picking up the crystal carefully between her index finger and thumb, Ge'annã painstakingly placed it into the indentation in the velvet pillow. Visibly drawing in a deep breath, Ge'annã stood slowly. Looking at Zandore she nodded once then resumed her place at Tynae's side.

After a brief exchange of looks, and presumably words, with Zandore; Ge'annã reached down, removing the crystal from the plush pillow. Carefully she set it atop Tynae's chest, directly over her heart.

Béo tried determining the color of the stone, but it was such a kaleidoscope of colors he could not assign it just one shade.

Without warning, the stone erupted with a multihued glow, and an entrancing melody filled the room.

Ge'annã beamed. "Amazing," she breathed.

Lowering his head until it was directly beside Tynae, Zandore closed his eyes. A low vibration began emanating from the dragons throat.

He's...humming. Overwhelmed by all that was happening, Béo stood so still you would have thought he was made of stone.

As Zandore hummed, the light surrounding the crystal began to expand. Slowly it inched over Tynae's entire body, eventually encapsulating her in a ball of ethereal light.

Zandore's hum melded perfectly with the beautiful music that seemed to come from the stone itself.

Gradually Zandore's hum became deeper. Béo felt the intense vibrations flowing through his body.

Eyes growing wide, Béo watched as the crystal began to sink into Tynae's chest. Turning to Kerszon, Béo opened his mouth, but the chief shook his head. Obeying the silent command; Béo resumed watching the crystal, along with its glow, slowly melt into Tynae's motionless form.

Tynae, still somewhere between worlds, became aware of her physical body. Was she alive? If she was, she was not awake.

Trying to clear the fog from her mind, Tynae's mystery man came back into view. He lovingly brushed his hand over her cheek, encouraging her to live. "That's it, my angel. Fight, breathe, feel the love for you flow through every cell of your being."

The sound of his voice was hypnotic. As his words trailed off, Tynae became profoundly aware of the unusual sensations flowing through her. Although she still stood outside her body, she could feel everything that was happening within her flesh. A look of bewilderment passed over Tynae's face as an odd tingling sensation flooded her person. It almost tickled. The sensation continued, warm at first, then her eyes got huge with terror. She was hot...very, very hot! Screaming, she dropped to her knees in agonizing pain, "It burns...fire...I'm on fire!"

There was only one who heard her heart-wrenching cries—the stranger standing beside her.

Dropping to his knees in front of her, the angelic stranger looked horror struck.

"Breathe, Tynae, please breathe," he begged.

He wants me to breathe? Confused she looked up at him as she lay writhing in pain. *How do I do that, how do I...ahhh, breathe?* Gasping, her body arched in pain. Looking at her mystery man with pleading eyes Tynae choked out, "HOW?!" Her airway constricted, allowing only small amounts of oxygen through. The pain was unbearable. "Fire...pain...kill me...Kill...me!!!"

"Dammit, Tynae, *breathe*! The pain will go away if you just *breathe*!" her angel demanded.

"I'm...burn...ing...he...lp me... I... ca....n't... br...brea...the...hel...p...lea...ahhh!!!"

The stranger moved as close to Tynae's energy as he could. With trembling hands he reached out, touching her frightened face. "Tynae, I cannot lose you again, I *cannot* live without you any longer. You are my entire world, my past, present, and most especially my future. Please, my love, you are my very life. I only exist because of your existence." The man gazed upon her with desperation. "Angel, you are so strong, you can do this, please, just BREATHE," he pressed urgently.

Tynae felt yet another strange sensation as her soul was yanked back into her body. The force was so tremendous it was disorienting. Her soul moved with lightning speed through what seemed like the entire universe. As her soul re-entered her body it felt like sinking into a tub of warm water.

Tynae's consciousness lingered in the other dimension as she lay in her body, *breathing*. Her mystery man stood by her side beaming with a brilliant smile as joyous tears rolled down his face.

Reaching up, Tynae gently wiped his tears. "Please don't cry," she whispered.

"I can't help it, I'm so happy." Leaning down, he tenderly pressed his warm lips to hers. Tynae did not protest.

"I love you, Tynae," he kissed her again. "I knew you would do it, you need me just as much as I need you." Her angel ran his hand over her hair. "Rest my love, I will see you soon, I promise." Kissing Tynae one last time, her mystery man brushed her face gently then silently vanished.

Watching her angel fade into nothingness, Tynae's soul ached with sadness. Slowly, everything around her began to fade and Tynae peacefully drifted out of her dream world.

Zandore's deep hum resonated through the entire room.

Béo stared intensely at Tynae. Her chest—it was moving...*she's breathing!* Relief washed over Béo like a wave of warm sunshine.

Studying Tynae once again, Béo looked her over. Her body had fully enveloped the crystal and its light.

Zandore's humming ceased. The magnificent creature opened his enormous amethyst eyes, examining Tynae.

Glancing up at Zandore, Béo was astonished to see the dragon, *smiling*?

Zandore positioned his muzzle near Tynae's face, blowing ever so slightly. Inhaling Zandore's encouragement, Tynae's eyes fluttered. Taking a second long draw of Zandore's breath, Tynae opened her eyes.

Was it possible for her to look more beautiful now than she had prior to jumping to her death? Béo still did not understand what had happened here.

Even with all the scratches, bruises and dirt still covering her, Tynae looked more like an angel now then ever before, and her skin...a glow emanated from every inch of Tynae's body as if encompassed by a nimbus.

With Tynae breathing steadily, Zandore nodded to Kerszon and quietly took his leave.

Odd, Béo made a mental note.

Watching in awe as the cuts and bruises covering Tynae's body vanished, Béo focused on her cheek. Béo's eyes opened wide as he watched the deep gash mend itself. In a matter of seconds the laceration was gone. All that remained was a small scar in the middle of her cheek. Béo glanced over at Kerszon, who looked like he was about to burst with joy.

Blinking her eyes, Tynae turned her head slowly.

Chapter 9
Awakening

"The body is a sacred garment."
~Martha Graham

"Where am I?" Tynae whispered.

"You are safe, My Lady," Béo answered.

Tynae turned toward his voice. "Béo? Is that you?"

Béo grinned. "Yes, My Lady."

Tynae managed a weak smile. "I would have recognized that stubble-covered face anywhere, blurry or not."

Béo couldn't believe his eyes. *There's the smile I love so much.*

"Where am I, Béo?" Tynae was clearly addled.

"You're in Calai, My Lady."

"Calai? What?" Closing her eyes Tynae rubbed her temples. Opening her eyes back up Tynae laid her hands across her stomach. Taking a deep breath she looked up at Béo. "That's not…no," she protested. "That's not possible, Calai? Calai does not exist, it's not real," she insisted, her voice quivering. "Béo, this is not funny."

Seeing Tynae on the verge of tears was destroying Béo. *Hasn't she been through enough?*

Lifting her trembling hands, Tynae carefully touched her face then slid her hand over her collar bone then her shoulder. "I feel so strange, my body…I hurt everywhere," her voice quivered again. "Everything is blurry, I can barely see, and…what's happening to me?"

Béo took Tynae's hand. "Relax, My Lady you are safe, and you *are* in Calai. Chief Kerszon, the leader of Calai is here as well," Béo assured.

Desperately Béo wanted to do something to take away Tynae's pain and fear, but was at a loss. Looking apprehensively over at the chief standing across the room, Béo made a silent plea.

Kerzon gave Béo a consoling nod.

Approaching Tynae's side, the chief looked down at her with deep compassion. "What is the last thing you remember, My Lady?" he asked softly.

Tynae furrowed her brow, "I…I don't really remember. I was at the ball, yes…then I was in the wood, and…" Tynae seemed to go somewhere else for a few moments. "Sir GWILLIM! He…they…ME, they were going…going to…kill *me*…" Tynae began breathing rapidly. *"Running, I, I was running, I couldn't get away from them, I ran and…and…I jumped…I…died…where am I? Why can't I see clearly? Why can't I move my body properly, what's happened to me?"* Fear weighed heavy on Tynae's face and words. "Béo, please, I am so scared, what is going on here?"

It was Kerszon who addressed Tynae. "Please relax, My Lady, you're safe. If you promise to remain calm, I will explain what happened once you entered the waters." Patiently Kerszon waited for Tynae's response.

With an audible exhale and a slight smile Tynae tightened her grip around Béo's hand. "Okay," she sighed.

Béo grinned softly glancing down at their interlinked fingers with wonder. It was understandable that Tynae would want to know what had happened. The fact that she was alive was unimaginable.

Kerszon recounted the events of the past nineteen hours. He told Tynae how she had come to be in Calai, why he had requested the assistance of so many Archimagi, and then he told her about Zandore. "The Archimagi did as much as they could, but it did not seem to be enough so we brought you here to Zandore," Kerszon explained.

Confusion passed over Tynae's beautiful face. "Zandore?" she repeated, "and magi? There are people that truly perform…magic?" she asked.

Kerszon smiled. "Yes, there are many beings capable of true magic. It is not just something from fairytales. As for Zandore, he's a dragon that has been with our people for nearly a million years. His magic is astonishingly powerful. We brought you to him and he was able to revive you. Now, here we are. You'll require a substantial amount of time to recover fully, My Lady, and you will be staying here with us in Calai. It is necessary for your safety." Kerszon's warning was subtle, yet clearly not a request. "Lady Tynae, I am certain you will have a plethora of questions as you recover and I will gladly answer each and every one of them that I can. But as for right now, many hours have passed since you came to us, and you really do need to get some rest." The chief's attention turned to Béo. "Béo, please take the princess to her room."

"Wait…" Tynae blurted out. "I'm sorry. Calai, it's real? I'm in a city…underwater?" she questioned with disbelief.

Kerszon chuckled, "Yes, My Lady, Calai is very real. We are the Greer and you are in a city that is indeed underwater. I give you my word, you *are* safe." Kerszon gently touched Tynae's shoulder. "You really do need to get some rest, Princess, please go. We will talk again soon."

Kerszon dismissed the Archimagi, but Tynae insisted that they wait. "Hold on, please," Tynae held up her hand. "I just want to thank all of you for saving me. I'm forever in your debt. Thank you so much." Tynae smiled her magical smile and everyone smiled back.

"Béo, a word please," the chief said.
"Yes, Sir." Béo lightly squeezed Tynae's hand, "I'll be right back."

One by one, each of the Archimagi left the room. Walking past Tynae, they whispered blessings upon her.

As the last Archimagus took his leave, Béo returned to Tynae's side. "Am I to carry her, Chief?"

"Yes, it will be the most pain-free way to get her to her room. She'll be staying in the Vu'tella chambers. Lady Tynae, there will be maids and a chancellor in your quarters at all times. They will help you with all of your needs, whatever they may be. Please do not hesitate to call upon them." Kerszon's voice was soothing.

"Thank you, Chief Kerszon, for everything you've done for me."

Kerszon inclined his head. "You deserve nothing less, My Lady," he said sincerely.

Feeling uneasy, Béo stepped closer to the princess. "Are you ready, Lady Tynae?" he asked apprehensively.

Tynae smiled at Béo. "Yes," she sighed.

Bending over Tynae, Béo paused. Despite her time in the water, and the dirt and leaves, she smelled phenomenal. Her scent was intoxicating. Picking Tynae up, Béo cradled her gently in his arms. She rested her head on his shoulder.

Béo was almost to the door when Tynae lifted her head slightly. "Wait, Béo. Chief Kerszon, would it be okay if Béo were to remain with me? I would feel much better if someone I knew were near by."

Béo was taken aback by Tynae's query. *Did Lady Tynae just request that I stay with her for the night?*

"Understandable, My Lady," Kerszon said. "He may stay with you for as long as you wish." Looking at Béo, Kerszon gestured toward the door with his head.

"Thank you," Tynae breathed, laying her head back on Béo's shoulder and closing her eyes.

Almost out the door, Tynae popped her head up once again. "Wait, one last thing, please," Tynae implored.

Kerszon chuckled, "Yes, Lady Tynae?"

"May I come back at some point in the future? I'd really like to meet Zandore and all the Archimagi who brought me back from beyond the veil." Tynae shakily held up her head awaiting Kerszon's response.

"I think we'd all like that very much, My Lady. I will see to it as soon as your strength has returned. Go now, rest," Kerszon insisted.

"Thank you again, Chief Kerszon." Grinning, Tynae laid her head back on Béo's shoulder.

"Sleep well, My Lady, I shall see you soon." Kerszon bowed.

Béo exited the chamber. He was very apprehensive about carrying Tynae. They would be walking for a while as her quarters were a fair distance away. "Lady Tynae, please tell me if I'm walking to fast or if I hurt you."

"I'm fine, Béo, really."

While walking Béo occasionally leaned forward, inhaling Tynae's sweet aroma.

"Béo, I'm sorry, I should have asked if you had prior commitments before I requested that you stay with me. I hope you don't mind."

Béo's head was still reeling from her initial request that he spend the night with her. At that moment, he considered himself to be the luckiest man on the planet.

"It will be my pleasure, Lady Tynae. You have always been a great friend to me. It is the least I can do for you." Béo could honestly not think of a better way to spend his days.

"And, Béo…"
"Yes, My Lady?"
"Thank you for saving my life, if not for you I would not be here." Lifting her head, Tynae kissed Béo lightly on the cheek.

For the first time in his life, Béo was thankful for the darkness of the long tunnels. Blood rushed to his cheeks so fast he thought his face might burst into flames.

"I'm glad I was there." Béo had never spoken truer words.
"Béo?"
"Yes, My Lady?"
"When I was unconscious, did you speak to me?"
Béo shook his head, "No."

"Odd, I thought I heard a man speaking to me, I could have sworn…" Tynae's words faded sleepily.

"No-one was talking to you, My Lady."

Béo could think of nothing else to say. No-one had been speaking except Chief Kerszon and he was not talking *to* her. He had read from the ancient scrolls in Antediluvian, a language exclusive to the Greer. Tynae would not have understood it.

I wonder if Zandore spoke to her. It would have been in her head and I would not have heard it.

"Are you certain?"
"Quite." *I think.*
"Okay…" sighing, she relaxed into Béo's shoulder.
Serenity washed over Béo. Every cell of his being became drenched with unfamiliar warmth that tingled as it surged through his body. It only took a fraction of a heartbeat for Béo to realize it was Tynae's energy mingling with his own. It was like nothing he'd ever felt.

Béo walked on quietly, enjoying the peacefulness, and allowing Tynae to rest.

Chapter 10
Dreams

"The face is the mirror of the mind,
and eyes without speaking confess the secrets of the heart."
~Saint Jerome

After walking for nearly an hour they finally reached their destination. Tynae had been quiet for some time. Béo presumed she'd fallen asleep. Carefully opening the door to Vu'tella, he tried not to wake Tynae.

Inside O'leana awaited their arrival. An older woman with ginger hair, O'leana was a genuinely caring soul. She would be Lady Tynae's handmaiden for as long as Tynae resided in Calai.

O'leana curtsied as Béo entered, "Good evening, My Lord."

Béo inclined his head. "Good evening, O'leana. Please turn down the bed."

Walking through the living area, into the bedchamber and over to the bed Béo carefully set Tynae down, pulling the covers over her.

Tynae nuzzled into her pillow. "Ahh, this feels nice," she muttered.

Pulling up a plush chair next to the bed Béo sat down. "I'll be right here if you need me, My Lady," he whispered.

"My Lord, I can stay with her," O'leana suggested.

"No, O'leana, thank you. Lady Tynae requested that I stay with her. You may return to your room. If she or I require your assistance I will call on you. Good night."

"As you wish, My Lord," O'leana curtsied. "Good evening."
Once O'leana was gone Tynae rolled over to face Béo.
"Béo?" Tynae spoke softly.
"Yes, My Lady?"
Tynae's smile was peaceful, "First of all call me Tynae, please."

"Yes, My La—I mean, Tynae," Béo chuckled.

"Second, why did O'leana call you *Lord*? I do not recall you ever telling me you were of noble descent."

Béo hesitated. "I don't like to be treated *differently*. I'm just a normal man."

Tynae shook her head, smiling, "you are anything but *normal*, Béo, but I understand what you mean."

"Besides," Béo added hastily, "if I had told you I was the 'White Prince of Calai', you would have thought I'd gone completely mental."

Snickering Tynae nodded. "True."

"So are you going to tell me the title of your father or do we have to play a game of questions?" Tynae inquired lightheartedly.

It took Béo a moment then he blurted out, "Chief."

"Was that an answer, or a sneeze?"

Taking a deep breath Béo repeated himself. "Chief," he said audibly.

Tynae looked perplexed. "Chief? As in Chief Kerszon?"

"Yes My..." Béo shook his head, "I mean, Tynae. Chief Kerszon is indeed my father."

"Huh, good to know." Yawning, Tynae stretched her arms. "I'm ready for sleep."

"Okay." Béo settled into his chair. "I'll be right here. Let me know if you need anything."

Tynae faded off to sleep quickly. Unfortunately, she woke several times, screaming.

"Is there anything I can do?" Béo asked distressed.

Rubbing her temple, Tynae let out a sigh. "Perhaps, would you please ask O'leana to come in here?"

"Of course." Bemused, Béo did as requested. He was back in a matter of minutes with O'leana.

"Yes, Lady Tynae?"

"O'leana, who is my chancellor?"

"Breck, My Lady."

"Would you please ask him to fetch Lord Béo's sleeping attire? Then I'd like you to help me change into a sleeping gown."

"Of course, My Lady, I will be right back."

"O'leana," Béo said.

"Yes, Sire?"

Béo glanced at Tynae, "Ask Breck to also bring me the *appropriate* attire for tomorrow as well."

The handmaiden gave Béo a 'knowing' nod. "Yes, My Lord."

O'leana left the room. There was a knock on a distant door, then voices.

"Breck will return shortly with your garments, My Lord," O'leana informed when she returned.

"Thank you, O'leana. I will step out while you assist the princess."

Béo paced outside Tynae's door while he waited.

The chancellor returned hastily. "Here are your clothes, My Lord. May I be of further service?"

"Thank you, Breck, no."

Breck bowed.

It wasn't long before the chamber door cracked open, "Will there be anything else, My Lady?"

"No thank you, O'leana that will be all. I'll see you in the morning."

Béo re-entered the room.

Passing Béo on her way out O'leana curtsied, "Good evening, My Lord."

Béo took his seat beside Tynae's bed once more.

"I hate not being able to see, this is so irritating." Tynae squinted. "I hope it's not permanent."

"I'm sure it's not," Béo assured.

"Did your nightclothes arrive?" Tynae asked, smiling. "All I can see is a big blur."

"Yes." Béo chuckled. "I even put them on."

"Getting cheeky are we?" Tynae teased. "You always make me smile, Béo," she said warmly.

"It wasn't necessary. I was fine in my clothes."

"There's no need for you to be uncomfortable." Tynae felt around her bed, "Is there an extra blanket in here?"

"Yes, would you like it?"

"Please."

Standing, Béo walked over to the wardrobe. "Got it."

Tynae sat up, leaning against the headboard. "I have a request."

"Anything, My La…Tynae." Béo walked to the foot of her bed.

Tynae grinned timidly. "Thank you. I want you to lay with me on the bed, atop the coverlet of course." Tynae patted the bed. "This way there will be no question as to my virtue or your chivalry," she said plainly. "Perhaps then I can actually get some sleep."

Béo did not respond. Overcome with surprise once again Béo stood rooted to the spot he stood upon, so very thankful Tynae could not see him clearly.

"Béo?" Tynae's face was heartbreaking. "Please don't make me beg," she said softly.

Regaining his ability to move Béo smiled sheepishly. "I'm sorry. Of course I will lay with you." Béo got on the bed beside Tynae.

Tynae's demeanor became serene. "Thank you. Please make yourself comfortable."

Tynae turned so that she and Béo faced each other, he could tell she was struggling to see.

"I have just one last request," Tynae said. "Would you please hold my hand? This has been an extremely long and trying day. I just need to know that I have a friend here while I sleep."

Overcome with compassion gazing into Tynae's stunning gray eyes, the reality of the day's events hit him, hard. *I almost lost her today.* Right then and there Béo dubbed himself Tynae's personal guardian, swearing an oath to himself. *From this day forward, I will not let Tynae wander from my sight. Even if it means dying, I will never allow anyone or anything to harm her ever again, for as long as I live.* Béo laced his fingers between Tynae's. "I will gladly hold your hand, My La..." Béo smiled, "Tynae. Sleep well," he said tenderly.

"Good night, Béo."

It took less than three heart beats and Tynae was fast asleep.

Béo's day had been equally as long. He knew that he too needed to get some rest, but how could he? He was lying next to the woman he'd loved from afar for years.

Béo watched Tynae as she slept. Her ethereal beauty was entrancing. *I love you so much, Tynae, please stay with me forever.*

Several hours passed while Béo watched Tynae slumber. Eventually his eyelids became heavy and he too succumbed to exhaustion.

As Tynae slept she found herself in a small quiet garden. Looking around, Tynae took in her surroundings. Soon she became aware that she was wearing a form-fitting royal blue gown. The material was unbelievably soft. It must have been sewn from the finest silk in the world. Inspecting her body further, Tynae realized her hair too had been transformed. It was pulled back in a long thick braid. She also felt a circlet around her head. Tynae's attention was drawn away from her attire when she saw a man approaching. He wore black suede trousers, a dark blue tunic, and black leather boots. Dressed quite simply in comparison to her, his status in no way was discernable. It mattered not to Tynae if he was a peasant, nobleman, or king.

Taking Tynae's face tenderly in his hands her mystery man kissed her gently on the lips. "I'm here, Tynae. I never left you. I never will."

Tynae melted into his arms. *Do I know this man? His voice, his touch, everything about him is so comforting and familiar, like an old friend.*

The man gazed at Tynae, as if in disbelief. Lovingly he touched her face, letting his fingers glide softly over her cheek, along her jaw, and down her neck.

Tynae was completely entranced by his striking blue eyes. Looking into them made her feel safe, like nothing could ever harm her. "Are you real?" Tynae asked.

"I am very real, my love."

"What is your name?"

"Ryedin."

"Where are you, Ryedin, are you in Calai?"

"I am wherever you are."

"How did you get into my dreams? Do I know you? Will we be together at some point?"

Ryedin chuckled, "So many questions. Are we not together at this very moment?"

Tynae arched a brow.

Ryedin let out a hardy laugh. "Never the patient one…some things never change. We will be together in due time, I promise. I love you so much, Tynae." He stroked her cheek. "You are the missing part of me. We make each other whole, you will see."

The man's words touched Tynae's soul. He spoke as if he knew her.

Brushing her cheek again, Ryedin smiled slightly. "I just wanted you to know that I'm still here, now get some rest," he insisted.

Tynae leaned into his warm touch as he brushed his hand under her chin.

Looking deep into her eyes Ryedin leaned forward kissing Tynae tenderly.

Not wanting him to stop, she wrapped her arms around Ryedin's neck.

He held her firmly.

She'd never felt so safe in all her life.

"Please don't go," she whispered.

Smiling brightly, Ryedin happily obliged. "I will stay with you for a time, my love," he said softly holding Tynae tight.

Taking Tynae by the hand Ryedin led her to an over-sized, over-stuffed lounge chair that sat amongst a beautiful array of colorful flowers near a small waterfall.

Together they lay on the chair staring into each others' eyes. Neither spoke, somehow words were not necessary.

Resting his forehead against hers, Ryedin gently stroked Tynae's cheek and her eyes slid shut.

"I love you," she whispered drifting into a peaceful sleep.

Tynae was unaware of how much time had passed, but it felt like hours, several relaxing and blissful hours.

"My love," Ryedin whispered, "It's time for you to go back."

Drowsily Tynae opened her eyes. "I don't want to go back," she told him, running her fingers through his hair. "I want to stay right here with you, forever," Tynae insisted, kissing his soft lips.

He smiled. "I would love nothing more, but you and I both have obligations we must see to." He stroked her face lovingly. "Soon we will be able to stay with each other, I promise."

His words didn't make sense, but she understood the part about staying with each other.

"Forever?" she asked.

"Forever," he assured resting his forehead on hers.

"I don't understand any of this," she sighed, "but I trust you with my life, nay my very soul and I have no idea why. So I will go, trusting that I shall see you again." Reaching up Tynae delicately touched Ryedin's face.

Wrapping his arms tight around Tynae's waist Ryedin pulled her tight.

Tynae looked into Ryedin's deep blue eyes. Leaning forward she pressed her mouth against his. "Please don't leave me," she whispered against his lips.

Gently pulling away, Ryedin smiled softly. "I'll never leave you, my angel, from this day forward we shall be together forever. Even if you don't recognize me I am always with you," he insisted, brushing her cheek.

"This will all make perfect sense to you in time. Things are different now, I've learned from my mistakes and we will no longer be kept apart." He took her face lovingly in his hands. "You will see me the next time you sleep, I promise." Pressing his forehead to hers, he grinned. "Now get some more rest, please."

With one last gentle kiss, Ryedin turned. Walking into a shimmering mist, he vanished just as quietly as he had appeared.

Standing alone in the beautiful garden Tynae was saddened by Ryedin's departure. She'd never had dreams like this before. *Could this possibly be real?*

Slowly the garden faded into darkness, and restful sleep settled in.

Chapter 11
Wherefore Art Thou

"We burn daylight."
~William Shakespeare

When Tynae did not show for breakfast King Yurgon went to her room to check on her, thinking she may have fallen ill.

Yurgon knocked twice, but got no answer. Slowly opening the door the king looked inside. Glancing around it was not only apparent Tynae was not there, but it was clear she had not slept in her bed.

Tynae had never spent the night away from the castle, and she would on no account slip away without telling her father first. Though she was not a child and did not need her father's permission, Tynae knew how he worried about her, and always told him where she was going.

Walking back to his study Yurgon wondered if he was over reacting, but the more he thought about it the more he became convinced that something was horribly wrong. This was incredibly out of character for Tynae.

Entering his study Yurgon pulled a thick green and gold cord that hung near his desk, summoning his guards.

Duke Gwillim along with four guards rushed to the king's study.

"Your Majesty." Gwillim bowed as did the other guards.

"Gwillim, have you seen Lady Tynae? She appears to have spent the night away from the castle." Yurgon's voice was calm.

Gwillim shook his head. "No, Majesty, last I saw her was at the ball. She was dancing with Prince Kaleal looking rather cozy. Is there something amiss, Sire?" Gwillim asked with concern.

"I'm not sure, but it is unlike Tynae to not sleep in her own bed. I want Darvah searched from top to bottom. Leave no stone unturned, and no room is to be excluded, not even my chambers.

Tear this castle apart brick by brick if you must, but find my daughter," the king demanded.

"Of course, Majesty." Gwillim turned to his soldiers. "Vangor, Rapheeon, go and gather every soldier you can find, then meet me in the courtyard."

"Yes, Your Grace." The men departed immediately.

Gwillim continued dispatching his men, "Dechai, find Enessa and Vinard. I want to speak with them. They may know something."

Acknowledging his orders, Dechai quickly departed.

"Dovic, you're with me." Gwillim turned to the king, "Sire, we'll let you know the instant we discover anything."

The king gave a half smile. "I know I can count on you, Gwillim."

With a bow Gwillim and Dovic turned to leave.

Baroness Arona entered as they exited. She and Gwillim exchanged a fleeting glance.

Gwillim suddenly felt nauseous.

How had he allowed things to get so far out of hand? However it happened, it was too late to turn back now. He was caught between a rock and a hard place, forcing him to play his part in this living nightmare. The deed could not be undone. There was nothing Gwillim could ever do to put right the atrocity committed by he and his men. If he did anything to betray the Baroness, his entire family would be slaughtered; babies, wife, elderly parents, nothing was sacred to Arona. She would dismember, disembowel, and decapitate every member of Gwillim's beloved family right before his eyes. Once satisfied she had completely driven him mad she may have allowed him the peace of death.

Once outside the study Gwillim put his hand up signaling Dovic to stop. Gwillim wanted to hear what Arona would say.

"What's happened, Sire? I heard the alarm, is something the matter?" she asked concerned.

Gwillim's gut twisted. Swallowing hard, he tried to subdue his gag reflex as pungent bile flooded his mouth. Arona and her facade sickened him. Gwillim didn't know if he was more repulsed by Arona's actions, or his own. *How are we going to pull this off? Why did Arona want Tynae out of the way so badly? Why didn't she have us kill the king as well? Are Tynae and the king not of the same name, same blood? Do they both not share the same vision for our lands? What does Arona have to gain by removing Lady Tynae?* Arona never let Gwillim in on her entire plan, just bits and pieces. He didn't know how she foresaw making any of it work. *What if she tells the king it was I and my men who plotted and killed the princess?* He hadn't thought of this until now. What little bit of color remained in Gwillim's face quickly drained. The thought of Arona turning on them had never occurred to him, but now that the idea had firmly implanted itself in his mind he became very ill. *Why did I not think of this before?* Unable to stomach anymore of the baroness' shite Gwillim jerked his head, letting Dovic know he was ready to leave.

"If we'd stayed there any longer we would have needed to get shovels to dig the king out from under all the manure Arona was dumping on him," Dovic commented, looking at Gwillim as they walked. "Your Grace, are you alright? You look...green."

Gwillim's face twisted as he swallowed, trying to remove the bitter taste that remained in his mouth. "I'm fine, let's just get this performance underway. The sooner the final curtain falls, the better," Gwillim spat.

Situated in the courtyard, Gwillim and Dovic awaited the return of the other soldiers. A fair bit of time had passed when King Yurgon joined them.

Dechai was the first to return, Vinard and Enessa following close behind. They appeared puzzled by what was happening.

With the king watching Gwillim was forced to play his role to the hilt.

Enessa had been Princess Tynae's Lady in Waiting for several years. Marrying later in life, Enessa did not have many years with her husband before he died. Alone and childless Enessa cherished the opportunity to be Tynae's handmaiden.

Where Vinard was concerned there was no secret that he and Tynae where the best of friends. The pair could be found together most days, even during his time off.

Gwillim broached the subject of the princess carefully, for Tynae was beloved by many. He did not know who was in on Arona's scam, who was completely innocent, or who his potential enemies were. Someone had told Tynae the soldiers were coming for her, he knew that for a fact. Whoever that was, could potentially reveal Gwillim and his men as Tynae's killers.

Gwillim decided to come at this from a, 'lets not get too worried *yet'*, stance. "Enessa, Vinard, we don't want you to be alarmed, we don't even know if anything is wrong, but no-one can find Lady Tynae and we are a bit concerned. Have either of you seen her this morning?" Gwillim's tone was friendly.

Vinard and Enessa looked surprised by this news.

Enessa looked from Gwillim to the king then back to Gwillim. "No, Your Grace." She shook her head. "The last I saw of her was at the ball last eve. She was with Prince Kaleal. She insisted that Vinard and I could go. She and the prince seemed to want some privacy so we took our leave." Enessa shrugged, "That's the last time I saw her."

Vinard nodded, "That's the last time I saw her as well."

Apprehensive, Enessa added, "I know it's not like her to stay out, but perhaps she and the prince snuck off someplace..." Enessa looked at Yurgon, "someplace without prying eyes perhaps?"

Vinard nodded in agreement.

Shaking his head the king rejected Enessa's hypothesis. "No, I spoke with Kal a few moments ago. She left the ball shortly after you, according to him, and she left alone."

"So neither of you have seen her this morning, is that correct?" Gwillim asked patiently.

"Correct," Enessa replied.

"That is correct, Your Grace." Vinard shook his head, "I have not seen her."

Yurgon sighed. "And neither of you have any idea where she is, or where she may have spent the night?" There was a pleading tone in Yurgon's voice that could not be missed.

Before Enessa or Vinard could answer, the side gate groaned as it opened. Everyone fell silent, turning.

It was Vangor and Rapheeon. They entered with nearly five hundred soldiers in tow. The soldiers dispersed themselves around the courtyard, quietly awaiting their orders.

All together there are about eleven thousand soldiers stationed in Pathrow alone, but currently half, if not more, were away. Some had been stationed with other regiments throughout Montronvarr for training, while others were on holiday, and some were just not home when Vangor and Rapheeon called on them.

Seeing that it was only the soldiers they were expecting, everyone resumed their previous conversation.

Looking at the king apologetically Enessa shook her head, "No, Sire, I have no idea where she may be."

"Nor do I," Vinard said.

The king nodded once. "Very well then, thank you. Enessa, you may go, Vinard please join your regiment."

Vinard bowed, quickly taking his leave.

Bowing her head, Enessa curtsied to the king. Turning to walk away, she looked back remorsefully. "I am truly sorry I could not be of more assistance, Your Majesty."

Yurgon gave Enessa a caring smile. "I know you love her as much as I, Enessa. Rest assured we will find her." The king's smile faded abruptly. "And if any harm has befallen her, you can bet your life that those responsible will suffer great consequences," Yurgon stated crossly.

Enessa grinned. "I have every confidence in you, Majesty." She nodded once more to the king than turned to Gwillim nodding to him.

Gwillim returned the gesture.

Before Enessa took her gaze from Gwillim she arched a brow then turned away.

Gwillim caught the subtle gesture, but wasn't sure what to make of it. His heart hammered and his palms began to sweat as he contemplated the possible meaning of her message. *Does she know something?* Startled, he gawk at Enessa as she walked away. *No, she would have said something to the king if she knew anything. I'm just being paranoid.*

A loud sneeze from one of the soldiers startled Gwillim, bringing him back to reality. Shaking off his paranoia, Gwillim quickly got back into character.

Pulling his shoulders back, Gwillim walked over to a large fountain that stood in the middle of the courtyard. Climbing atop the bricks forming the base of the fountain, Gwillim could now be seen by all the soldiers.

Gwillim addressed his army. "Gentlemen, Lady Tynae has not been seen since last evening, we need to search every inch of the grounds and the castle. We will not stop until we find her. I will remain in this area. You are to return to me the instant you find anything. Break into groups of three, search every, and I mean every inch of Darvah. Send all the people you come across, this means maids, cooks, bishops, *everyone*, send them to me. No-one is to leave this castle until I have personally questioned them. Assuming I find their answers satisfactory, they will be free to come and go as they please. I expect at least one person from each group to check in occasionally, and all of you are to return here at dusk."

The soldiers stared awkwardly at Gwillim.
"What are you waiting for? Go!"

Quickly the soldiers broke into groups as ordered, then moved out.

As his men departed Gwillim glanced up, spotting Arona looking down from her study.

Wearing a smug smile she stroked Tynae's ring as she stared out of her window. Arona watched proudly as the first bits of chaos ignited. It was evident by her smirk she was quite please with herself.

Arona gave Gwillim a slight nod. He returned the gesture then made it a point not to look in her direction again for the rest of the day…*Witch.*

The day passed slowly as Gwillim interviewed every member of the king's staff.

Yurgon came out periodically to see how things were progressing. The king's growing concern was becoming more evident.

Soldiers began returning to the courtyard as twilight dawned. They were instructed to join the king and Gwillim in the hall of Naviyd. Once all the soldiers where seated King Yurgon addressed them. "Thank you for your diligence today men. I was hoping we would find some trace of my daughter by now, but I will not give up hope. I will not stop searching until Tynae has been found, and returned here to Darvah. We've managed to locate several more of your counterparts throughout the day. They will pick up where you left off." The king looked at Gwillim who stood to his right. "So now I will turn the floor over." Yurgon stepped aside, "High Constable."

"Thank you, Sire." Gwillim bowed to the king. "I must repeat what His Majesty has said. Thank you for your diligence and we will not stop until we find Princess Tynae. For those of you just coming on duty you will be searching the Forest of Nombin tonight. For those of you finishing up, we will apprise you of any progress we make first thing in the morning." Gwillim glanced at the king then continued. "If tonight's search proves unsuccessful we will begin searching all of Pathrow tomorrow. Goodnight gentlemen, we will see all of you back here at dawn."

Gwillim remained with the king until all the soldiers had gone. "Will there be anything else, Your Majesty?" he asked politely.

The king shook his head. "No, Gwillim thank you, you may go home to your family. Be sure to give those beautiful children of yours a big hug from me, and get some rest." Yurgon's voice was somber.

The king's demeanor was heartbreaking, but Gwillim managed a thoughtful smile. "Thank you, My Liege. We will find Lady Tynae, I give you my word. You try to get some rest as well. I'll see you at dawn." Bowing Gwillim took his leave.

Thank God, I just want to get the bloody hell away from Darvah, the king, and especially Arona. Not ready to go home and face his wife just yet, Gwillim took refuge in the armory. He lit no candles. Sitting in the dark he replayed the day's events in his mind.

It was quite late when Gwillim was finally ready to leave. He made his way quickly toward the gates leading to the city, but stopped abruptly when Arona stepped out of the shadows. Lost in thought and caught off guard, Gwillim automatically drew his sword, almost running her through.

Realizing who it was, Gwillim sheathed his weapon. *Shite! What the bloody hell does she want now?* "Baroness Arona, I apologize, I mean, Your Highness. You should never sneak up on me like that, especially at this hour," Gwillim warned.

"I suppose it is rather late. I will forgive your shortcoming this time," Arona said smoothly stepping closer. "I just wanted to congratulate you on your impressive performance today. I almost believed Lady Tynae was going to be found, and all was going to return to normal once more." Arona laughed coldly taking another step forward, now standing chest to chest with Gwillim. "Keep up the good work, Your Grace…" she purred sliding her cold hand over Gwillim's cheek.

Gwillim wanted to jerk away, but knew better.

"And you will be rewarded handsomely."

Arona looked Gwillim over like a prize stallion.

Adding to Gwillim's dismay, Arona had clearly taken a personal liking to him.

This nightmare just keeps getting better and better doesn't it? He growled inside his mind.

Gwillim switched on a smile. "You're much too generous, Your Highness," Gwillim sputtered, choking back the bile accelerating up his throat.

To Gwillim's relief others were heading toward them.

"I'll see you soon, Gwillim. Keep up the excellent work." Arona ran her fingers through Gwillim's hair as she walked past him.

Gwillim shuddered, disgusted by her icy hands touching him. *They remind me of a decaying corpse.*

Turning quickly, Gwillim left before whoever was headed his direction had a chance to reach him. He did not want to speak with anyone, nor did he wish to resume his role in the ongoing theatrical production, or tragedy as it were. *This day's role-playing is over. All I want to do is get home.*

Once beyond the gates of Darvah Gwillim looked around, ensuring no-one was watching he ran home.

His beautiful wife Layanne greeted him at the door with a warm smile and gentle kiss. "Did you find Lady Tynae?" she asked eagerly.

Gwillim sighed, "No, my love, but men continue to search for her as we speak. If tonight's search is unsuccessful we will continue our search tomorrow, and every day thereafter until we find her." *Will the lies ever end?* "Are the children in bed?" he asked already knowing the answer, but needed a change of subject.

Layanne chuckled. "It's quite late husband, of course they're in bed."

Gwillim smiled at Layanne, running his hand tenderly over her shoulder. "I'll be right back." He kissed her forehead.

"Would you like something to eat?" Layanne called after Gwillim.

But Gwillim did not answer. He was already in his children's room. Lovingly he stared at his daughter and son as they slept peacefully in their warm beds. He was thankful for their existence and could not imagine his life without them. Gwillim loved his children more than life itself and knew that he would not hesitate to kill anyone who tried to harm or take them away from him.

It was in that moment of adoration that Gwillim realized exactly what he had done to his king, what he had *taken* from him. His only child, the light of his world, and his single reason for living...he had in essence taken his kings very life.

Kneeling down beside his daughter's bed Gwillim stared at his precious little girl. She rolled over and Gwillim's heart shattered. In her small hands she clutched her most cherished dolly. It had been a gift from her favorite person, Princess Tynae. Closing his eyes Gwillim shook his head slowly. *Please forgive me.*

Reaching out Gwillim touched his daughter's baby soft hair. "My perfect angel," he whispered, "I love you so much." Leaning forward he kissed *his* princess gently on the cheek.

Walking over to his son's cradle, Gwillim gazed down watching his baby boy. His two perfect tiny pink lips curved into a wide grin, showing his toothless gums as he dreamed and giggled. *What a wonderful time of life,* Gwillim thought. "I love you, my little warrior," he said quietly.

Bending over the edge of the cradle he kissed his son's forehead.

Gwillim crept out of the room, careful not to make a sound.

Standing in the doorway looking back at his two sleeping angels, Arona's plan suddenly became painfully clear. Gwillim's world plunged into absolute darkness in a single heartbeat. *I will let no harm come to you, even if the cost is my life.*

Gwillim walked to the cooking area where Layanne waited for him. "You did not answer me. Would you like me to fix you something to eat?" she asked again.

Grinning, Gwillim shook his head and walked over to his wife.

"No," he answered, wrapping his arms around Layanne, "I just want to hold you close and never let you go."

"Are you okay, Gwillim?"

Gwillim smiled softly. "I'm fine. It's just that these kind of events remind us how the ones we love can be here one instant and gone the next."

Layanne ran her fingers through Gwillim's long hair. "I know exactly what you mean, my love."

The couple stared tenderly at one another.

Leaning forward Gwillim kissed his wife passionately. Layanne was Gwillim's entire world. He loved her more than life itself.

"Come on, let's go to bed. It's been a long day and I want to lie with my beautiful wife."

Exchanging a sly smile that only couples know, Gwillim scooped Layanne up in his arms.

Layanne giggled, "My, I'm sad Lady Tynae is missing, but I do like this."

Wrapping her arms around Gwillim's neck Layanne pressed her lips to his. Their kiss impassioned, neither came up for air as Gwillim carried Layanne to their bedchamber, bumping into walls all the way.

Chapter 12
Discovery

"The only joy in the world is to begin."
~Cesare Payese

When Tynae awoke the next morning she realized that she felt *different*. It was more than just feeling rested or healed. She felt—*alive*!

Sitting up Tynae rubbed her eyes and stretched. To her great pleasure her vision had fully returned. Taking in her surroundings, Tynae was surprised at how grand her room was.

Hearing a crackle she turned her attention toward a large fireplace nestled into the wall to her left. This fireplace was different from any she'd ever seen, most were made of brick or some type of stone, but this one seemed to be an actual part of the wall.

Movement in her bed drew Tynae's attention to the body lying beside her. Though Béo's back was toward her the steady rhythmic sound of his breathing assured Tynae he still slumbered deeply.

Careful not to jostle too much, Tynae climbed out of bed. Glancing at her bedside table she noticed a single white rose. Picking it up, she inhaled its sweet fragrance. Looking at Béo thoughtfully, she smiled. *He's always been so kindhearted.* Setting the flower back down, Tynae began exploring her new surroundings, heading straight to the fireplace. The wall the fireplace was laid within was rather curious as well. Running her hand over it, Tynae quickly realized the wall was not just the color of slate, it was slate. Looking up, she saw the ceiling too was made of the same rock. *We're not only underwater, in the coldest ocean in the world, we're under ground?* She pondered. *It should be freezing in here, yet it's as comfortable as a warm spring day.*

Tynae inspected the fireplace further; it was not built against the wall or into it. It actually *was* the wall.

A large white marble mantel was anchored above the unusual fireplace. Veins of gray and dark brown ran through it, with hints of green and gold flecks. Atop the mantel was an intricately detailed miniature forest, part of it actually carved directly into the wall. Tiny animals were meticulously sprinkled throughout the forest, like delicate jewels.

The pocket sized trees had birds the size of ants perched in the miniscule branches. Bushes with teensy flowers filled a chunk of the forest floor. There were even tiny boulders. The animals had such detail that Tynae wondered if they were the real thing frozen and shrunk to fit in a new environment...*Can they do that?* Looking closer, Tynae saw lace-like ivy climbing the bases of the lifelike trees.

Looking even closer still, Tynae spotted a pack of wolves lying beneath a tree. Longingly Tynae stared at the miniature wolves, recalling her last day with *her* wolves in *her* forest. Tynae touched one of the animals lightly. "She knew," Tynae whispered, thinking of Xantara.

Not wanting to think about any part of home Tynae tore herself away from the hearth, walking toward the back of the room, the wall opposite her bed. Moving slowly, Tynae ran her fingers along the slate. Expecting it to be cool she was surprised to find it warm to the touch. Trying to take everything in Tynae admired several paintings hung throughout the room depicting gardens and seascapes.

Reaching the back of the room Tynae looked up in awe. It wasn't so much a wall as it was a stained glass window. The huge glass wall was made up of multiple colors; blue, purple, and green, were the most dominant. The window had a Celtic Fleur de Lis in the top most center with two hearts entwined directly beneath it. Purple roses adorned the outer edges of the glass masterpiece. Tynae absentmindedly traced one of the glistening roses with her finger tip. Sunlight appeared to be shining through the glass. *That's impossible,* she thought, *we're leagues underwater and underground to boot. There can't be sunlight down here, can there?*

Tynae continued her excursion. Walking to the sitting area located in the middle of her room, she became aware of the floor for the first time when her feet made contact with a snow white rug, made from animal fur.

Looking around at the rest of the room, Tynae realized the floor in general was made of dark wood, as were the two couches and three chairs in the sitting area. All the furniture was covered in plush royal blue velvet. Several ornate white pillows with purple, blue, and green glass beads and threads of gold mimicking the stain glass window where perfectly placed on the furniture.

Looking up Tynae saw a golden chandelier. It too was adorned with purple, blue, and green glass beads, and held thirteen stubby candles.

Sitting down on one of the chairs, Tynae scanned her room. Several flower filled vases where spread throughout. The arrangements were remarkable. *They smell exquisite,* she thought. *How odd, all my senses seem to be incredibly heightened.* After sitting for a spell Tynae resumed her inspection. Standing up she made her way toward a writing desk that stood opposite the fireplace. Tynae marveled at the wall on this side of the room. It was made of russet colored earth, and the desk was actually physically growing directly out of the wall. "This is such a peculiar place," she mused quietly.

Tynae ran her hand across the finely polished dark wood of the desk. A blank piece of parchment lay in the center, almost beckoning to be tickled by the quill perched in the corner of the desktop beside an inkwell. This brought back more memories of home and of the many friends Tynae corresponded with regularly. *Will I ever see any of them again?* Tynae shook off the sadness before it could grab hold. She would not allow herself to become depressed.

As far as she was concerned everything happened for a reason and she was more than thankful to still be alive after the events of the prior eve. She did not know why she had been spared, or why her life was undergoing such dramatic changes. But she accepted them, albeit tepidly, she accepted them nonetheless.

Tynae refused to look backwards, after all life is about moving forward and learning from our past, not dwelling on it. She knew all too well that those who live in the past never truly live at all, simply because they can not see today for the genuine gift that it is. "Perhaps if it were wrapped with a giant bow," she often said, "maybe then they would take a little time to appreciate it and enjoy it for the *present* it truly is."

Pushing her feelings of sorrow aside once again, Tynae focused her attention back on her wonderful room. Looking toward the dressing area in the corner, she saw two huge armoires growing out of the earth like the desk. She wanted to have a peek inside, but didn't want to risk it. She feared that one of the doors would inevitably squeak, and wake Béo.

Walking back to her bed, Tynae picked up the rose on her night table. Inhaling deeply she closed her eyes. It felt as if the essence of the rose were somehow permeating every cell of her being. With an audible exhale Tynae set the flower back on the table and gingerly climbed into bed.

Fluffing her pillows slightly Tynae sat in bed looking up at the breathtaking mural carved into the wooden canopy. The workmanship was flawless. Gazing around Tynae admired the rest of the handsome four-poster. Purple velvet curtains adorned the bed, held to the posters with thick golden ropes that looked like pure gold.

While Tynae admired her surroundings Béo rolled toward her.

Looking at his unconscious form Tynae realized he was still sleeping. *He looks so peaceful lying there, almost angelic.*

Cocking her head Tynae looked at Béo curiously. Her new vision allowed her to see that which she had never seen before.

Béo was more handsome than she remembered, and there was a radiant glow about him.

Has that always been there? She wondered. *It has been a while since I last saw him, but certainly I would have noticed such a vibrant aura.*

Tynae almost jumped out of her skin when Béo awoke.

Yawning sleepily Béo stretched his arms and legs. When he finally got around to opening his eyes he quickly realized Tynae was already awake.

Anxiously sitting up he wiped the sleep from his eyes. "My Lady, did you need something? What may I get you?" he asked hastily.

Tynae held her hand up. "Relax, Béo, I just woke up. No, I do not need anything. I'm fine," Tynae reassured, "and please, call me Tynae, remember."

Slightly embarrassed, Tynae was thankful Béo hadn't caught her staring at him.

"Guess what?" Tynae was smiling from ear to ear.

Béo smiled back, "What?"

"I can see again and I'm better than I was before." Pure elation coated her words.

Straightening up, Béo interlocked his fingers. Stretching his arms out in front of him, he popped his knuckles then froze for a second. Looking puzzled he turned to Tynae. "What do you mean, *'better than before'*?" He scratched his stubble covered cheek.

Tynae shrugged, uncertain how to explain her new and improved self. "It seems that all my senses are keener than they've ever been. I can see clearer and further than I ever have, and the detail I can see is astonishing," she said excitedly, "and smell! I can smell things, things that I could never have smelled previously."

"Like what?"

"Well," Tynae looked around at the numerous vases, "I can distinguish the individual smell of each flower in every one of these bouquets." She smiled, "It's amazing." Tynae settled back into her pillows, taking in every aspect of her room.

Béo smiled exuberantly.

Suddenly, Tynae sat bolt upright. "You don't think it's only temporary do you?" she asked, almost panicked.

Béo's smile widened. "No," he chuckled shaking his head, "I do not think it's temporary. Father said Zandore possesses a very powerful magic, so I'm certain him healing you has a *little* something to do with your changes." Béo threw back the covers, climbing out of bed. "Which reminds me," Béo held up a finger. "Tell no-one of Zandore. No-one knows he exists—hell, up until last night *I* didn't even know he still existed." Béo stood in front of the crackling fire.

"Okay."

Béo smiled reassuringly at Tynae who looked a little taken aback.

"Don't worry, father will…"

The last thing Tynae heard Béo say was something about his father. When Béo had gotten out of bed Tynae's attention was drawn away from his words and directly to his form. She took in every aspect of Béo's masculine physique. His cinnamon brown hair, striking blue eyes, fair complexion, and even though he had on his sleeping attire she could clearly see the silhouette of his muscular body, thanks to the firelight behind him.

Warming himself Béo turned sideways.

Tynae blinked twice as she got an eyeful.

Oh my…

Catching herself Tynae quickly looked down at her hands, blushing crimson. *What am I doing? I've never looked at any man this way.*

"I'm going to get changed," Béo said, walking into the lavatory.

"Okay." Tynae barely glanced at him. *What does all this mean? So much has changed in just one day.* She was just beginning to realize how much her life and her world had been forever altered. Sitting, Tynae contemplated the palm of her hand, hoping the redness in her face would dissipate before Béo came back in. Straightening up Tynae sniffed the air. Something smelled delicious. "Yumm."

"Excuse me?" Béo asked emerging from the lavatory.

"Béo!" Blood flooded Tynae's face. "I… I didn't see you there! Breakfast, I was talking about breakfast. It smells scrumptious." Tynae tossed back the covers, "Join me? Please."

Béo rushed to Tynae's side before she had a chance to stand up, taking hold of her arm.
"Béo, I'm fine, really. I've never felt so strong," she assured.
Disregarding Tynae's affirmation, Béo grabbed her robe off the chair beside the bed helping her put it on. "I'm not going to take any chances when it comes to *you,* not after yesterday." Béo scrutinized Tynae carefully. "As a matter of fact," a broad smile crossed his handsome face, "I don't think I'll let you out of my sight ever again...and yes, I'd love to join you for breakfast." Béo smiled, "After you." He gestured toward a small dining table near the stained glass window.

Tynae rolled her eyes, grinning. "Thank you," she shot Béo a sideways glance walking past him. "I think."

Without warning Tynae turned, looking Béo dead in the eyes. Her swift movement caught Béo off guard, causing him to almost topple over. She took a step closer, "One should never make promises they can not keep," Tynae breathed silkily.

Béo stood rooted to the spot.

Chuckling, Tynae stepped back shaking her head. She knew full well no-one could ever accomplish such a feat. *"Never let me out of your sight,"* she laughed. "That's a good one." Looking at Béo Tynae smiled knowing he meant every word he spoke. "You really are something, Béo. Come on." Tynae tugged Béo's hand, leading him over to the dining table.

Béo pulled out Tynae's chair.

"Thank you." She sat down. "By the way, I told O'leana I wanted a bath this morning so if you need to leave, feel free." Tynae tried to keep her tone nonchalant, but there was a definite poutiness in her words. Tynae did not want to be left alone, but insecurity and apprehension were unfamiliar emotions for the independent princess. "I'm sure there are matters you'd like to tend to." Tynae forced a grin.

Sitting down, Béo smiled at Tynae. "I do have a few things I should take care of," he said, "but I will return as soon as I've finished."

Tynae perked up instantly. "Great!" she said a little too exuberantly, "I mean," she gathered herself, "you don't have to rush back on my account. I'll be fine here." Tynae smiled, biting her lip in an attempt to control her childish grin.

"I..."

Before Béo could get his words out there was a knock on the door, it was O'leana with breakfast. She served the pair then left them to eat in private.

Tynae grinned at Béo, "You were saying?"

"I was just going to say that I won't be long, I promise," Béo assured.

"Thank you." Tynae knew he was expediting his errands on her account. "The food looks great doesn't it? Let's eat. I'm starving."

After taking only a few bites Tynae stared at her plate, poking at her breakfast with her fork.

Béo set his fork down. "Tynae, what's wrong?" he asked sympathetically.

Setting down her own fork Tynae looked up at Béo somberly and sighed. "Béo, may I ask you about last night?"

"Of course," he put his hand on hers. "But I may not be able to answer all your questions. I am not yet a part of the Greer government and as such my father does not share many of the goings on of Calai with me."

Tynae nodded. "I understand." She smiled slightly. "Do you know why Gwillim attempted to kill me or why Baroness Arona wants me dead?" Tynae was unsure if she really wanted to know the answer.

Béo looked as miserable as Tynae felt. "I'm sorry, I do not."

Tynae sighed. "That's okay. I hadn't really expected you to know the answer, but I had to ask." Tynae fidgeted in her chair. "Is my father safe or...?" Tynae's throat constricted as she realized Arona may have ordered the same fate upon her father as she had for Tynae.

"Your father is fine, this I do know for a fact. But it is my understanding that he believes you to be..." Béo looked down, pausing for a moment. Looking back at Tynae he squeezed her hand slightly, "missing, and soon he will believe you to be..." Béo took a deep breath, "dead," he said plainly. "It must unfortunately stay this way for now. Everyone's safety depends upon it." Béo watched helplessly as Tynae's expression turn to heartbreak. "I'm so sorry, Tynae," he said softly.

Forcing a half smile, Tynae struggled to hold back her tears. "It's okay, I understand, really, but my poor father," her voice quivered slightly. Tynae and her father were incredibly close. She knew he'd be devastated at the thought of his only child being dead.

Tynae was quickly becoming homesick. She missed her father, his hearty laugh, and the tight bear hugs he often gave her. She would do whatever was necessary to keep him safe, but that didn't make the situation any easier. Tynae stared off into space for a heartbeat then her eyes met Béo's.

He smiled slightly. "Did you want to know something else?"

"No," she sighed, "I can save my other questions for the chief. As long as I know my father is safe, that's all I really care about."

Picking up her fork Tynae dug into her meal. "This food is really delicious," she said brightly.

Béo looked a bit taken aback by Tynae's sudden change of demeanor, but said nothing.

As they ate, there was another knock at the door.

"Enter," Tynae called.

O'leana poked her head in, "My Lady, Chief Kerszon was wondering if he might have a word."

Tynae smiled, "Of course. When…"

O'leana stepped aside, allowing Chief Kerszon to enter the room.

Tynae's eyes got huge. She thought the chief wanted to see her in his study, not that he was standing outside her door. The princess tried standing up so fast that she nearly fell over.

The Chief put his hand up. "Please don't get up on my account, Lady Tynae." Kerszon crossed the room.

Tynae sat back down. This was the first time she had actually seen Chief Kerszon properly and not as a blur. "Chief Kerszon…"

Tynae's words were cut short when Kerszon raised his hand once more. "Call me Kerszon please, or Chief, whichever you prefer. I do not expect you to be so formal with me, after all we are equals." Kerszon smiled.

Tynae was slightly stunned. Most people she knew who held a title of any sort insisted on being addressed as such.

Tynae beamed! "Very well, *Chief*, and I would prefer that you call me Tynae."

"I think I can do that," Kerszon replied. "I stopped by to…"

Looking at Kerszon, Tynae couldn't help but stare. He stood over a full meter and was stunningly handsome—*now I know where Béo got his looks from*—and though he wore a pair of tan suede britches; he did not wear a tunic. She could see the defined outline of every muscle on his perfect body. He was a living, breathing image of a god.

Tynae's eyes slowly traveled up Kerszon's washboard stomach, over his muscular chest, glanced across his rippling shoulders, and past his neck. The next thing Tynae knew she was looking into Kerszon's piercing green eyes.

Realizing he had been speaking to her, Tynae felt her face flush three different shades of red…she hadn't heard a single word the chief had spoken. Tynae never took her eyes from Kerszon's. "I am so sorry," she said ashamed.

The chief merely laughed. "I am well aware that you are not accustomed to our way of life. Please do not be embarrassed," Kerszon grinned.

Tynae nodded her head graciously. "Thank you, Chief." Kerszon stood a few feet from her and Béo. Tynae knew he was waiting on her to respond to whatever he had said. She tried to stop the corners of her mouth from turning up, but to no avail. A huge grin planted itself firmly on Tynae's face. "Umm, what was your question? Because I didn't hear a single word you said," she confessed.

All three laughed as Tynae made light of her faux pas.

Tynae pulled out the chair beside her. "Please, sit with us."

"Thank you." Kerszon graciously accepted the invitation, taking a seat. "I just wanted to see how you're feeling today."

Tynae lit up. "Oh, I feel amazing. I've never felt so good in all my life. I can see the finest details on things even from a distance, and I can distinguish individual aromas amidst several other fragrances." Jubilation permeated Tynae's words.

Kerszon beamed as he listened to Tynae eagerly describe her astounding recovery.

"I feel strong and rested. Like I told Béo, I feel ALIVE, it's absolutely phenomenal."

The broad smile on the chief's face said everything. "That's wonderful, Tynae. We were all so worried about you. Everyone will be elated to hear that you're doing so well." Kerszon stood.

"Are you leaving already?" Tynae asked, also standing.

"I'm afraid so. I just wanted to stop by for a progress report. I have to get back to my duties and the others will want to hear how you're doing. What do you say to supper a week from tomorrow?" Kerszon smiled.

"That sounds marvelous," Tynae said brightly.

"Wonderful. I'll let everyone know and I'll have O'leana inform you of the exact time." Taking a step toward Tynae, Kerszon put his hands on her shoulders. "I am overjoyed you are doing so well, my dear."

"Thank you, Chief. If not for you," she glanced at Béo, "and, Béo of course," she looked back to Kerszon, "the Archimagi, and Zandore, I would not be here. If not for all of you I would be no more. I owe my life to you. I'll never be able to thank you enough."

"You're so much stronger than you know, Tynae, but you're quite welcome, sunshine. We were more than happy to help." Kerszon's words sounded vaguely familiar, unable to place where she'd heard them before, Tynae dismissed the brief bout of déjà vu.

"We will see you soon. Until then, My Lady," Kerszon took Tynae's hand, kissing it softly, "be well."

Tynae bowed her head, "You as well, My Lord."

Kerszon nodded his head to Béo, "Son."

"Father," Béo returned the nod.

Once Kerszon departed O'leana came in. "Your bath will be ready momentarily, My Lady."

"Thank you, O'leana."

"Well," Béo stood up, "that's my cue to get out of your hair."

Tynae walked Béo to the door.

"I'll be back in a bit. Enjoy your bath." With a wink Béo departed.

O'leana walked to the lavatory, opening the antique looking door...Tynae followed.

It was warm and steamy inside, exactly how Tynae liked it. Seeing the room clearly for the first time, Tynae realized the entire chamber was made of marble and all the fixtures of pure gold. She also realized that the floor beneath her feet was oddly warm, not cool or cold the way marble should be. Tynae's eyes wandered to a corner where her tattered dress lie in a heap, exactly where Tynae had asked O'leana to leave it the night before.

"My Lady, this is Koralie and Sireeon." The two handmaidens bowed their heads.

Tynae nodded, "Pleased to meet you both."

O'leana assisted Tynae in removing her nightgown.

Stepping down into the oversized bath, Tynae sank into the warm rose water. It felt and smelled incredible.

"Does the temperature suit you, My Lady?" Koralie asked.

Tynae settled in by the edge of the bath. "It's perfect, Koralie, thank you."

O'leana, along with Koralie and Sireeon, proceeded to bathe Tynae. When they were finished they allowed the princess time to soak undisturbed.

When Tynae was ready to get out, O'leana dried her with a towel then helped her with her robe.

"May I please see my dress?" Tynae pointed to the corner.

"Of course." Sireeon grabbed the crumpled mass, handing it to Tynae.

Tynae examined the shredded remains of her once beautiful gown. There wasn't much left and what small bits remained where covered with her blood.

"Thank you." Tynae handed it back to Sireeon. "You may dispose of it."

"As you wish," O'leana responded.

Together, the four women walked to the dressing area in Tynae's sleeping chamber.

"My Lady, our attire in Calai is not what you are accustomed to. We can have clothes made specifically for you if you wish," O'leana offered.

Tynae peered inside the over stuffed armoire. "I don't want *special* clothes made for me. I wish to wear the same clothing as the Greer." Tynae turned to O'leana with a smile, "So, what do you suggest?"

"Well, My Lady, for a woman of your status, grace, and beauty, you'd wear an outfit like this." Reaching into the huge wardrobe, O'leana pulled out something golden and held it up.

Tynae stared at two pieces of shiny gold material. The part that was to be worn on the top half of her body looked like it was barely enough material to cover her breasts, and the piece that went around the waist was short and somewhat sheer.

Blood rushed to Tynae's cheeks as she stared at the tiny outfit. "Wow!" Tynae breathed. "Well, when in Calai," she muttered. Taking a deep breath, Tynae looked at O'leana and smiled. "I think it's absolutely beautiful. I'll wear it," she said cheerfully.

O'leana returned the smile. "It will look lovely on you, Majesty. There are other customary pieces as well that Chief Kerszon sent along with it. May we dress you in the full attire befitting a Lady of Calai?"

Tynae glanced inside the wardrobe again, stunned by the chief's generosity. "Chief Kerszon sent *all* this?"

"Yes, My Lady."

"I would be honored, yes. Thank you." Tynae sat down and her handmaidens went to work.

When finished the maids led Tynae to a large mirror.

Tynae's eyes grew wide when she saw herself. She had never seen her hair so straight, it reached all the way to her waist, and in it was long strands of golden thread. The makeup on her face made her appear flawless and upon her forehead were golden jewels. The gold material covering her chest crisscrossed, tying in the back and around her neck. There was nothing else to it. Her entire mid-section was exposed. The sheer material covering Tynae's bottom half simply wrapped around her waist, tying on the side. Even her undergarments were made of shimmering gold material. Other pieces adorned Tynae's body. Gold chains wrapped around her waist, ankles, and arms. One of the two things that had not been lost or destroyed during Tynae's flight for her life was a beautiful pair of long golden earrings. These had been a birthday gift from her father a few months prior, and went perfectly with her new attire. The other thing was a dagger, which Tynae insisted on strapping to her thigh, as she never went anywhere without it. The finishing touch was a soft perfume that smelled of jasmine and ginger.

A knock came at the door just as the women finished.

"Enter," Tynae called out.

Walking into the room, Béo could not see Tynae. Sireeon, Koralie, and O'leana stood in front of her. When they stepped aside, Béo's mouth fell open. Walking further into the room, Béo's eyes got huge. He literally tripped over his own feet.

Trying not to giggle, Tynae lowered her head and fidgeted with a gold chain around her waist. Taking a deep breath, she looked up at Béo innocently. "Does this mean you approve?" she asked shyly, doing a little spin.

Seeming to be tongue tied, it was a few moments before Béo spoke. "Umm...Greer fashion...it...it suits you...rather, well...you are..." Béo looked Tynae over slowly, "magnificent."

"Thank you, Béo," Tynae said timidly.

Distracted by Béo's scorching eyes, Tynae jumped with a start when O'leana addressed her. "My Lady, would you like me to prepare supper for you and Lord Béo this evening or will you be dining in one of the halls?"

Tynae fiddled with some flowers in a vase beside her, attempting to conceal her awkwardness. "I'm not sure," Tynae looked at Béo, "what would you like to do?"

Béo thought for a second. "I think we should dine in. O'leana is an excellent cook."

O'leana curtsied. "Thank you, My Lord."

"Then dining in it is," Tynae reiterated.

O'leana bowed, "Very well, I shall have supper ready and waiting for you. Will there be anything else, Majesty?"

"No, O'leana, thank you. We will see you this evening."

Bowing, the three maids took their leave.

Tynae turned her attention back to Béo. "If you're not too busy today, would you mind showing me around Calai?" Tynae looked around her room. "I still can't believe it really exists and that I'm actually here."

Béo's smile was dazzling. "I'd love to show you our city, and whatever you want to know about the Greer, just ask." Béo looked somewhat concerned, "Are you sure you're not tired?"

Tynae smiled, "Positive. I feel as though I could swim a thousand leagues and still have energy to burn." Tynae put her hand on Béo's arm, "I promise, if I get tired I will tell you."

Béo shook his head. "How can I resist those eyes?" he joked, "Okay. Let's get started then, but first I want to show you around Vu'tella."

Tynae looked confused.

Grinning, Béo answered her impending question, "Your chambers."

"My chambers..." This confused Tynae even more, "Oh, okay." *What could possibly be so exciting about a few rooms?* She wondered.

Béo opened the door leading from her sleeping chamber to the rest of the dwelling.

Stepping through the doorway, Tynae could not believe her eyes. Never in her life had she seen such a place. Astounded, Tynae marveled at her unique room.

Directly in front of her, slightly to the left was a traditional sitting room, dining area, and cooking area. Beyond that was a long hall which she assumed led to the servant's quarters. But, the area to her right was unlike anything she'd ever seen. A waterfall cascaded down out of the wall, flowing through a vibrant, living, scaled-down forest taking up more than half the huge room. Lush green shrubs were everywhere. Long vines with gorgeous purple flowers crept over the stone walls and a rainbow of blossoms blanketed the floor of the mini-forest. But the part that truly amazed Tynae was the wall made out of clear glass, looking out into the depths of the sea.

Grinning, Béo walked to the head of a trail leading into the forest. "Come on," he held out his hand.

Tynae followed eagerly.

A wide stream flowed off the waterfall, zigzagging through the center of the forest. A quaint bridge crossed the stream, allowing access to the other side. Drawing closer to the window the ground transitioned from dirt and moss to something green and shimmering. Kneeling down, Tynae scooped up a handful of the shiny earth, "It's sand."

Béo chuckled, "Yes."

"How odd."

"There's a waterfall flowing out of the wall, and it's green sand that baffles you." Béo laughed again.

Tynae shrugged, "Well I suppose it's because I've seen waterfalls before, but I've never seen sand of this color."

"Get used to it, it's pretty much the only color of sand we have here in Calai."

Soft lounge furniture was perfectly positioned in the sandy area so that one could look out the window or enjoy the forest scenery.

Tynae walked up to the huge window, almost pressing herself against it. She giggled watching a large turtle carelessly drift by. It seemed to wave hello with its flipper.

Standing in awe, Tynae admired the amazing sea garden outside the glass wall. It abounded with colorful coral, fish, sea flowers, and hundreds of other plants and sea life Tynae had never before seen.

"Béo, this is unbelievable. Is it magic?" she asked with wonder.

"No," Béo grinned, "it's all very real."

Wiggling her toes in the warm sand, Tynae knew she'd be spending many hours in this forest.

"Are you ready to see the rest of Calai?" Béo asked.

"Oops," Tynae giggled, "I'm sorry. I got distracted. It's just so captivating." Tynae tore herself away from the window and the pair walked out of the forest. "Yes, I'm ready. If my room is this remarkable I can't wait to see more of Calai." Before walking out the door Tynae turned, casting a glance around her room once more. *Wow.*

Chapter 13
A Whole New World

"Joy is not in things; it is in us."
~Richard Wagner

Walking through the halls, several people passed Tynae and Béo. All inclined their heads toward the couple.

Tynae observed the passing people with curiosity. *That's odd,* she thought. "Béo?"

"Yes?"

"Why are your clothes so different from everyone else's?"

Béo wore suede trousers, a simple dark green tunic, and soft suede boots. His two day old stubble was still intact and his long dark hair flowed down his back.

Béo laughed out loud. "I had no idea you'd be so agreeable to our attire, so I wore what you were accustomed to seeing me in when I visited Pathrow. To be honest, it's a bit uncomfortable. Do you mind if I change?"

Tynae grinned, "You mean to tell me, that after all these years I've never seen you in your own clothing?"

Béo shrugged.

Tynae's brow rose "Hmm." She eyed Béo slyly. "Seems there's much I don't know about you, *Lord* Béo, White Prince of Calai," she teased. "Now that I'm here in Calai, for however long, I hope we'll get to know each other a lot better."

"I'd like that too, now that you know we *exist!*" They both laughed. "I don't have to keep secrets from you any longer."

"Well let's go to your chambers so you can get changed," Tynae pressed.

When they reached Béo's quarters, they were met by Ezro, Béo's chamberlain. Bowing deeply, Ezro greeted the pair. "Good afternoon, Majesties." His voice was surprisingly deep. Ezro looked at Béo. "What may I assist you with, My Liege?"

An older man, Ezro was tall and slender with silver hair, and his mannerisms were highly refined.

Béo smiled at Tynae. "Have a seat or look around, whatever you'd like, I'll be right back." Béo turned to Ezro. "I wish to get out of this," Béo gestured to his clothes, "and into my own attire." Before the chamber door was shut Béo was pulling his tunic over his head.

Tynae chuckled. "If it's any consolation," she spoke loudly toward the shut door, "our clothes look really nice on you. I was thoroughly convinced you were human."

Wandering around Béo's dwelling, Tynae noticed how different it was from her own. It was simple, yet regal and masculine. *He must like to read,* she thought, glancing at the many bookshelves throughout the room; all of which were stocked to maximum capacity with a wide variety of books. *Hmmm, I'd like to borrow a few of these.*

Tynae turned when the chamber door opened.

Béo walked out of his room looking quite comfortable in his 'Greer' attire.

It was Tynae's turn to be stunned, her jaw dropped when she saw Béo. He wore a loincloth, and a few leather straps around his biceps, wrists, and calves...little more. Tynae's eyes about popped out of her head. *Shite!* She proclaimed silently, *his body is a master piece.*

"Isn't this much better?" Béo asked, sounding relieved.

Blinking, her mouth agape, Tynae was completely and utterly taken aback by his clothing, or lack thereof. She could not remember how to put words together to form a simple sentence. Her mind was totally blank. "Well, umm," she stammered. A girlish giggle escaped Tynae. Instantly she clamped her hand over her mouth, eyes wide from embarrassment. She felt like every molecule of blood in her body was flooding into her face, making it feel like an inferno. Mortified by her reaction, Tynae wished desperately that she could melt into nothingness...*Oh dear god, Tynae you are making an arse of yourself, pull it together.* It took every ounce of effort she had to regain a minute bit of composure.

Taking a deep breath, Tynae gulped down the knot sitting in her throat and forced herself to look at Béo. "Ahh yeah." She fought back another giggle. Tearing her eyes from Béo, Tynae focused on the ceiling for a minute before she dared to look directly at him again. "It looks...much, much..." Tynae bit her lip, "more comfortable," she blurted out, knowing she wouldn't be able to contain herself much longer. Tynae smiled so hard it hurt. Fearful she might say more than a *lady* should, Tynae continued biting her lip.

"What?" Béo asked confused, "Is there something wrong with what I'm wearing?"

"I..." Tynae coughed trying to disguise the giggles that just wouldn't go away. "I just wasn't ready to see..." She coughed again, looking Béo up and down. *Oh god.* "So...much of you." Tynae's voice broke on the last word. Straining to look at anything other than Béo's muscular body Tynae took a deep breath, clearing her throat. "Shall we umm, be on our way then...?" Tynae turned toward the door, "I'm dying..." Tynae accidentally locked eyes with Béo. She could tell he was loving every second of this.

"Yes?" he asked in a courtly manner.

Biting her lip, Tynae tore her gaze from Béo once more, staring up at the ceiling, as if inspecting it for leaks. With another forced gulp, Tynae finished her sentence, "to see this beautiful city of yours." Tynae nodded at Béo awkwardly, "Mhmm."

An inscrutable smile crept across Béo's face. "Okay." Béo opened the door. "After you, *My Lady*," he teased smoothly.

Trying not to look at Béo as she passed him, Tynae tripped over his foot.

Béo reached out to catch her, at the same time Tynae reached out, grabbing hold of him.

Chest to chest, Tynae had her arms wrapped around Béo's neck. Catching his scent Tynae inadvertently lurched forward pressing her nose against his neck, inhaling deeply.

Shocked by what she'd done, Tynae began laughing so hard she fell to the floor. *Oh my! I've completely lost it...he must think I'm an absolute nutter.*

Béo was right there on the floor beside her laughing 'til his sides hurt.

With tears streaming down her face, sides splitting in pain, Tynae tried to talk. "I...haa...have no...haaaha...idea...ahhh..." taking a deep breath, Tynae tried regaining herself. Crimson faced, Tynae was positively humiliated by her behavior. Catching her breath she was finally able to speak. "I think when the Archimagi and Zandore were working their magic; weaving my fibers back together they may have crossed a few...or broken several." Tynae shook her head, "I have no idea what has come over me...Oh my gosh," Tynae drew in a deep breath. "I am so sorry, Béo, if you do not wish to be seen in public with me I will completely understand."

Gaining control of himself, Béo looked at Tynae with disbelief. "Are you kidding me? You are too much fun! I can't remember the last time I laughed this hard." Standing up, Béo wiped the tears from his eyes then helped Tynae up. "I don't know what to expect next, you're fantastic!" Béo's smiled broadly at Tynae. "Let's go, there's much I want to show you."

To Tynae, Calai looked to be an intricate maze of tunnels and corridors. Some made of gray bricks and others of earth and stone. Once they reached what appeared to be the center of Calai it opened into a massive expanse. The city was nestled snugly in a valley surrounded by a magnificent mountain range. It was as if someone had picked out the most pristine piece of land in the world and covered it with a magic bubble, preventing all deterioration.

Smiling, Béo opened his arms wide. "Welcome to Calai."

The pair stood at the bottom level of the city.

Looking up at the mountains, Tynae saw they had been carved into a remarkable fortress. There were many levels above them, several with numerous passageways, others with actual dwellings protruding from them. The only inconsistency was to her right. Instead of having multiple levels, it remained a solid mountain with an extremely large arched doorway at the base. Two large ponds were on either side.

"This is amazing," Tynae breathed, trying to take it all in. With her new vision little escaped her sight. Throughout the city was a kaleidoscope of flowers, trees of all sizes, statues, hedges, and fountains. Green plants crawled along the walls for as far as she could see. Which, she reminded herself, was actually quite farther than most. To Tynae's surprise there were even birds and butterflies flittering around. Looking up at the top of Calai, Tynae saw the glass-like dome that protected them. Somehow sunlight shone through, glittering brightly upon the heart of the city. "It's a perfect replica of the world above. I could easily forget I'm underwater," she said in wonder.

Hundreds of people were a bustle in Calai. Some shopped, while others sold their goods. Couples walked hand in hand as their children ran in front of them giggling and chasing one another. Smiling at the wondrous world before her, Tynae looked at Béo bright-eyed. "This is the most perfect place I've ever seen."

Directly in front of them was the market. Merchants with wooden carts sold everything you could possibly imagine: jewelry, clothes, food, armor, weapons, and these were just the carts Tynae could see. There were many more merchants further out. Naturally Tynae was drawn to the merchant who sold jewelry.

With a deep bow, the merchant greeted the royal pair. "Good morning, Your Majesties."
Béo nodded.
"Good morning," Tynae responded cheerfully.
The merchant was quite friendly.
"See anything you like, My Lady?"
Tynae smiled, "Just looking."
"And how are you this fine morning, My Lord?"
"I am quite well, Ildrai thank you."
Béo looked at Tynae, "Ildrai here makes the finest jewelry in all the land, both above and below the sea."

Ildrai bowed, "You are too kind, Sire."

"I only speak the truth." Béo smiled. "It seems that fine craftsmanship runs in the family. Ildrai's son Glaxor makes our swords. You would be hard pressed to find a better blacksmith. His workmanship is superb, and his swords are nearly indestructible."

Tynae looked impressed. "I'll be sure to see Glaxor before I leave Calai—wait," Tynae turned to Béo with a puzzled expression. "Am I allowed to purchase merchandise from your city?"

"Of course you are."

Tynae continued looking at Ildrai's goods. "That necklace there," she pointed. "Is it diamond or crystal?"

"Ah, Her Majesty has an eye for true beauty, 'tis a diamond of the highest quality, seven carratus."

"That is exquisite, Ildrai. Did you cut the stone as well?"

Ildrai bowed his head. "Ay, 'tis one of a kind, My Lady," Ildrai answered proudly. "Would you care to see it?"

Tynae's eyes grew bright. "Please. Is the chain platina?"

"Yes." Ildrai looked impressed. "Her Majesty is familiar with precious metals?"

"A little, enough to know platina when I see it and that it's extraordinarily rare."

The chain from which the pendant dangled was grayish – white with a slightly bluish tinge. The bluish tinge is how Tynae knew what type of metal it was. From the chain hung a faultless pink diamond in the shape of a heart. Behind the heart was a key also made from platina. Etching covered the key, giving the impression of delicate lace.

"I've never seen anything like it, Sir." Tynae examined the rare gem, turning it over in her hand. Holding the heart up to the light, it sparkled with millions of facets and the color was absolutely brilliant. "It truly is breathtaking," she said, handing the piece back. "Here you go, thank you for letting me see it, Ildrai."

Ildrai took the necklace with a bow. "You are quite welcome, My Lady."

Enthusiastically Tynae turned to Béo, accidentally looking at his bare chest. She quickly moved her gaze to his eyes. "Okay, what's next?"

Before he could answer Tynae spotted something. "Ooh, I want to go over there," she said excitedly, pointing to the middle of the city. "Come on!"

Chapter 14
Tiny Package, Big Surprise

"Woman is a miracle of divine contradictions."
~Jules Michelet

Grabbing Béo's hand, Tynae pulled until they were running.
Béo laughed, "Where are we going?"
"You'll see."
Although there were many people in the city, most were in the market place. A majority of the area was open with the exception of shrubs, trees, and benches strategically placed throughout.

Arriving at their destination, the pair stood in a large dirt clearing. Several small round arenas where marked off by meter high walls made from rock and earth.

Tynae was as excited as a child on her birthday.
Béo chuckled.
"What?" Tynae was truly bewildered, "What's so funny?"
"Sword's, Tynae?" Béo questioned skeptically, "Really?"
They where standing in the training arena used by Calai's swordsmen.
Tynae narrowed her eyes, "Do you know nothing about me Béo?" she asked critically.
"I thought I knew quite a bit about you, but obviously I'm missing something."

"How do you protect yourselves so that no-one gets injured?" Tynae looked around. "I don't see any shields or armor."

Raising his hand, Béo beckoned for someone. A small creature standing across from the couple immediately came over, accompanied by what Tynae assumed was his pet.

The creature bent in an exaggerated bow. "Your Majesties," the little being spoke with a squeaky voice, "good day to you both."

114

Tynae was delighted to meet the small and charming stranger, "Good day," she replied.

"Good day, Tingy," Béo grinned.

Tingy was a tiny little thing, barely reaching Tynae's waist. His alabaster skin had a rosy glow, and his large bright blue eyes gave him an innocent, almost child-like appearance. His eyes stood out like beacons against his pale skin. Slightly pointed and miss-matched ears sat high on the sides of his head. One stood straight up, while the other drooped lazily. He wore wee little britches that were tan, and a small beige tunic.

His pet was fluffy like a milkweed puff. Sky blue in color, with iridescent wings, it was about the size and shape of a grapefruit. It too had big blue eyes that almost seemed too large for its petite body. It flew beside Tingy as he walked. When Tingy stopped his pet landed on the wall beside him.

"They're far too cute for words," Tynae whispered to Béo. "What are they?"

"Later, I promise," Béo whispered back.

Béo motioned toward the little being now standing before them. "Tingy here places a spell on us."

Tynae looked slightly alarmed, "Spell?"

Béo smiled. "Yes, it prevents the blade of the sword from penetrating our flesh," Béo explained.

"Okay." Smiling, Tynae opened her arms slightly, "Tingy, what do I need to do?"

Béo looked at Tynae in total disbelief. "You're really serious?"

Grinning at Béo playfully, Tynae ignored his comment then looked back at Tingy.

"You need do nothing, Majesty, I do all the work."

"Very well, if you would please," Tynae requested sweetly.

Tingy inclined his head, "Yes, My Lady," he said in his chipper voice. Closing his eyes Tingy moved his hands slowly in opposite directions creating large circles. Lowering his arms, Tingy opened his eyes.

"Is that it?" Tynae asked.

"That is it, My Lady."

"But I felt nothing."

"You're not supposed to feel anything, or maybe I should say very few people do."

Tynae eyed her skin, "I don't look any different." Then she felt her skin, "I don't feel any different either." Picking up a small blade from the stone wall beside her she poked her arm with the tip. Nothing happened. "Huh." Tynae looked at Béo, "nothing can penetrate my flesh?"

Béo chuckled, "Nothing."

"Okay." Tynae ran the full length of the blade down her arm. Nothing happened…Tynae's smile became exuberant. "I can feel the cold steel against my flesh, but…" Tynae ran the knife down her arm again, pressing hard, "fascinating. Thank you, Tingy."

"Now where do I get my weapon?" she asked eagerly.

"There," Béo pointed to a three-walled shed, "Come on." Béo looked at Tynae seriously as they walked over to the hut, "We're actually going to do this. You're going to pick up a sword and fight *me*?"

Tynae chuckled. "Yes, Béo, we are *actually* going to do this."

The variety of swords to choose from was large. After trying a few different sizes and weights, Tynae decided on a heavier blade. Turning to Béo, Tynae smiled slyly. "Choose your weapon, *My Lord*," she teased bowing. "Choose wisely," she cautioned with a wink then fluttered away thrusting and swinging her sword.

Looking bewildered, Béo watched Tynae for a moment. Shaking his head he chuckled turning back to the swords. "Never a dull moment indeed," he muttered picking up a weapon.

"I heard that."

Laughing, Béo headed to the ring Tynae had chosen.

There were several rings located in the large dirt clearing, each surrounded by a wall made out of stone.

Tynae snickered to herself, "poor boy has no idea what he's getting himself into," she muttered beneath her breath. Getting a feel for her sword, Tynae gamboled around the arena.

Tingy and his pet perched themselves on the wall. "Would it be okay with you if we watch, Your Majesty?" he asked politely as Tynae danced by.

Tynae smiled at them, "Feel free," she called out.

Working her way to the middle of the ring, Tynae smiled a wicked smile looking directly at Béo. "I promise to take it easy on you," she teased.

Settling into a crouch, Tynae beckoned Béo to the middle of the sparring arena with a crook of her finger.

Grinning wide, Béo shook his head and chuckled. "You asked for this."

"Yes, I absolutely did." Tynae gestured with her hand, "Come on big boy, let us see what you got."

Facing each other, the two grinned.

Without warning, Tynae sprang like a giant cat out of her stance.

Out of sheer instinct, Béo threw his sword up, blocking Tynae's blow.

"Damn!" Béo barked.

Their swords collided in mid air, ringing out, and the sparks began to fly.

Tynae matched every one of Béo's strikes, as he did hers.

He clearly was not holding back and that's exactly the way she liked it.

Tynae spun to her left. Béo twisted to his right. Sparks flew everywhere as the pair battled.

Tynae moved with lightning speed.

The pair circled each other like hunter and prey. Tynae may have looked like the prey, but she was playing games with this hunter.

Tingy clapped wildly, and his little pet jumped up and down every time Tynae got the better of Béo.

Passersby saw the unusual pair fighting and a crowd began to gather.

Tynae leapt toward Béo again, their swords locking overhead. Chest to chest, eye to eye, they were in an intimate dance. Pulling her sword back Tynae spun around, twisted then did a back flip right over the top of Béo's head. Before he had a chance to even realize what had happened, she'd gone in for the kill.

In one swift and smooth movement, Tynae pulled the dagger out that was strapped to her thigh. Pressing herself against Béo's back, she grabbed a hand full of hair, pulled his head back slightly, and put her blade to his throat. "Gotcha," she whispered in his ear.

The exuberant spectators, including Tingy and his pet, jumped up and down clapping and hollering.

Letting Béo go, he turned to face Tynae.

She wore a smug smile.

Raising her brows Tynae sashayed, pacing in front of him, "Care to go for round two?" she asked in a sultry tone, holding up two fingers.

Béo looked at Tynae like she was touched in the head. "A man can only take so much humiliation, love," he said with a smirk.

"Ah, come on," Tynae pleaded, wearing a pout. "Please, just one more?" Batting her eyes innocently, she held up her index finger and mouthed the words, *just one*.

Béo stared intensely at Tynae, contemplating her request. After a moment or two, his face softened and he let out a loud laugh. "I guess if it's you doing the humiliating, I can survive one more go." Béo grinned. "Second and *final* round," he submitted taking his place in the center of the ring.

Tynae began to circle Béo slowly.

He followed her every step.

She was certain his only goal now was to somehow redeem himself.

With their audience steadily growing Tynae quietly mouthed, "Ready?"

Ready or not, Tynae lunged forward, spun, and with a resounding boom their swords collided. The force was such that Tynae was certain the spectators could feel the vibrations.

The crowd screamed with exhilaration, cheering on the pair.

They both moved with such speed and agility that they were almost blurs. Béo feigned left then lunged right; but Tynae saw it coming. Their blades crashed overhead, showering them in sparks. Disengaging with a flourish, Béo riposted. Tynae parried once more then fluttered away.

"Yeaaaaa!"

Back and forth they went, both drenched in sweat, each trying to hammer the other down.

Swinging her sword behind her back then over her head, Tynae thrust her blade forward, locking eyes with Béo as their swords met. Sparks showered down with each powerful strike, both grinned hugely. Neither could best the other.

Stomping their feet, the crowd yelled and screamed wildly.

Taking a step back, Béo swung his sword hard. Tynae crouched down at the last second allowing the strike to breeze over her head.

"Owwww!" the crowd jeered leaning back.

The couple's choreography was flawless.

Tynae moved quickly lunging and striking at Béo. He blocked and parried easily. Swinging her sword low Tynae aimed for Béo's legs, with lightning speed he leapt straight up into the air narrowly avoiding the blow.

"Yeeeaaa!"

Prowling around each other, the pair moved slowly in a circle.

Without warning, both leapt forward at the exact same moment. Their swords and bodies collided in mid-air. Their blades struck with such force it sounded like thunder. Everything moved in slow motion as the couple seemed to hang in the air for a split second. "I'm winning," Tynae whispered breathlessly in Béo's ear.

Landing on the ground with a thud, Béo nearly fell on his face.

The crowd howled with laughter.

Tynae winked. Twisting around, swinging her sword over her head, she thrust at Béo. He blocked her blow yet again.

Her next move was a complete blur; wielding her blade in such a manner that Béo's sword flew out of his hands. Spinning around Tynae extended her leg, kicking Béo's feet out from under him, throwing him flat on his back. In a flash, Tynae was on his chest, dagger drawn and at his throat. Panting Tynae smiled, looking down at him. Leaning over she whispered, "I think I win." She kissed Béo on the cheek. "You're a good sport, thank you." Tynae stood up.

Remaining on his back, Béo stared up at Tynae with disbelief, trying to catch his breath.

Grinning, Tynae offered Béo her hand to help him up. He willingly accepted with a broad smile.

The onlookers were still stomping, clapping, and yelling as loud as they could. They couldn't get enough.

Béo dropped to his knees in front of Tynae, bowing in mock worship.

"Yeaaa!" The crowd ate it up, roaring with laughter.

Tynae curtsied to the onlookers playfully.

Jumping up, Béo grabbed Tynae, threw her over his shoulder and ran off with her. Lifting her head, Tynae waved to their audience as Béo carried her away.

Tingy was waiting for them in the area fighters go once competition is over.

When they got over to Tingy, his little arms were wrapped around his middle. He was doubled over roaring with laughter.

Straightening up Tingy looked at Béo, "My Lord, such a graceful loss I have never witnessed," he said, still laughing.

His laughter was contagious. Tynae turned away in an attempt to conceal her giggle.

"Thanks, Tingy." Béo eyed Tynae with what was supposed to be a scornful glare, but his smile betrayed him.

Tynae stood smiling back at Béo. Biting her lip, she fought to not burst out with laughter.

"Some cool water?" Tingy offered, holding out two large wooden cups.

"That is perfect! Thank you." Tynae accepted a cup.

"Thank you." Béo accepted his drink likewise. "Please remove the shields from us Tingy," Béo requested, smirking playfully at Tynae, both still panting.

"Of course, My Lord." Tingy continued to silently chuckle, his little body shaking.

Tynae almost giggled, but successfully stifled it. "Thank you, Tingy, I'm sure I'll be seeing you again," she said with a jovial smile.

Béo let out a laugh that sounded more like a bark. "Not any time soon, you can be *sure* of that. I'll need some time to recover." Béo rubbed his bum pretending to be in pain. "These bruises on my ego may take a while to heal," he teased.

Tynae laughed. Shaking her head she rolled her eyes at Béo then turned to Tingy. "Good bye, Tingy, *I* will be seeing you soon." She set her cup down.

Collecting himself, Tingy bowed to Tynae. "Good bye, My Lady, I look forward to our next encounter," he said merrily.

Béo laughed, shaking his head. "Come on, let's grab some dinner."

"That sounds great," Tynae said. "No hard feelings?"

Béo shook his head, "No hard feelings." He opened his arms.

Smiling, Tynae accepted his gesture. Walking over to Béo, she wrapped her arms around him.

Holding her tight about the waist, Béo whispered in her ear, "You're all sweaty, *My Lady,* allow me to cool you down."

Tynae pulled back, but Béo didn't let go.

Smiling devilishly, he held his mug over her head.

Tynae eyed the vessel, shaking her head. "You'll pay for it later," she warned.

Béo raised his eyebrows, continuing to grin. "I know," he said un-phased pulling Tynae tight to him. "I've missed your company," he said in her ear, pouring his mug of cold water down her back, causing her to arch.

To his surprise, water flowed freely over the top of his head at the same time.

"I've missed you, too," she said, pouring a carafe of water Tingy had snuck to her over Béo's head.

Tynae burst out laughing at the shocked look on Béo's face.
"Tinnngy!" Béo shouted.
The little guy was standing off to the side laughing hysterically, watching the couple at play. He contained his laughter temporarily when Béo hollered at him.
"Good-bye, Tingy," Béo and Tynae shouted, walking away still laughing.
Once the couple had gotten a short distance away from the fighting arena they heard Tingy burst out, howling with laughter.

Tynae had to put her hand over her mouth to keep from laughing out loud.

Béo glared at her with mock anger. "Okay, *My Lady*, you have some explaining to do," he wagged his finger at her.

Tynae looked amused. "My abilities with a sword are known throughout Pathrow and beyond. I can't help it if you don't keep up."

Béo was clearly entertained by all this. His smile never faded. "Is that so? I guess I'll have to listen to the gossip a bit more carefully from now on." Shaking the water from his hair he sprayed Tynae.

"Hey!"
Laughing, they made their way to the market.

Chapter 15
Chemical Reaction

"The meeting of two personalities is like
the contact of two chemical
substances: if there is any
reaction, both are transformed."
~Carl Jung

When the couple got back to the market place, there were loads of people around.

"It's getting awfully noisy and crowded here. I think someplace a little quieter would be nice, don't you?" Béo asked.

Tynae smiled, "Sounds fantastic." At this point, she would gladly go anywhere Béo wanted to lead her.

"Great, let's grab some food and head to the Forest of Ataraxia."
"Forest of..." Tynae looked confused, "What?"
Béo grinned, "It means Forest of Tranquility."
"Oh... okay, sounds perfect." Tynae successfully concealed her nervousness. The thought of being alone with Béo was both exhilarating and terrifying. She had never been so taken with a man.
When they reached the food carts, Tynae saw several choices.

Béo headed for a particular merchant. "This guy is great! Henley McDugle is his name. He has food all wrapped up and ready to go. We call his stand, "Ye Old McDugle's."

Tynae looked rather impressed. "That is really quite convenient, isn't it?"
"Ay. Would you prefer ox or chicken?"
"Mmm," Tynae sniffed the air. "Either, they both smell terrific."
"Okay, I know just what to get, come on." The pair walked over to McDugle's.

"Greetings, Your Majesties. How may I serve you this fine day?"

"Good day, Henley. May we get a bit of everything?" Béo requested cheerfully.

"Of course."

Their food was ready in a matter of minutes.

"Here you go, My Lord." Henley handed Béo a leather pack.

"Thank you." Taking the pack, Béo swung it over his shoulder.

Walking off, Tynae eyed the bag quizzically.

As was becoming the norm, Béo answered her impending question before she had a chance to ask it.

"I come here frequently. I just leave my pack here. It makes life much easier."

"Okay." Tynae chuckled.

Stomach rumbling, Tynae suddenly realized she too was quite hungry. "How far is the forest from here?"

"Well that all depends." Béo looked slightly smug.

With a clever smile Tynae narrowed her eyes. "Oh? On what, pray tell?"

Béo's smile became cunning. "Well, you see that tunnel over there," he pointed, "the one with the green crystal over the top?"

"Yes," Tynae answered eyeing Béo suspiciously.

"That's the tunnel we need to take, so how fast you run will decide how fast we get there," Béo teased with a cocky, yet playful attitude.

A complacent smile spread across Tynae's face. "Is that so?" she asked coolly, "Are you challenging me to a race...*My Lord*?"

"Maybe...Are you game?"

Tynae was the smug one now. "So, once I'm in the tunnel where do I go? After all, I can't wait around for you all day," she goaded.

Béo guffawed. "Are you that confident you're going to beat *me*?"

"Maybe," she taunted. "Are you scared?"

"Never! Once you're in the tunnel you take the first right. It leads straight to the forest."

Tynae nodded. "All right. So what do I get if I win?"

"What would you like…*My Lady*?" Béo inquired with a bow.

"Hmm," Tynae looked around. "I like that outfit over there." She pointed to a cart with loads of colorful clothes.

"The red one?"

"Yes."

"Done."

Tynae's smile began to hurt, but she couldn't stop. "And, *My Lord*, what is it that you desire should *you* happen to win?"

Looking Tynae dead in the eye he said, "The same thing."

Tynae burst out laughing. "I'm not sure it would be very flattering on you."

"Ah, but I am quite certain it will look *stunning* on you."

Finding herself speechless, Tynae was positive her face was ruby red.

Béo grinned, "Come on."

The two walked over to the garment maker.

"Majesties," The merchant bowed.

"Adi," Béo picked up the outfit Tynae had chosen, setting it in front of the merchant, "Send this along with the usual accessories to the Vu'tella chambers." Béo turned to Tynae, looking her up and down. "Include a little something *extra,* befitting a woman of such extraordinary beauty."

Tynae looked at the ground in an attempt to conceal her embarrassment.

Adi responded with a curtsey, "As you wish, My Lord."

Béo nodded. "Thank you, Adi. Good day."

Béo and Tynae each looked like a cat that had swallowed a canary as they walked off together.

"Alright, stop here," Béo directed.

"Are you ready, *My Lady*?" he asked in a silky voice.

Grinning, she nodded once. "Oh, yeah…you?" she purred cunningly.

"Let's dance." Béo wore a Cheshire cat smile. "Ready, set, GO!"

They both took off like a bolt of lighting.

There were several obstacles between the starting point and their destination.

Béo clearly had the advantage, knowing what was where and what was on the other side of walls and bushes.

Tynae moved with agility and speed leaping over benches, bushes and even hurdled over a small flock of sheep. She was clearly in the lead, but Béo wasn't far behind. Reaching the entrance of the tunnel first, Tynae immediately took the first right. She almost died from embarrassment when she nearly ran into Chief Kerszon. Eye's wide with alarm, Tynae stopped as fast as she could, managing to bring her body to a complete halt just in time. "Oh!" She gasped. "Chief Kerszon, I'm so sorry."

Kerszon looked at Tynae with curiosity then saw Béo running toward her. "Are you racing my son?" he asked with an impish smile.

Tynae looked over her shoulder anxiously, then back at Kerszon. "Yes, Chief." She danced on her tip toes like a child.

Kerszon burst out with laughter. "Go woman!" He gave Tynae a slight push.

She didn't need to be told twice. Like a shot, she was gone.

Béo sped past his father, but the race was already over.

Waiting patiently at the edge of the forest, sitting on a rock, Tynae grinned.

"What took you so long?" she teased. "I'm starving!"

Béo snickered. "I think I had better give up on trying to best you at anything." Extending his hand, Béo helped Tynae off the rock. "Let's go further in, I know the perfect spot." Stepping in front of Tynae, Béo led the way.

Tynae took in the vision before her. *That's the finest architecture I've ever seen.* "Mmmm."

Béo turned around, "What?"

Wide-eyed and beet red, Tynae slapped her hand over her mouth and shook her head. "Nothing," she muttered. "Just lead the way." She nearly choked on her words.

Shaking her head slightly, Tynae silently giggled. *What is wrong with me?*

Tynae wasn't certain, but she was fairly sure Béo was wearing a massive smile.

The bushes and trees got thicker as they moved deeper into the forest. In the distance Tynae could here a waterfall. It was clearly autumn in Calai as it was in Pathrow. The forest of Ataraxia was going through its fall changes. The vast array of leafy shrubs and shaggy ferns thrived here as did a multitude of blossoming flowers exploding in a symphony of colors. Beneath their feet, crisp golden leaves carpeted the moist coffee colored earth. Tiny striped chipmunks darted past as the pair walked. The animals' puffy little cheeks filled to capacity, looking as if they'd burst at any moment, made Tynae giggle. Continuing to follow Béo, Tynae watched as the sleek critters ran about the wood zealously, darting from hole to hole. They chattered at their fellow chipmunks and any would be thieves, telling them to '*stay away*!' Briskly they scampered to each of their caches as if following a treasure map committed to memory. Once assured that their stash was still safely hidden, they added their new found riches.

When Béo finally stopped they were standing in front of a gorgeous waterfall. Stunning lilies, thick ferns, and spongy moss carpeted the ground around the falls.

"How's that for a view?" Béo pointed to an area behind Tynae.

Turning around she gasped, "It's beautiful."

The valley below them vibrated with life as far as the eye could see. Hundreds of ancient trees, bushes and ferns were scattered throughout the forest floor. Vibrant wild flowers added magnificent splashes of abstract color. Sapphire water from the waterfall they now stood next to flowed like honey through the thriving jade valley. Several animals, some foreign, some familiar, frolicked about in the forest below. Watching the animals gambol around Tynae's smile slowly widened. She observed the forest meticulously. Beaming with comprehension she turned to Béo. "It's the full size version of the forest in my room," she said brightly.

He nodded. "It is."

Tynae cast around the valley once more then turned back to Béo. "The view is magnificent."

"Yes, I agree wholeheartedly." Béo never took his eyes from her.

Tynae blushed. She was fairly certain they were not talking about the same thing, but was unwilling to press the matter.

Pulling a blanket from his bag Béo laid it out. "Let's eat," he motioned for Tynae to have a seat as he set out their food and drink.

They ate beside the waterfall, talking and enjoying the beauty of their surroundings.

"That was fantastic," Tynae said stretching out and looking around. "What do you call this waterfall?"

"Kaûma. It means calm."

"Kaûma," Tynae repeated, "I like that. Some of your words are so different from ours. Why is that?"

Béo grinned, shaking his head. "They're not different, just ancient. Most of your language was derived from ours. There are just some things we choose to use the original words for. Names are powerful."

"How so?"

Béo smiled. "I don't know that I'm the right person to explain that to you."

"That's okay," Tynae said unfazed. "Do you come here a lot?"

"Yes." Béo smiled, "This is one of the spots I come to when I need to think, clear my head, or just get some peace and quiet."

Tynae cleaned up, putting the cloths their food had been wrapped in back inside Béo's pack.

Side by side, they laid on the blanket looking toward the heavens. Mist from the waterfall fused with the fragrance of the surrounding flowers floated weightlessly through the air. The smell was intoxicating. Where the sky was supposed to be was the top of the dome encapsulating Calai. The liquid world above them was a stunning shade of indigo blue. The light from the sun broke through the waters surface, making everything it touched glitter. They could see hundreds of fish and marine life swimming above them in the shimmering water. Jelly fish drifted by, mimicking puffy white clouds. Hundreds of small fish darted to and fro like tiny sparrows playing a game of tag. And the occasional large fish looked like a soaring eagle.

"This is simply marvelous." Tynae sighed, "I could lie here all day."

"Well we can do that if you'd like, at least until dusk. It would look rather bad if I didn't have you back to your chambers in time for supper, not to mention you need to get your rest." Béo turned to Tynae, "Speaking of which, how are you feeling?"

Tynae smiled. "I feel phenomenal. I should die more often."

They both chuckled.

Tynae looked at Béo. "I'm really glad I ended up here. I've always treasured your friendship, Béo, and now I get to know you on a whole new level. Thank you."

Rolling onto his side, Béo propped himself up on his elbow. He watched Tynae with reverence.

Tynae looked into Béo's eyes. It was as if a chemical reaction had occurred. She was so far out of her element, but she couldn't help herself. Caught up in the moment, she reached up, brushing her hand over Béo's cheek, his stubble rough against her skin. Slowly she explored Béo's handsome face. Spellbound, Tynae slowly traced Béo's perfect lips. He kissed her finger softly. Tynae's heart leapt. Her hand seemed to have an agenda of its own, sliding slowly back over Béo's cheek, tenderly caressing the curve of his neck then creeping its way into Béo's soft hair. Her fingers entwined with his long locks, allowing her to gently pull him toward her.

Their eyes slid closed as their lips met. There was so much more than just a spark between them. It was an out of control wildfire, burning with a fury. Béo slid his tongue between Tynae's warm lips. He tasted sweeter than she ever could have imagined.

Béo suddenly pulled back, "Tynae! I am so sorry."

Disappointment and abashment flooded Tynae as she fought back tears of rejection. Rolling onto her side, she absentmindedly played with a wildflower. Fidgeting gave her the perfect excuse to gaze at the ground instead of at Béo. "Sorry for what? I pulled you to me." Tynae's tone conveyed her confusion and sadness. "Clearly you are not attracted to me."

"What?!" Béo snapped. "That is the most absurd thing I've ever heard. What man in his right mind would not be attracted to you?" Béo moved close to Tynae, "I'm sorry." Tenderly he slid his hand under her chin, lifting her head. They were looking into each others eyes once more. "What I meant to say was that I have never been more attracted to anyone in my entire life. I think you are the most amazing, beautiful, and intelligent person I've ever known." Béo's words were compassionate.

A fragile smile slowly materialized on Tynae's face. "Then kiss me," she whispered.

Béo looked deep into Tynae's eyes. Would he refuse her? Slowly he ran his hand down Tynae's arm, his touch gentle. *Is this really happening*? She wondered for a split second. Rolling onto her back as Béo leaned forward; passionately they melted into one another. She pressed her warm lips softly against his. Tynae's hand slid through Béo's hair smoothly, she allowed the flow of her hand to continue gliding across his warm flesh, over his muscular shoulders, down to the small of his back. Without a second thought, she pulled his body tight against her. His smoldering bare skin felt like silk against her half nude body.

"Slow down, angel," Béo said lightly, pulling back gently.

Tynae felt giddy. "Sorry," she apologized, only half embarrassed.

Standing up Béo flattened his disheveled hair. "Let's go for a walk before we get ourselves in trouble," Béo suggested with a chuckle, offering Tynae a hand up.

"Fine, lets go," she grumbled grabbing hold of his hand. "You know..." Tynae glanced out of the corner of her eye, "It really doesn't help that you people run around half naked," she teased.

Chapter 16
Secrets

"A joyful heart is the inevitable result
of a heart burning with love."
~Mother Teresa

Wearing a sly smile, Tynae looked at Béo. "So, why is it that out of everyone I've seen here in Calai, you and I seem to have the least amount of clothing on? Oh, and your father, too," Tynae shook her head recalling her earlier faux pas. "Lord, how could I forget him?"

Raising his eyebrows, Béo returned the mischievous smile. "I was wondering when you were going to ask about that. In Calai, the higher your status or rank, the less you wear." Béo let out a boisterous laugh. "I have no idea why that is, it's just the way it's always been. Besides myself, my father is the only other high ranking male, and *you* are the only high ranking female in all of Calai. It's been over a century since Calai housed a female with such a status." Eyeing Tynae, Béo's smile became crafty. "I must say, our attire has never looked so good on anyone."

His comment caused Tynae to fidget.

"I'll admit I'm still a bit confused. I've never heard of a culture like this, but it is what it is." Tynae smiled dropping the subject.

Béo took Tynae's hand lacing his fingers through hers. Gazing into her eyes, he drew her hand to his lips, kissing it tenderly.

Tynae thought her heart would batter its way right through her chest it began pounding so hard.

Continuing to hold Tynae's hand, Béo led her through the forest, showing her all his secret spots.

Time passed too quickly for the couple's liking. With a stolen kiss here and there, it was time to head back for supper.

Working their way back down the mountain, Béo became lost in thought.

"Is something wrong, Béo?" Tynae asked. His silence concerned her.

He looked at Tynae apprehensively. "I'm not sure how my father would feel about…you and me."

Tynae heard genuine trepidation in Béo's voice. She smiled with understanding. "Would you like to keep this," she pointed to him then herself, "*Us*...a secret for now?"

Béo looked rather morose. "Would you mind?"

Hearing the embarrassment in his tone, Tynae knew Béo felt bad for asking her to hide their relationship.

"I understand. I don't want to make your father angry either. Mum's the word." She gave Béo a wink then jumped in front of him. Pulling him close, she got up on her tip toes and whispered in his ear, "Race you down the hill." Bouncing back, she stuck out her tongue, spun around, and was gone.

Tynae was a quarter of the way down the mountain before Béo reacted. Shaking his head, he chuckled. "It's impossible to be upset with you around," he shouted. Laughing, Béo took off after her.

When he reached the bottom of the hill, Tynae was leaning against a stone wall wearing a bashful grin. "I'm sorry," she said, "I couldn't help myself."

Smiling slyly, Béo narrowed his eyes and shook his finger at Tynae. Taking a step closer, he placed his feet just outside of hers and leaned forward.

Their bodies almost touching, Tynae felt their energies fuse together.

Taking the tiniest of steps forward, Béo placed his left hand on the wall beside Tynae's head and the other on her bare shoulder. Leaning closer still, his face was just centimeters from hers.

Looking up into Béo's smoldering gray-blue eyes, Tynae's breaths became uneven. Béo's eyes burned with a fierce fire, mesmerizing Tynae.

His gaze moved to her nude shoulder his hand sat upon. Gently caressing her, he slowly slid his hand down her arm.

Tynae's heart began to pound out of control.

Leaning forward, Béo softly touched his lips to her naked shoulder. "That wasn't very fair," he breathed.

His searing breath tingled against her exposed flesh. Closing her eyes, Tynae struggled to remember her own name.

Kissing his way slowly across her collar bone, Béo paused at the hollow of her neck. "Do you always play dirty?" he whispered.

"No," she exhaled.

Resuming his crusade, Béo kissed his way up her neck.

Tynae's head drifted to one side, allowing Béo full access.

Béo's hot breath slid silkily over Tynae's bare skin like warm liquid, sending goose bumps over every inch of her sweltering body.

Kissing along the edge of her chin, Béo followed her jaw line until he reached her ear. Breathlessly he spoke. "Are you going to do that again?" he whispered. His warm lips brushed softly against Tynae's electrified flesh, sending bolts of lightning through her.

Tynae opened her mouth to speak. A soft moan was all that came out.

Béo lightly kissed either cheek, stopping just shy of Tynae's crimson lips. Gently he brushed his soft lips against her anticipating mouth, teasing her with his tongue.

Oh god...

"You see," he said, his lips barely grazing hers, "I can play dirty, too."

The fiery heat from his words danced over her expectant lips.

Taking his hand from the wall, Béo slid it to the nape of Tynae's neck. Gently grabbing a fistful of hair, he pulled Tynae tight against his bare chest, while his other arm constricted around her waist. His impassioned kiss took her breath away.

Reaching up, Tynae slid her arms around Béo's neck then wrapped her leg around his thigh.

His hot bare flesh pressing against hers made her yearn desperately for him. Pressing her hips into Béo's, she could feel just how much he wanted her. Her longing for him was equally intense. They couldn't get much closer, but that didn't stop Tynae from trying. Lacing her fingers in Béo's hair she pulled him tight to her. Their bodies melded together.

"Tynae," he said, their lips still pressed together. "We mustn't." Taking Tynae's face gently in his hands, Béo reluctantly removed his lips from hers.

Both breathless, they stared into each others eyes.

As Béo stroked Tynae's cheeks with his thumbs, a smile spread across her face. Béo smiled back.

"We really need to get going, angel," he reminded her.

"Oh yeah," she breathed, having forgotten people other than they existed in the world.

Standing up straight, Béo gestured with his head toward the entrance to the forest. "Shall we?"

Heading out of the forest Tynae giggled.

"What's so funny?"

Tynae rolled her eyes. "I was just thinking we were lucky no-one saw us."

Béo laughed mischievously. "I took care of that before I got down the hill," he confessed.

Tynae wasn't sure what he meant.

Giving Tynae a sideways glance as they walked, he answered her unasked question. "I placed a spell on the entrance into the forest. No-one would have been able to get in."

Tynae looked at Béo out of the corner of her eye. "Impressive."

Béo pulled open the large wooden door that led from the forest back to Calai, "After you, My Lady."

Tynae bowed her head, "Thank you, Sire."

They walked in silence for a moment or two, but Tynae couldn't let it go. "So, was that my *punishment* for tricking you?"

Béo tried keeping his voice stern. "It was. Did you learn your lesson?" he replied with a grin, failing miserably at his attempt to be intimidating.

"Hmm, I'm not sure. I may need to be disciplined a little more, maybe even a *lot* more," she sniggered. "I might *accidentally* slip up and do it again if my punishment isn't severe enough."

"I'll have to see to your discipline personally then," Béo said firmly. "We wouldn't want your actions to go unpunished. After all, one must learn from their mistakes." He smiled slyly, glancing at her sideways.

Walking back to Tynae's chambers, they talked and joked enjoying every second they spent with each other.

Entering Vu'tella, the couple was laughing, paying no attention to what was going on around them. They were a little surprised to see O'leana and Sireeon still preparing supper.

"Good evening, Princess Tynae, Lord Béo," the women greeted.

"Good evening," the couple unintentionally spoke in unison. The two looked at each other in surprise then exchanged a crafty smile.

O'leana walked over to a table. "This arrived for you earlier, My Lady." O'leana held up Tynae's *prize*.

Admiring her bounty, Tynae noticed Béo watching her. Crimson blood flooded her cheeks.

Turning back toward O'leana, Tynae commented on her new outfit. "It really is beautiful isn't it? I won it," Tynae declared.

O'leana appeared baffled. "Won, My Lady?"

"Yes." Tynae glanced at Béo, blushing yet again then looked back to O'leana. "Lord Béo here bet me he could beat me in a foot race."

O'leana's brows rose slightly. "And *you* won?" O'leana glanced over at Béo who nodded in confirmation. "Lord Béo is, or I guess I should say *was*, the fastest person in Calai...until now. You must be incredibly fast, Lady Tynae. That is impressive." O'leana smiled.

"Thank you, O'leana," Tynae said graciously, "and you cleared something up for me as well."

"I did? What is that, Majesty?"

Tynae donned a smirk, "Lord Béo here seemed awfully confident when he challenged me, now I know why. But I guess one really can't blame him, I suppose he was only trying to redeem himself after I beat him," Tynae glance at Béo, "twice," she teased holding up two fingers, "in the sword arena." Tynae looked over at Béo.

O'leana burst out with laughter. Putting her hand over her mouth, she quickly regained herself. "You mean to tell me, that you beat Lord Béo at swords as well?" O'leana was clearly taken aback.

With an innocent grin, Tynae nodded.

O'leana eyed Béo suspiciously. "And you didn't *let* her win?" she asked maintaining the utmost respect.

Béo barked out a laugh, "Absolutely not."

"My, my, it will be a new world around here with a woman who can best a man. A man who cannot be easily bested by other men at that. This is refreshing." O'leana grinned.

Both women looked at Béo.

Wearing an innocent puppy-dog smile, Béo just shrugged.

"A whole new world indeed," O'leana shook her head. "Would you like for me to put this with your other clothes, My Lady?" She picked up Tynae's new outfit.

"Yes, and I should like to wear it when we go to supper with Chief Kerszon next week," Tynae said decisively. "He said he would tell you the specific day and time."

"Yes, Majesty, Chief Kerszon did mention it. I will let you know as soon as the evening is confirmed. I shall see to it that everything is perfect for that night, My Lady."

Tynae nodded with a smile. "Thank you, O'leana."
"Tis my pleasure." O'leana bowed her head.
Sireeon looked at Tynae from the cooking area. "My Lady, your supper is ready. We were not sure what you would prefer, so we prepared both duck and lamb. I hope that is all right." Sireeon sounded slightly concerned.

Tynae smiled. "It's perfect, Sireeon, thank you."

After the maids had served the couple Tynae dismissed them.

"As you wish, My Lady." The women curtsied to the royal pair then turned to leave, "Oh!" O'leana turned back abruptly. "I made a sweet treat. It's in the *is*bux. I do hope you enjoy it."

Dawdling no more, the two women disappeared down the hall to their rooms.

Tynae smiled at Béo who was standing next to the table holding out her chair.

He smiled back.

Tynae was anxious to be alone with Béo, now that they had moved to a new level in their relationship.

Chapter 17
Table for Two

*"The first duty of a man is the seeking after
and the investigation of truth."*
~Cicero

Going to take her seat Tynae swept her hand lightly over
Béo's cheek. He closed his eyes as her touch washed over him.
Fire raged through his entire body.

"Thank you," she sighed, sitting down.

Béo sat in the chair beside her, "Would you like some wine?"

"Please."

Their fingers touched as Béo handed Tynae her goblet.
Palpable electricity flowed between the two like a raging river.
The powerful current immobilized the pair. Frozen, they glanced
at their fingers then at each other.

Tynae gradually removed her drink from Béo's hand. "Thank
you," she said timidly, her words echoing slightly in her goblet
as she took a sip of wine.

Béo watched Tynae as she admired the feast set before them.
He had loved this woman, his friend, from afar for so many
years; but he'd never felt anything like he was experiencing now.
He'd often imagined what it would be like to have Tynae by his
side as his queen, but now he was certain. *I want to spend the
rest of my life with this woman. If I had any doubts before, there
are absolutely none now.*

Tynae took a bite of food.

"O'leana really is a great cook," she complimented, after
swallowing her food.

"That she is," Béo agreed, taking a bite of duck. "So, what
did you think of your first day in Calai?"

Tynae's eyes still held the excitement of the day's events.
"It's fabulous here. I have never seen anything like it. I can see
why the Greer remain underwater. Why would you ever want to

leave this place? *Everything* is absolutely perfect here." Tynae's words implied much more than she had said aloud.

Having caught her unintended implication, a smile of confidence crossed Béo's face. "I'm glad you think so."

Tynae shifted slightly in her seat. "Is there anything this place doesn't provide?"

"If there is, we've yet to discover it." Béo extended a small basket to Tynae. "Care for another?"

Tynae held up her hand, "No thank you." Stabbing a baby tomato with her fork, Tynae looked at Béo. "Have you tried this tomato salad? It's almost sweet enough to be dessert. I've never had such delicious food." She sounded a bit surprised.

Béo smiled. "The Fãbbiano family oversees all our farmers and their crops. Nettie and her family have learned how to naturally stimulate the growth process of many plants and how to grow all manner of crops throughout the year instead of seasonally. The Fãbbiano's have been our lead farmers for centuries. They take great pride in getting everything they grow just right."

Tynae held up her fork slightly, brandishing a bite-size tomato, "Kudos to them, job well done!" She put the tiny tomato in her mouth. "So, is this just one large city?"

"No, it is an entire nation." Béo took a bite of bread.
Tynae took a sip of wine. "Are there other cities?"
"Yes, but most live in one general area." Béo grinned, taking another bite of food. "I'm sure you want to talk about more than food and territory."

"I do, but where to start? I suppose I'll begin with simple questions." Tynae thought, cutting her slice of lamb into bite size pieces. "I know," she said enthusiastically, "Tingy."

Béo didn't understand the question. "What about him?" He took another bite of food.

"Well he's clearly not human." She nibbled on some bread.

"Oh…" Béo chuckled, "I don't know why, but I keep forgetting you've only been around humans. He's a Nanic."

Tynae almost fell out of her chair. "Nanic?! I thought they were extinct."

Béo grinned. "Clearly they are not, but I think it best if father fills you in on that one. He is a fascinating tale weaver. I can answer basic questions about the Nanic though." Béo offered.

"Hmm," Tynae straightened her napkin. "Okay, I did not know they were magical beings, is their magic like yours? Not that I know a whole lot about magic to begin with."

"Their magical abilities are different than those of human magi, but their magic is very powerful all the same." Béo took a bite of food.

"How so?" Tynae cut into her helping of duck.

"I'm not completely clear on that. I only know that when they're born all of their powers are fully developed, unlike ours that we have to hone and perfect. Their abilities are rather exceptional. We have yet to duplicate their defensive spells. Fortunately for us, they are more than happy to help in any way they can. I think they feel that they owe us, but we expect nothing from them."

"Why would they *owe* you?"

"That's the story father will be sharing with you." Béo took a bite of tomato.

"Oh okay, I can't wait for supper next week!" Tynae said with anticipation. "He is too precious."

Béo cocked his eyebrow, "My father?"

Tynae choked on her bite of food. "He is a rather handsome man, but I meant Tingy."
Béo chuckled at his mistake.
"Tingy is precious," Tynae reiterated. "What was that fluffy little thing that was with him, a pet?"
"Yes," Béo answered with a massive grin. "It's called an ickel. They are a bit rare. Anyone who possesses magical powers

can have one as a pet. They are able to retrieve items magically and are excellent at detecting when people are concealing ill intentions. They're extremely loyal and a few have even been known to lay down their life to save their master."

Tynae grinned, "They are just as precious as the Nanic. Do you sell them here in Calai?"

"We do. Nhiooh, Tingy's little sister, she breeds and sells them. You tell her the color and traits you want and she makes it happen." Béo grabbed the bottle of wine, "More?"

Tynae held out her goblet. "Just a little please. Tingy has a sister? Is she as cute as he is?"

Béo laughed boisterously. "Nanic's are not pets, Tynae. And yes, I dare say she is even cuter than he."

"I know they're not pets or something to be owned, but up until the last twenty-four hours…well it's just all very exciting. I'm sorry." Tynae apologized for her naivety.

"Don't you dare apologize!" Béo's voice was almost angry. "You've done nothing wrong. I'm the one that needs to remember that until today you've known not of no beings other than humans. This must all be very strange to you," he said with concern remembering how upset she became when told she was in Calai.

"You would think that, wouldn't you? It is all a bit odd really, but somehow not totally unexpected. It's like things I've always suspected on some level or another are being confirmed one by one." Tynae looked around the room, "Now, what to ask next?" She tapped her fingers rhythmically on the table. "Time," Tynae blurted out.

"It's almost seven."

"No, not what time *is* it…How do you tell what time it *is*?"

"With numbers…how do you tell time?" Béo chuckled.

"Getting cheeky are we?" Tynae laughed. "In Pathrow…well not just Pathrow, in all of Montronvarr, we have sundials positioned throughout the cities. At night we use candles and sometimes hour glasses. Most of our cities have a church with a bell tower. The monks see to it that the bell is rung every hour on the hour. In smaller towns a 'town crier' announces the time." Tynae took a sip of wine. "I've seen no sundials. Clearly they would not work down here. And I've heard no criers or bells."

Béo sat his fork on his empty plate. "Your right, we do not use any of that. We have water clocks. You see that vase over there?" Béo pointed to a tall clear cylinder filled with water. A stoic stone dragon encircled the container. "The water is calibrated. As each hour passes, the cylinder slowly fills. There are notches etched in the glass indicating the time. After a while, you just know what time it is by where the water level sets. When midnight strikes, the water empties and the process begins again."

Tynae stared at the vase. "That's water? Why is it golden-orange?"

Béo chuckled. "There's almost always a touch of magic when Calai is involved. The color of the water coincides with each of the seasons. It is now autumn, and that's the color someone deemed best depicts the season. The larger clocks in the heart of the city signify the specific month and season. You will find water clocks everywhere throughout Calai. They are all interconnected."

"The hours are still the same, correct?"

"Yes..." Béo smiled. "I know. Some things must seem very different. Trust me; the differences are only slight at best. Are you ready for dessert?"

Tynae's attention was drawn back to Béo. "That sounds lovely."

"You think of your next question." Béo stood, sweeping his hand lightly over Tynae's nude shoulder as he walked past. "And I'll get our dessert. What would you like to drink, meol, juice, or water?"

Not turning, Tynae touched her shoulder lightly. "I have no idea. You choose."

"Okay," Béo said happily, tinkering around in the cooking area. "I'm glad you're so open to trying new things. You're really going to like this...I hope."

Béo set Tynae's dessert down on the table then went back to get their drinks.

Tynae looked curiously at the contents in the clear bowl in front of her. Picking up the bowl, she looked at it from all angles, even the bottom. The contents in her bowl kept changing colors. "What is this, exactly? It looks like there's a rainbow in my bowl." Setting her bowl down, she turned to look at Béo. He was still getting their drinks.

Béo loved the childlike innocence that flooded Tynae's face every time she discovered something new. "It's called chamae'leon puduc. It's quite unique. The flavor changes every time the color does, and as you can see the color changes every few seconds," he explained brightly.

"That is different," Tynae said absentmindedly. "What are these?" She pointed to two long objects protruding from her puduc.

"You eat the puduc with them instead of a spoon. They are called koekie's. The brown one is chocolate and the white vanilla. You'll notice there's a groove down the center. Every time you take a scoop of puduc you take a bite of your koekie as well." Béo came back to the table, bringing with him two large steins. He set Tynae's in front of her then took his seat.

Tynae picked up her large cup peering inside. Her drink resembled milk, but was bright yellow. Tynae looked at Béo curiously then sniffed her drink.

Her caution amused him.

"What is it?"
"Just try it," he urged with a chuckle.
Tynae raised a brow then took a sip. "Mmm," her approval echoed in her mug as she swilled her tasty drink.

Béo let out a barking laugh. "Slow down, there's more if you like it that much."

"Is that…" Tynae set down her stein, "Banana milk?" She wiped away her creamy mustache.

"It does taste like banana milk, but it's meol. It comes from the berry of an inkuhl bush. Try the puduc," he urged.

Grinning, Tynae eagerly picked up her vanilla koekie and took a scoop of her prismatic puduc. "Mmm, oh my gosh! I've never tasted anything like this," she said, mouth full of puduc and koekie. "It's marvelous!"

"What flavor did you get?"
Tynae swallowed her food. "My first bite tasted like fresh strawberries, and the next sweet blueberries."
"If you let it sit in you mouth the flavor will continue to change."
Tynae looked like a child with a new toy.
"Told you you'd like it." Béo beamed.
Eating their dessert and drinking their meol, the two continued to talk.

Tynae looked around her room. "Ahh, the crystals throughout the city. How do you get them to glow so bright?"

"We had nothing to do with the brightness of the crystals. They create their own energy," Béo explained, while Tynae continued to eat her puduc. "The energy that radiates from the crystals is tremendously powerful and over time we have learned to harness it. The crystal needs to be cut in a precise manner in order to maintain the energy."

"Where do the crystals come from?" Tynae glanced up at a large crystal hanging from the ceiling like a chandelier. "I've never seen anything like them."

Béo chuckled. "That's because they only exist in Calai."

"Well, that would explain why I've never seen or heard of them before." Tynae giggled. "Do you have a specific name for them?"

"Meenakara, it means precious gem of energy. It is how we survive underwater, so to us it is incredibly precious." Béo took a sip of his meol. "Without the meenakara we would die."

"How so? Could you not create energy in other ways if you had to?"

"It is not just the energy that it provides. It is what makes the Greer...well, Greer," he shrugged. "But that's an entirely different story and it's getting late, we don't have time for that tale this evening. What else? Keep it simple, please. We'll have loads of time for the more colorful stories, just not tonight." Béo grinned.

"Colorful," she repeated. "That reminds me; tell me about the different colored crystals throughout Calai. What do they represent? Or is that complicated, too?"

"No, that's fairly simple. I can explain that one, but is there anything you don't notice?" Béo chuckled.

"I'm sure there is plenty I don't notice, but this is all so new that I'm trying to take in every little detail that I can," Tynae said honestly.

"That makes sense." Béo tried to imagine what all this must be like for Tynae. "First you have to understand, Calai is enormous. I've not even been to all the boundaries. Of course, there are places I'm not allowed...for now anyway. The colors define different regions within Calai. It gets incredibly dark down here once the sun goes down, so we use colored crystals to indicate where each tunnel leads." Béo thought for a moment. "Okay, let's see. There are seven colors in total, six mark the different domains and one, the clear, is used for lighting all over the city. There is green, blue, yellow, orange, red, purple, and clear. The green crystals are usually where things grow such as the forest and our crops. We also have our live stock there because they graze on the grass that's grown near the forest. "Red is fairly simple. It's for anything directly related to Chief Kerszon; the Archimagi, council members, visiting aristocrats, pretty much anything that has to do with the running of our nation basically."

"I didn't notice. Do you reside in a red area?"

"Yes, only because I've chosen to follow in my father's 'civil' footsteps. Had I chosen another trade I would reside somewhere else." Béo got up. "Would you like some more meol?"

"Just a touch, thank you," Tynae handed Béo her empty stein. "You could have chosen to *not* be the next leader of Calai?"

"Yes and no, but that's another complicated story. Let's stick to the crystals for now."

Tynae smiled, "Okay."

Béo continued his explanation as he got their drinks. "The purple region is where our healing gardens are. We have our conventional flowers and plants in the green areas, but the flowers used for medicines and potions, as well as the flowers that have healing properties, are in the purple areas. The crystal caves are also in the purple region. Here you go." Béo set Tynae's drink in front of her then took his seat. "Let's see, then there's yellow. Yellow is where the Nanic reside, no-one else. Then there's blue. Blue is one of my favorites. It houses the ice forest."

Tynae took a sip of her meol. "Ice forest?" she asked intrigued.

"Yes, I'll take you there soon if you'd like."

"I'd love that." Tynae's childlike enthusiasm was back. Her bright eyes ensnared Béo, causing him to lose his train of thought.

Tynae grinned. "That still leaves orange."

Her voice brought Béo back. "Right, orange, that's where we mine for metals, minerals, and gems."

"Okay." Tynae's brows pulled together. "So where does everyone live, and who lives in the massive homes carved into the cliffs?"

"We live where our 'trade' is. If you're a farmer you live near your crops in the green region. If you're a black smith or a jewelry maker you live in the orange region and so on. The dwellings carved into the cliffs are typically occupied by the leaders of the different clans."

"Clans?"

"Yes, each skill or profession is broken into categories. There are officials that lead or oversee each group, or clan as it were." Béo emptied his stein. "If father needs to discuss something in regards to crops or mining, he only speaks to the person who oversees that particular clan. Father and all the clan leaders meet once a month in order to discuss affairs of the nation. That's the basics." Béo winked at Tynae. "You'll learn more over time."

Taking her last bite of puduc, Tynae looked puzzled. "Where does everyone eat at night? Surely the market is not open past sundown."

"There are dining halls on every floor where people maintain dwellings, but most people prepare their own meals."

"Perhaps we could dine at one of the halls tomorrow?" Tynae suggested.

"Of course. Maybe Jubryi will dine with us. He's a friend of mine. I know he's dying to meet you." Béo grinned slyly.

Béo's last comment left Tynae looking baffled, but she said nothing about it. "I would like that very much. Now, not to change the subject, but there is something that's been bothering me," Tynae told Béo.

"What's that, love?"

"How am I to pay for items I wish to purchase while I'm here? I no longer have access to my gold or property." Tynae spoke with genuine concern.

"You may have whatever you desire. Don't worry about payment. My father and I will see to your debt," Béo told her simply.

Tynae cocked her head, giving Béo a skeptical look. "Is that you or the chief talking?"

"Both. I will make certain father tells you so himself the next time he sees you." Béo spoke with his rare 'Chief' voice.

"That does not set well with me, Béo. I do not like to count on anyone other than myself to pay for my debt. Working for my keep is acceptable to me."

"You'll do no such thing! It is not *acceptable* on any level. This is me talking, but I promise you my father will agree with me vehemently," Béo assured sternly.

"We shall see," Tynae grinned. Standing up, she took the dirty dishes to the cooking area. Turning around, she ran smack into Béo who was standing directly behind her. "Ohh, I'm sorry, I didn't hear you get up."

Béo slid his arms around her waist. "No need to apologize. It worked out just how I planned," he confessed, wearing a mischievous smile. Running his hand over Tynae's beautiful face, Béo leaned forward pressing his lips to hers. Her warm lips parted. Their tongues danced together seductively.

"Let's put out the candles and lanterns so we can take this to the other room," Tynae breathed against Béo's lips.
The two reluctantly pulled apart.
Tynae started to walk away to put out the candles.
"Wait," Béo grabbed her arm, "watch." Clapping his hands twice, Béo sent a bluish-white cloud of mist shooting from his palms. It zoomed around the room, extinguishing every flame; except for one…Theirs wasn't so much a flame, as it was an inferno.

Béo reached for Tynae's hand and together they walked into her bedchamber.

Closing the door behind them, Tynae approached Béo slowly. Seductively, she ran her hand softly over his bare chest.

Before she could go any further, Béo gently put his hand on top of hers. "Tynae, I will not besmirch your virtue," he warned solicitously.

Tynae smiled at his gallantry. "I would expect nothing less from you, Béo. But if I choose to *give* you my virtue, well that is my choice to make." She spoke like the true royal she was. "I am the one who must live with my choices, aren't I?"

Béo didn't know how to answer.

Tynae kissed Béo on the cheek. "Don't look so worried," she grinned. "I do not plan on having my way with you," she said walking away.

Béo stood staring at Tynae as she grabbed her nightdress and headed into the lavatory. Just before she closed the door, she poked her head out, "Not tonight anyway," she teased with a wink then closed the door.

Béo heard Tynae's amused laughter echo off the marble in the bathroom. He stood there staring at the lavatory door, looking utterly mystified by her words, but intrigued all the same.

Chapter 18
Patience and Virtue

"Love isn't a decision. It's a feeling.
If we could decide who we love, it would be
much simpler, but much less magical."
~Trey Parker and Matt Stone

Tynae emerged from the lavatory wearing a mischievous smile and her nightdress.

Béo too was dressed in his night attire and waiting for her.

Tynae giggled. "Sorry, I couldn't help myself," she confessed playfully.

"That's okay; it keeps things interesting to say the least." Béo's innocent smile turned into an impish grin. "Besides, I'll get you back," he said smoothly.

The two exchanged an enthralling look, but said nothing. Both clearly had something on their mind, but neither was ready to admit it quite yet.

Pulling back the covers on her side of the bed, Tynae glanced at her night table. "Where's?" she looked around the room, "never mind, it's over there." She pointed to a slender crystal vase on a table in her sitting area. It held a single white rose.

The pair climbed into bed, each in their respective places, Tynae below the covers and Béo atop.

Béo clapped his hands together. The bluish-gray mist shot out of his hands once again, bolting around the room extinguishing all the flames except the one in the fireplace and the one smoldering between the couple.

"Béo?" Tynae said softly.

His heart skipped a beat. His name on her lips was the sweetest sound he'd ever heard. Rolling onto his side to face Tynae, Béo saw the intense sparkle in her eyes and radiant glow about her skin. *I mustn't touch her, I mustn't touch her*...Swallowing his heart, which had become lodged in his throat, Béo began to breathe again. "Yes?" he choked out.

Tynae crooked her finger, beckoning him to the middle of the bed were she lie.

I mustn't touch her, I mustn't touch her...Béo slowly scooted toward her until their foreheads were touching. "What is it, my angel?" he breathed, praying she couldn't hear the thudding of his heart beating uncontrollably.

Tynae ran her hand tenderly over his cheek. "Nothing, I just wanted you closer. This is perfect," she said quietly.

Béo automatically closed his eyes, absorbing the energy from her loving touch.

Tynae moved a little closer, they were now just a lips distance apart.

Béo didn't need to open his eyes. He could feel her energy drawing him to her.

Tynae pressed her moist lips to his.

Béo hadn't intended on what happened next, but his desirous feelings for Tynae got the better of him. Everything about her drew him in; her smell, her touch, even her voice.

Her kiss was impassioned, yet gentle.

Grabbing Tynae's hair at the nape of her neck, Béo pulled her tight against him. He felt her heart pounding against his.

Tynae's fingers wove themselves into Béo's hair. The two became lost in the moment.

A loud pop from the fireplace brought Béo back around. "Stop," he muttered.

Her lips moving determinedly over his, Tynae didn't acknowledge Béo's words.

"Tynae, please, we can't."

"Why?" she asked breathlessly, her hot breath washing over his lips.

Béo reluctantly managed to break their connection. "Because I won't, at least not right now, please try and understand. I want you more than you could ever imagine, but we must wait," Béo insisted, regaining his determination.

Tynae huffed, giving Béo a comprehending grimace. "I understand," she conceded. "But if you keep kissing me like that, I'm going to have to club you over the head, tie you to my bed, and have my way with you," she warned with a giggle. "Let's get some sleep," she sighed.

Tynae's warning took Béo by surprise. He'd never heard a woman, much less a woman with Tynae's status, speak in such a manor. He kind of liked the idea. But being the gentleman that he was, he elected not to say another word about it. Instead, he extended his arm nearest Tynae out. "Come here," he whispered.

Scooting over, Tynae curled up in Béo's arms. She carefully tucked her head on his shoulder and rested her hand on his chest.

Béo reached over with his opposite hand, tenderly pushing Tynae's hair out of her face.

"I can live with this…for now," she said softly, "You know…"

Béo gently placed his index finger over Tynae's lips. Instantly she stopped speaking, looking deep into Béo's eyes.

"I do *know* this is not something you do or have ever done for that matter. I know you much better than that, Tynae. And no, it does not diminish my respect for you on any level." Béo let his finger slowly slide from Tynae's lips.

"Thank you," she breathed. "But how did you know what I was going to say?"

"Honestly, I'm not sure, I just knew." Béo ran his hand gently over Tynae's arm. "So much has changed and I understand none of it."

Tynae smiled warmly, "That makes two of us."

The couple kissed delicately. "Good night," she sighed.

"Good night."

Sleep came faster than expected, and with it Tynae's mystery man.

Tynae found herself standing in *their* beautiful garden once again. This time she wore a blood red gown, accentuating her full bosom. Rubies adorned her body from head to toe.

Looking around, Tynae noticed a foggy gray mist at the edge of the world she was now in. *Was that there the last time?* She wondered.

A figure slowly became visible within the thick fog bank. "Hello, my angel," called a man.

Tynae's heart fluttered when she heard the enchanting voice. It was distinctly familiar yet entirely new. Emerging from the opaque mist, the man wore a warm and alluring smile.

Tynae beamed. "Hello..." Tynae's expression changed to alarm and her words fell short.

Her mystery man's smile became a large grin. "What is it, angel?"

"I don't remember your name," she admitted highly embarrassed.

The man chuckled, now standing directly in front of her. Reaching out, he placed his hands gently on her face. Tenderly he pressed his lips to hers.

His name suddenly became completely irrelevant, considering she couldn't even remember her own.

"Ryedin," he breathed against her mouth.

Pulling back slightly, Tynae looked at the man with utter bewilderment. "Huh?"

"My name," he chuckled, "it's Ryedin."

"Oh. Sorry," she tittered, "lost my brain for a minute there. 'Ryedin', I won't forget again."

"No worries, love. Care to sit?" Ryedin gestured toward the chaise lounge they'd sat upon the last time they were here.

"Of course," she accepted with a smile.

Taking Tynae by the hand, Ryedin led her over to what was now *their* spot.

Ryedin pulled Tynae close as they sat. "How was your day, my love?"

Tynae proceeded to tell Ryedin all about the day's events and the many new things she'd learned.

Before she knew it, he was telling her it was time to go back. "I don't want to go, you know I don't," Tynae protested as they stood up.

"And you know that you must," he argued lovingly. "If I had my way, you would stay with me every second of every day." He pulled Tynae close, "But that is not possible, is it?"

"Unfortunately, no," Tynae sighed

Ryedin pressed his lips against Tynae's erotically. Lost in the moment, Tynae's breath became embarrassingly loud.

Ryedin pulled away just slightly.

Tynae stood there, chest heaving, breathless and never wanting to let this man out of her sight.

"I must go, and you must rest," he told her firmly.

"Okay," she said submissively, like a little child being told to do something for her own good.

Ryedin kissed her gently, brushing his hand over her cheek. "Sleep sweet, my angel."

"You as well, *my* angel."

Ryedin turned, walking away. He was almost to the cloud bank when Tynae cried out nearly panicked, "Ryedin?"

He turned with a heartwarming smile. "Yes, my love?"

His sparkling eyes mesmerized her so; she almost forgot what she was going to ask. "Will I see you again tomorrow?"

"Of course, my love, as I told you before, I will never leave you. Please don't fret. I have always been and will always be here for you." Blowing her a kiss, Ryedin vanished into the gray mist, and the garden around Tynae quickly faded to black.

Tynae found herself back in Calai, snug in Béo's arms, and more confused than she had ever been.

How can I feel such strong emotions toward a dream? She looked at Béo sleeping peacefully. *How can I dream of another man when I have one here that I love so much? Could Ryedin possibly be Béo? Though they appear different, they are somehow the same.*

Tynae decided not to worry about her dream man and the world they shared. After all, what harm ever came from a dream. Tynae nestled snuggly into Béo's arms, falling into a peaceful slumber of her own.

Chapter 19
True Love Never Wanes

"I show you doubt, to prove faith exists."
~Robert Browning

Dawn's light shone upon the forest of Nombin, the leafy canopy shattering the sun's golden beams into millions of warm, glistening fragments. Thin threads of steam rose from the forest floor, as the sun's warm rays gently kissed the morning frost.

Sluggishly, hundreds of tired soldiers meandered their way back to Pathrow. When the soldiers returned to the castle of Darvah they found a large breakfast awaiting them, along with their replacements. Slowly, but surely, all the soldiers trickled into the hall of Naviyd until it was filled to capacity with bodies and chatter.

King Yurgon waited until a majority of the men had finished their meals before he addressed them. The king took his place behind an ornate dais standing in the center of a large wooden stage. "Good morning, men," Yurgon spoke in a monotone voice. "I must assume that none have significant news or I would have heard by now, but I do wish for the three colonels to give a brief summary of the night's events so that we are all up to speed." The king took a seat in his thrown-like chair that sat atop the stage. Gwillim sat to Yurgon's right in a smaller, yet equally ornate chair.

The first to stand was Colonel Haremon, leader of the 2nd, 4th, 5th, and 29th regiments. With a bow of his head, he addressed the king. "Majesty, I am sorry we bring no news of Lady Tynae's whereabouts. My men and I checked every inch of the wood we were assigned and beyond." The colonel awaited his dismissal.

Yurgon nodded. "Very well, Haremon." Yurgon's voice was barely audible. "Thank you."

Haremon nodded, taking his seat.

Colonel Jardah, commander of the 3rd, 12th, 31st, and 82nd regiments was the next to stand.

Bowing to the king, he began his report. "I'm afraid we do not have much to report either, Sire. We searched all the shallow lakes and ponds throughout the forest. Standing shoulder to shoulder my men and I walked every inch of the pools. Perhaps it is encouraging news that we found nothing, Your Majesty."

Yurgon nodded. "Thank you."

The third and final commander stood, Colonel Batu. He commanded the 1st, 6th, 7th, and 13th regiments. He and his men were known for their uncanny ability to find those who were believed to be untraceable, both friend and foe.

Batu bowed to the king. "I'm afraid we have little to report as well, My Liege, but we did find these." Reaching into his pocket Batu pulled out what appeared to be a large handful of rubbish. "May I approach, Your Majesty?"

"By all means."

Batu walked up to Yurgon. With shaking hands he carefully laid the mess on a small table that sat between the king and Gwillim.

Yurgon sorted through the jumble.

The king looked up at Gwillim then to Batu, trepidation evident in every line of his aged face.

"Where did you find this?" he asked calmly.

Staring at the table Gwillim's heart began to race. Taking a deep breath he attempted to calm himself.

"We found them all over the forest, Your Majesty. The majority was found in the thickest part of the wood. They were stuck to bushes and branches throughout the whole of the forest…and we found this." Batu reached into a leather satchel that he carried and pulled out another piece of fabric, this one was different than the rest. Batu handed Yurgon the large chunk of blood-stained material then stared at the floor.

Why did we not see any of this? Gwillim's heart pounded wildly, *we searched the forest methodically, covering our tracks.*

With a trembling hand, Yurgon took the cloth. Clutching it in his fist he stared at it for several heartbeats…Finally he spoke, not looking up. "Did you find anything else?" The king's quiet words shook slightly.

Batu hesitated then looked at his king. He opened and closed his mouth three times before words actually formed on his lips. "It is unclear if it is anything at all, Majesty, but the long grass in the meadow near the overhangs was slightly flattened." Batu paused running his hand through his long blond hair. "The path led directly…"

Yurgon lifted his head, "Yes?"

"To the cliffs," Batu explained, clearly distressed. "I wish I could tell you something that would set your mind at ease, My Lord, but I can only speak of that which I know."

"I understand, Batu, please continue."

"The flattened area was very wide, it must have taken several bodies to make it. It could never have been made by just one," Batu rationalized, "perhaps it was created by a pack of wolves or maybe a family of deer resting for a spell."

It was evident Batu was grasping at straws. It seemed that no-one was ready to believe that Lady Tynae was gone.

Yurgon smiled slightly. "Thank you, Batu. You may take your seat."

King Yurgon looked out at the concerned faces of his men, all sitting quietly looking back at him. He stood, "Thank you, everyone. There is still work to be done here. My daughter is alive. I know it. I can feel it. You are the best soldiers in the entire world. I know you will find her." Yurgon's strength and determination had returned.

King Yurgon's faith in his men and in his daughter reignited the soldiers' determination.

Standing in unison, the soldiers placed their arms over their chests forming an "X" with their arms. Together they thumped their breast plates with their fists and shouted "kaelorah!" three consecutive times.

This was their motto. It meant: 'With allegiance we fight and with honor we die'.

King Yurgon's smile was genuine this time. He mimicked his men. Placing his arms over his own chest, he responded to his soldiers' devotion by shouting, "sinauf tornen."

This was a blessing that meant: 'Bless you who fight with loyalty, with a safe return home'.

"Batu, give Gwillim the exact coordinates where you found this." Yurgon acknowledged the blood-stained material in his hand. "We'll send another company out to comb the forest this day. Perhaps fresh eyes may see something that may have gone unnoticed in the dark. As for the rest of you, you'll receive your orders from the constable. You will be searching all of Pathrow today."

Yurgon turned to Gwillim. "The floor is yours, High Constable."

Yurgon took his seat while Gwillim dispatched the soldiers.

Gwillim spoke with Batu and his men at length then called for Captain Kabool to join them.

Kabool was the commander of the 85th company, a subdivision of the 13th regiment. Kabool was to lead the search party that was returning to the Forest of Nombin.

Gwillim then met with the commanders of each regiment, going over a map of Pathrow. Having a port and being the capitol of Montronvarr, Pathrow was a bustling metropolis. The map was divided evenly into one hundred segments. No less than two squads of men were sent to each sector.

Gwillim dismissed the soldiers from the previous night's duties, some volunteered to stay. "I appreciate the gesture men, but you need your rest. Plenty of soldiers were brought in throughout the night. We will all meet up again at twilight. Good rest to you all."

Once the last soldiers had departed, Gwillim turned to Yurgon.

The king had remained in his chair atop the stage. Clearly immersed in bitter thought, Yurgon still clutched the shredded material Batu had given him.

With soft steps, Gwillim crossed the wooden stage walking over to the king. "Sire, do not give up hope." His words carried a genuine heartfelt sentiment.

The king smiled softly at Gwillim. "Never," he said resolutely. "I was just thinking about this dress." Yurgon looked thoughtfully at the cloth. "I had it commissioned specifically for that night." He ran his hand over it. "I picked out this material myself." Yurgon looked back at Gwillim. "There was so much more that was supposed to happen. I'm just afraid…"

The king glimpsed the blood soaked material then focused on Gwillim again. "I may be a king, but I am only human, and she is still my daughter. I am her father first and foremost, not her ruler." Yurgon sighed. "Rest assured, I will not let fear take root." Yurgon set the remnants of his daughters last night in Pathrow down. "You know what it's like, Gwillim. I've seen you with your little ones. You love them like I love Tynae. I know you would die before you would allow anything to happen to them, even if it meant betraying me. Would you not?"

Gwillim's stomach almost turned inside out. "Betray you? Wha…"

Yurgon tilted his head with a smirk, "Don't tell me you would never betray me Gwillim."

He knows!

"Sire, my oa…"

Yurgon cut him off, "Sworn oath, undying allegiance, blah, blah, blah. If you knew the lives of your children were on the line, you would kill me to save them…I know you would. I would do the same."

Gwillim let out a soft chuckle, shaking his head. "Ay, Sire, I suppose you are correct."

"I know I am."

"But, My Lord, Lady Tynae, she's different. She would die or exchange her own life for another and never think twice about it," Gwillim said with admiration.

Yurgon beamed at Gwillim's statement, "That she would. She is like no other. My daughter is incredibly strong, Gwillim. I know that if someone tried to harm her, she would fight vehemently 'til the death. I would bet my life on that, nay my very soul. In the end, if she is no more I will accept that fact. But if her end was brought about by those with evil intent, they will rue the day they came into existence when I am through with them. I am not Tynae. I do not see all things the way she does." Yurgon's voice became uncharacteristically harsh.

"Ay, Sire that is an understatement. If she has been harmed…" Gwillim paused knowing this would make the delivery of his lines appear more dramatic. "Or worse, I pity the poor soul or souls that will have to answer to you and your soldiers." Narrowing his eyes, Gwillim clenched his fists. "The bloody bastards will beg to be drawn and quartered," he assured with a growl.

Hearing footsteps echo on the stone floor, Gwillim turned to see Baroness Arona casually saunter through the doorway. Gwillim bowed. Once fully in the room, Arona curtsied to the king and Gwillim.

"There is good news, I hope?" she asked expectantly.

"I'm afraid not, my dear." Yurgon informed sadly.

Arona flung herself upon Yurgon's chest. Her shoulders shaking as she sobbed.

Yurgon ran his hand compassionately over her back. "There, there, love. We will find her."

Arona turned her head slightly to look at Gwillim. With a wicked smile, she gave him a wink.

Without skipping a beat, she resumed her almost convincing impression of a caring human being.

Gwillim's stomach turned and before he could stop it, he was doubled over. His body convulsed violently as he coated the stage with his morning meal.

Grabbing a woven basket Yurgon slid it under Gwillim. "Shall I call for the doctor?" Yurgon asked, concerned.

Gwillim held up his hand, shaking his head. "No, I'll be fine," he managed to gag out between expulsions. Once his stomach had expelled every last bit of food, he was able to catch his breath and stand up. "Something just isn't setting well with me," Gwillim muttered coldly.

Gwillim inspected the floor he'd camouflaged with chunks of his breakfast. "I'm sorry, Sire. I will clean up this mess."

Yurgon patted Gwillim on the shoulder. "Nonsense, perhaps you should go home and rest a spell."

"No!" Gwillim snapped, "I mean, no, Sire, I'm fine. I'm sure it was just something I ate. I feel much better now."

Yurgon eyed Gwillim in a fatherly manner. "If you're sure."

"I am," Gwillim maintained convincingly. "I just need to wash up. Was there anything else, My Liege?"

"So be it. I appreciate your commitment, Gwillim, thank you. No, there's nothing else. You may go." The king turned to Arona, who was still sniveling, wrapping his arm lovingly around her.

Gwillim almost gagged again. "I'm fine," he argued, desperate to take his leave.

Yurgon looked at Gwillim doubtfully. "You must assure me that if you continue to feel ill you will rest."

Gwillim nodded, fighting to keep his gag reflex in check.

Yurgon started to speak, but Gwillim threw his hand up cutting him off.

"Okay," he grinned weakly. "I promise, I will rest or see the doctor if this persists," Gwillim affirmed.

Having gotten his way, Yurgon grinned. Nodding his head once in thanks, he let the matter drop.

Gwillim bowed then quickly made his way to the loo. Leaning over a water-filled basin, he splashed cold water on his face. Nerves somewhat calmed, Gwillim examined his reflection in the water. *Dammit man, get a grip on yourself! You need to push all this self-righteous crap aside. The deed is done. That cannot be changed, so you better get used to that. Your life and your family's lives depend on it,* he reminded himself.

Gwillim successfully convinced himself that from this day forward every time his conscience started to get the better of him, he would bury those feelings. There was no way to undo what had been done. He accepted that now. *From this moment on I can never look back.*

Grabbing a towel off the sink, Gwillim dried his face and hands. Setting off, he joined his men in the city. Together their performances were spectacular. The soldiers searched every building, field, puddle, and hole while Gwillim questioned every person young and old with evident concern and tact.

Chapter 20
Confessions of the Soul

"I love you, and because I love you, I would sooner have
you hate me for telling you the truth
than adore me for telling you lies."
~Pietro Aretino

Tynae lay on her side still wrapped snug in Béo's arms, her head on his shoulder.

The tantalizing smell of breakfast greeted the couple.

Béo yawned. "It smells like morning's arrived," he said with an air of disappointment, running his fingers over Tynae's arm lying across his chest.

"Mmm, do we really have to get up?" Tynae stifled her own yawn. "I'd be content lying in your arms for the entire day."

Béo ran his hand atop the blanket covering Tynae's back. "I would love nothing else, but…"

Tynae placed her finger over Béo's lips.

"I know, I know," she sighed deeply.

Turning to look at Tynae, Béo still could not believe the woman he'd loved for so long now lay in his arms. Her beauty continued to astonish him. It seemed as if she became more and more breathtaking with each passing day.

"Tynae, I have to tell you something," Béo announced in an unusually serious tone.

Tynae's eyes grew wide. "You're betrothed to another, aren't you?"

Tynae's accusation caught Béo so completely off guard; he almost burst out with laughter. In his attempt to stifle his chuckle he ended up snorting. Smiling, he shook his head. "No," he said, amused, "Don't be silly."

"Oh," Tynae sighed. "Then do tell. What's on your mind?" She ran her fingers through his hair.

Béo took a deep breath. "I've been thinking." *That's a good place to start, yeah...I have been thinking.* "I've been thinking, so much has happened in the past few days. Well, that's an understatement." He laughed. "Anyway it's...well it's made me very aware of how precious and unpredictable life truly is." Béo swallowed. "There are many things I have put off or even avoided doing because I'm always waiting for the 'right time', but I've realized that the *right time* will never come. There will never be a day or time when everything is 'perfect'."

Tynae listened intently.

Béo could see she had no idea where this was heading. Turning onto his side Béo was careful to keep Tynae cradled in his arm. Lovingly he brushed her cheek.

She looked at him with such love. He could feel her soul touch his. The warmth, the peace, the fluttering of his heart...It was the most amazing sensation.

There was a slight shake to Béo's words. He was clearly nervous. "Though I risk losing you forever by speaking what may be considered too boldly, I must tell you how I honestly feel." Hesitating for three heartbeats, Béo consciously filled his lungs with air. *Here goes nothing.* "I love you, Tynae," he exhaled. "I have for years, and after the events of late I can go no longer without telling you my true feelings. After almost losing you the other day I realize just how precious each and every moment is...tomorrow may never arrive." Béo's words trailed off as he gazed at Tynae.

Tynae slid her hand along Béo's shoulder. Caressing the curve of his neck she gently pulled him to her. Her rose petal lips pressed against his mouth. She kissed him once, twice...her tongue gently tracing his lips.

His heart raced as their kiss consumed him.

Pulling back slightly, Tynae looked intensely at Béo. "I love you, too," she whispered.

These were the sweetest words Béo had ever heard. *I'm going to marry this woman,* he thought to himself, *nothing will ever come between us again.* The pair lay staring at one another when a knock at the door caused them both to start, hurdling back to reality. Quickly they moved to their respective sides of the bed.

"Enter," Tynae called out, trying to suppress the girlish giggle desperately fighting to burst out.

Entering the room, O'leana curtsied. "Majesties, breakfast is ready. Would you like us to serve you?"

"Please," Tynae said blandly, biting her lip. She did not dare to look over at Béo, if she had any hope of maintaining her lady-like demeanor.

Once all the food had been placed on the table, O'leana and the other handmaidens departed.

With the maids gone Tynae looked over at Béo. Both erupted with laughter.

"We should get up." Béo threw off the covers. "I'm sure we're already the talk of Calai, we need not give them any more fuel for the fire."

Tynae sighed. "You're right of course," she admitted reluctantly, tossing her covers off.

"Of course I am."

Sitting on the edge of the bed, Tynae glanced at her bedside table. Grinning she picked up a freshly cut white rose, smelling it.

Walking to her side of the bed, Béo offered a chivalrous hand.

Tynae eyed his hand. Setting her rose down, she looked up at him. With a crooked smile, she grabbed hold of Béo's night-shirt, pulling him to her.

She was much stronger than he would have imagined. Falling over on top of her Béo caught himself on his hands, careful not to crush Tynae.

Lowering himself until his lips and body barely brushed against hers, Béo smiled wickedly. "Yes, *My Lady?*"

"Shhh," she pressed her lips to his.

Béo knew he should protest, but could not rouse the willpower.

The couple performed a perfectly orchestrated dance. Béo grabbed Tynae around the waist as she wrapped her arms and legs around him. Together they rolled. She was now on top of him.

Béo twined his fist tight in Tynae's hair. Her breathing was fast becoming loud as she pressed her body tight against his. Erotically, fervently, their tongues danced together.

Reaching down, Tynae began pulling up Béo's night shirt.

"No," he said breathlessly. Béo loosened his grip on Tynae's hair. Sliding his hand over her back, their tongues continuing to cavort.

As their kiss finally slowed Tynae swiftly yanked herself off Béo's body. She lay on her side next to him, chest still heaving.

Looking thunderstruck, Béo gawked at her. "What was that?"

"Sorry, love." She smiled. "Stopping wasn't the direction I was headed. It was either quick like removing a bandage," she laughed, "or not stopping at all."

"Is your faith in me truly that slight?" Béo asked with a boyish grin.

"It has nothing to do with my faith in *you*. It's me. I don't know what to expect from myself from one moment to the next these days."

Tynae's words carried an emotion Béo was not used to hearing from his always confident princess, uncertainty. Béo rolled onto his side. Smiling at Tynae he ran his hand over her cheek.

Tynae closed her eyes.
"Come on, our food is getting cold," he said lightly.
"Okay," she sighed, sliding out of bed.

Béo was at her side in a flash helping her with her robe.

Together they ate. "So what's on the agenda for today?" Tynae asked.

"I figured I'd let you choose. Healing gardens or ice forest?" Béo asked, taking a bite of eggs.

Tynae contemplated her choices. "Hmm, let's visit the healing gardens. I've always been curious about potions and..."
There was a knock.
"Enter," Tynae called.
O'leana entered with a curtsy and a smile. "Is there anything I can get for you?"
"No, O'leana, thank you, but we'll be done soon and I'll be ready for my bath." Tynae grinned.

"Very well, My Lady, just let me know when you're ready." O'leana bowed, departing once more.

When Tynae turned back to Béo he was staring at her with a serene expression. Tynae cocked her head slightly. "What?" she asked innocently.

He shook his head, "You're just..." He smiled. "I love you," he confessed once more reaching out, touching her hand. Now that he had said it and knew she felt the same, he would be sure to tell her those three little words any time he felt like it.

Tynae smiled, blushing slightly.

Béo got up, holding out his hand.

Taking his hand, Tynae stood.

Béo pulled her tight to him.

Tynae secured her arms around his neck. Leaning forward she whispered in his ear. "I love you, too."

Her breath wafted over his skin causing goose bumps to explode over every inch of him.
Tynae leaned back just enough to gaze into Béo's eyes; automatically their lips were drawn together as if magnetized. They exchanged a brief, but passionate kiss.
"I'll be back soon," Béo said softly pulling away.
Her smile was that of an angel, he was sure of it.

"Okay," Tynae breathed.

Béo slid his hands down Tynae's arms, not wanting to let go until he absolutely had to. Slowly he backed away from her, until just their fingers where touching. Bending over, Béo kissed each of Tynae's hands lightly.

Before Tynae joined her handmaidens, she picked up her white rose. Breathing in its sweet fragrance, she smiled as she thought of Béo. Setting down the flower she went into the lavatory.

This day's attire was fun and colorful. When Tynae inspected herself in the mirror she did a double take when she saw hot pink tufts of color running through her hair.

Koralie rocked nervously on the balls of her feet, nibbling on her finger nails as Tynae looked in the mirror. The bright outfit had been Koralie's *bright* idea. "Do you approve, My Lady?"

Tynae spun around, looking at herself in the mirror from all angles. "Oh yes, I do like this," she gushed, admiring her new outfit.

The material was black and bright pink with pink crystals and just as revealing as the previous day's attire. The top had a knot in the middle and a thin strap that went over one shoulder. Pink crystals hung from silver threads over her abdomen. The skirt had a wide beaded pink waistband that came to a point, from it hung several large pieces of sheer material alternating in color, pink and black.

"It's so vibrant. I love it!" She spun around again. "We would never wear anything this colorful in Pathrow during the day." Tynae continued inspecting herself in the mirror for another moment then dismissed her maids. "Thank you, ladies. You may go, and if you have nothing else to do you may have the remainder of the day off."

"Do you not wish for us to prepare supper?" O'leana asked.

"No. Béo and I will be eating..." Tynae appeared confused, looking at O'leana she chuckled, "well I'm not sure where, but not here."

"Very well, My Lady, enjoy your day."

The three maids curtsied and left.

Anxiously awaiting Béo's return Tynae strolled through her personal forest.

"Hello?" a male voice called.

Tynae's heart skipped a beat. "I'm in here," she shouted.

Béo made his way to Tynae, who sat admiring the sea garden outside her huge picturesque window.

"I spo..." Béo's words ceased when Tynae stood.

Her expression fell blank, "What's wrong?"

It took a heartbeat or two before Béo spoke. Smiling, he walked up to her. "Nothing," he sighed, wrapping his arms around her waist. "You...you look absolutely gorgeous. I don't know that I will ever get used to your stunning beauty."

Shaking her head, Tynae rolled her eyes. "Now you're the one being silly. I'm no different than any other woman."

Béo looked at Tynae incredulously shaking his head. "I'm not going to argue with you. I know you don't see yourself the way others do. This is one of your most endearing qualities, my angel, and it's what makes you all the more attractive."

Tynae blushed slightly. "Thank you. Were you going to tell me something?"

Béo's brow furrowed. "Huh?" Realization flashed across his face. "Oh yes, I spoke with Jubryi, he said he'd love to have supper with us tonight. I told him we'd meet him at seven."

Tynae beamed. "Great, I can't wait to meet him, but right now I really want to see more of this extraordinary city of yours."

"Shall we get started then?" Béo held his hand out.

Tynae took his hand, "Absolutely."

When they reached the door, Béo pulled Tynae to him. Placing his hands gently on her cheeks, he whispered. "It will be hours before we can do this again." Leaning forward, he kissed her softly. Once…twice…each kiss lasting slightly longer than the previous, thrice… "Let's get out of here…" Béo barely managed to pull himself away from Tynae. "Before I change my mind," he said half-serious. "I may just buy you a club while we're out today," he joked.

"A club?" It took a second for Tynae's words to come back to her from the previous night. "Oh right." She laughed, "Hmm."

Chapter 21
Life Lessons to be Remembered

"Each decision we make, each action we take,
is born out of an intention."
~Sharon Salzberg

The people of Calai welcomed Princess Tynae with open arms, treating her as if she'd lived among them her entire life. Although people ogled her once in a while, it was never disrespectful. It was certainly no different than being in Pathrow.

Reaching the heart of the city, Béo and Tynae headed straight for the first tunnel with a purple crystal over the entrance.

The moment they'd entered the tunnel, all the noise from the city faded into silence.

Grinning, Tynae looked at Béo. "Why did it get so quiet, so fast?"

"Like I said, you miss nothing. It's a spell. Many of the plants that grow in this area are particularly sensitive to different types of vibrations. Most prefer a peaceful and soothing atmosphere."

"Vibrations? I don't understand." Tynae probed as they continued to walk.

"Yes. Sounds, feelings, emotions, they all carry an..." Béo searched for the right words. "'Energy', if you will. Energy, though invisible, has a vibration that every living thing, be it a person, plant or animal can feel, even if unaware of it. Inevitably everything will eventually react to the energy that surrounds it."

Tynae said nothing, but Béo read her uncomprehending expression.

"Does a tree not bend its mighty trunk to the gentle will of the wind, or an abused animal eventually turn against his abuser. And does not a loving human willingly give his life for the one he loves? Would you not agree that all of these reactions are a direct result of the energy the 'thing' was constantly surrounded by?"

"Yes," Tynae nodded, "I can see that."

Béo went on, "If someone is in a foul mood, they are not permitted to enter this area. There are spells at the doorway preventing people from entering if they harbor negativity of any sort."

"How come?"

"Because most, if not all, that grows in these gardens will either be turned into a potion, antidote, or some form of elixir that will inevitably be digested and absorbed by someone, or something."

The path the couple was on led to a large wooden door that looked as if it took at least three very large men to open it. Drawing closer to the door, Béo held up his hand, palm toward the door. The sound of clicking and clanking bolts being unlocked could be heard. Approaching the heavy entrance, it silently drifted open.

Tynae seemed surprised, which was understandable. After all, magic was not real in *her* world, much less something one used on a daily basis.

Without skipping a beat, Béo continued his explanation.

"You see, the herbs here are so powerful that they will transfer to their consumer that which they themselves possess. If they have taken in anger they will deliver anger. If they have taken in only love and joy, then that is all they can give," Béo said matter-of-factly.

Standing beside a silver door, Béo smiled eagerly. "After you, *My Lady*," he gestured with his hand.

Walking through the doorway, Tynae found herself standing in a very bright and oversized circular vestibule known as the 'sword room'. Looking up, she probably expected to see a stone ceiling with an illuminating crystal. Instead she saw the clear blue water of the Calain Sea through the dome protecting this magical place.

Then she noticed the floor.

Tynae stepped back to get a clear view at the inlayed design. The entire floor was a brilliant cobalt blue with the exception of the middle. There was a huge sword inlayed directly in the center of the floor. Running from wall to wall, the blade was at least one meter wide. The hilt was accented with golden flames flaring out. An amethyst the size of a goose egg lay flush with the floor creating the pommel. The sword lay atop a set of glistening white wings. The words *Proeliators Iussu Otium* were written in gold, forming an arch over the wings and sword. In addition, the words Praedo Umbra ran along the bottom half of the circle.

"This is stunning," Tynae said, gradually making her way around the cylinder room, admiring the design from all angles. "What does this mean?" She pointed to the words.

Béo grinned. "The words around the top mean 'Warriors of Peace,'" he said simply. "It's who we, the Greer, are, and the words along the bottom mean 'Destroyer of Shadows'. It's what the sword has been aptly dubbed, but when it is spoken about it is referred to as 'The Sword of the Guardian'."
"Why is that?"
"Because only a true guardian of humanity may wield it."
Tynae looked at Béo with astonishment. "Oh," she breathed.

Tynae got down on her hands and knees to examine the masterpiece. "The blade looks like silver, yet it looks like..."

"Light," Béo finished her sentence. "Only light can destroy darkness," he pointed out, "hence the name, 'Destroyer of Shadows'."
"It's simply amazing," she muttered resuming her examination. "It actually looks like it's glowing. And the silver and gold inlayed into this— it's the purest I've ever seen." She ran her hand over the seamless floor. Bending over even further, Tynae examined the huge amethyst so closely her nose almost touched it. "This stone, I've never seen one this large fully intact much less flawless." With a scrutinizing eye, Tynae looked

around at the exceptional floor she sat upon. "There's not a single tool mark, anywhere," she murmured. Straightening up a little, Tynae ran her hand over the iridescent wings. "They're made from opal!" she gasped. "The workmanship is overwhelmingly intricate. I just can't believe anyone could make something so…so…I'll say beautiful, but that does not do it the justice it deserves, and the flawlessness." Tynae stared for a moment more then began to get up off the floor. "How long did it take to…" Gasping, Tynae dropped back down to the floor. "No! It can't be!" She ran her hand over the blue substance covering a majority of the floor. "I thought this was glass!" She looked up at Béo, "Is this…*no!*" She shook her head disbelieving, looking at the blue floor again then back to Béo, "Sapphire?!"

Béo was smiling from ear to ear. "Yes, it most certainly is," he extended his hand out to help Tynae up, "And sixteen years."

"Excuse me?"

"You started to ask how long it took to make. It took sixteen years," he answered with a chuckle.

"Wow," she sighed, staring at the floor. "That does not surprise me in the least. Did Ildrai make it?"

Impressed and a little surprised Béo's smile widened. He hadn't expected Tynae to remember the jewelry maker's name. "Ay and his son."

"It's simply phenomenal," she said, still gazing at the floor. "Does this sword truly exist?"

Béo shook his head, *she misses nothing.* "Yes, well, maybe. There's a legend that says it does anyway. The sword's true name is 'Guardian of Souls', but we've never seen it, and no-one knows where it is. It was lost during the war of Animus. It may have been stolen or it may have been taken by the God above." Béo shrugged. "It is said that the Creator himself forged the sword, combining all the elements of the world, and whosoever wields 'The Sword of the Guardian'—in His name—can control not only the elements, but time itself. Father or maybe Zandore would probably be the best ones to talk to about it."

"I'll do that," Tynae said.

Once she was able to tear her eyes away from the floor Tynae turned, finally noticing the rest of the room. "Why is…Are those…" Tynae looked at Béo skeptically, "Doors?"

Before them stood seven glittering, translucent doors. All were a dazzling bright color, each fading seamlessly into the next. The rainbow of doors covered half the circular room.

Béo chuckled. "Love, you are a strange one. Most people notice the doors first, the floor second, and the ceiling last. They are indeed doors, each leads to a different type of growing area. If what we grow wants soft soothing music we keep it separate from the flora that desires total silence or an upbeat atmosphere."

Tynae gazed at the prismatic doors. "Oh, I see." Enthusiastically she turned to Béo, "So, which door are we going through?"

"You pick."

"Really? Well, hmm…" With deep concentration, Tynae studied each of the doors carefully. After a minute or two she turned to Béo. "Green…I think."

"Are you sure?"

Tynae re-thought her choice for a minute. "Yes," she nodded. "Definitely, the fourth door," she said with confidence.

"Excellent choice."

Puzzlement coated Tynae's face as she looked carefully at the doors. Reaching out she felt the glistening material. "It's solid—it feels like glass."

Béo just grinned.

"How do you get in? There are no handles or latches?"

Béo took Tynae by the hand, "Come on."

With a wave of his free hand, the green pigment began to ripple like water.

Chapter 22
What's in a Name?

"Names, once they are in common use,
quickly become mere sounds,
their etymology being buried, like so many
of the earth's marvels, beneath the dust of habit."
~Salman Rushdie

Tynae looked at Béo like he was touched in the head. "You expect me to walk *through* that?"

"Do you trust me?"

"With my life," Tynae answered without hesitation.

Béo took a step closer to the quivering liquid. "Touch it," he encouraged.

Tynae looked from Béo to the doorway then back.

Béo gestured toward the door with a wink.

Slowly Tynae reached out, her fingers were almost touching the door when Béo suddenly grabbed her around the waist and shouted, "BOO!"

Tynae leapt into the air. "You arse!" she yelled, punching his arm.

"Owww!" he chuckled rubbing his shoulder. "I couldn't help myself…Damn, woman, you've got a wicked right hook."

Tynae shot him a glare that was somewhere between 'you got what you deserve' and 'don't you forget it.' Reaching out once more, she warily touched her fingers to the door, it didn't feel like anything.

"Do you honestly think I would ever put you in harm's way?" Béo asked seriously.

"No," Tynae grimaced, "of course not. But all of this is still so strange."

"Naw, just new," Béo corrected. "There's nothing strange about it, it's just been tucked away neatly until the time was right for you to learn about it."

Tynae smiled. "And now is the right time?"

178

"Apparently so," Béo grinned. "Let's go."

Side by side, the couple walked through the liquefied glass. Tynae considered shutting her eyes, but forced herself to keep them open. Everything appeared green while they were walking through the door, but nothing else seemed to happen.

Once on the other side everything appeared normal again and Tynae saw the most incredible flowers she'd ever laid eyes on. The blossoms were all different shapes, sizes, and colors. Looking around she also saw several small creatures fluttering about. They resembled butterflies, birds, and an assortment of insects; but nothing like the creatures she was used to. Vividly red bugs resembling bees buzzed around. Shimmering pink bird-like creatures fluttered about, and a few dazzling blue insects meandered over the leaves of the plants the couple stood beside. "What are they?" she asked, as a tiny pink creature danced in the air above her.

"They are birds and insects like any other. They were just created to live among these particular flowers."

The couple had been wandering among the blossoms for about an hour when they noticed someone kneeling in one of the flower beds.

Tynae leaned toward Béo, "Who is that?" she whispered.

"That is Dame Chenoa. She is Sir Demric's wife, and the sole caretaker of the gardens of Leideyja. I'll introduce you. I must warn you though, she is not like anyone you have ever met," Béo said in hushed tones.

Tynae looked at Béo with a confused smile. "What do you mean?"

"You'll see," he raised his eyebrows mischievously.

Dame Chenoa was a striking older woman. Her long white hair had subtle streaks of emerald green running through it. This was striking against her olive complexion. She wore a long tan skirt made of animal hide, and a colorful loose-fitting top.

Chenoa looked up from her gardening as the couple approach. "Ah, young Béo," Chenoa said cheerfully, standing to greet her guests. "And you must be Princess Tynae. Calai is all a buzz about you, my dear," she said, dusting the dirt off her hands.

Tynae inclined her head politely. An unsettling feeling pervaded the air. Tynae was certain she was being sized up by Chenoa.

"Dame Chenoa, this is indeed Princess Tynae. My Lady, this is Dame Chenoa."
Chenoa gave a small curtsy.
"Your Grace," Tynae bowed slightly.
"Grace sh'mace, just call me Chenoa, girl." Chenoa spoke to Tynae as if she had known her all her life.

"Chenoa it is." Tynae grinned.

"My, you are a pretty little thing, aren't you?" Chenoa walked around Tynae, inspecting her. "Mhm, mhm, yes, yes, I see," she muttered slowly circling around Tynae.

Slightly panicked, not knowing what to think of the woman sniffing around her like a curious pup, Tynae locked eyes with Béo.

Béo noticeably suppressed a laugh. Closing his eyes slightly, he shook his head. His silent message was understood, *just relax. She's harmless.*
Tynae had the sneaking suspicion this type of behavior was commonplace for Dame Chenoa. Now she understood what Béo had meant, *she is not like anyone you've ever met.*
The old woman stopped in front of Tynae. "Do you know the meaning of your name, girl?"
"Meaning?"
"Yes, every word has a meaning. Take my name for instance—Chenoa. It means '*white dove*'," Chenoa informed proudly.
"Oh, that is quite lovely isn't it?" Tynae shook her head, "No, I don't know the meaning of my name. I've never really given it any thought to be perfectly honest," Tynae admitted, slightly embarrassed.

"Of course you haven't," Chenoa said in a matter-of-fact tone. Chenoa looked Tynae up and down, reading her once again. "Your name means 'love'." Chenoa turned to Béo, "It really is quite fitting, isn't it?"

"It is?" Tynae questioned.

Chenoa grinned at Tynae. "You are something very special and quite unique, but you don't know that, do you?"

"Umm," Tynae stuttered, not understanding the eccentric woman's riddles.

Chenoa chuckled, never taking her eyes from Tynae. "You still have much to learn. You will have many choices to make, and none will be simple. Much is still to change, young one." The woman looked at Tynae curiously. "You will come to be known by many names."

Béo seemed to tense up as Chenoa spoke.

"I can most definitely see why it is *you* that has been chosen," Chenoa said with approval.

Tynae's brow furrowed. "Chosen?"

Béo took a slight step toward Chenoa, "Dame…"

"Béo!" Mouth agape, Tynae froze in terror, eyes wide. "Where'd he go? He just vanished into thin air!"

"Relax girl," Chenoa said calmly. "I trust that our young prince explained to you how these gardens work."

"What?!" Tynae looked around frantically, "Yes…I don't know." Tynae turned around, "Where is he?" She looked at Chenoa, "Where did he go?"

"Did he tell you that no-one is permitted in here if their energy is not positive?"

"Oh that." Tynae continued looking around, "Yes. What does that have to do with anything? Where is Béo?"

"There is a spell placed among my gardens. Anyone emanating negative energy, even in the slightest, is automatically ejected."

"But…"

"Relax child, or you will be next. I can only prevent you from doing a disappearing act of your own for a few more moments. Our young prince may return as soon as he has his emotions in check…I suggest you get yours sorted quickly."

Just as Chenoa spoke her last word Béo came into view, walking up the path they had been on earlier.

Seeing that Béo was fine, Tynae relaxed immediately.

"You know better, boy," Chenoa said to Béo as he re-joined them. "This is a place of peace and tranquility, not paranoia and nerves."

Turning her back on Béo, Chenoa resumed her conversation with Tynae. "Where was I? Aww, yes, chosen. But you will understand that in due time. And as I was saying, there will be many choices along your path. Your choices will affect many." Chenoa continued to look at Tynae, reading her like a book. "You must find balance and in that you will find peace. This, young one, will allow you to discover your *true* self…" Chenoa stared at Tynae as if she'd stumbled across a word she couldn't pronounce. "How do you feel about war, child?"

Her question threw Tynae. She had to think about it for a moment. "Honestly, I'm not against it, but I am for peace."

"You are wise beyond your years, young one." Chenoa sounded impressed. "May I offer you a piece of advice, dear?"

"Please," Tynae said eagerly.

"When you wish to see something for what it truly is, close your eyes. See with your heart and feel with your soul, for with thine eyes closed you shall see clearly."

"I'll remember that."

"Yes, you will," Chenoa said plainly. "So you have a desire to learn about this magical world of mine; potions, elixirs, and such." Chenoa stated this as a fact, rather than a question.

Tynae glanced at Béo with surprise.
He just shrugged.
"I do," Tynae chuckled.
"Well let us begin with the flower set out before us, they are used for…."

The three spent the entire day discussing many different flowers, what they could be used for, and the multitude of ailments they could treat.

"Thank you for a fascinating day, Chenoa, but we must get going," Béo said.

"Ah, right, supper with Jubryi. He is a good lad." Chenoa looked at Tynae, "He will make a fine husband."

Tynae smiled politely, surprised that Chenoa knew of their supper plans and a bit appalled that she would imply that another man would make a good mate when Béo stood beside her.

"I look forward to spending much time with you, young one. Come back when you are ready. Good evening, Majesties." Chenoa bowed then quickly departed.

The two looked at one another bewildered and laughed.

"Wow! That was…" Tynae shook her head, "well, definitely different, but quite enjoyable none the less."

"Are you sure?" Béo asked with concern.

"Absolutely. She was great, and she's right. I do want to come back and learn more."

Béo laughed, "Whatever you want, my angel."

The two made their way out of the garden.

"Where did you go when you disappeared?"

"Back to the sword room."

"Did it hurt?"

Béo chuckled, "No."

"Why did you disappear in the first place?"

Béo took a moment to answer. "I just thought she might be upsetting you, and that made me nervous."

Tynae laughed. "She seems harmless enough. I found her rather interesting. Is she a fortuneteller?"

"She's a sage and potion maker."

"Sage? I've never heard that term"

"A sage is a profoundly wise person whose possession of wisdom, judgment, and experience is prized, revered, and greatly

183

respected. She is able to see the future, but I don't know how or why. I've never spent much time with her."

When the two reached the sword room Béo stopped, wrapping his arms around Tynae.

"Mmm, I like this," she whispered.

"I just needed to hold you for a moment." Béo pulled her tight. "I don't know how I feel about sharing you with all these people," he teased. "I've enjoyed having you all to myself."

The couple allowed their lips to mesh together for a brief moment.

"I am not going anywhere," she assured, running her hand over his stubble-covered cheek. "I love you."

Béo smiled adoringly, "I love you. Let's get out of here. Jubryi will never let me live it down if we're late."

Chapter 23
The Beginning of a Beautiful Friendship

"When the character of a man is not clear to you,
look at his friends."
~Japanese Proverb

Walking into the Quenby dining hall, where the couple was supposed to meet Jubryi, Béo scanned the tables looking for his friend. There were at least one hundred small square tables situated throughout the great hall, each with a small flickering candle. Large lanterns hung throughout the hall, creating warm fires and bright light.

A loud voice boomed, "OY!"
Béo turned toward the shout. "There's the old sod," he said with a huge grin.

Tynae shot Béo a sideways glance then looked to where he was pointing. A striking man was holding up a stein and smiling widely.

"Come on," Béo urged enthusiastically. He went to grab hold of Tynae's hand then thought better of it.

Béo would never admit to it, but he was a tad concerned Tynae might pay heed to Chenoa's counsel. He was well aware that Jubryi was the epitome of tall, dark, and very handsome. Jubryi had never met a woman he couldn't have. With long dark hair which he wore pulled back, and stubble in tact, just the way Jubryi liked it, he looked incredibly masculine. Every feature on this man appeared to be chiseled. His cat-green eyes looked like light shown from behind them against his sun kissed bronze skin and even though he was not royalty, Jubryi wore little more clothing than Béo.

Jubryi stood to greet the pair. "My Lady," he bowed then turned to Béo. "You're bloody barmy if you think I'm gonna bow to you, little brother." Jubryi chuckled, clapping Béo on the shoulder.

185

"If you bowed to me I'd *know* you'd gone mad, you toss pot," Béo jeered back.

Tynae flinched when the two men grabbed each other in a bear hug.

"Tynae, this is Jubryi. Believe it or not, he is my oldest and dearest friend. Jubryi, this is…"

"I know who this is, you sod." Jubryi took Tynae's hand, kissing it lightly.

Wearing a brilliant smile, Tynae gave Jubryi a nod.

"Sit down, sit down. I was under the impression we were going to eat, not stand around making small talk." Waving for the server Jubryi ordered more ale and requested two additional steins.

"How the bloody hell are you?" Jubryi asked Béo.

"Wonderful," Béo glanced at Tynae.

"I can see that, brother," Jubryi said slyly.

Jubryi turned to Tynae. "So you're the little darlin' that's stolen my brother's heart?" he teased.

Tynae giggled, glancing at Béo. "Suppose so, but he's done some stealing of his own."

"Really?" Jubryi looked at Béo. "Been a naughty boy, have we?" There may be some hope for you yet," Jubryi said proudly, clapping Béo on the shoulder.

"So, Lady Tynae…"

Tynae cut him off, "Just 'Tynae', please."

Jubryi raised his eyebrows. "Ah, one order of royalty, hold the etiquette. You are a rarity, lass. Are you sure you want to be wasting your time with this one?" Jubryi jerked his thumb toward Béo.

Tynae smiled slyly. "He's far from a waste of time, Jubryi. You may be surprised to know that he is more than enough man for me…that is saying a lot." Tynae winked at Béo. "But, if ever I feel the need to slow things down, I'll be sure to call on *you.*"

Jubryi clutched at his chest. "Ouch, touché, love, touché." Jubryi smiled broadly. "And a sassy lass to boot, you've gotta love it," Jubryi chortled.

Béo was a bit bowled over. He'd never seen this side of Tynae.

"So, *Tynae*, how do you like this fine city of ours?"

"I love it! Although there are quite a few things I must grow accustomed to."

Jubryi took a drink of ale. "Such as?"

She shrugged, "Well, magic for one."

Jubryi nodded, "Yeah, I suppose that would be a bit odd for one who didn't even know it existed," Jubryi mused. "It will all become quite standard in no time, love." Jubryi turned, "Ah here's our food. I hope you don't mind. I took the liberty and ordered for all of us."

Tynae smiled her magical smile. Béo grinned, knowing the effect this had on most men.

"Not at all," Tynae said looking at Béo with a questioning expression.

Two servers pushed another table up to theirs to hold what appeared to be an endless supply of food.

"Are we expecting others?" Tynae asked.

It was Béo who responded. "Naw, this is all for him, our food hasn't even come out yet," he laughed boisterously.

Jubryi punched Béo's shoulder, "Shut up, you git, you're just envious."

"Envious? Of what?" Béo chortled, "Your ability to eat an entire ox in one sitting?"

Jubryi narrowed his eyes, shaking his head, "You pratt, you exaggerate far too much." Jubryi looked at Tynae innocently, "It was only half an ox," he corrected.

Tynae practically choked on the gulp of ale she'd just swallowed she started laughing so hard.

"Aha, here's your food, brother." Jubryi grabbed a large bowl, setting it in front of Béo.

"Very funny," Béo said sarcastically serving himself some salad from the bowl.

"So will you be bringing your lady love to practice tomorrow?" Jubryi asked.

"If she'd like," Béo smiled at Tynae.

"What practice?"

"We're both on Calai's vorbix team," Béo boasted.

"Vorbix?" Tynae asked, "What the bloody hell is *vorbix*?"

Both men started laughing.

"You're the luckiest man alive, little bro," Jubryi said with admiration.

Béo touched Tynae's hand resting on the table, "I know, trust me. I know."

"What the ruddy hell are you two on about and what exactly is vorbix?" she demanded in jest.

"Would you like to explain it to her?" Jubryi asked.

Béo shook his head taking a bite of lamb. "By all means, be my guest."

"Okay. So we have five teams here in Calai. Each team is comprised of thirteen players: four bläker's, two wards and seven chacier's. The wards only job is to guard the goals, and the bläker's—that's what I am—a bläker," Jubryi stated proudly puffing out his chest. "They have two jobs, two of the bläker's stay within ten meters of the goals at all times to assist the wards, and the other two run with the chacier's. We get to bloody up anyone who tries to get near our teammate who has the rucx."

Tynae raised an eyebrow at the alien term. "Rucx?"

Grinning Jubryi picked up his tankard, draining it yet again. "Ahh," slamming the heavy metal stein down on the thick wooden table, he wiped his mouth with the back of his hand. He laughed, "That's one of the balls we use, I'll explain that part in a minute. Let's see, whose left?" he mused, staring at the ceiling, rubbing his chin.

Béo looked at him with a wily smirk. "Chacier's, perhaps?" Béo reminded him sarcastically.

"Oh, yeah, that's right," Jubryi mocked innocently. "The chacier's, that's what lover boy here, is. They kick and chase the ball in an attempt to score. With me so far?" Jubryi took a bite of ox.

"I think so," Tynae nodded.

After taking a swig from his freshly refilled tankard, Jubryi continued. "Okay, there are seven goal hoops that stand upright. The hoops vary in height and size. The ones furthest out have the biggest opening and are lowest to the ground. As you progress toward the center goal, each goal gets higher and the opening gets smaller. The smallest and highest being the center goal post. Still with me?" Jubryi stabbed a piece of ox with his fork.

Tynae nodded. Finishing her bite of food, she gave a brief recap. "Thirteen players, seven goals, got it."

"Now, the objective is to get your points from three hundred thirty-one down to zero."

"I've never heard of a game like this," Tynae said captivated.

"Every time you get the ball through a hoop, you subtract points. But getting it through the goal is only half the battle. You have to get to the goal first," Jubryi grinned cunningly. Emptying his tankard in one long swig, he refilled it again.

"I don't understand. Is scoring difficult?"

Howling with laughter, the two men slammed their tankards together, "Huzzah!"

"Damn near impossible, lass, and your fella here," Jubryi punched Béo's shoulder so hard he nearly fell off his chair, "is something of an ace. He makes it look like child's play," Jubryi bragged proudly.

Straightening up Béo grinned, giving Jubryi a curt 'thank you' nod.

"Well it's true, little brother," Jubryi insisted.

"You see, darlin' there are two types of balls. There's the rucx, which is of medium-size, about the size of a melon. That's the one we kick and shoot through the goals. Then there's another ball, it's called a barbul. They're the size of a walnut and they're wicked little bastards." Jubryi took a bite of food and

189

swig of ale before continuing. "There are several barbuls on the field at any given time and they're a bloody pain in the arse they are," Jubryi barked.

"What's so bad about them? Their just balls aren't they?" Tynae asked innocently.

Slamming his tankard down, Jubryi looked at Tynae with utter disbelief. He looked at her as if she'd spoken a foreign language. "Blimey! What's so bad about them?" Jubryi turned to Béo, "What's so bad about them, is she serious?" he asked aghast.

Shrugging, Béo simply smiled. He knew how obsessive Jubryi could get when it came to vorbix.

"The bloody little bastard's only purpose is to pelt your arse, which they usually do. And when they hit you they make you do some really mental stuff, sometimes costing you the bloody damn game. Which they've done to our team on several occasions, thank you very much." Jubryi looked at Béo, "I was right bloody there I would have made that goal," he shouted slamming his fist on the table. "Damn little bastards!"

Tynae chuckled at Jubryi's animated outburst. "What on earth do you mean 'they make you do *mental* stuff'?"

"When the little buggers hit you, you get jinxed, and it stings like ruddy hell. They can make you literally freeze solid as ice in your tracks, move in slow motion, shoot you with lightning bolts, all kinds of barmy stuff," he ranted.

Béo chuckled. "Come on, they're not all beastly," he insisted.
"True," Jubryi lightened up a bit. "I do have to admit, some are pretty bloomin' brilliant. There's some that make you move incredibly fast, and others that enclose you in a ring of fire. I bloody love that one," Jubryi roared. "No-one comes near you when you're surrounded by a blaze'n inferno," Jubryi barked, throwing his head back and howling with laughter. "Problem is you never know what frak'n jinx a barbul carries 'til the li'l bastard hits you. And if that's not annoying enough, they have the worst dispositions you could possibly imagine." Jubryi

motioned for the server. "More ale and keep it come'n, Gar'kon," he ordered.

The server bowed, "Sir. Yes, Sir."

Tynae shook her head. "Perhaps I misunderstood you. Did you say *disposition*? As in, personality?"

"That's correct, love, they have personalities all right. They're usually dreadful ones at that. Most of them are moody ol' codgers. Others cackle like banshees and laugh in your face as their cronies pelt your arse." Jubryi grinned at Béo. "They really do enjoy their jobs don't they?" He used the opportunity to take another swig of ale and bite of food.

Béo nodded. "Mmm, certainly seems that way," he agreed, mouth full of food.

"And if the flying little bastards don't get you, the vortexes will," Jubryi blurted out.

"Now I'm getting confused. Vortexes?"

"Little swirling holes of hell. You never know when or where they're going to open up, as if the giant one in the middle of the field wasn't bad enough. Small vortexes open up randomly and suck the ball away from you, then spit it out on some random part of the field," Jubryi explained roughly. "Then…then there's the giant swirling pit of doom in the middle of the field." Jubryi drew a giant circle with his finger on the table. "It has a gravitational pull that the rucx is constantly being drawn toward, and if you get too close you and the ball get sucked in. Shocked the bloody hell outta me last time, but it was one hell of a ride," he barked. Turning to Béo he held up his stein. "Huzza!" they shouted.

Jubryi held his stein out toward Tynae. "Huzza!!!" the three shouted as Tynae clanked her stein with theirs.

Tynae took a large swig from her tankard then wiped her mouth with the back of her hand. "Is there no way to block the barbuls?" she asked.

"Sure, with a scrawny little piece of rawhide they call a gauntlet," Jubryi said scathingly. "You only get one and it's a bit difficult to keep track of the hundreds of barbuls hurtling around the field at any given time when you're trying to stay on top of the rucx." Jubryi picked up his ale, downing half his tankard in one gulp.

"That's it, that's the basics of vorbix. Will you be joining us tomorrow?" Jubryi asked with a huge grin.

Tynae took another swig of ale. "Absolutely," she said enthusiastically. "Do the teams have names?"

"Of course they do. I can't believe I forgot to tell you the names. Well, as I said there are five teams, each team represents one of the earthly elements and a direction."

"Direction?"

Jubryi grinned. "You know north, south, east, west..."
"Oh, okay," she nodded with understanding.
"So the Lijfbreeth Sylphs represent east and air." Jubryi must have noticed the confused look Tynae had. "Their name means Breath of Life," he explained. "The Lacertusféuer Salamanders represent south and fire; they are the 'Great Lizards of Fire'. Next are the Kejanpa' Islithra Dragons, 'Warriors of Peace and Balance', representing center earth and space. The Watomandare Undines or 'Commanders of the Water', represent west and water. Last, but not least, are the Garder'erdeu Gnomes, 'Guardians of the Earth' who represent north and earth." Jubryi recounted the names of each team to himself, ticking them off on his fingers. "Yep, that's all of them." He grabbed his tankard.

Tynae took a sip of her own ale. "Are you both on the same team?"

Jubryi pounded his large fist on the table. "Bloody well better believe it, lass, Kejanpa' Islithra Dragons. Ain't any finer team, darlin," Jubryi stated proudly.

Tynae's curiosity was never-ending. "So how are the teams chosen?" she asked, taking another swig from her tankard.
Jubryi grinned. "A mirror," he said smoothly.
Tynae raised a brow, "A mirror?"
"Yes, the mirror of Tryggth. It's used for many different things, but when used for team selections you must stand before it. It does not show what is on the outside; it verifies what is on

the inside. It reflects who one truly is. Once it has determined what lies at your very core, the mirror then reflects the team you are most suited to be on," Jubryi explained.

"How does it know?" Tynae asked bewildered.

"Your energy, it pulls it from all around you then reads it somehow. I'm not really clear on how it works, but so far the teams have been evenly matched."

"Remarkable," Tynae praised with fascination.

"Did you want to try out?" Béo asked earnestly. "You'd be the first woman on a team," he said with a grin.

Tynae shook her head heartily. "No thank you. I think I'll sit this one out. Being a spectator might be refreshing for a change," she giggled.

"Suit yourself," Béo grinned. "But if you change your mind, just let me know."

"Will do," Tynae muttered into her tankard, polishing it off.

The three sat for hours, laughing, joking and talking. They even had a belching contest that Tynae participated in. She was unanimously declared champion. No-one had noticed the passing of time, but the smell of breakfast caught their attention.

Tynae yawned.

"We should probably turn in for the night—or morning to be more precise," Béo suggested.

Jubryi looked at the couple suspiciously. "So he really sleeps in your chambers?" he asked with adoration.

Tynae smiled slyly. "Yes, he does, and he sleeps in my bed, too. What of it?" she challenged.

Jubryi marveled at Béo.

Béo knew his friend would have done anything to trade spots with him. It was usually Jubryi with the beautiful woman, but this was one woman Jubryi would never have.

Jubryi looked at Tynae longingly. Shaking his head, he changed the subject. "Not a thing. So we'll see you at practice then?"

Tynae smiled her heart-stopping smile, "Most definitely."

Jubryi took Tynae's hand, kissing it lightly, "Adieu, My Lady, sleep well."

Tynae blushed. "You as well, kind Sir," she gave a small curtsy.

"Take good care of her, young úlfur. She's one of a kind," Jubryi reminded Béo.

Béo looked at Tynae, "You have no idea."

Tynae just grinned at the comment.

The two men clapped each other on the shoulders. "See you at practice," Béo said.

Jubryi nodded once then they parted ways.

Chapter 24
Realization

"Learn from yesterday, live for today, hope for tomorrow."
~Albert Einstein

"Did you enjoy yourself?" Béo asked as they walked.

"I did. That was the most fun I've had in quite some time. I miss hanging out with the men," Tynae admitted.

"You hung out with *men* in Pathrow?"

"Specifically the guards. I trained with quite a few of them. I was just a member of the team when I was with them…just one of the men."

"I don't know if that's humanly possible, angel. For you to be one of the men that is," he smiled.

Tynae chuckled. "Oh trust me, it is. And I rather enjoy it."
When the couple reached Vu'tella, Tynae's handmaidens were waiting.
"Good morning, My Lady, you're up early," O'leana commented.
Tynae stifled a yawn. "Actually, we're just getting in."
"Oh," was all O'leana said.
"I plan on sleeping, so you may go." Tynae yawned again, "If you would return around midday that would be lovely."

"Would you like us to help you change into your night dress?" Talia asked.
"Please."
Before Tynae crawled into bed, she looked at her night table. "Where'd my ros…oh, there it is," she pointed to the writing desk. "Thank you, ladies. Good night."
Béo joined Tynae after he'd changed into his nightshirt, lying atop the coverlet.
"Hi," she sighed, once he'd settled.
"Hello, my angel," Béo gazed into Tynae's warm eyes.

The two held one another as if they hadn't seen each other in years. Their lips came together, the kiss impassioned.

Béo pulled back, brushing Tynae's cheek. "We need to get some sleep," he reminded her.

Tynae sighed. "I know. Hey, can I ask you just one thing."

"Of course."

"Why does Jubryi call you brother? Are you related?"

Béo chuckled. "No, but we've known each other since we were babies. Our mothers were the best of friends. We were even born on the same day." Béo shrugged, "Neither one of us has siblings...hell, I don't think we could be any closer, even if we did share the same parentage. We deemed ourselves brothers when we were three and have never seen ourselves as anything less." Béo smiled.

"But he looks a bit older than you."

"That's because he has chosen to age his body. Like I said before, we are human just like you. What most humans have not figured out yet is that aging is a process that occurs in the mind. It is not necessary, it is purely a choice."

"That's very interesting," Tynae said. Her mind flashed to Vinard, *I used to have a 'Jubryi'*. Not wanting to think of home, Tynae quickly pushed the memory away. "Let's get to sleep." She nuzzled into Béo's arms. Looking up at Béo, Tynae kissed him lightly. "I love you," she breathed.

"I love you, too," he whispered pulling her tight. "Sweet sleep, my angel, sweet sleep."

Tynae's sleep came swiftly.

"Hello, my love," Ryedin said affectionately, greeting Tynae as she entered *their* world.

She smiled brightly at the sight of him. "Hello." She rushed into his arms.

Ryedin pulled Tynae close in a tight embrace. Their lips quickly meshed together and Tynae was home.

When they finally pulled apart, Tynae noticed her surroundings. "Where are we?" she asked excitedly, realizing they were not in their garden.

Ryedin grinned. "We are on the shores of a wondrous coast. That is all I can tell you, angel."

Tynae understood that he could not tell her any more than what he had already said. Although she didn't understand why, she truly trusted this man. Looking down, Tynae examined this night's attire. She wore a long thin pale pink gown made of the purest silk. Her hair was in a long plait and she was barefoot, as was Ryedin.

Ryedin wore his usual attire; leather trousers, and a tunic, this one fawn beige.

"Come on," Ryedin grabbed Tynae by the hand.

Together they ran along the shoreline, hand in hand, until they reached a small cove.

Stopping, Ryedin grabbed Tynae about the waist and dropped to the ground. Together they lay on the sand, holding each other and panting.

Eventually Tynae rolled off Ryedin. Sitting beside him, she looked around.

Ryedin ran his hand softly over Tynae's back as she admired their surroundings. The beach they were on was remarkable. Tranquil turquoise water, glittering ivory sand as far as the eye could see, and it sat at the edge of a lush green forest. "This place is magical, like something straight out of a fairy tale," she sighed. Tynae turned to Ryedin. "Why did you bring me here?" she asked suspiciously.

He grinned broadly, "You'll see."

With a slight, but firm tug on Tynae's arm Ryedin pulled her to him. His soft supple lips found hers, their tongues danced seductively together. In an attempt to get closer Tynae hitched her leg over Ryedin, climbing on top of him.

Ryedin placed his strong hands on Tynae's shoulders pushing her back slightly. "I want nothing more than *you* in every possible way, but I will not have your flesh in that way until we are husband and wife," he said plainly.

Tynae took a deep breath. "What if that day never comes?" she asked brooding.

"Have faith, my love," Ryedin reassured, brushing his hand over Tynae's face. "It will come sooner than you think."

Tynae continued to frown. "I want to believe that, I truly do, but you're...just a dream."

"Am I?" Ryedin smiled slyly. "Are you sure you do not see me in your waking hours?" he asked. "If you did, would I then cease to be a dream?" Ryedin let out a soft chuckle. "I know you do not understand, my love, but in due time you will, so until then I will gladly remain nothing more than a dream to you." Wearing a cunning smile, Ryedin stood up. "Come on," he held his hand out.

Tynae's breath caught in her throat. Ryedin's eyes had her entranced. "Okay," she breathed, taking his hand. Together they walked further down the beach. When they stopped they were at the forest's edge. Ryedin made a clicking sound with his tongue.

Smiling, Tynae gazed at Ryedin with curiosity, "What are you doing?"

Ryedin smiled back. "Just wait, you'll see." He made the noise once more.

Tynae heard a rustling sound coming from the forest. Ryedin's smile grew.

"Shhh," he said softly, putting his finger to his lips.

Standing perfectly still, Tynae watched the wood carefully...then she saw it—an amazing black stallion—at least she thought it was a stallion. The mighty black animal drew closer. Tynae gasped, putting her hand over her mouth. Beaming she looked at Ryedin with downright disbelief. "Is that? No...I've never..." Tynae looked from Ryedin to the magnificent creature and back. "Black? I never knew they…I mean." Tynae collected her thoughts. "Is this real? Are they real? I've always heard they were white," she whispered, "at least in fairy tales."

A stunning black unicorn stepped out of the shadowy forest, walking toward the couple.

"They are very real, they are not just in fairy tales and most are white now, but this is their sire. He and one other have propagated the species you now know as white unicorns."

Tynae looked confused.

Ryedin chuckled. "Fret not, angel, you'll understand when you meet his mate. But you will not meet her today." The marvelous creature now stood no more than a meter away.

"Lady Tynae, it is my pleasure to introduce you to Tarak the Mighty." Tynae bowed her head to the majestic animal. Ryedin continued his introduction, "Your Grace, may I present Her Majesty Princess Tynae Brimon Le'jonrey Du'Vonaire of Montronvarr, the Bringer of Joy."
Tarak bowed to the princess.
"You may pet him if you'd like."
"Are you sure?" Tynae asked awestruck.
"Absolutely," Ryedin assured with a grin.
Reaching out, Tynae rubbed the side of the magical beast's long face. He earnestly pushed his head against her hand, clearly enjoying her touch.

"Care to go for a ride?"

Tynae looked at Ryedin with great enthusiasm, "Really? I'd love to."

Ryedin made the clicking noise once more. This time a large chocolate brown horse came striding out from the forest. "This is Gideon," Ryedin said proudly, patting his mount.

"A pleasure, Gideon," Tynae said.
This horse too bowed.
"Shall we?" Ryedin gestured toward the unicorn.

Tarak lowered himself so Tynae could climb onto his back. Together the couple rode for hours. Ryedin took Tynae through the entire forest and up into the mountains. Reaching the summit they dismounted. Together they enjoyed the divine view of the valley below.

Tynae stood with her back against Ryedin's chest.

Wrapping his arms tight around her Ryedin softly sighed, "You need to be going soon, my angel."

Tynae closed her eyes as Ryedin pressed his warm lips against her bare neck. "I was afraid of that," she breathed.

Dusk soon arrived and it was time to leave. Walking over to Tarak Tynae rubbed his muzzle, giving him a kiss. "Thank you for allowing me to ride you."

The thickset stallion lowered his head in a graceful bow.

Tynae then walked to Gideon, running her fingers through his soft mane. "You are a fine, fine horse," she complimented, then glanced at Ryedin. "Take good care of him while I'm gone, won't you?"

The horse neighed.

Walking up to Tynae, Ryedin wrapped her securely in his arms.

She looked into his peaceful blue eyes, "As usual I don't want to leave."

"And as usual I must insist that you go, and remind you that it is only temporary, my angel." Ryedin tenderly kissed Tynae.

Apprehensively, Tynae watched as the iridescent fog slowly rolled in. Knowing it was there to take her angel away from her, yet again. She tightened her grip around Ryedin.

"I'm sorry, my love, we must part ways. I will be right here waiting for you the next time you close your eyes. I'm just an angel's breath away." Ryedin took Tynae's face in his hands, kissing her determinedly.

His kiss, his touch, everything about him took her breath away. Tynae pulled away from him sharply. "You!" she gasped.

Ryedin looked at her, smiling his angelic smile. "What is it, my love?"

Realization had hit Tynae and it hit her hard indeed. "*You!* You were the one I heard when I was dead…*You* led me back!" she said, stunned by her revelation.

"Yes," he breathed.

Tynae gently ran her hand across Ryedin's cheek. "You are my light. You were the light that led me out of the very darkness of death."

"I have always been here, Tynae, and I will always be here. In time you will understand all the silly riddles that seem to elude you at the moment." Ryedin brushed Tynae's cheeks with his thumbs. "Funny thing, time, isn't it? We get so wrapped up in our lives that we become blinded to what is truly going on all around us. One day we're innocent little children playing hide-n-go-seek with our friends and crying over lost toys. In the next moment we find ourselves somewhere in the middle of our life wondering what great purpose we may serve."

Ryedin seemed to be speaking of something very specific, yet it was just another riddle to Tynae.

"You can never know what particular event will change the direction of your life forever, possibly impacting the course of history itself. It's usually the small events. You know, the ones you believe to be the least significant, that change the world as we know it." Ryedin lovingly examined Tynae's face as he stroked it. "Every single person has a permanent place in history, they just don't know it. The passage of time comes so quickly that you become oblivious to the fact that you, your life, and your actions are truly becoming a genuine part of the history of the world. Be it as simple as the roots of your family, or as grand as changing the fate of humanity for all time. Either way, we all have our proper place, don't we?"

Tynae knew Ryedin's question was rhetorical.

Ryedin marveled at Tynae. The fire burning between them was unmistakable, their love tangible, and the longing for each other painful. "And my place is at your side, *my queen*," he whispered, continuing to hold her face firmly in his hands. "You are *my* angel," he sighed, pressing his forehead against hers. "My one and only love," he breathed. "I must go." Ryedin smiled lovingly. "We will see each other tonight." Placing one last kiss upon Tynae's lips, Ryedin walked into the mist. "I love you, Tynae. I truly do love you." His words faded, as did he.

"I love you, too," she called out, uncertain whether or not he had heard her.

The ache, the longing, the painful emptiness that came every time they parted was not only back, it was growing stronger. Standing on the mountain top, alone, feeling hollow, Tynae felt like she was barely breathing as the wind swept past her...

Everything faded into blackness.

Chapter 25
Birds of a Feather

"Friends are the siblings, God never gave us."
~Unknown

Once again it was the sweet smell of O'leana's cooking that roused the couple from their slumber.

When they woke Tynae was still securely wrapped in Béo's strong arms.

Béo stretched trying to wake-up. "Time to get up already?" he yawned.

"Must be," Tynae answered, pulling in a deep breath and stretching. Tynae looked at Béo serenely, "Good morning, my love."

"Good morning, my angel." He kissed her softly.

My angel? Why did he just call me that? He'd called her angel and my angel previously. This wasn't unusual. But she remembered what Ryedin had said about being with her in her waking hours. *Is this his way of confirming he and Béo are one and the same?*

Smiling, Tynae almost jumped out of her skin when someone knocked at the door. After re-starting her heart, she quickly scooted to her own side of the bed and called out, "Enter."

O'leana stuck her head in the room. "It's noon, Majesties. Would you like your meal now or would you prefer to wait a bit?"

"Now is fine, thank you."

Tynae had only been in Calai a matter of days and already the couple had established a routine. The two would eat their meal in the privacy of Tynae's sleeping quarters then Béo would leave to tend to his personal affairs, while Tynae bathed and dressed. And to Tynae's extreme pleasure there was always a single white rose sitting on her bedside table when she woke. Although she truly took pleasure in her new freedom, and was thoroughly enjoying the luxury of exploring her new world at her leisure, she was not yet used to having no set schedule, no mandatory meetings and no future goals for her life. This would have to be dealt with soon. Tynae was the sort of woman who needed to have a purpose, wanted to make a difference, and would settle for nothing less.

Once again Tynae dismissed her handmaidens when they'd finished dressing her. Today's attire was purple. Tynae had never been one who enjoyed being fussed over and now that she had a man in her life she cherished every second of alone time they could get.

Upon Béo's return, he greeted Tynae with a loving embrace and an ardent kiss. Béo held Tynae tight, their lips moving in perfect unison. When they finally came up for air Béo smiled. "How would you like to spend the day? We have several hours before I need to be at practice."

"Truthfully, I'd like to stay here until it's time for us to leave. I thought we could explore my lovely wood some more," she gestured toward the miniature forest in her dwelling. "Don't get me wrong, I want to explore every bit of Calai, but hiding away behind closed doors for an afternoon would be kind of nice, too. Wouldn't you agree?"

"Sounds perfect to me."

"In all honesty," Tynae said in a serious tone. "Even though I'm used to the stares and all the unnecessary attention, it doesn't mean I enjoy it. Why don't people understand that we are no different than they? Sure, our jobs and our lives are very public, but that's the only difference really," she said, frowning slightly. Tynae grabbed Béo's hand as she spoke and together they walked to the heart of her forest. "They work just like we do, be it for themselves or someone else. They make budgets just like we do. They figure out how best to run their businesses and they tend to their customers needs just like we do. And at the end of the day they go home to their families." Tynae sighed. "We do the exact same thing, except our business involves running an entire nation and our customers are our subjects. As such, they depend on us to be truly sincere, morally ethical, and just minded. As does any customer that gives a merchant a large chunk of his or her wages. It's all the same really, it's just the scope of the scale on which we work is a bit larger."

Béo laughed heartily, "A bit larger, is that how you see it?"

Tynae chuckled. "Okay, it's grandiose compared to their jobs. But still, we basically do the same thing. You don't think yourself better than they, do you?"

Béo shook his head, "Never."

Relieved, Tynae smiled then laughed. "I don't know how I got so far off base. Bottom line is that I enjoy a bit of solitude every now and again."

Béo laughed. "No worries, my love, I enjoy learning about you. Besides, your fairness is why your people love you so."

"Loved," she corrected.

Béo nodded serenely, "Loved."

Tynae pulled the oversized chaise up to the picturesque window, refusing Béo's help when he tried to move it for her. "I am quite capable of moving a chair," she insisted. Once she got the chair over to the window she pushed it until it was against the glass. Climbing onto the cushion Tynae patted the seat beside her.

Getting into the seat Béo pulled Tynae into his arms, her back was against his chest. For hours they sat, Béo pointing out and naming the multitude of different fish, plants, and sea life.

"Hello?" called a male voice from within Tynae's chambers.

Tynae looked at Béo with surprise.

"Hello?" the voice called again.

Béo grinned widely. "It's Jubryi," he told Tynae. "In the forest," Béo shouted, "just follow the path."

The pair sat on the edge of the chair waiting.

Jubryi had a huge smile on his face when he came into view. "So, this is how the other half lives," he joked.

Tynae raised an eyebrow.

Jubryi chuckled, "I'm just joking, jeez, ease up," he opened his arms wide.

Smiling broadly, Tynae stood, walking over to Jubryi.

"There now, that's better isn't it?" Jubryi held her in a tight bear hug.

"Watch it," Béo warned, "she's got a mean right hook."

"This tiny little thing?" Jubryi looked Tynae up and down.

"Perhaps we should discuss this in the battle arena," Tynae suggested.

Jubryi let out a howl of laughter so loud Tynae was certain the people in heart of the city heard it.

"That would be an interesting match," Béo mused, holding back a sinister smile.

"You're serious?" Jubryi asked, looking from Béo to Tynae.

Béo shrugged. "What can I say? She's not like most women, and I refuse to be the one that denies her anything. I've learned to pick my battles with this one carefully. If you're afraid to face her in the ring just tell her 'no'," Béo taunted.

Jubryi raised his brows. "Afraid? You've got to be joking. Just name the time and place," he countered.

Tynae smiled, "How 'bout tomorrow then?"

Jubryi faltered for a second, clearly caught off guard by Tynae's response.

"You're on. Don't expect me to take it easy on you just 'cuz you're a girl," he warned.

"I'd be upset with you if you didn't try your best, Jubryi." She grinned mischievously.

Looking puzzled, Jubryi eyed Tynae suspiciously.

"I promise, I don't cheat," she assured.

Jubryi narrowed his eyes, "This should be fun." He laughed heartily again.

"Shall we place a wager on it then?" Tynae goaded.

"What would you like to bet?"

"I'll have to see if there's anything I fancy in the market place," Tynae replied. "And what might *you* care for if you happen to win?"

"Hmm, I'll need to think on that a bit. I'll let you know later," Jubryi winked. "Shall we be on our way then?"

"Give us just a second alone please," Béo requested.

"Yeah, yeah," Jubryi teased, waiving off the couple like an annoying bug. "I'll wait by the door."

Béo looked at Tynae, slyly pulling her to him. "I love you," he whispered.

"I lov…" Tynae's response was cut short by Béo's warm lips pressing passionately against hers.

After getting their 'kissing fix' they joined Jubryi.

Jubryi examined Tynae carefully as she stood beside Béo. "You know, I'm going to have to come up with a nickname for you," he informed her.

Tynae laughed. "Is that so?"

"Mmhm, sure is," Jubryi gave her a wink. "Come on, let's get out of here before I have to douse you two with cold water."

Leaning over so only Béo could hear him, or so he thought, Jubryi whispered, "Not that I can blame you, brother. I'd never leave the room if she were my girl."

Béo chuckled quietly, grinning at Jubryi's approval.

The three walked together to the heart of the city. Jubryi teased Tynae the entire time.

God, how I miss Vinard and his endless ribbing.

Once within the city, they walked to the huge double doors that were always guarded. It took all three guards to open just one of the enormous wooden doors. Once the trio stepped through the entrance, the guards closed it behind them. They were now standing in a long and somewhat darkened corridor. When they emerged from the tunnel Tynae was shocked when she looked up and saw hundreds upon hundreds of seats in a colossal amphitheater.

"It's bare right now, but on Saturday when we play it will be decorated with the colors and shields of all the teams," Jubryi informed. "Why don't you go pick out a seat while Béo and I get changed. We'll be out after our teammates arrive."

Tynae smiled, "Okay."

Walking away from the two men, Tynae suddenly realized that this was the first time she had been completely on her own since she'd arrived in Calai. Strolling through the amphitheater trying to pick out the perfect seat, an odd sensation tingled in the pit of Tynae's stomach. The feeling was one she could not recall having ever felt before. For the first time in her life, Tynae felt insecure.

Climbing a steep staircase in the middle pitch, Tynae perched herself in the closest row of seats to the center of the field. She looked around while she waited for the team to come out. The stadium held seating for thousands. *I wonder if all these seats will be filled come game day. I cannot imagine that there are that many people in Calai.* The clear dome over the city allowed the sun to shine bright upon the perfectly manicured grass. *The turf holds no magical appearance,* Tynae thought. *It just looks like an ordinary playing field of green grass...all be it perfectly manicured; it appears to be ordinary grass all the same.*

Tynae heard the sound of echoing laughter as the team walked through what she could only assume was a bricked corridor.

The first one onto the field was Béo. Spotting Tynae he sprinted over to her. Squatting down he placed his hands on her knees. "Hello, my love," he whispered.

Tynae beamed at him. "Hi," she breathed. "I like your uniform," she ran her hands over his leather covered shoulders. Glancing toward the field, she noticed the entire team staring at her and quickly put her hands in her lap.

Béo looked over his shoulder then back at Tynae, "Don't worry about them."

The entire team wore dark brown sleeveless tunics made of satin. Their shoulders and chests were covered with pieces of hard leather that formed perfectly to their bodies. The single gauntlet they wore was short. Their loincloths came to a point at their knees and were cut high on the sides. Their soft suede boots reached the middle of their calves and each player had a bright yellow number in the middle of his back. Béo's number was seven.

"Thanks," he said. "If you get bored, you don't have to stay."

Tynae narrowed her eyes, "Are you trying to get rid of me?" she asked in jest.

"Never," he said seriously.

"Come on! Are we practicing or doing our nails?" Jubryi hollered.

Tynae had the sneaking suspicion he was the only one who would ever dare speak to Béo that way.

Shaking his head Béo chuckled. "He's not known for his patience. I'll see you in a bit." Blowing Tynae a concealed kiss Béo joined his teammates.

The men huddled on the field then broke into two teams of six. One person guarded the goal area. They were all very good at what they did, and Jubryi seemed to thoroughly enjoy tackling the other players whenever the opportunity presented itself. Tynae had not asked who the team captain was, but it quickly became apparent that it was Béo who called all the shots. He was also the one who scored most of the goals, one after another. He never missed.

The men moved agilely and with great speed as they passed the ball back and forth—so fast that Tynae could hardly keep track of it. *Oh my gosh, this is only practice and it is completely enthralling. I can't wait to see the real thing!*

After what Tynae was sure had been several hours of practice they called it a day.

Béo hurried over to her. "I'm going to wash up and change. I won't be long then we can go grab some nosh."

Tynae smiled brightly, "Okay."

Running, Béo caught up with his teammates.

Before she knew it he was back. Taking the seat next to her Béo didn't seem in any rush to leave. "So what did you think?"

"I loved it," she beamed. "I've never seen anything so exhilarating."

Béo eyed her suspiciously. "You're not just saying that, are you?"

Tynae shook her head. "Never," she said sincerely. "I can't wait to see the real thing. Are you the team captain?"

"I am," he said humbly. "The guys asked if we'd join them for supper. We don't have to if you don't want to."

"I'd love to."

"Really?" Béo sounded surprised. "Great. Let's go. They're meeting in the Quenby dining hall."

Jubryi met them in the corridor they had entered through earlier. He tapped Tynae playfully on the shoulder with his fist.

She punched him back.

"Bugger, girl! You do have a bloody wicked right hook," Jubryi chuckled.

Béo laughed. "Told you so, but you never listen to me."

Walking to the dining hall, Jubryi rubbed his shoulder. "So what'd 'cha think, girly?"

"I loved it! I can't wait to see an actual game."

Chapter 26
Just One of the Boys

"A man's character is his fate."
~Heraclitus

When the trio entered Quenby hall Béo's teammates hollered, "Huzza!"

Béo and Jubryi raised their fists into the air, "Huzza!"

The men had put several tables together in a corner area. Tynae and Béo sat down in the only two seats that were side by side.

Standing behind a teammate, Jubryi pulled his chair out from under him. "Find another chair, mate, this one's mine," he said, sitting down beside Tynae. Jubryi's intimidating size prevented many from challenging him.

"Really, Jubryi?" Tynae said crossly, "That was rather rude, don't you think?"

Reaching across the table Jubryi grabbed a tankard and filled it up. "No," he took a long drink. "See this?" Jubryi pointed to some marks on the side of the chair.

Tynae had to look really close to make out what they where. "Is that…" Tynae looked at Jubryi incredulously, "your name?"

"Yes it is," Jubryi said smugly. "So you see, this IS my chair."

Shaking her head Tynae had to laugh.

Béo leaned in so Tynae could hear him. "You think that's bad," he said. "Jubryi's scratched his name into more than half the chairs in here."

Tynae looked at Jubryi with disapproval.

With a proud nod, Jubryi held up his stein, "Sure have."

Tynae just shook her head.

Smiling, Béo patted her leg under the table. "You'll get used to it, I have."

Béo stood up. "Gentlemen," Béo had Tynae stand, too. "It is my pleasure to introduce to you Her Majesty Princess Tynae Brimon Le'jonrey Du'Vonaire, the Bringer of Joy from the great nation of Montronvarr. Lady Tynae, this is…" Béo began on his right, working his way around the table; "Ulric, Willoughby, Adish, Jalil," the men respectfully inclined their head to Tynae as they were introduced, "Pe'er, Rafiq, Vecenté, Ebrem, Heath, Edvard, Matteo, and you already know the toss pot sitting beside you," Béo said jovially taking his seat.

Tynae could tell her presence was putting a damper on the mood. *Great, nothing like royalty to bring the party to a crashing halt...thanks Béo.* Looking at the uptight men she smiled. "Lighten up, my status changes nothing." They all just smiled back politely. Tynae sighed, knowing what she had to do. It was a bold move and she never would have done it in Pathrow, but she wasn't in Pathrow any longer and she wasn't about to be know as 'the mood killer'. Tynae grabbed Jubryi's stein out of his hand.

"Hey!"

"Oh hush, you can get more." Taking a huge gulp, Tynae slammed the tankard down and wiped her mouth with the back of her hand. The belch that followed was just an added bonus. *Vinard would have been proud of that one.*

With disbelief, the men looked from one to another then started howling with laughter.

Tynae grinned. "That's better. Tonight I'm just one of you, agreed?"

"Agreed," the men said in unison.

Jubryi handed Tynae her own tankard. She held it up, everyone followed suit. "Huzza!!!" Accomplishing her objective Tynae took her seat.

The night was filled with lots of laughter, crude jokes, and gallons of ale.

Somewhere in the middle of all the fun, Tynae leaned toward Béo. She whispered "I was just wondering," she kept her pitch low, "my bet with Jubryi, I don't want to...I mean...well, is there an amount I should not go past when it comes to a prize?"

It only took Béo a second to figure out what she meant. "I'm going to take care of it actually. If you don't mind, that is?" Squeezing her hand under the table, Béo gave Tynae a wink.

The noise was such that the couple could not discuss the matter at length as Tynae would have liked. "Sure," she agreed.

"So!" Slamming his fist on the table, Béo got everyone's attention. "Did captain brash here," Béo jerked his thumb toward Jubryi, "Inform you that he and Lady Tynae have placed a little wager?"

"Really?" one teammate said.

"He hasn't mentioned it," said someone else.

"Jubryi, you cocky bloke, what kind of bet would ye be make'n with such a fine lass?"

Béo's grin grew wider. "Seems that Lady Tynae is a bit of a gambler herself and has challenged Jubryi to a sword fight."

Recognizing a few of the men from when she and Béo had sparred, Tynae wondered if they would tell Jubryi of her skills. She had her answer within a matter of minutes thanks to her new and improved hearing.

Willoughby leaned in close to Edvard, "She kicked Béo's arse the other day. She is going to wipe the floor with Jubryi."

Edvard smiled mischievously, "Oh, I'll pay good money to see a woman take Jubryi down. This is going to be excellent."

"Really?" asked Willoughby loudly.

"Truly," Béo replied.

"What's the wager?" Edvard shouted.

"I will be furnishing the prize." Béo raised his hand, motioning for a man sitting across from them to join their group.

The gentleman walked over. "My Lord," he bowed.

Tynae did not recognize this person.

"Lady Tynae, this is Glaxor, Ildrai's son."

After bowing to Tynae, Glaxor laid a long parcel on the table.

Béo opened the package, withdrawing its contents.

"This, lady," Béo inclined his head to Tynae, "and gentlemen, will be the prize." Béo held up a magnificent silver sword.

Jubryi's mouth visibly fell open.

"Anyone who cares to join us we'll be meeting at the sword arena tomorrow at noon," Béo announced.

Wanting to see the sword, everyone stood. Each admired it then passed it around.

"I'll be there!" said Ulric.

"I wouldn't miss it!" Jalil exclaimed.

"This I've got to see!" Adish laughed.

"I can't wait to see this, I'll be there," Heath barked.

The man standing next to Béo nudged him with his elbow, leaning in so only Béo could hear him. "Bloody bastards doomed and doesn't even know it. You know I'll be there," Rafiq chuckled.

Having seen Tynae and Béo's sparring match, Willoughby seized the chance to make some easy money. "I'll be there, and I'll put two drablun's on Lady Tynae."

"Two drablun's? You're on!" Ebrem exclaimed. "I'll be sure to get there early and save you a front row seat. This will be the easiest money I've ever made." Ebrem inclined his head toward Tynae, "No offence intended, My Lady."

Tynae smiled, "None taken. Besides, it's not about who wins or loses it's about having fun," Tynae said in the most naive voice she could muster.

Ebrem nudged his neighbor, leaning over, "Words of a true loser if I ever heard 'em," he whispered to Matteo.

Matteo shook his head. "I don't know, Ebrem, I've heard things about her."

"Like what?" Ebrem asked skeptically.

Looking around the table, Tynae caught the two men's eyes…they stopped talking.

Simultaneously the rest of the men stopped, too.

"Tell me," Tynae decided to take advantage of the temporary silence. "Do they serve crow here in Calai?" she asked smoothly.

"Ooohh," the men all groaned.

"And a battle of wits to boot," Edvard muttered to Willoughby.

Willoughby chuckled. "Jubryi is so far out of his league on this one. He won't know what hit him."

Tynae shrugged her shoulders. "I was just wondering," she said innocently.

The men laughed boisterously at her boldness.

Wearing a huge grin Jubryi threw his arm around Tynae. "You gotta love her."

Once the men stopped laughing, everyone resumed their conversations.

Béo talked with Glaxor for a bit, while Tynae sat nursing her ale, shrewdly eavesdropping.

Still chuckling, Matteo leaned toward Ebrem. "Rumor has it she beat Béo in a couple a bouts the other day," Matteo informed.

"Please," Ebrem said sarcastically. "He's in love with her, can you not see that? He let her win."

Matteo shrugged his shoulders. "You say so, it's your bollocks...I mean drablun's," he corrected with a grin.

"Doesn't matter, Jubryi's been drooling over that sword ever since Glaxor put it on display. He could never afford it, even if he saved every cent he made for the next ten years. I don't care how good she is, he's bigger, faster, better, and he wants *that* sword. He will win." Ebrem took a swig of ale. "You should put some money on this."

Matteo shook his head. "Nah, that's too rich for my blood, but I'll definitely be there. I wouldn't miss this for the world."

Tynae recognized Matteo. He had been front and center when she and Béo had fought. Unless he was blind, he knew Béo hadn't let her win. Glancing across the table Matteo noticed Tynae looking at him. He gave her a wink. She inconspicuously raised a sly brow in acknowledgment.

Finishing off her drink, Tynae set down her stein and stood up. "Well men, it's been fun, but I need to get to bed." She looked at Béo. She could only imagine the comments his teammates where dying to say, but didn't dare. Several of the men started to stand, but Tynae raised her hand. "It's alright, don't get up. We'll see you gentlemen tomorrow." She gave everyone a wave.

"Night," Béo said, grabbing the sword off the table.

"Don't get too used to that being in your room, lass." Jubryi nodded toward the prize.

Tynae just smiled as she and Béo departed.

"So," Tynae looked at Béo seriously as they walked back to her room. "Is there someplace I can get my hands on a silver platter and a stuffed crow?"

Béo started laughing so hard he had to stop walking. "God I love you," he said catching his breath. "I think I might be able to help you with that." They continued walking.

"So why did you pick the prize?" Tynae asked suspiciously.

Béo glanced at her with a sly grin. "Because I want him to really try, so he won't later say that he let you win. I know how much he wants this sword. Female or not, he won't go easy on you when it comes to this." He held up the sword.

When they got back to Vu'tella, Tynae quickly changed into her nightdress. Tired, she wanted to get some rest.

"Good night, my angel." Béo kissed Tynae gently. "I love you."

"I love you, too." She nuzzled into *her* place in Béo's arms. "Good night," she sighed drifting off.

Tynae walked out of the mist and into a twilight lit forest.

"Hello, my angel." Ryedin greeted with a loving smile and a passionate kiss.

The couple spent the next several hours walking through the woodland, laughing, discussing life, holding one another and kissing often. Tonight's visit to her dream world was a simple one. No surprises, no new creatures, just the two of them in the sanctuary of the wood.

Once again the time to part came much too soon.

Waking briefly, Tynae found herself lying back in her own bed. Running her fingers softly through Béo's dark hair, Tynae laid staring at her sleeping prince. She couldn't understand why he took on such a different appearance and different name in her dream-world, but she was convinced that Béo and Ryedin were one and the same. *Who really understands the mind anyway?* She thought. *They are just dreams after all.*

Chapter 27
Sugar and Steel

"If you obey all the rules you miss all the fun."
~Katharine Hepburn

The next day when the couple reached the sparring arena, Béo was certain half of Calai had turned out to watch the bout.

Smiling nervously, Tynae leaned toward Béo. "What are all these people doing here?" she asked, barely moving her lips.

Béo shook his head. "Normally I would say that when the vultures smell fresh blood they start circling, but in this case..." Béo looked around. "Well, love, I'd say this crowd is evenly split. Half are here to see you kick Jubryi's arse and the other half, well I'm sorry to say it, angel, but they're here to see a woman," he gave Tynae a knowing look, "get knocked back into the 'cooking area' where she *belongs.*"

Tynae stopped dead in her tracks. Hands on her hips and brow cocked, she glared at Béo. "Excuse me?"

Béo flinched when he saw how Tynae was staring at him. "What? Don't look at me that way." Béo looked away briefly, feeling like a child who'd just been reprimanded. "I didn't say I agree with them, I'm just telling you why so many people came to watch," he clarified. "Don't kill the messenger," Béo joked. "Come on."

Narrowing her eyes, Tynae didn't move. "What exactly *are* your feelings on the matter?"

Béo took a step closer to Tynae. "Angel, I do not have a problem with the fact that you can kick my arse," he chuckled. "I prefer that you stand beside me, not behind me. The whole damsel in distress routine has been done to death. But..." he said holding up a finger, "Being needed every now and again is always nice, too."

Tynae leaned even closer, whispering in Béo's ear, "I need you more than you will ever know," she grinned. "Come on."

Approaching the arena, Jubryi became visible. He was talking with Ebrem and some other teammates standing at the front of the crowd.

"Ah, here comes my prize now!" Jubryi said loudly, gesturing to the sword Béo carried.

Tynae ignored the comment.

Tingy trotted over to Tynae the instant he saw her. "Majesty, is it true? Are you really going to fight Commander Jubryi?" he blurted out, clearly alarmed.

"Commander?" Tynae hissed. "Commander!" she repeated harshly, turning to Béo.

Béo laughed. "He's not the 'commander' of anything, Tynae, relax. Do you honestly think I would keep something like that from you?" Béo questioned, smirking. "It's just what Tingy calls him."

Tynae considered Béo's words for moment then comprehension crossed her face. "Ohhh, I'm sorry," Tynae frowned. "I shouldn't have behaved like that."

"Don't worry about it. It's completely understandable," Béo rationalized.

Tynae looked down. "Yes, Tingy, I'm fighting 'commander Jubryi' today," she told him calmly.

The little guy looked worried, but said nothing.

Béo knelt down, getting close to Tingy. "In addition to the protection shields I want you to also put up a charm preventing other magic," he instructed.

"Of course, My Lord," Tingy bowed.

Walking over to select her sword, Tynae looked at Béo curiously, "Other magic?"

Looking around, Béo made sure no-one was listening. "I want this fight to be fair. You'll know if someone tries to use magic, because colored flashes will appear," he told her quietly. "No need to worry though, it won't harm you."

Tynae looked over the sword selection. "Do you really think...?"

"Yes," Béo cut her off, "I do, so don't be surprised when bright flashes appear out of nowhere…That's the one you used last time," he pointed.

"Ahh, thanks." Tynae picked up the sword. Fingering the hilt, she got her grip just right as they walked back to the arena.

"You ready to do this?" she taunted, walking past Jubryi.

"Absolutely!" Jubryi countered.

The fighting duo walked to the center of the arena. Both stood silent while Tingy worked his magic. When finished, Tingy bowed to the princess then left the ring. He perched himself beside his ickel, who sat on the wall next to Béo's teammates.

Béo stepped into the center of the ring. "The rules are basic," he announced loudly, "the first one to administer a positive death blow wins this." Béo held the superlative sword up over his head.

Gaping at the prize, Jubryi's eyes lit up.

"May the best man…or woman," Béo bowed slightly to Tynae, "win!"

The crowd cheered.

"Let's get this over with, lass. I have a new sword to break in."

Béo could tell Tynae was blocking out everyone and everything. Taking her stance, she zeroed in on her prey. "Let's go, big boy," purred the tigress.

"Play nice you two," Béo warned before walking away. Staying inside the ring, Béo walked over to where Tingy sat and leaned against the wall. With crossed arms and a smug smile, Béo was one hundred percent confident that *his* woman was about to teach *his* best friend a major life lesson.

"Majesty," Tingy leaned close to Béo.

"Yes, Tingy?"

"Are you sure this is a good idea?"

Béo chuckled. "Yes, Tingy. This is an excellent idea. I would never put the princess in danger."

"If you're certain, Sire."

"I am, Tingy. Now relax and enjoy the show."

Béo watched Jubryi's expression fade from cockiness to confusion as Tynae prowled around him slowly, then launch herself at him.

The air rang with the clanging of blades.

During the first blows of the match, Jubryi focused on his defense. He quickly discovered Tynae was more than an aptly qualified opponent.

The crowd roared as the pair settled into the rhythm of swordplay.

Béo chuckled to himself, knowing it would only be a matter of minutes before Jubryi figured out just how much trouble he was in…big trouble.

Béo knew Jubryi was well practiced when it came to swords. Not great when they were younger, Jubryi had gotten much better over the years. Better or not, Béo knew if Tynae could best himself, she would certainly surpass Jubryi.

Watching Tynae was incredible. Her speed, her strength, the way she maneuvered her sword…Béo had never seen a fighting style like hers.

Of course Jubryi had the advantage of brute strength, but Tynae had speed and agility on her side.

Jubryi lunged, she parried. Tynae lunged, he stumbled.

Swords slammed, sparks flew, and the exuberant crowd shouted.

For several minutes Jubryi tried to get past Tynae's defenses. It was clear he'd expected a quick defeat and an easy humiliation, not an equal opponent.

Numerous bright flashes appeared in the air directly behind Jubryi.

"Tut, tut, Jubryi!" Béo shouted. "It appears that someone doesn't believe you can beat a *girl* on your own."

Swords locked Tynae stepped close to Jubryi, saying something.

Béo had no idea what she'd said, but he did notice Jubryi's falter.

Leaping back, Tynae swung her sword, Jubryi blocked, and sparks rained down. The sound of the crashing blades echoed.

The exhilarated crowd screamed.

Tynae kept everyone guessing. It was impossible to predict her next move. Several times Béo thought she was going one direction only to see her veer the opposite way. All the while, she was viciously hammering away at Jubryi. Momentarily their weapons caught high in the air, locking. Tynae disengaged with a flourish. With lightning speed she slipped her sword past Jubryi's defenses, slashing at his throat.

Jubryi scarcely managed to dodge the strike. "Wonderful strategy," he praised loudly countering with a backhanded blow.

Tynae thrust her blade up vertically, catching his blade before it made contact.

The crowd was in a frenzy hollering at the top of their lungs.

Jubryi tried the aggressive approach next. Taking several steps forward, he forced Tynae backward. He lunged, she block, then parried.

Clapping their hands franticly, the crowd chanted, clearly cheering on their favorite.

Jubryi lunged again. Tynae parried then struck out with her blade. Jubryi blocked.

The crowd began stomping their feet in a rhythmic fashion, boom, boom, boom...boom, boom, boom.

Taking aim at the princess' legs Jubryi swung his sword hard and low. Tynae leapt gracefully into the air allowing the blow to breeze past.

Jeering, the crowd clearly did not condone the cheap shot.

Blinking as if coming out of a daze Jubryi continued to go for the death strike.

"Show her your je ne sais quoi!" Béo shouted. This was what Béo had dubbed Jubryi's so called 'secret maneuver'.

Jubryi nodded with understanding.

Tynae must have decided it was time to bring the fight to an end. Laying on the speed she moved gracefully, maneuvering herself to Jubryi's side. With a spin and kick to the crook of Jubryi's leg, she dropped him to his knees with a thud. With uncanny speed Tynae unsheathed her dagger. Stepping behind Jubryi, she grabbed a fistful of hair. Pulling his head back against her heaving chest, she ran her blade across his throat. Letting him go, Tynae walked back in front of her opponent.

Sitting on the ground panting, Jubryi looked up at Tynae, shaking his head.

The cheering crowd roared with the voice of a thousand lions.

Béo and Tingy walked over to the worn out pair.

Jubryi looked at Béo. "I think she broke my quoi," he groaned.

Béo let out a hardy laugh.

Tynae offered Jubryi a hand up, which he graciously accepted.

"Lass, you truly can fight. I stand corrected." He bowed deeply.

Bending down, Béo whispered something to Tingy then motioned toward Ebrem.

Jubryi stepped aside, allowing Béo to award Tynae her prize.

"I declare Lady Tynae the winner!" Béo shouted, holding up Tynae's arm. Letting her arm go, Béo carefully handed the princess her new sword.

The crowd went wild, chanting, "Tynae, Tynae, Tynae! Yeaaa!!!"

Looking thoughtfully at her prize for a moment, Tynae turned to Béo. Leaning forward she began to open her mouth, but Béo stopped her.

Putting his hands on her shoulders, he leaned forward so he could talk in her ear. The crowd was still yelling so loud this was the only way she'd be able to hear him. "Tynae, it's your sword, do with it what you will." Taking a step back, Béo gave her a small nod.

Tynae mouthed the words, "Thank you," then turned to Jubryi, smiling sincerely. "It really is exquisite isn't it?" she said with admiration.

"Ay," he replied softly.

Tynae laid the sword across her hands, holding it out, "It's yours."

Jubryi looked at her with sheer disbelief. "But you won it, lass, fair and square," he said incredulously. "It's yours."

"It was never about the prize, Jubryi. I only wanted to earn my place."

"You are truly one of a kind, My Lady. If it was my respect you were after, you've won it in aces." Jubryi glanced at the sword in Tynae's hands. "Béo, are you okay with this?" Jubryi asked.

"It's hers to do with as she pleases."

Jubryi looked at Tynae. "Are you certain about this?"

Tynae smiled her magical smile. "Positive," she placed the sword in Jubryi's hands. "Besides, you're doing me a favor. It's too big for me." Turning to the crowd, Tynae motioned for Jubryi to stand beside her.

The crowd applauded her generosity.

Béo took a step toward Tynae. When she looked at him he gestured toward Tingy, who was carrying something large and shiny in his tiny arms.

Tynae nudged Jubryi in the side. He was lovingly admiring his new weapon.

"Yah, lass?"

She gestured toward Tingy.

Jubryi glanced over. "What's the little guy up to? Come on, let's get a closer look."

224

The trio walked over to Tingy, who stood in front of Ebrem holding a lidded silver platter.

Béo took the platter. Setting it on the stone wall, he removed the large lid. In the center of the dish sat a huge, perfectly-sculpted, black crow made out of cake and icing.

"I believe it's time for you to eat this," Béo said smugly.

Laughing, Ebrem shook his head. "I'm a big enough man to admit when I've been horribly wrong!" Ebrem conceded loudly. "Lady Tynae, please accept my apologies. You are an exceptional fighter."

"Apology accepted." Tynae smiled, eyeing the crow. "Jubryi, I'll let you have the honors."

Grinning from ear to ear, Jubryi set his new sword off to the side. Jubryi carefully picked up the crow's head in both hands. Taking a step forward, he mashed the cake in Ebrem's face, taking extra care to thoroughly shove it up his nostrils. Jubryi howled with laughter as did the crowd.

"As I recall, Mr. Cockiness," Ebrem said, scraping a pile of black frosting off his face. "You too thought she would easily be bested."

"Yeah and she kicked my arse," Jubryi chuckled.

"That she did, and I don't have a problem sharing!" Ebrem said.

By the time it had registered to Jubryi what Ebrem meant, he too had a snoot full of black frosting.

Tynae merrily joined in. Grabbing a handful of cake, she smashed it in Jubryi's face.
"Oh, so that's how it is!" Jubryi teased, grabbing more cake.
Tynae's eyes got huge, "Oh, no you don't." She turned to run, but Béo stepped behind her to prevent her from leaving. "Ahh, that's not fair!" she giggled in protest. Jubryi pressed both his hands against her face, twisting.
Béo laughed so hard he dropped Tynae's arms.

"Think it's funny?" Tynae scoffed, shoving a pile of cake in Béo's face.

By the time the cake was gone, every member of the team, plus Tynae, was covered from head to toe with frosting.

"What do you say to supper with us again tonight?" Ebrem asked Béo and Tynae, scraping a fresh coat of icing off his face.

Accepting a handkerchief from Tingy, Tynae cleaned her face off. "I'd say that before I do anything, I need to bathe," she giggled.

"As do we all," Matteo agreed.

Tynae glanced at Béo, who nodded. "We'd love to," she said. "Same time, same place?"

"That works! We'll see you at seven then," Vecenté said.

A majority of the crowd was still assembled. Several people congratulated Tynae as she and Béo departed.

"I was thinking we could have a light dinner in my chambers," Tynae said as they walked to Vu'tella.

"Sounds great! I'm starving."

Everyone stared at the frosting-covered couple as they passed.

"What a sight we must be," Tynae asserted.

"What a sight, indeed." The pair laughed.

Tynae tugged at her outfit, "I hope they can clean this."

"I'll be back shortly," Béo told Tynae, when they reached her room. He gave her a quick peck on the cheek and was gone.

When Tynae stepped through the door O'leana gasped, running over to her.

"I'm fine, O'leana. I was just attacked by a crow," Tynae giggled.

O'leana looked baffled.

"Long story, but the crow was made of cake and now I need another bath." She licked some frosting off her fingers.

Talia went to run the water while Tynae and O'leana selected fresh clothes. Tonight's outfit was black with gold beading and just as revealing as ever.

By the time Béo returned, Tynae was all cleaned up and O'leana had prepared a late dinner.

"Are you sure you don't want us to stay?" O'leana asked.

"No thank you, we're having supper out again," Tynae informed her maids. "We shall see you tomorrow."

"As you wish." The maids bowed, "Good day, Majesties."

The couple sat to eat their dinner.

"So, *your* sword should be ready in about a month or so," Béo informed with a smile.

Tynae looked at Béo. "Sword? What sword?"

"I knew you'd give Jubryi the other one, so I commissioned Glaxor to make you a sword of your own."

"You knew? How?" she asked between bites.

"I know you better than you realize. You are far too kind…" Béo re-thought his last words. "Well, not too kind, you just care about everyone. I knew you'd let him have it once you knew how much he wanted it, and to be honest he could never have afforded it." Béo took a bite of food. "And he would never have accepted it from me, not even as a gift."

Tynae set her fork down. "That is really sweet, thank you, but you didn't have to do that," she said gratefully.

"I know I didn't *have* to, I wanted to. Which reminds me, Glaxor asked me to bring you by. He needs to take a few measurements."

"Okay." Tynae resumed eating her meal.

"So we have a few hours to kill, did you have anything in mind?" Tynae asked.

Béo grinned. "Actually I did, and I thought we'd stick to the seclusion theme for just a bit longer."

Tynae giggled, "Really…So what exactly is it that you have in mind?"

"I thought you might like to see Calai from the outside."

Tynae thought about what Béo said for a minute, but couldn't figure out what he meant. "Outside?" she asked nervously.

Béo nodded. "Yes, outside the dome, in the water."

Tynae's face fell slightly. "You mean…" Tynae pointed up. "I mean…" She couldn't organize her thoughts. Finally she swallowed the lump in her throat and shook her head. "I don't do very well underwater, Béo…I mean I can swim, but I just don't…"

Béo laughed jovially.

Tynae couldn't figure out what she had said that was so funny. "What?"

Béo caught his breath. "Do you mean to tell me that there's actually something you're not good at?"

"There are several things at which I am *not* good at," Tynae grinned, "and yes you have stumbled upon one."

Chapter 28
Fear Discovered

"Not by age but by capacity is wisdom acquired."
~Titus Maccius Plautu

Béo chuckled. "Don't worry, love, we're taking a versaire."
Tynae's brows knitted together. "What's that?"

"It's an enclosed vessel. Our scouts use them when they go on long missions, but we also use them when we want to show visiting dignitaries our city from the outside. I just thought it would be something you might enjoy," Béo explained thoughtfully.

"Will I be able to see it properly? I thought there were spells around Calai preventing people like me from seeing it?"

Reaching into a leather pouch that hung at his waist, Béo pulled out a small glass vial which he handed to Tynae. "Here, drink this," he said. "It will allow you to see what others cannot for the next twenty-four hours."

Tynae looked at Béo with a crooked smile. Taking the vial she removed the cork, "Cheers."

Swallowing the draft in one pull Tynae smacked her lips. "Tastes a bit like honey. What are we waiting for? Let's get out of here!"

The couple stopped by the sword shop for Glaxor to take Tynae's measurements then headed to the far side of the city.

Entering a corridor with a red crystal over it, there were several paths leading off the main corridor. Each had a guard stationed in front of it. All the guards bowed as the couple passed.

Finally entering a cavern with a large lake in the middle of it, they crossed a bridge walking further back.

"Your chariot, My Lady," Béo extended his hand toward a row of what looked to be several glass covered boats bobbing at the waters edge.

Tynae beamed. "They're amazing, is that glass, how do they work, who...?"

"Whoa, whoa, slow down, one question at a time, love." Béo laughed. "Their cover is made of the same material that shields our city. They run off the energy of crystals, and several of our finest engineers created them." Béo grinned. "Did I answer all your questions?"

Tynae giggled, "For now." She looked around. "How do we get in? I don't see a handle."

"Watch." With a wave of his hand the cover on the versaire nearest them lifted. "After you," he smiled.

Holding onto a narrow railing Tynae carefully stepped into the craft.

Béo followed immediately behind. Seated, Béo waved his hand once more; closing the cover.

The two seats which sat side by side were flush with the floor. One could easily sit with their legs outstretched, bent, or even crisscrossed if they so desired. A long crystal-looking pole extended out from the center of a panel directly in front of them.

Tynae eyed the panel. It was covered with an array of buttons and other unfamiliar gadgets.

Béo pushed a small yellow button and all the gadgets lit up, glowing blue. With the push of a few more buttons and the twist of a knob or two they were off.

Slowly the versaire submerged until there was several feet of water above them, making it nearly impossible to see. Béo pressed another button, turning on a bright light in the front of the versaire. The illumination allowed them sight several meters in front of them. Next, he pushed the long lever forward and they began to move.

Various crystals below them and attached to the walls helped light the underwater cavern they traveled through. Gliding slowly, they moved toward a huge set of gates. Six underwater guards protected the gates, each bowed as they passed.

This was the first time Tynae had ever seen a Greer in their aquatic form. They wore what appeared to be short trousers that tied at the knee and were very snug. Their weapons were similar to pikes, but the poles were not wooden and there was a blade on both ends.

"Are those…" Tynae stared intently at the guards, "gills…and fins?"

"Yes," Béo said quietly.

"Their eyes…they're solid back."

"It enables us to see with unhindered vision while under water. Does it bother you?"

Tynae quickly realized Béo must have thought she was bothered by the sight of the guards. "No, not in the slightest. I find this all very fascinating."

Béo seemed to breathe a little easier.

"You'll have to tell me all about gills and such eventually." She smiled, "but right now I just want to enjoy the ride."

Passing through the gates Tynae looked up, seeing what seemed to be nothing but leagues and leagues of water overhead. "Umm, Béo?" Tynae breathed.

"Yes?"

"If for some reason we were to say…uhh, break down…" Tynae tried to keep her tone nonchalant, "I wouldn't have to swim, would I?"

Béo apparently heard the fear in her voice. "Relax, my love," he put his hand on hers. "You're safe and we've never had a versaire breakdown," he assured.

"Maybe so," Tynae's heart began to race and her breathing became shallow, "but there's always a first time for everything," she argued, staring transfixed at the unfathomable liters of liquid surrounding them.

Slowing the versaire, Béo twisted in his seat. Putting his hand on Tynae's chin, he gently turned her head toward him. Her gaze remained locked within the oceans depths. "Tynae, look at me," Béo said in a soothing voice.

Gripping the sides of her seat, Tynae's knuckles turned white. Reluctantly she tore her gaze from the lung crushing fluid enveloping them.

"If you're not comfortable we can turn back," he said sincerely. "Do you trust me?"

Immediately Tynae realized just how silly she was being. Béo would never do anything that had even the slightest possibility of harming her and she knew it.

"With my soul." Taking a deep breath Tynae leaned forward, giving Béo a kiss. "Let's explore," she grinned.

Béo grinned back. "That's, my girl. Now, let me show you what this thing can really do." Pushing a lever all the way forward, they flew through the water.

Finally relaxed, Tynae was able to enjoy herself. Calai was behind them and the wide open ocean before them. She knew they'd been traveling for a fair bit of time, but it seemed to only have been a matter of moments.

Béo slowed the vehicle.

Their versaire floated silently through the water. Fish of every color and size swam around and beside them. Kelp, vibrant sea flowers and other plant life grew in droves.

Béo guided the versaire to an enormous reef.

Tynae pointed, looking at all the new life she never knew existed before that day. "You're so fortunate," she said with admiration.

Béo's brows pulled together. "How so?"

"You, your life...You've had nothing hidden from you. You've always known of all these wondrous things. I know every time you show me something new I say how amazing it is, but to me it is all truly, truly amazing and I really have never seen anything like it before in my life."

Taking Tynae's hand in his, Béo kissed it tenderly. "I can't make up for what's been kept secret from you. But I will show you every inch of the world that I am aware of, if you will allow me."

"I'm counting on that," she smiled.

"Here, let me show you something." Béo positioned their craft in the center of the reef. Shutting everything down, they floated peacefully with the sea life. "There's a lever on the right side of your seat, pull it up."

Tynae did as instructed. When she pulled on the lever Béo pushed the back of her seat down to the floor.

He did the same with his seat.

Together their seats formed a very comfortable, very large cushion. Something like a bed.

"Look," Béo said flipping over onto his stomach.

Turning around, Tynae saw that the floor of the vessel behind their seats was transparent like glass.

The pair got comfortable.

Crystals on the bottom of the versaire illuminated everything under their craft.

Lying on their bellies, they watched the countless forms of sea life below them. Some seemed completely alien in form. It was a fairy tale world of bright colors and ever-changing patterns. There seemed to be a billion years of evolution in this one spot.

Tynae felt as if she'd entered another world, a world of never-ending wonders. "What's that little creature there with its tail wrapped around that plant?" she pointed. "It's so different. It looks like a cross between a skeleton and perhaps a dragon. I've never seen anything like it."

Béo grinned. "We call them Soul Guardians or Dragons of Ordum. Ordum was the first chief of our people. It is believed that he actually created the tiny creatures in an effort to guide the souls of those who perished at sea, giving them safe passage and protection until they met their final destination. Some cultures believe they are affiliated with the god of the seas and as such symbolize great strength and power. Either way, most view them as symbols of good luck." Béo continued, "They are interesting little creatures. As you can see, they look nothing like any fish known to us. It is believed that when they choose a mate, it is for a lifetime. It is actually the male of the species who carries and cares for their young."

"Fascinating," Tynae breathed. "What are those?!" she gasped, directing her attention to several creatures cleverly disguised as rocks that begin moving sideways.

Béo laughed. "Those are called swift warriors. They've learned how to camouflage themselves in order to fool their pray, and escape hunters much the way true warriors do. Their body is akin to that of a warrior's shield, and contrary to their appearance, they are quite fast."

"Wow!" she said bewildered. "With that moss all over them, I thought they were actually rocks," she chuckled.

Béo pointed to something in the middle of their window. "You see those little pink and yellow tube-like flowers there?"

Tynae leaned closer to the glass, "Yes."

"The plant is called 'a wind flower' or 'daughter of the wind'. They have a symbiotic relationship with a select few species of fish. Normally, the flowers sting anything that touches them. Their sting is highly poisonous, but you see those little orange and white fish swimming in and out of it. They've learned how to protect themselves against the plant's defense system. They help the flower by eating matter off of it that would otherwise destroy it," he told her.

"Really?" she said bewildered. "How do they keep from getting stung?"

"We believe they cover their bodies with bile and this prevents the sting from affecting them. The fish have turned the flower into their own personal fortress," Béo chuckled. "Smart little buggers. Wouldn't you say?"

"Absolutely! That's amazing…it's all amazing. How do you know all this?"

"I've spent many hours out here, watching and exploring. Plus our scientists have spent centuries upon centuries researching sea life. Mind you, we've barely even begun to discover what's here; but reefs are fairly simple to study since we can get so close to them."

"I keep forgetting how old you are," Tynae said. "Not that it makes a difference," she added quickly.

"I understand," Béo put his hand on hers.

Tynae stared at the plethora of thriving sea life below them with wonderment. "Wow, I never knew so much life existed underwater. When it comes to the sea, I guess I've always just thought fish lived in it and nothing else," she mused.

Béo smiled, but said nothing.

Several hours passed and it was time to return to Calai.

Rolling onto his side Béo looked at Tynae. "We should start heading back, love. We can return here whenever you'd like."

He must have noticed the disappointment on Tynae's face. "Would you like to steer this time?"

"Me? I have no idea where we are or which way to go."

"There's no wrong way, angel and I know exactly where we are."

Tynae's smile got huge, "Okay."

"It'll cost you though." Béo wore a Cheshire cat smile.

Tynae played along. "What is the toll, Sire?" Tynae propped herself up on her elbow, smiling slyly.

"A kiss."

"Is that all?" Tynae asked. "I think I can afford that." She was only too happy to oblige.

Leaning over, Tynae ran her hand across Béo's bare chest. Leaning even further, she pressed her lips to his. The heat from their searing kiss rocked her to the core.

Reaching around, Béo grabbed Tynae's waist. Pulling her tight to him, her breasts pressed tight against his bare chest.

The versaire steamed up as they became lost in their impassioned kiss, almost losing all control.

Béo would have to thank his tailor for such a well constructed loincloth the next time he saw him. As of late, he was putting it to the ultimate test.

Managing to pull away from each other before they did anything far too brash, Béo looked at Tynae with such love in his eyes it almost made her cry.

"I love you, Tynae, you know that, right? It's not about sex, or your money, or any other material possessions you have. It's *you* that I love," he said breathlessly, his words genuine.

His sentiment caught her off guard. "I know that, Béo, I've never questioned the validity of your feelings for me," she brushed his cheek tenderly.

"Good," he sighed, "I just wanted to make sure that that was perfectly clear."

After setting their seats back up, Béo showed Tynae the basics on how to control their versaire.

Tynae eagerly took control of the levers. She seemed to have a natural hunger for speed as she sent the versaire zooming through the water, pushing it to its limits.

The time soon came to return home. Béo directed Tynae on which way to go.

When the city came into view Tynae gasped, slowing the versaire. She looked at Béo with disbelief. "Oh my god, Béo, it is truly breathtaking."

The kingdom was huge. From up above, it looked like something only seen in paintings, flawless paintings, at that. The city of Calai was neatly nestled in the valley of a never-ending mountain range, chiseled perfectly into the rocks. The landscape was greener than any Tynae had ever seen. The dome-covering the vast territory seemed to go on forever as they slowly drifted above it. There were rolling green hills and vast valleys, sapphire blue lakes, endless mountain ranges, and countless waterfalls cascading down, surrounded by rainbows.

"This must be what heaven looks like," she sighed. "Where in the city are those lakes and falls?" she asked, "I've never seen them."

Béo smiled. "There is much you have not seen yet. I told you Calai is vast...some might even say infinite. It certainly feels like that at times. Don't worry, love, you will see as much of Calai as I am able to show you," he said factually. "Do you mind if I take the controls? We're almost home and it gets a little tricky up here."

"By all means." Tynae released the 'magic' lever.

Béo slowed their craft to a crawl as they passed a large reef near the shield of Calai.

"Do you know what that is?" he pointed.

"A reef," she asserted cheekily.

"Ha, ha," he laughed. "Yes it is a reef, but which reef?"

Tynae shrugged, "Should I know?"

"Probably," Béo smiled. "It's the reef outside your window."

"OH!" She turned to see if she could spot her room, but it was impossible to see into any of the windows.

Once back in Calai the couple headed straight for the dining hall.

"Huzza!!!" The men all shouted as the couple walked in.

Tynae was please to see they had not fallen back into their 'a princess is in the room' demeanor.

Jubryi had two open seats next to him. It seemed that he liked keeping Tynae as close to him as possible.

"Hey there, brother...and" Jubryi pulled out Tynae's chair for her, "Phelan."

"What did you just call me?" she laughed.

"Phelan, that's one of your nicknames. It means 'little wolf'. I figured since you're with this young pup..." he elbowed Béo jokingly.

"Dare I ask what else you plan on calling me?"

Jubryi laughed, "Jack. It's simple, but fitting."

"Jack? How on earth is that 'fitting'?"

"You know those children's jack-in-the-box toys?"

"Yes..."

237

"Well you never know when it's going to spring open or what may pop out. Kind of like you, full of surprises. I thought it was perfect."

Tynae laughed, Jubryi had clearly put a lot of thought into this. "Okay, I can live with that."

Jubryi reached for Tynae. "You're just so adorable. I just wanna grab ya and…"

Tynae stopped him. "Jubryi," she warned, raising a brow and pointing a finger. "If the next word out of your mouth is noogie, you're in for another arse woopin."

Jubryi laughed heartily. "See," he pulled Tynae into a giant bear hug. "You're such a spitfire." He kissed the top of her head.

Tynae started laughing, as did all the men. It warmed her heart to know Jubryi thought so highly of her. There was no doubt he would always keep life interesting.

Chapter 29
Admiration Abounds

"Gratitude is one of the least articulate of the emotions,
especially when it is deep."
~Felix Frankfurter

Still standing, Jubryi raised his huge hands. "Pipe down you lot, I have something I'd like to say." He looked at Tynae with a seriousness rarely seen. "Lady Tynae, you taught me something this day. It is possible for a woman to be equal to, or even better than a man. I have never met anyone like you, female nor male. You're as delicate as a cherry blossom, yet as strong as a fearsome dragon." Jubryi looked around the table. "We all think you're pretty amazing."

Tynae smiled timidly at the men.
Everyone held up their steins, "Here, here!"
"We wanted to give you something special." Jubryi picked up a small wrapped box. "So the boys and I got together, once we were icing free..." everyone laughed, "and made you this."

Tynae accepted the box. "Thank you," she said softly. Carefully she unwrapped the gift. Looking up at Jubryi then around the table at the men, Tynae's eyes seemed to well up. "It's lovely," she sighed, removing the gift from its box. Tynae held in her hands a beautiful gold and silver bracelet. Petite trinkets dangled from the bracelet and between each trinket was a small golden ball.
"I've never seen anything like it, what are these called?" Tynae pointed to the tiny objects.
"We just call it a bracelet."
"It is so much more then that, it is positively charming...that's what I will call it, a charm bracelet," Tynae declared proudly.
"A charm bracelet it is." Jubryi held his hand out, "May I?"
"Of course." Tynae set the bracelet in his hand.
"Remember I told you about the mirror of Tryggth?" Jubryi asked.

"Yes," Tynae nodded.

"Well, another function the mirror has is to show us our animal of destiny."

Tynae's brows knitted together.

"Every person, magical or not, has an animal they are most akin to. To make a long story short, here in Calai our animal is very important to who we are, and to what we are to become." Jubryi laid the bracelet flat in his palm. "Each one of us is represented here," he pointed to the twelve tiny animal 'charms'. "Each of us made a trinket of our animal and we made one for you, too." Jubryi smiled at Tynae. "After discussing it, this is what we came up with this," Jubryi pointed to a tiny silver sword that had a pair of silver wings attached to it. "We considered giving you an animal, but we figured we'd let the mirror do that," Jubryi added with a smile.

Tynae picked the bracelet up, "You made these today?" She thoughtfully touched each of the tiny animals.

"Yes," Jalil answered.

"They're exquisite."

"Well, we got the bracelet itself from Ildrai," Matteo added.

"Why the sword and wings?" Tynae asked, examining her tiny charm.

"Because you are both an angel and a warrior," Rafiq told her simply. "It just fit."

"I'm flattered." Tynae looked closely at her gift. "What are these?" She pointed to the little gold spheres hanging between each charm.

Jubryi looked at Tynae. "Those, lass, are barbuls. Remember, the balls with attitude?"

"Vaguely," Tynae teased.

"Those are miniature versions of the little bastards," Jubryi said bitterly. "We figured since we are all on the same vorbix team it was only fitting."

Tynae chuckled. "This is wonderful!" she said looking at all the men. "Thank you so much...Jubryi, which one is yours?"

He pointed to a large bird like creature dangling beside her wings and sword.

Tynae did not recognize the animal, but decided she'd ask him at a later date what exactly it was.

Tynae handed the bracelet to Jubryi. "Would you please put it on me...*vittles*?" she poked him on the shoulder.

"Vittles?"

"Sure, you're always eating and..."

Jubryi looked affronted.

"Come on Jubryi," Tynae laughed. "You can out eat anyone here."

"Yeah," Jubryi smiled wide, "your right."

Jubryi secured Tynae's bracelet around her wrist. "Oh, if you didn't notice there's one remaining space." Jubryi looked at Béo, "It's yours, little brother, right here next to Tynae's wings," he pointed.

Béo nodded with gratitude.
Tynae admired her gift lovingly.
"My Lady..." Edvard started to say.
"Tynae," she corrected.
"Of course, Tynae, come sit with us." He patted the seat between himself and Matteo. "Béo has you to himself everyday and Jubryi...well he's not very good at sharing," Edvard joked.

Tynae laughed. Walking to the other side of the table she sat in the seat they'd pulled out for her.

Jubryi moved into Tynae's seat beside Béo so they could talk.

"So, do all women from Montronvarr know how to use a sword?" Edvard asked with admiration.

Tynae shook her head. "Naw, I'm a bit of an oddity in my world," she laughed.

"You may be a rarity, possibly even a phenomenon; but you could never be an oddity," Vecenté interjected.

"Ain't that the truth," Jubryi added.
Tynae nodded graciously.

"Ah, here's our food and ale," said Willoughby.

"Would you tell us about your world?" Pe'er, the youngest member of the team asked. "Most of us have never been to your land."

"Gladly," Tynae smiled, "but first my stein needs filling."

"I'll take care of that." Heath grabbed Tynae's tankard.

Tynae glanced at Béo who sat diagonally across from her, giving him a wink. Jubryi smiled slyly at her gesture. She smiled back with a 'so what'cha gonna do about it' look. While Tynae told the men about Montronvarr and Pathrow her stein never ran dry, nor did anyone else's.

Jubryi glanced at Tynae as he spoke to Béo. "How do you do it, brother?" Jubryi asked.

"Do what?"

"Leave her sleeping chamber?" he laughed, nudging Béo.

"You cannot be that single minded, brother," Béo said.

"If I had a woman that looked like that I don't know that my mind could ever be else where." Jubryi admitted, looking at Tynae again.

"Have you not learned that there is much more to her than looks?"

"Of course…but she's so breathtaking," Jubryi said, without taking his eyes away from her.

"Ay," Béo agreed looking at Tynae, too. "It might interest you to know that we have not done what you've been led to believe," Béo admitted.

"Then why did she say…?" Jubryi eyed Tynae curiously.

Béo chuckled. "To shut you up, you toss pot."

Tynae laughed. Her timing seemed to go along with Jubryi and Béo's conversation more than her own.

Jubryi looked crestfallen. "Then do you even sleep…"

Béo stopped Jubryi. "The only part that was not true was the part that compromised her virtue."

Jubryi glanced at Tynae then looked back at Béo. "Does she reject you?" he asked in a tone bordering on hopeful.

Béo's laugh came out like a bark. When he glanced at Tynae, she blushed scarlet. *Can she hear us?* "Hardly," he admitted. "To be totally honest I've been the one that keeps stopping."

"Why the bloody hell would you do something like that, you sod?" Jubryi asked with disbelief.

"Her *honor,* Jubryi," Béo said plainly.

Béo need not say more. "I understand completely, and as much as I hate to admit it," Jubryi nodded, "I would probably do the same thing. It is impossible to know her and not thoroughly respect her."

This led their conversation in a whole new direction.

"So what happened that night you brought her here? No-one has really said anything about it," Jubryi inquired seriously.

Béo hated thinking about that night. "Her people tried to murder her," he said somberly.

"Why would anyone want to harm *her?*" Jubryi asked looking at her once more. "I'll kill'em," he growled.

"Calm down, Jubryi," Béo whispered, glancing at Tynae. "I'm not sure why they want her dead. I only know that for her safety, everyone must believe that she is truly gone."

Jubryi looked confused. "How'd they bring her back then? She appeared…dead when I saw her in your arms."

Béo's heart ached when he thought of how she looked that night. "The magi," he mused softly.

"Really?"

"Well it took all of them, but they brought her back from beyond the veil. For this I am eternally grateful."

"How does your father feel about you and…" Jubryi gazed at Tynae, who was laughing and talking with the other men.

Béo shrugged. "I don't know."

"Is there any reason he wouldn't give you his blessing?"

"Yeah, there's this little issue of her being…" Béo caught himself just in time. He had almost said, 'the chosen one'.

"Yes?" Jubryi asked, waiting for Béo to finish his answer.

Béo looked at his friend. "Jubryi, she's the future queen of the most powerful nation in the entire world, and I'm the future Chief of Calai. How could we possibly manage that?" Béo asked with a pleading tone.

"Does she have to return to Montronvarr?" Jubryi asked.

"That's just it," Béo shook his head, "I don't know."

"Well then I guess the next thing to ask is would you be willing to give up your station as Chief?" Jubryi pressed.

"In a heartbeat," Béo admitted without even thinking about it.

"That settles it then, for god's sake, Béo, we're immortal! Have a few boys and let them carry on for your father."

"I never thought about it like that," Béo mused.

Jubryi punched Béo in the shoulder. "Of course you haven't, little brother," Jubryi laughed. "That's what I'm here for."

Jubryi always saw things differently than Béo—somehow in a simpler way.

Béo stared with adoration at Tynae. Was it really possible for him to have his cake and eat it too? There was only one way to find out.

Jubryi waved his hand in front of Béo's face, snapping his fingers. "Hello, anybody home?"

Béo shook his head. "Sorry."

"So you'll talk to your father then?"

Béo smiled. "Absolutely," he said firmly.

Vecenté joined Béo and Jubryi; the three discussed the upcoming game for a time.

Tynae walked up behind the men, putting her hands on Jubryi and Béo's shoulders. "I'm getting tired, Béo, are you ready to leave?"

"I am," Béo stood. "We'll see you all on Saturday."

Tynae held up her bracelet. "Thank you again."

Jubryi stood too, holding his arms open wide. "May I give you a hug, Jack, Jack?"

"Of course," she grinned.

Jubryi held Tynae in a tight bear hug. "Thank you for the sword, Tynae," he whispered in her ear.

"Don't mention it." She gave him a kiss on the cheek, "Enjoy it...Vittles."

Chapter 30
Gifts of Love

"There is no remedy for love but to love more."
~Henry David Thoreau

The couple got back to Vu'tella in record time.

Grabbing her nightdress, Tynae headed for the loo.

"Hang on," Béo said, grabbing her arm. Taking the nightdress he tossed it over a chair and pulled Tynae into a tight embrace. "You were amazing today."

She grinned, wrapping her arms around Béo's neck. "How so?"

"You gave Jubryi the sword, you faced your fears, and most importantly," he looked at her with a huge grin, "you got into a wicked food fight."

They both laughed.

"Like I said before, never a dull moment when you're around, my angel."

"Hold on," Tynae looked a little confused. "What fear did I face today?"

"I do believe you have a fear of water."

"Ah," she chuckled. "So I do. I don't know that I really faced my fear though. It's not as if I actually went into the water." Tynae kissed Béo's chin. "But it was a really great day."

"Do something for me?" Béo asked.

"Anything," she breathed.

"Close your eyes."

"Why?" she asked, eyeing him suspiciously.

"Please. You said 'yes'."

"That I did." Tynae conceded, closing her eyes.

Béo gently kissed each of her eyelids. "Thank you," he whispered. "Now stand right here and don't move."

Tynae sighed, "Fine."

Béo walked away. "No peeking. Are you peeking?"

"I'm not peeking," Tynae giggled. "What's this all about?"

"You'll see."

"Okay," he said, standing in front of her once more.

"May I open my eyes?"

"Yes."

Béo held in his hands a small perfectly polished box made of a red wood.

"Is that for me?"

"It is." Béo placed the container in Tynae's hands.

Tynae ran her hand over the smooth lid. "Did you craft this?"

"I'd like to take credit for it, but I cannot. I did commission it, though."

Tynae opened the box. Inside were four velvet-lined compartments. Nestled in one was a tiny onyx wolf.

"Oh, Béo, I love it." She picked up the petite wolf. "Is this your animal?"

"Yes."

"Did you make it?"

"I did," he brushed her cheek, "especially for you."

"When? You've been with me all day. I think I would have noticed you chiseling a stone."

Grinning, Béo shook his head. "We don't use chisels to create things like this in Calai."

Tynae flipped the tiny black wolf around in her hand. "Every feature is so finely detailed. The hairs of its coat, the pupils in its eyes..." Tynae looked at Béo, "How then?"

"Like this, *Phelan*." With a wink, Béo extracted a white marble-sized rock from the leather pouch that hung at his waist.

Tynae observed Béo with curiously.

"It's an opal," he said, "watch."

Béo closed his hand around the stone. When he opened his hand a few seconds later there was a miniature white wolf lying on his palm, slightly smaller, yet a twin to his onyx wolf.

Tynae picked up the trinket. "How?" she breathed amazed.

"Magic of course."

"Can you make anything?"

"Yes, but it's easiest to make your own spirit animal. Would you like me to join them?"

Tynae nodded, "Please."

Béo put the white and black wolves in the palm of his hand, closing his fingers. When he opened his hand the body of the petite white wolf stood in front of the form of the larger black wolf. The two, now fused side to side.

Tynae ran her finger over the wolves. "They're perfect."

"Yes they are." Béo smiled. "We'll take them to Ildrai tomorrow so he can add them to your bracelet." Béo placed the melded wolves into Tynae's jewelry box. Taking the container from her, he set it on a table. He removed the lid entirely then pushed a small button at the bottom of the box.

Tynae turned when she heard the first note from her elegant box reverberate through the room. "It plays music, too?" She beamed.

"Do you like it?"

"I love it." Tynae listened to the tune. "What song is this, I don't believe I've ever heard it?"

"That's because I only just finished it in the past few days. I composed it especially for you." Béo grinned. "Do you like it? I call it 'Angel in the mist'."

"I adore it."

Béo pulled Tynae into his arms. Slowly the couple began swaying to the melody.

"I love it here," Tynae whispered, laying her head on his shoulder.

Béo smiled softly, "In Calai?"

"No, here," Tynae whispered, running her hands over his broad shoulders, "In your arms."

Béo held her tighter. "It's exactly where you belong."
Resting his cheek against her, he inhaled her distinct fragrance.

The couple finally called it a night.

Crawling into bed Tynae took her spot in Béo's arms.

It was only supposed to be a tender, goodnight kiss. But the instant her soft lips pressed against Béo's anticipating mouth they became entangled. Their kiss frenzied. Their hands moved earnestly over each others bodies. Their passion for each other consumed them…Béo's love for Tynae stopped them.

"Wait," Béo said breathlessly as Tynae's lips continued to press against his sweltering flesh. "Tynae," he pushed her back slightly. "I won't," he insisted sternly.

"I'm sorry." Tynae collected herself. "I know I'm supposed to be demure and proper, but you bring something out in me. A side of me that is free and cares not what etiquette mandates." She ran her hand over Béo's chest. "I know I should sleep alone, but I don't want to do that either." Tynae kissed Béo's cheek. "I promise I'll behave."

"Not too much, I hope," Béo teased.
"Never," Tynae said slyly.
"I love you, Tynae." Béo stroked her face. "I love you so much...Sleep sweet, my angel."
Tynae sighed. "I love you, too, goodnight."

The blackness of Tynae's sleep slowly faded into warm orange and golden rays of the afternoon sun. This night, Tynae found herself standing on the perimeter of the glorious forest that edged the sea shore. Tarak greeted her. The splendid black unicorn had a plush blanket draped over his back, and to it was pinned a letter. The gallant stallion bowed to the princess.

"Hello Tarak," Tynae said, removing the letter from the blanket. Tynae examined the wax seal. It was a dragon.

My Dearest Angel,

I find myself temporarily detained. Tarak will stay with you until I am able to join you.

Until then, my love, know that my affection for you grows with every beat of my heart.

Though the pang of absence has shattered my soul, it is your undying love and affection that heals me.

Written by the man who is now and has always remained yours.

Faithfully for all eternity,

Ryedin

Tynae read and re-read the letter, his words touched her soul. Folding the letter, she carefully tucked it under her corset. "I guess it's just the two of us, Tarak." Tynae rubbed the unicorn's jaw.

Tarak knelt down.

Hitching up her long amethyst gown, Tynae climbed onto his back. The silver trim of her dress showed distinctly against his shimmering black coat.

The unicorn took Tynae deep into the wood. They rode high into the mountains until they came to an enormous clearing at the summit. The remnants of a once grandiose castle stood in the center of the clearing.

Dismounting, Tynae walked around the ancient ruins. The dilapidated walls and fallen columns were covered with ivy and moss. Huge trees had taken over, shading most of the area. Walking through the historic grounds, Tynae ran her hand over the cool bricks. Somehow this reminded her of home.

Hearing the clip clop of hooves, Tynae turned excitedly in anticipation of Ryedin's arrival. It was not Ryedin. To her amazement it was a sublime white horse. The celestial animal came straight to Tynae and Tarak, joining them.

"Is this your mate, Tarak?" Tynae asked.

The stallion neighed.

"I will take that as a yes." Smiling brightly, Tynae bowed graciously to the white mare.

The mare knelt, spreading a pair of enormous white wings.

Tynae gasped. "You truly are divine," she said with awe.

Tarak and his mate stayed near by as Tynae explored.

Finally the glistening fog came, and out of it stepped, quite literally, the man of her dreams.

Tynae ran to Ryedin, wrapping her arms around his neck and kissing him passionately.

"Hello, angel."

"Hello," Tynae sighed.

Taking Tynae by the hand, Ryedin walked to where the horses stood. "Lady Tynae, this is, Lady Asria."

"My Lady," Tynae bowed. "I am very honored to make your acquaintance."

Ryedin looked at Tynae. "Tell me, my love, have you ever flown?"

"Flown? Do I look as if I have wings?" Tynae laughed.

"Come on." Ryedin led Tynae over to Asria, assisting her atop the winged horse then climbed on behind her.

"Ryedin," Tynae spoke nervously.

"I won't let any harm come to you, my angel, please set your fears aside."

Tynae took a deep breath. "Okay."

"That's my girl."

Wrapping his arms securely around Tynae's waist, Ryedin gave Asria a light prod.

The horse gained speed with each step she took. Soon Asria was in a full run, headed straight for a cliff.

"Hold on, love," Ryedin shouted so Tynae could hear him.

Hold on…what else would I do, throw my hands up in the air? Wide-eyed, Tynae's heart raced uncontrollably. Reaching the cliffs edge, the horse launched herself into the great blue sky. Clutching onto Asria's mane for dear life, Tynae let out an ear splitting scream. It was the most exhilarating, yet terrifying experience of her life. It took some getting used to, but once Tynae felt comfortable she loved the bird's eye view of her extraordinary dream world. They flew over canyons and waterfalls, rivers and lakes.

They even flew through a canopy of puffy white clouds. While soaring over the forest, a falcon glided along side them.

Tynae leaned back against Ryedin's chest as they floated through the sky.

When Asria finally landed it was in the same clearing they had taken off from.

Ryedin helped Tynae dismount.

"That was fantastic!!!" she said, ecstatic.

Ryedin beamed.

"Thank you so much, My Lady." Tynae ran her hand over Asria's side. "So is this Tarak's mate?"

"Indeed," Ryedin inclined his head.

Tynae looked at Ryedin with a peculiar expression. "I still don't get it," she said looking at the two animals then back at Ryedin. "How did unicorns become pure white if their sire is black? And now I'm wondering why they don't have wings."

"Well the wings are easy enough. It's just like when we have children. Our offspring have some traits from their father and some from their mother. There are unicorns that have wings. They're just harder to spot, especially since they spend a majority of their time in the sky.

"As for the fact that *most* unicorns are white, they owe that blessing to their parent's undying and absolute love for each other. You already know that in nature a wildebeest mates with a wildebeest, and a giraffe mates with a giraffe." Ryedin looked over at the two horses that were canoodling and smiled. "Although they were of different breeds they were of the same race. Both came from regal blood lines which under ordinary circumstances would have been ideal. But their herds had been feuding for centuries, for reasons neither side could even recall. Nevertheless, they were forbidden to be with each other."

Taking Tynae by the hand, Ryedin began to walk around the ruins. "They loved each other so much that they agreed to leave the valley of Tasnimdeza and never return. They gave up everything to be with each other, never looking back. Anything that extraordinary can only create something equally as extraordinary, and for this reason they were blessed with offspring as pure as their love," Ryedin explained with adoration as he led Tynae to a stone bench under an archway of red roses where they sat hand in hand. "Their horn, hair, blood, and in Asria's case, feathers, all possess supremely powerful magical properties." Ryedin stared at Tynae.

Understanding registered on Tynae's face. "Is this…" she glanced around, "Is this place Tasnimdeza?"

"Yes," Ryedin smile.

Looking around Tynae frowned slightly. "What happened?"

"Their families never did learn to co-exist and in the end destroyed not only themselves, but the home and land they cherished. It's taken hundreds of years for this place to heal itself, but it's well on its way."

"That's really sad," Tynae said. "But if they had never planned on returning why are they here now?" Tynae laid down on the stone bench, resting her head on Ryedin's lap.

"It is quite sad." Ryedin ran his hand over her hair. "But what's even more disheartening is that the races and generations that followed never learn from the mistakes of their past. As for them coming back, Tarak and Asria returned in hopes of inspiring peace between their families. They had hoped that their beautiful children would force the elders to see how ridiculous their behavior was, and what they'd missed out on by forcing the couple to flee." Ryedin sighed. "It was too late. The only thing left was rubble. Tarak and Asria decided to stay and their offspring joined them. Together, with their love and magic, they've helped nature heal much of this place." Ryedin looked around. "It's amazing what a little bit of love can do, isn't it?" he declared, marveling at their surroundings.

"It can change the world," Tynae breathed.

"That it can, my angel, that it can." Ryedin smiled down at her, stroking her cheek.

Running her hand over Ryedin's hand, Tynae's new bracelet jingled.

"You know what's missing from this?" He pointed to the tiny wings and sword.

She smiled. "What's that?"

"This…" he waved his hand over her bracelet.

Tynae's eyes got wide as she watched a spark of bright white light encircle *her* charm. It didn't hurt her; she could not feel it, though she could sense something from it. Eventually the spark faded. At first when she looked at her charm she could see no difference. Upon closer inspection she observed something that had not been there previously, a tiny amethyst on the hilt of her wee sword. Examining the new addition she noticed something else. Tynae watched in amazement as the wings on her charm gradually changed from silver to white.

Tynae looked at Ryedin. "Now it looks exactly like the…"

"Guardian of Souls?" Ryedin grinned, "I just thought you might like something to take back with you."

Tynae sat up. "You mean it will not disappear once I leave this place?" she asked excitedly.

"Not at all," Ryedin grinned.

Tynae admired the new addition to her already cherished gift. Ryedin sighed.

"It's time for me to go isn't it?" She tried to conceal her sadness.

Ryedin looked at her lovingly. "Yes." He brushed his hand softly over her cheek.

"Why were you not here when I first arrived?" she asked.

"I…" Ryedin considered his answer then shook his head. "I cannot say. I'm sorry," he confessed, clearly with a heavy heart.

Tynae smiled acceptingly. "Don't worry about it, my love," she said. "I understand that there are things you cannot tell me."

Ryedin grinned with appreciation. "Thank you for understanding. In time you will know everything, I promise." Leaning forward, he pressed his soft lips to hers.

She parted his moist lips with her supple tongue. Grabbing Ryedin's hair, Tynae pulled him tight to her, pressing her body to his. His touch, his taste, his smell, they were all so familiar, so welcoming, yet so frustrating. Their kiss became fevered, bordering on frantic, both clearly longed for so much more.

Every time he touched her, every time he was near her, her soul became more attached to him.

Ryedin reluctantly pulled away from Tynae. "I'm sorry."

"Don't be sorry," she touched his face tenderly. "I know in time we will be as one." Tynae did not know why she spoke these words. She only knew they were true.

"That we shall," he said with his angelic smile.
"Will you be here when I arrive tomorrow?" she asked.
"You can count on it."
Kissing her once more, Ryedin walked into the mist.

When Tynae awoke the next day she inspected her miniature sword. Her heart danced when she saw that the tiny amethyst and white wings were still intact.

Béo and Tynae visited Ildrai later that afternoon. He placed their entwined wolves on Tynae's bracelet beside her tiny sword and wings.

Over the next few days, Tynae and Béo spent much time exploring the liquid world outside of Calai.

Chapter 31
Ships, Sails, and Scandalous Tales

*"False words are not only evil in themselves,
but they infect the soul with evil."*
~Plato

The knock of the wooden gavel echoed throughout the court room. "This session of Montronvarr parliament is now open."

Gwillim stood to address King Yurgon and his council. "Sire, it has been beyond a week and we have found no trace of Lady Tynae anywhere, except in the forest. I think it is safe for us to assume at this point that she has been abducted. Perhaps it would be prudent for us to discreetly send out search parties to investigate within other nations."

Yurgon had gotten little sleep, if any, in days and looked it. "I have considered that." Yurgon took a deep breath, running his hand over his chin. "Assemble fifteen hundred search parties. They are to consist of three men each," the king instructed.

Gwillim nodded. "Yes, Sire."

Yurgon turned to the head of his navy. "Calder, I want thirty ships ready to go by week's end. They need enough supplies to sustain their crew and passengers for…" Yurgon silently deliberated the length of time that would be considered pragmatic for such a mission. "Six month's."

The King was asking a bit much. Getting that many ships and supplies ready in such a short period of time would require everyone to work around the clock for the remainder of the week.

Yurgon's focus was on Tynae, putting a complete plan in place, and finding her. Here is where the king's mind would linger during this session of parliament.

Yurgon stood to depart. "Calder, meet me in the war room in an hour's time. And Gwillim, join us as soon as you have an idea of how you're going to assemble the search parties," the king ordered.

Both men nodded. "Yes, Sire."

Yurgon paced in his war room. Under normal circumstances *war* was the only thing this room was used for. Every wall was covered with a full scale map. The floor, which also had a large map etched upon it, was comprised of movable tiles. This was so that mock ships, troops, and weaponry could be moved, positioned, and re-positioned for optimal visual presentation. Determining the best routes and least occupied territories when venturing into unfamiliar lands could very well mean the difference between defeat and victory. Several windows on almost every wall of this room provided ample lighting. Furniture in the room was sparse. There were a few chairs. A large wooden table used by the military leaders to lay their maps upon. And several wooden shelves that housed the small replicas of vessels, armed soldiers, and artillery used for battle simulations.

Continuing to pace, Yurgon studied the world beneath his feet carefully. Hearing footsteps down the hall, he glanced at a clock.

There was a rap on the door.

"Enter," Yurgon called.

"Your Majesty," Calder bowed.

"Calder," Yurgon replied. Walking over to his high back chair, he gestured to the chair beside him.

Calder took a seat.

"I trust you have been brought up to speed on the current situation?" Yurgon asked dryly.

"I have, Sire. I am truly sorry."

"Thank you," Yurgon said politely. "How was your trip from Brantin?"

"It was unusually smooth for this time of year and completely without incident."

Yurgon nodded. "This is good to hear. It has been some time since I've been to Brantin, lovely place. And your family, are they enjoying your new assignment?"

Calder smiled. "Very much, Sire, Brantin is the pearl of the sea."

"Wonderful. I'm glad. That wife of yours has been very tolerant of your time away and the constant moving from port to port. I felt the two of you had earned a little corner of paradise."

With a grin, Calder nodded in appreciation once more.

"Well let us get to it, shall we. I have no reason to believe that Tynae has been kidnapped for ransom or that she has run off," Yurgon said plainly.

The king stood, resuming his aimless pacing around the room. "The truth of the matter, Calder," Yurgon stopped, looking at the man directly. "There is more evidence that she has…perished, than gone missing." Yurgon stuttered over his words. This was the first time he had admitted aloud what he'd been dwelling upon for the past week. Yurgon shook his head, taking up walking in circles again. "Perhaps I'm being a fool, wasting precious resources and taking men away from their families." Stopping at a window the king clasped his hands behind his back. He stared outside at nothing in particular. "Perhaps I am sending you off in search of a ghost," he muttered. Yurgon turned sharply on one foot. "Do you think I am being foolish?"

"If it were me, Sire, and it was my daughter that was missing." Calder shook his head sympathetically, "I would never stop searching until I found her, breathing or not."

Yurgon managed a tired smiled. "I appreciate your candor." The king resumed walking around the room once more. "Tell me what you feel you can do in six months time. How much sea can you cover?"

Examining the foreign lands upon the walls, Calder did silent calculations in his head. "Well, if it were possible to ready forty ships instead of thirty we could send ten ships to each quadrant of the globe, and if we sent the men out in parties of two instead of three they could cover more land." Calder slid his hand over the unfamiliar countries represented on the walls. "Six months time is a bit daunting. In order to get the men to as many places as possible the ships will have to stop in numerous ports. This means we must reach our first harbor by the second month, drop the men, their supplies, and their steeds then continue on without delay." Calder examined the lay of the lands meticulously. "If we could make our final port two weeks prior to the four month mark, my men could have a break and the soldiers could search for Lady Tynae in every town they pass on their way to rejoin the ships. Bear in mind all this is contingent on Mother Nature's cooperation. The season of ice is rapidly approaching."

Yurgon nodded. Stroking his beard he considered Calder's proposal. "You're certain you can get to all the major out-lying countries in this time?"

"Yes, definitely…weather permitting."

Yurgon liked the sound of this.

A knock came at the door. "Enter," the king said.

"Ahh, Gwillim, just in time. Have you dispatched orders to the companies?"

"Ay, Sire I have. All the soldiers I have called up will be in place and ready to mobilize in the next forty-eight hours."

"Very good," Yurgon acknowledged. "Calder and I have been discussing how we will move forward with this operation. Calder, explain to Gwillim what you have worked out."

Opening the door of his war room, Yurgon addressed the guard standing outside. "Grayson, have Aron and Weston report to me immediately," he ordered.

"Yes, Sire."

Closing the door, Yurgon rejoined his captains. The three men discussed how the troops were to travel, and more importantly, how they would travel the countryside looking for Lady Tynae without drawing attention to the fact that the future queen of Montronvarr was missing.

Another knock came.

"Enter."

Aron and Weston came into the room. Both bowed to their king then the other two men.

"Ready ten more ships, Weston, for a total of forty," Yurgon ordered.

Weston's expression fell slightly. "Yes, My Liege," he looked at the floor.

Calder stepped forward. "Weston, go to my ship, The Elizaveta, ask for Bodee. Tell him that I wish to speak with him. I will have him assist you. He knows how to ready a ship faster than anyone I've ever known."

Weston smiled gratefully. "Thank you, Sir." He turned to the king, "Will there be anything else, Sire?"

Yurgon shook his head. "No, you may leave."

"Calder, please tell Aron which countries you would like to have laid out," Yurgon pointed to the floor, "and where you would like them placed."

Weston opened the door to leave, "Sire…"

The king turned to see Prince Kaleal standing in the doorway. "Kal, what are you doing here?" Yurgon walked over, greeting his unexpected guest.

"After speaking with my father at length, we've both agreed that what is best for Montronvarr is to find Princess Tynae and return her. I have come to offer anything you may need; ships, soldiers, gold…whatever is necessary." Yurgon considered Kal thoughtfully. "Kaleal, I know how you feel about my daughter and I appreciate your help, but I cannot and will not, force her to marry you because you have aided in her rescue."

Yurgon wanted to make it clear to Kal in no uncertain terms, that his assistance, though respected, would not guarantee him the princess' hand. Tynae, and only Tynae, would choose her husband.

Kaleal smiled. "I love Tynae, this is true. But I assure you, Sire, the offer is not a ruse to ensure her hand. It is genuine. My only desire at the moment is to see Lady Tynae returned safely to Pathrow."

The king extended his hand to the prince, "I accept your generous offer."

Yurgon and Kal walked over to where the other men stood. "Gentlemen, this is Prince Kaleal Daariq Gannath Trevongwee the Benevolent of Mithtalray, son of King Brennon Fettri Palaton Trevongwee the Ardent."

The men bowed to Kal.

"Prince Kaleal, this is Duke Gwillim of Montronvarr. He is Commander-In-Chief of my Army and this is Count Calder also of Montronvarr. He is the fleet Admiral of my Navy."

Kal inclined his head, "Gentlemen."

"I will send Taisiya to my father at once," Kal told Yurgon. Yurgon knew what Kal was talking about, but the others did not. Kal must have noticed the confused looks on the faces of his new acquaintances. "My falcon," he added.

Their understanding was evident.

"Before I departed, I ordered that twenty ships be readied. If you accepted our help, father would deploy them immediately," Kal informed. Staring at the floor Kal examined the sailing route they were planning. "We could rendezvous here," he stepped on a tile, "on the first night of the voyage." Kal looked at Calder.

Calder nodded with approval. "That would work."

"If we dropped anchor for an hour or two, we could meet with the captains of my ships and explain their assignments," Kal suggested.

Calder and Gwillim both nodded. They obviously liked this plan and clearly welcomed the extra man power.

"It is settled then," Yurgon said, "send Taisiya to your father, and please express my immense gratitude."

"Yes, Sire," Kal bowed.

The four men discussed tactics, shipping routes, and cover stories for many hours.

Yurgon had supper served in the war room.

When the evening hours turned into dawn the men finally turned in. Yurgon offered Kaleal a room in Darvah, but he chose to return to his ship.

The next several days were spent locked in the war room perfecting strategies, time frames, and groupings of soldiers.

Gwillim saw to it that he and his fellow assassins would travel together at all times. Gwillim was beginning to settle into his role as 'caring and loyal soldier' very well. His phony stories and untruthful words now flowed quite easily. His conscience had quieted down tremendously once he had received his first installment of gold from Baroness Arona. Gwillim was now certain that when they returned from their pointless pursuit he would be able to weave tales worthy of the treacherously sly canine he was quickly becoming. He and his fellow conspirators were looking forward to getting away from the dreariness of Pathrow, even though it was they who created the misery that now plagued their city. They planned on turning the six month excursion into an extended holiday. All expenses paid.

Chapter 32
Gratefulness

"Gratitude is merely the secret hope of further favors."
~Francois de La Rochefoucauld

The next few days passed quickly, and for reasons unknown to Tynae, she was feeling quite nervous about that night's supper with the chief.

She had met with many dignitaries from all over the world and had never felt like this. Perhaps it was the fact that she was going to meet the most powerful Archimagi in the world. She was still trying to wrap her mind around Calai's existence, and magic was the most difficult part to absorb. Or maybe it was because she would be spending an entire evening with her *beau's* father. She knew the feelings between her and Béo were apparent to most. If Kerszon did not already know, it would only be a matter of time until he did.

Sitting in her warm bath, Tynae's mind swirled with questions. *How does Kerszon feel about me? Would he approve of Béo and me being together? Will Kerszon think I'm good enough for his son? What if he forbids us to be with each other?* Tynae was working herself into a tizzy and there were still several hours to go before supper.

"Is something the matter, mistress?" O'leana asked, wrapping Tynae's robe around her.

Shaking her head, Tynae smiled. "Just nerves, I'll be fine." Walking to the dressing area Tynae looked at her clothes that had been set out and grinned. "I still can't believe that I won this," she chuckled, admiring her *prize*.

"Well, I think it will look beautiful on you, My Lady," Sireeon grinned. "Let's get started, shall we?" Her handmaidens spent the next few hours weaving thick threads of gold into Tynae's dark hair. Once that was done, they fashioned her hair atop her head in perfect ringlets, letting a few pieces cascade around her face and down her back. The look was quite elegant.

The deep red fabric of her lavish prize was striking against Tynae's olive skin. This outfit was rather extravagant compared to the previous ones. The top had intricate beading with pearls, crystals, and threads of gold. She did not wear gold chains around her waist with this outfit as with the others. There was no need. The beading on her top cascaded down over her abdomen. The waist of the skirt was covered with the same intricate detail and beading. The skirt was made of a soft flowing material that moved like wisps of smoke. With bands of gold the maids attached blood red scarves to Tynae's arms. They flowed from her wrist, to her bicep, along her back and to her other arm. Around her ankle they fastened an anklet bejeweled with rubies. *This must be the something* extra *Béo requested,* she thought, grinning to herself. They did her make-up next. Tonight even her face would be adorned with jewels of gold. The last thing they applied was her perfume, and as if on cue, a rap came at the door.

O'leana opened it and Béo entered.

"We're almost finished. Give us just a few more minutes…Wait until you see her," she added in a whisper.

Tynae viewed herself in the mirror.

"Oh, my," she raised her hand to touch her face.
O'leana pushed her hand down. "No touching, My Lady."
"Sorry, I've never seen make-up or hair like this," Tynae turned in a circle in front of the mirror. "It's brilliant."
Tynae turned to her three maids. "Thank you for all your help, ladies. You are free to return to your own dwellings for the evening. I'll see you tomorrow."

O'leana started to open her mouth, but before she could get a single word out Tynae opened the chamber door. With an expectant smile Tynae pulled the door open a little further, raising her brows. "That will be all," she insisted, still holding onto the door knob.

"As you wish, My Lady," O'leana bowed her head and the three maids departed.

Tynae shut the door behind the women. She wanted just a few moments alone with Béo before they set out for the evening. She knew all too well how these social gatherings worked and knew it would be many hours before they would be alone again.

"What do you think?" She purred, walking toward Béo, stopping right in front of him and turning slowly.

Béo stared at Tynae. "*Wow*! You are…breathtaking," he said, not taking his eyes off her. Stepping forward, Béo put his hands on Tynae's arms. Pulling her to him, he kissed her cheek softly.

Tynae's heart raced, her breath caught in her throat as Béo's warm lips slowly inched over her skin.

"Love," he breathed, his hot breath sending a surge of electricity through her. "We need to leave right now." His words had urgency in them, but his lips lingered on Tynae's flesh. Moving slowly, wantonly, he kissed down her throat, along her collar bone and across her shoulder.

Tynae's heart beat frantically which made it difficult to speak, but she managed to get out a few audible words. "I…I thought…we still had…a spell." Her head turned as Béo's warm tongue slid over her neck. "Did…ahh…did the time change?" she asked breathlessly.

Béo took a small step back, away from Tynae. He smiled. "It's not that..." he looked her up and down, slowly. "If we don't get out of here right now, I will *not* be held responsible for whatever I may do next."

Realization crossed Tynae's face. "Oh..." She grinned. "Okay, but I just need to do one last thing," she held up one finger. Stepping forward she closed the splinter of distance between herself and Béo. It was her turn to admire him. Delicately she slid her hands over Béo's chest. She felt his body shiver. Tynae became lost in the passion Béo held in his eyes. With her tongue, she traced his sweet lips. Wanting more she slid her tongue gently into his mouth. Pressing her body tight against his, her fingers tightened…Tynae attempted to step away from Béo, but found she couldn't move. Looking down she saw the beading from her top had snagged on Béo's silk tunic. "Shite!" Tynae spat loudly.

"Excuse me?" Béo laughed.

"Don't act like you've never heard the word before," she jabbed.

"Oh, I've heard the word plenty, just not from the mouth of a *lady,*" he teased.

Tynae shook her head. "Don't start, just unhook us," she urged, beginning to panic.

Béo looked down, examining their awkward situation. "It appears that a thread from my tunic has attached itself to one of the beads on your..." Béo looked at Tynae uncomfortably.

"Breast, Béo...it's okay to say the word...breast."

Every time Béo reached to unhook the thread he pulled his hand back. Béo looked at Tynae with pleading eyes. "Perhaps umm, maybe you should do it. I don't think I can undo it without touching..." Béo looked down at Tynae's breasts, "You know."

His adolescent discomfort was priceless. Tynae bit her lip. He was too adorable. She tried to unfasten the string, but couldn't unhook it. She tried taking a step closer to Béo allowing the thread to hang slack, but that didn't help either. Tynae looked at Béo apologetically. "I'm sorry, but I don't know what else to do, so just stand still." Tynae pushed herself tight against Béo. He tried to look as if he were not enjoying the awkward situation, as she wiggled and finagled around. Finally she managed to unfasten their clothes from each other. "There," she proclaimed, sounding flustered. Straightening herself up, Tynae looked at Béo. "You know what?" She giggled. "I think you're right. We really do need to get out of here, *now.*"

Chuckling, they set off to Kerszon's chambers.

Walking through halls Tynae had never traveled before, Béo pointed out paintings and statues explaining their significance.

"By the way, I really like this." Tynae gestured to Béo's clothing. He wore tan leather trousers that were rather fitted, accentuating his tight bum, and a long sleeved red silk tunic that exposed his magnificent chest. On his feet were soft suede boots.

"Thank you. We, my father and I that is, wear red when we are entertaining guests of nobility. I'm glad you like it," he grinned.

"So, what should I expect this evening?" Tynae asked, inadvertently revealing her nervousness.

"Well, I'm sure everyone is going to want to know how you're feeling. What changes, if any, are happening to you and then who knows," Béo shrugged.

Tynae took a deep breath.

"It will be fine. You can do anything." Béo grinned widely, "I'm convinced of that."

Tynae smiled at his confidence in her. "Thank you."

Béo took Tynae's hand, kissing it. "Don't be nervous, angel, I'm right here." Stopping he looked Tynae in the eyes, "I won't leave your side."

"Promise?"

"I promise," he vowed sweetly.

Taking a deep breath, Tynae grinned at Béo then the two resumed walking. Tynae was in no particular hurry.

It seemed like the further they walked the fewer people they saw, until they arrived at a long hall. The floor was covered with a rich red carpet. Oversized paintings hung upon the walls, and statues lining either side of the walls appeared to be guarding the paintings. The statues varied, some were made of bronze and others of onyx. Each figure was clearly that of a warrior. Each warrior was accompanied by an animal. Tynae saw panthers, wolves, tigers, falcons and several other creatures. The warriors wore golden loin cloths. Each statue grasped within each of its hands a long spear. Extending its arms out to the side, together with the statue beside it, they formed an 'X' with their weapons.

"Are these statues of real people?" Tynae asked.

"Yes, past chiefs, and with them is their power animal."

"I see."

Béo stopped at the very last set of statues and turned to Tynae. "We're here," he said lightly.

"What?" Tynae looked around at the brick walls, paintings and statues. "Here where?"

"My father's residence," Béo chuckled. "The doorway is concealed," he nodded toward a particular painting.

"Oh," Tynae laughed, "I should have known."

Béo smiled softly, this calmed Tynae's nerves a bit.

"I don't know why you're so nervous, my love, please relax," Béo urged in his soothing voice. "It's going to be fine."

Tynae nodded, fidgeting with her bracelet. The butterflies in her stomach had not only taken flight, they were threatening to revolt.

Leaning forward Béo kissed Tynae on the cheek. Taking both her hands in his, he tenderly kissed each one.

The warmth of his lips on her skin made Tynae's entire body feel as if it were going to melt.

Lowering his arms Béo squeezed Tynae's hands lightly, slowly letting her hands slide out of his. With the wave of his hands, two of the statues drew in their spears. The painting they guarded shimmered briefly then transformed into a large ornate door. Opening the door Béo bowed slightly, "After you, My Lady."

Tynae fixed a smile on her red lips, stood tall, and walked over the threshold. There had been an audible buzz of conversation in the room, but when Tynae entered it became deathly quiet. All eyes focused on her. Tynae flashed a smile, and everyone smiled back.

Chief Kerszon's voice boomed from across the room. "Welcome, Lady Tynae and Lord Béo."

Conversations resumed.

"Thank you, Chief," Tynae said politely, trying desperately to tame the jellyfish now using her stomach as a trampoline. Tynae had never been this nervous in her life.

Kerszon walked over to greet the couple. Taking Tynae's hand, Kerszon delicately kissed it. She curtsied. "You look lovely, My Lady. Our attire is rather stunning on you."

Blushing, Tynae looked at the floor briefly. "Thank you, Chief, it is my *prize,*" she admitted bashfully.

Kerszon smiled, looking at the couple with curiosity.
Béo wore his Cheshire cat grin.
"Ah." Understanding crept across Kerszon's face, "The race?"
"Yes," Tynae replied with a slight quiver in her voice.
"I believe in this case, we all won," Kerszon said, his eyes lingering on Tynae, perhaps a moment too long.
Béo cleared his throat.
Kerszon blinked. "I'm sorry, My Lady. It has been quite some time since I have seen a woman of such stature," Kerszon admitted in a gentlemanly tone.

Tynae grinned slyly. "That's okay, Chief. One good faux pas deserves another, I always say," she teased.

Kerszon chuckled. "I like this girl! Good evening, Son," he said with a huge smile.
Béo smiled at the Chief. "Father," he said cordially.
"Please, come in, join us." Kerszon insisted in his jovial tone. "Our feast will be ready soon."
Tynae glanced over at Béo.

He gave her a wink.

Béo and Tynae followed Kerszon into the lounge, joining the others.

Kerszon cleared his throat and the room instantly quieted. "I would like to formally introduce Her Majesty, Princess Tynae Brimon Le'jonrey Du'Vonaire 'The Bringer of Joy', daughter of His Majesty, King Yurgon Ellar Le'jonrey Du'Vonaire 'The Gentle', and future Queen of the great nation of Montronvarr."

Everyone bowed to Lady Tynae.

She graciously returned the gesture.

"Tynae, please take a seat," Kerszon said with a warm grin. "We have many questions and I'm sure you have a few of your own."

Tynae gave a slight nod. "Thank you, Chief."

The room they were in was enormous. There were many large, over-stuffed chairs, as well as several couches varying in size. Sitting on the edge of a smaller couch, Tynae placed her hands in her lap, and Béo sat beside her.

"These, My Lady, are the Archimagi who helped bring you back from beyond the veil," Kerszon gestured to the people sitting in the room then proceeded to introduce each person. "Starting here on my right we have Nuri and his wife Safara. Their specialty is Fire. To their right are Keb and his wife Kiah. They are earth."

Each person nodded to Tynae as they were introduced.

She did likewise, all the while fidgeting with her bracelet.

"Across from them are Aldare and Drayea. They are water. And next we have Caremon and Havel. Air is their forté. Over by the fire we have Eron and Tao. They are our peace makers. And our last couple next to the door is Jeevan and Karasi. They concentrate on life. Let's see. Across the room here we have Kijani. He wields magic for our warriors and next to him is Laida. She works with the peacemakers. She is love. And last, but certainly not least, is Ge'annã. She is our most powerful healer and her specialty is…well, everything," Kerszon chuckled. "That's everyone."

Standing up, Tynae looked at each and every person in the room, this included Béo and Chief Kerszon. "Thank you once again," she said gratefully, inclining her head. Tynae sat back down, returning her attention to Kerszon. "Chief, you mentioned *specialties*. I don't understand."

"Ah, well. You see, Tynae, magic can be a tricky thing. You can work in many different areas, but it is wise to specialize in a specific craft. This is what our Archimagi have done and this is what makes them the most powerful of all the magi in the world."

Unthinking, Tynae rubbed the tiny entwined wolves on her bracelet. "Do all couples specialize in the same thing?"

"Not always. But if two Archimagi that specialize in a particular skill do unite, they become incredibly powerful. Of course there are people like Ge'annã who are so powerful on their own that uniting with another would have very little, if any effect on her magic." Kerszon grinned at Ge'annã who didn't seem to notice he was speaking about her.

"I see," Tynae said, finding this all incredibly intriguing. "How did so many magi come to be in Calai?"

Kerszon glanced at Béo.

"I'm sorry," Tynae looked at Béo then back to the chief. "Should I not have asked that?"

"No, that's fine," Kerszon said casually. "Calai is one of the most secure places on the planet. This is where they choose to reside."

Tynae nodded with understanding. It made perfect sense.

Jeevan had been watching Tynae intently since she had arrived. A lull in the conversation presented him with the opportunity to address her. "I must say, Lady Tynae, you look beyond restored. You look positively radiant," he commended, grinning.

Funny how love can do that to you. "Thank you, Jeevan, I feel incredible," Tynae beamed. "I have no idea what you did, but I hope it doesn't wear off."

Though everyone smiled, odd glances were exchanged. The reactions did not go unnoticed.

Ge'annã was the next to speak. "We have found that when we," Ge'annã looked at her fellow magi, "as Archimagi, assist in the healing of another being, magical or otherwise, for an extended period of time, as we did you…we inadvertently transfer some of our abilities to them. Needless to say, we exercise extreme caution when it comes to those whom we choose to *heal*," Ge'annã said in a monotone voice. "With you it was a fairly easy decision. We believe in what it is that you represent, and what you will fight for."

Smiling serenely, Tynae considered herself very privileged to have had such a great honor bestowed upon her. "I am forever grateful that you found me worthy of such extraordinary gifts. Thank you again," she bowed her head.

Chapter 33
Tales of Lore

*"Those who cannot remember the past
are condemned to repeat it."*
~George Santayana

A set of double doors by the large hearth opened and a tall slender man stepped out. "Supper is served, My Lord."

"Thank you." Kerszon stood, "Shall we?" The chief leading the way, everyone followed.

The dining room was lit by candles, torches, and crystals. The table was long and covered in the finest of linens. Each chair with its high back and red velvet seat resembled a throne. Exotic flowers filled the entire room with their sweet perfume. The crystal stemware looked as if it was cut from diamonds. Utensils made of gold were set beside exquisite white china trimmed to match. From one end of the table to the other, the food was artistically positioned. The center piece, a whole hog, had been roasted to perfection, even the apple in its mouth shown like a flawless ruby. There were numerous other dishes. Tynae recognized some of the cuisine, but most she did not. It all looked and smelled heavenly.

Kerszon was the first to take his seat, at the head of the table, naturally. He requested that Lady Tynae sit to his right.

Béo pulled out Tynae's chair for her.

Once she was seated, he took the seat beside her.

Everyone else seemed to know where to sit without instruction.

When Tynae went to place her napkin on her lap she accidentally brushed Béo's hand with hers.

Clasping her hand in his for just a second, they exchanged a crooked smile then returned their attention back to the table.

273

With a bright smile, Tynae turned to Kerszon. "Chief, everything looks absolutely delightful."

"Thank you," Kerszon gave her a nod. "The Nanics never let me down," he added with a smile.

Tynae set her goblet down. "Oh, that reminds me. I met Tingy the other day," she said in a delighted tone. "That was the first time I'd ever seen a Nanic. I didn't think they...I mean...I was told...they had been hunted to extinction," Tynae reluctantly stated her last few words in a reserved voice.

Kerszon grinned at Tynae again. "Tingy's a great lil bloke isn't he?"

Tynae nodded. "He really is."

Kerszon took a sip of wine. "As for the Nanic race, I will admit that it was a close call. At one point they were being killed in droves. Having been long-time allies with the Nanic, we offered them refuge here in Calai. They've been here ever since," Kerszon declared proudly.

Tynae marveled at Kerszon's statement. "Would you please tell me about their race? I know so little about them. I knew vaguely of their existence, but knew not of their magic. I was led to believe they were more like wild animals, not civil beings."

With a twinkle in his eyes Kerszon smiled at Tynae.

"Gladly, My Lady, but first," Kerszon looked at his guests, "everyone, please help yourselves, enjoy," he insisted in his jovial tone.

Everyone happily did as instructed and began serving themselves.

Béo leaned toward Tynae. "What would you like to eat, My Lady?" he asked quietly.

The warm air from his spoken words danced lightly over her skin. The sensation sent such a jolt through Tynae she almost fell out of her chair. Slowly she turned to face Béo.

He was forced to look at the floor when he saw the hunger in her eyes. It was evident that what she craved was not food.

Heart pounding like thunder, Tynae was certain the entire room could hear it. Taking a deep breath, Tynae pulled herself together. "It all looks so good." She eyed the food. "I will definitely have some of the hog, you choose the rest." She gave Béo a scorching look.

Turning his attention toward the feast upon the table, Béo put a plate together for Tynae with an array of different foods.

"Mmm," Tynae took her plate. "Thank you, this looks fantastic."

Kerszon smiled. Everyone now served; he was ready to begin his story. "Let's see, where shall I begin?" Kerszon mused. "I suppose the basics would do best. The Nanic are only happy when serving others. They do this by choice, not by force or imprisonment. They belong to themselves. They are not owned and they will not allow themselves to be mistreated or abused. While they may look different from you and me, they are exactly the same. They have feelings and emotions. They bleed, fall in love, have children, and die," Kerszon explained. "So when the people, particularly King Romgor, started treating them as slaves they attempted to leave those whom they served. This did not go over well. People thought themselves to be the 'masters' of the Nanic and began killing entire Nanic families."

The food was as delicious as it looked and smelled. Tynae ate slowly, listening intently.

"News of the murders spread swiftly across the countryside. When the surviving Nanics learned of their slain brethren, they unanimously decided to cut all ties with humans." Kerszon paused taking a bite of food and sip of wine. "Their objective was to return to their homeland, Firvy. King Romgor had other plans. Enraged that *his* servants were revolting against him, he decided to kill every last one of them. Discovering the Nanic's plan, Romgor blocked every possible passage from Tuvarda, ordering that all Nanics be killed on the spot. That's when Vesic, the leader of the Nanics, sought asylum with us here in Calai. Together we devised a plan to smuggle the surviving Nanics out of Tuvarda. We managed to pull it off without any more losses and they've been here ever since. They are quite happy I might add." Kerszon grinned, taking a sip of wine.

Tynae wrinkled her brow. "King Romgor? He ruled over two hundred years ago. Did you personally help the Nanics?" she asked, slightly perplexed.

A sly smile crossed Kerszon's face. "Ay, My Lady, I did indeed."

Tynae smiled back. She wanted so badly to ask Kerszon how old he was, but thought better of it, asking a different question. "How did you get the Nanics out of Tuvarda without detection?" she asked. "The fortification that now surrounds Tuvarda was anew two hundred years ago. It's impenetrable to this very day. Even if you could get in, the city is always overflowing with soldiers and spies." Tynae smiled at Kerszon, "Clearly you did get in, and out. Do tell how you accomplished this, Chief," she urged, bright-eyed.

Kerszon's grin broadened. "It really wasn't all that difficult to be perfectly honest. We are a bit more skilled in the art of magic than most, and have the ability to temporarily control the thoughts, feelings, and actions of others," he said matter-of-factly. "This is a prowess we do not like to use often, but when necessary we do what we must...but I'm jumping ahead of myself; let me back up a touch." Kerszon took a bite of meat then continued his tale while Tynae listened spellbound.

"Vesic was in search of a place to hide himself and his fellow Nanics. He approached a church in hopes of finding sanctuary. They of course turned him away. Romgor had decreed anyone caught helping the Nanics would be put to death immediately. As Vesic left the church, the last of his fleeting hopes obliterated, an older priest stepped out from an unseen passage. Motioning for Vesic to follow him, the priest led him outside. Once outside, the priest spoke quickly and in hushed tones. He told Vesic of a disguised entrance that led to a secret labyrinth beneath the church. No-one ever asked the priest why he seemed to be the only one that knew about these tunnels, or how the tunnels came to be, they were just grateful for his help. Traveling only at night, cloaked in darkness, all the surviving Nanics successfully made their way to the maze under Tuvarda." Kerszon paused taking another bite of food and sip of wine.

Tynae used the opportunity to slip in a question. "Where did the tunnels lead?"

"The maze is said to be vast and is presumed to span beneath more than half the city. Alas, it had only the one discreet doorway. We know there must have been a purpose to the maze, but we can only speculate as to what it may have been."

"What happened next?" Tynae asked riveted to her seat.

"Unfortunately, shortly after the Nanics took up shelter under the church; Romgor's men started patrolling the area of the forest where the hatchway was concealed. The Nanics became trapped within the tunnels. The good news is that neither Romgor, nor any of his men ever discovered the Nanics sanctuary."

Tynae ate slowly, engrossed in every word of Kerszon's fascinating tale.

"One of the tunnels led directly to a small hatch within the church, barely big enough for a loaf of bread. The priest that had told Vesic of the labyrinth would leave food there for the Nanics, but there were so many of them that the food was never enough. Without the ability to go out and hunt, they would soon starve to death. Vesic did the only thing he could. Risking his life, he sent a message to me." Kerszon took a bite of food. "Time was scarce. The Archimagi and I quickly devised a plan then set off to Tuvarda. We entered the city as travelers, traders, peasants, and even animals. Once inside the city walls, I met up with Vesic at the church where he and the rest of the Nanics hid."

Tynae hung on Kerszon's every word.

"We told them of our plan, explaining how we would transfigure some of them into children or animals. For others, we would make them invisible and put them into our carts. Delighted by what we proposed, one by one, we got each and every Nanic out of Tuvarda. Some of us took the shape of hawks, eagles, and owls, turning the Nanics into mice, squirrels, and hares. You understand, anything that would be considered fare for such large birds of prey. Carefully we flew them to safety." Kerszon took a bite of bread.

Tynae stared. "You did this in broad daylight?"

"We did."

"How did you get the guards away from the doorway?"

"We didn't," Kerszon grinned. "They, shall we say, took a bit of a nap."

"Oh," Tynae chuckled. "How many Nanic were there?"

"Over ten thousand."

"Really?! Please continue."

"Well, we turned others into goats, sheep, and cattle. This allowed us to lead quite a few out at one time. By night fall we had rescued every Nanic from Tuvarda. We brought them to Calai, allowing them respite and sustenance. I spoke with Vesic and told him that if he and the other Nanics wanted to return to Firvy, we would escort them there. If they wished to stay in Calai, we would safeguard them for as long as they remained."

"Did any of them leave?" Tynae asked.

"None. Not at that time, anyway." Kerszon lifted his goblet taking a long sip of wine, his eyes bright as he watched the fascination play on Tynae's face.

Enthralled by the story Tynae's brows furrowed. "If they have children and they've been here for hundreds of years wouldn't there be...well, a lot of them by now?"

The Chief laughed. "Yes, My Lady, but there is plenty of room here in Calai. To this day we have thousands of acres that remain uninhabited. While it is true that most of them did choose to stay here, there were a fair few that returned to Firvy eventually. The older Nanics generally return to Firvy in their twilight years," Kerszon explained. "If and when they choose to return to their homeland we personally escort them back. Firvy is not a desirable place for humans, or any other living creature for that matter, to inhabit. And because all Nanic's are believed to be extinct no-one ever bothers them."

"Is Vesic still here in Calai?" Tynae asked.

"Ay," Kerszon nodded, "he is."

"Might I meet him someday?" she asked with fascination.

Kerszon smiled. "Of course, I'm certain his entire clan would love to meet you."

The rest of the evening was filled with simple conversation and laughter.

Hours passed and it was getting late. Many of the Archimagi started to excuse themselves for the evening.

Tynae used this to her advantage. She was dying to get out of there so she and Béo could be alone. "Chief, the meal was fabulous and the company superb, but I am getting a bit drowsy. I hope we can do this again," Tynae smiled.

Kerszon beamed. "Yes, the hour is getting late, and yes, we will most certainly do this again soon. We still have much to learn about each other." Taking Tynae's hand, Kerszon kissed it.

She curtsied.

"May I extend an offer to you, Tynae?" Kerszon asked.

She smiled. "By all means, Chief."

"Your new abilities, would you like to sharpen them?"

Tynae lit up. "Absolutely."

"I know that over the years you have become quite accomplished with the sword."

Tynae shot Béo a sideways glance.

"Okay, so most everyone except for me knew that you were skilled with a sword," Béo admitted.

Kerzon laughed. "Would you like to add hand-to-hand to your bag of tricks?"

"Indeed I would!" Tynae replied enthusiastically.

"Wonderful." Kerszon grinned. "Béo, I would like for you to introduce Tynae to Demric when the new week begins."

Béo nodded. "Yes, Father."

"Chief?" Tynae said.

"Yes, sunshine?"

"When might I meet Zandore?"

Kerszon thought about it. "How does next week sound?"

"I think my schedule is fairly open," Tynae said playfully.

"I'll see to it then." Kerszon smiled. "Will you be joining us tomorrow at the game?"

"Absolutely, I can't wait," she said excitedly.

"Fantastic, you'll be sitting with me. Béo, you can drop her here before you leave, can't you?"

"Of course." Béo grinned at Tynae.

Béo and Tynae each thanked Kerszon for a lovely evening then bid him farewell.

"Sleep well. We shall see you both tomorrow."

Chapter 34
Souls Intertwined

"Love is, above all else, the gift of oneself."
~Jean Anouilh

As the chamber door closed behind them, Béo grabbed Tynae's hand and they were off. Running and giggling as they went like a couple of adolescents through the corridors.

Because of the late hour, there was no-one about. They'd run through five different passageways before Béo stopped. Grabbing Tynae around the waist, he pulled her tight, pressing his lips hard against hers. They moved in unison, their passion raging.

Standing on her tip toes, Tynae wrapped her arms around Béo's neck.

Their bodies were on fire.

"Tynae wait…" Béo said breathlessly.

Refusing to stop, Tynae grabbed a fistful of hair, pulling him back to her.

"Wait please…" Béo begged, ardently kissing her between words. "We have...to stop...if...someone...sees...us."

Tynae pulled back slightly. "I don't know what it is that you do to me! I just can't help myself." She eyed his chest, running her hand over it. "But you're right, of course. Let's get back to Vu'tella."

With one last kiss they set off.

"Can we run?" Tynae asked hopefully.

Chuckling, Béo shook his head. "Patience is not one of your strong suits is it?" he teased.

Grabbing each others hands, they were off in a flash and back in Vu'tella in a matter of minutes.

Leading Béo straight to her bedchamber, Tynae closed and locked the door behind them.

Turning her full attention on Béo, she looked like a lioness ready to pounce on her prey.

Only a few steps away Béo threw his hands up, "Tynae, wait."

His request exasperated her. "What *now*?" she asked peevishly.

Béo studied the floor beneath his feet. "We can't," he confided in devoutly hushed tones.

"Excuse me?" Tynae questioned incredulously.

"It's not that I don't want to…" Béo raised his head looking at Tynae. He had a fire in his eyes that was unmistakable. "You have *no* idea…" he breathed then dropped his head, resuming his inspection of the floor and sighing, "But we can't."

"You said that already," Tynae reminded him. "Why not? All these mixed signals are very disorienting. I feel like my head is spinning out of control. I don't even know what emotions I'm supposed to be feeling…mad, sad, hurt, or maybe just insane. Am I reading you wrong? Are you even interested in me *that way*?"

"I'm interested in you in *every* possible way." Taking a few steps forward, Béo closed the gap between them, running his hands over her arms. "It's your virtue," he said sincerely. "Remember?"

The expression on Tynae's face went totally blank then she doubled over with laughter.

"I'm serious," he asserted.

Taking a deep breath, Tynae pulled herself together, "To hell with my *virtue*, Béo! I realized something after *dying* the other day. Life is short...well it might be anyway. My point is; you just don't know when you might be taken from this place. If I had died, I would never have known love nor passion…I've never felt like this for anyone and I no longer want to take life for granted." She ran her hand lovingly over Béo's cheek. "I want to live this life to its fullest." Looking at Béo with pure love and understanding Tynae sighed. Taking him by the hand, she led Béo over to the couch where they sat down. "I don't want to do this…just to do it," she explained as she agilely climbed on top of Béo's lap, her knees on either side of his thighs. Tenderly taking Béo's face in her hands she looked deep into his eyes. "I am irreversibly, incontrovertibly, and most absolutely, in love with *you*."

Béo ran his hands over Tynae's bare back. "I love you, Tynae, I have for years. If this is what you want…I just think we should wait…like I said before…I don't know if my father will condone us being romantically involved. I would not feel right pretending that you are just my *friend* when we're among others." Béo's words were pained.

"Béo, I'm alright with us being *friends* when were not in this room. It's the way it will have to be for now. Stop denying me and love me." Tynae implored with pleading eyes that burned into Béo.

That was the end of their discussion.

With eyes ablaze Béo grinned. Shaking his head he sighed. "You're going to be the death of me, you know that, right?" he teased lightly. Sliding his hands into Tynae's hair Béo removed the pins holding it in place, allowing her long hair to cascade down her back. Seizing a fist full of hair, Béo pulled Tynae to him. His lips molded hungrily to hers.

There was no stopping this time.

Tynae's mouth explored Béo's body eagerly. Kissing along his jaw line until her lips found his ear; she grazed his lobe with her teeth. Seductively she slid her tongue down his neck, nibbling and kissing every inch of him.

Maintaining his grip on her hair, Béo pulled Tynae's head back. She was a puppet in his hands. Her neck fully exposed, Béo kissed her throat.

Slowly raising her head Tynae gazed longingly into Béo's gray-blue eyes.

Béo's mouth moved slowly back up the column of Tynae's throat, teasing every inch of flesh his lips touched.

Reaching Tynae's lips, he seized them with a virility that set her ablaze. Their lips moved in perfect unison, searing fire pulsating through their bodies.

Pulling Tynae tight against his chest Béo stood up.

Instinctively Tynae wrapped her legs around Béo's waist as he walked.

Reaching the bed, he carefully set her on the floor.

Grabbing hold of Béo's tunic, Tynae pulled it over his head tossing it aside. Tynae gazed at Béo, devouring every inch of his body with her eyes.

Slowly Tynae walked around Béo, sliding her fingers over his warm flesh.

Closing his eyes he drank in her delicate touch. *Oh god...*

Standing back in front of Béo, Tynae wrapped her arms around his waist pulling him tight against her. Looking into his eyes Tynae slid her fingers softly down Béo's back. Slowly her fingers found their way to the front of his body. Leaning forward, she kissed his hard body.

Turning, Tynae gave Béo an inviting look as she crawled to the middle of the bed like a seductive tigress. Beckoning him with the wave of her finger, her eyes had an unmistakable hunger.

Fortunately Béo was in command over his urges or Tynae's clothes would have been ripped to shreds by now…Béo crawled across the bed to get to Tynae.

Who was the hunter, who was the prey?

When he reached her he went straight for her neck. Lacing his fingers in her hair he pulled her head back, gently exposing her delicious flesh.

Closing her eyes, Tynae turned her head giving Béo maximum access. He kissed his way up her neck until he reached her ear. "I love you, Tynae," he whispered, his hands gliding over every inch of her exquisite form. Everything about this woman was sheer perfection.

An audible exhale was her only response.

Clothes removed, Béo hovered over Tynae's beautiful form. The current pulsating between their bodies surged and flowed like ocean waves crashing against rocks.

Tynae's sweet scent overwhelmed every one of Béo senses. His body flooded with desire, dancing dangerously close to the edge of control.

Bodies and lips pressed together, pure love coursed through Béo's heart causing it to explode with light, shattering all boundaries and barriers. The sensation was breathtaking. Béo's gaze burned deep into Tynae. He was full of yearning, yet still he waited. "Are you sure," he whispered.

"Positive," she purred.

Béo smiled softly. This was all the encouragement he needed. "Mmm, I'm not sure where to start," he admitted eyeing every inch of her body. "You're so tiny."

Tynae gasped then let out a chuckle, punching Béo in the arm. "You never tell a woman she's *tiny* when you're gawking at her chest. How rude. What if I said that while I was looking at…?" Tynae eyed Béo's groin region, "well you get the picture."

It took Béo a second to realize what he had said. "Oh, I didn't mean it that way."

"I know," Tynae grinned. "And by the way," her gaze wandered below Béo's waist again. "Kudos," she purred.

Béo grinned proudly.

"I didn't mean…You're not tiny there." Béo clarified, admiring Tynae's ample breasts. "Those are perfect, and far from being tiny. It's just that you're so petite, I don't want to hurt you." Béo explained, running his hands lovingly over Tynae's velvety skin.

"I'm far from being a delicate flower," Tynae said, "You know that."

Béo did know that. Tynae had undeniable strength, cunning smarts, and damn if she didn't have *all* the right parts. Leaning down Béo kissed Tynae with ravenous desire. He had never wanted anything more than he wanted her at that very moment. Settling himself between Tynae's warm thighs, Béo kissed a path down her neck. Using his entire mouth, he kissed a trail to her firm, yet supple breasts. His voracious mouth and warm tongue pulled quiet moans from Tynae. Béo continued kissing Tynae, teasing her with his lips, teeth and tongue.

As he ran his hands over her yearning body, caressing her, she gasped. Arching her back she let out a low moan, sounding like a purr.

This was the most hypnotic music Béo had ever heard.

Béo continued his journey down Tynae's tight abdomen, kissing, licking, and nibbling as he went. Reaching her thighs he lightly ran his fingers along the inside. Caressing her flesh he gently nudged her legs apart.

Tynae inhaled deep with anticipation. "Easy, lover," she whispered.

His tongue and fingers teased Tynae's body lovingly. Her scent, her taste, her sheer beauty was almost more than he could bear.

Tynae writhed and moaned at Béo's touch.

He nearly came undone over her uninhibited response to him. Tynae's thighs began to shake and Béo needed more.
Bringing Tynae to soaring heights her moans of pleasure turned to cries of passion, echoing through Vu'tella and weaving into Béo's soul. He'd never heard such a beautiful sound.
Tynae shivered as waves of pleasure consumed her body.

Breathless, Tynae looked at Béo, who wore a smug grin. "Well aren't we the arrogant one?" she taunted.

Béo leaned over Tynae, his haughty grin still in-tact. "Hell yeah, is *my* lady not a well pleasured lady?"

Tynae grinned wickedly. "Hell yes I am," she complimented. "Would you like a round of applause?" she teased.

Béo kissed Tynae passionately. "All I need is you."

Tynae looked at Béo dreamily. "I'm all yours, Béo. I always have been."

"Are you certain?" Béo asked, his body hovering slightly over hers.

Slowly sliding her hands over Béo's form, Tynae reached the small of Béo's back pulling him to her, raising her hips to meet his.

"Yes," she moaned, arching as their hearts, minds, and bodies merged into one.

Béo slowly slid into Tynae until her moist warmth sheathed him fully. Overflowing with ecstasy, Béo let out a low throaty growl.

Tynae moaned as her eyes slid shut.

Their bodies pressed tight against one another as they made love for the very first time.

The passion, the love, the completeness they felt was other-worldly. They made each other whole.

The pair spent the night hopelessly entwined in each other's souls.

Chapter 35
Insubordination

"She had an unequalled gift of squeezing big mistakes
into small opportunities"
~Henry James

Dawn approached far too quickly.

"Tynae?" Béo spoke softly. "Are you awake?"

"Mmm, yes," she murmured, lying blissfully on Béo's warm chest listening to the rhythmic beating of his heart.

"We need to get dressed."

"I know." Tynae sighed, propping herself onto her elbow. Staring into Béo's eyes, she ran her hand over his chest while he gently slid his fingers over her back. "Is something wrong?" Tynae asked. "You seem a bit distant."

"No, not at all…well, maybe."

"Talk to me, please," Tynae requested softly.

"I love you, Tynae, I want you to be mine forever, but I don't think we'll be allowed to be together. At least not as anything more than *friends,* as far as the rest of the world is concerned."

"Why do you think that?"

"Tynae…there are things which I cannot tell you. It's not that I don't want to, but..." Béo stopped speaking, closing and opening his eyes as if in slow motion, carefully contemplating his next words.

The lovers stared into each others eyes, souls connected.

Béo tenderly ran his hand over Tynae's face. "As future chief of Calai I'm just not able to. Do you understand what I'm trying to say?" Frustration fused with Béo's words.

As the once future queen of Pathrow, Tynae understood exactly what Béo meant. Even though she would never become queen, now that she had been *killed,* Pathrow still held many secrets she would never divulge to anyone, not even Béo. Tynae smiled softly. "Béo, I do understand, trust me. I will not push you for an explanation. Let's just enjoy the time we have with each other and if a day comes that we must go our separate ways, well," Tynae swallowed hard, "I guess we'll deal with it then." Leaning forward, she kissed Béo lightly on the lips. "Let's get dressed and get some sleep."

They changed into their appropriate sleeping attire, and Béo took his *proper* place atop the coverlet.

Hand in hand, they fell asleep.

Standing in their garden, Ryedin waited for his *queen*. Tynae loved the thought of being *his* queen.

Neither one spoke, they just fell into each others arms, allowing their lips and hearts to entwine.

"Hello," she breathed when they finally came up for air.

"Hello, my angel."

"No forest today?" Tynae asked.

"Not today." Ryedin held out his hand, "Shall we?"

Tynae put her hand in his, and the two walked around the garden grounds. "So, you're going to a vorbix match and you'll be learning hand to hand combat," Ryedin said cheerfully. "You are in for an exciting week."

"I know, I can't wait," Tynae beamed.

"You'll love vorbix," he said enthusiastically, "it's the best game ever."

"Of course you think that," she grinned. "You really like playing don't you?"

Ryedin smiled brightly, "I love it. When I'm out on the field it's the most freeing feeling. Kind of how you feel when you walk through the forest, you know, no etiquette, no bowing. Okay, it's a little different, everyone wants you to kick the other team's arse," Ryedin laughed. "But the feeling of just letting everything go is exactly the same. During a game there is no bowing or royal etiquette and rank is out the window…everyone is equal on that field."

"The masks we wear to please everyone." Tynae chuckled, "And it's the simplest things in life that truly make us the happiest," she mused.

"If you'd like I can train you here in *our* world," Ryedin offered.

Tynae's brow furrowed, "Train me, how?"

"Hand-to-hand," Ryedin clarified. "Or anything for that matter; the bow, bow on horse back, whatever your heart desires, my angel."

"Will it help me in the real world?"

"Of course, everything you learn here you will remember forever."

"That would be great. Once we're done with hand-to-hand, I'd love to learn the bow," she said eagerly.

"Then it shall be, My Lady," Ryedin said with a slight bow.

"Can I wear…" Tynae looked down at the long gown she wore. "Well, anything other than a long dress?"

"Not a problem." Ryedin smiled slyly, "Would you like to start your training today?"

Tynae's eyes lit up. "Could we?"

"Certainly," he grinned. "Close your eyes."

Tynae eyed Ryedin skeptically, "Okay."

The few seconds Tynae had her eyes shut seemed uneventful.

"Open your eyes."

Tynae looked around, nothing appeared different. "Why did you have me close my eyes?"

Ryedin gestured toward her body.

Glancing down, Tynae flinched when she saw her new attire, "Oh my!"

"Is this more of what you had in mind?"

Tynae laughed. "I'm not sure what I had in mind, but clearly it's what *you* had in mind." She now wore fitted black leather trousers, a short black shirt that clung tight to her figure, a white corset over her mid section and long black leather boots.

"I can change it, if you'd like."

"No, I like it," Tynae admitted, "a lot." She remembered how she had ogled Béo in his tan trousers just a few hours earlier. "Besides, I'm sure there's a bit of payback here."

Ryedin just smiled. "Let's get started then." He began by showing Tynae the basics; blocks, punches, and a few kicks. "You're really good. Want to get even better?" he teased.

"Of course."

"Do you trust me?"

"With my soul."

Taking a leather strap from around his waist, Ryedin tied it around Tynae's eyes. He proceeded to teach her how to feel his energy and how to block him before he was able to touch her.

Twilight soon came and with it the enchanted fog.

Ryedin looked at Tynae.

"I know, I know, it's time for me to leave," she said gloomily.

Ryedin took her in his arms. "Did you have fun?"

"I did."

"We'll pick up where we left off tomorrow night. Have fun at the game. Oh, and star gazing," he added.

"Star gazing?"

"You'll see." Ryedin stroked her cheek. "I love you, angel, so much."

Ryedin's words made her soul ache. "I love you, too."

The couple held each other, arms tight around one another, souls entwined. "You make me whole," he whispered.

"And you me."

Ryedin kissed her forehead, "Goodnight, angel, sleep sweet."

"Goodnight, my prince. Dream of me," she said with a peaceful smile.

"I always do," he replied, "I always do."

The black fog faded and Tynae woke briefly. She was in Béo's arms once again, although she was fairly certain she had never left them. Lying there staring at him, she became confident

that life just couldn't get any better. Closing her eyes, she faded
back to sleep.

Awaking the next morning Tynae was thankful to see Béo
lying beside her. He'd become her rock, providing a sense of
security she had never felt before.

Rolling onto her side, Tynae was startled to see O'leana
standing in her room.

Tynae's venomous glare made it more than clear to O'leana
that she had greatly overstepped her boundaries.

Handmaidens do not enter into their mistress' room
uninvited.

Tynae was far too bothered at this point to go back to sleep.

"Ready my bath," Tynae snarled.

"Yes, My Lady," O'leana's voice faltered. "I shall have it
ready momentarily."

"Let Lord Béo sleep, he's got a game today and needs his
rest," Tynae growled scornfully, climbing out of bed.

"My Lady I…I am so sorry," O'leana stammered over her
words, following Tynae into the lavatory.

Spinning around to face O'leana, Tynae stared fiercely at her
maid. Tynae chewed on her cheek, fighting not to say the harsh
words she was aching to spew. "O'leana, I didn't get much sleep
last night. My dreams kept waking me…" she lied. "I just want
some quiet, please." Tynae managed to keep her tone to a low
roar.

Once disrobed, Tynae sank into the hot water. O'leana,
Koralie, and Sireeon did their jobs without another word.

When Tynae came out of the lavatory Béo was gone. She
was confident he would return shortly. Walking over to her
wardrobe, Tynae looked thoroughly through the clothes that had
been placed within it. Now, slightly calmer, Tynae was able to
speak with a monotone voice. "I would like to make a request,"
she said in a faintly harsh tone.

"Anything, My Lady." O'leana plainly wanted to appease her mistress.

"I will be engaging in hand-to-hand combat and need clothing that will allow me to move easily. I want something like a skirt; only it will have short trousers attached underneath and the top needs to be thicker than these small ones. Black should work nicely."

"As you wish, My Lady," O'leana bowed.

Tynae turned her full attention on O'leana, looking her dead in the eyes, "One more thing."

O'leana swallowed hard. She must have known what was coming. "Yes, Majesty?"

"Why were you watching us?" Tynae asked crossly.

O'leana shook her head. "I'm not sure why I did it, My Lady. I suppose I'm just..." O'leana stopped, clearly unsure if she should finish her sentence.

"Go on," Tynae pressed tolerantly.

"Master Béo, My Lady, I just don't want to see him get hurt. He is still so young." The maid gave Tynae a soft smile. "But I can see how much you love each other." O'leana looked shamefully at the floor. "I am truly sorry, Majesty."

Tynae was taken aback by O'leana's observation. *Are our feelings for each other that apparent?* She wondered.

Tynae stood tall, all but ignoring the accusation. "I can appreciate your concern for your future leader, and I realize that you do not know me. After all, I am nothing more than a stranger in your world. But you should trust Lord Béo to be intelligent enough to know who and what is right for him," Tynae said indignantly.

O'leana continued to stare at the floor. "Of course you are correct, My Lady."

Tynae remained calm, yet wanted to get her message across, leaving no room for misinterpretation. "Never," she said sternly, "enter my room to spy on me ever again. If you feel that there is a problem, talk with me directly. Do I make myself clear?"

Tynae's words were smooth and decisive. This was not an order, or even a command; it was a decree that was to be followed from this day forward, no questions asked.

Shamefaced, O'leana's gaze lingered on the floor. "Yes, Majesty, I understand completely. It will never happen again." Remorse was evident in her voice.

"Thank you," Tynae said, satisfied with O'leana's response. "Now, please help me choose something appropriate to wear for this afternoon's match."

After rifling through the wardrobe for only a few moments, O'leana extracted a remarkable peacock blue outfit. The material on the skirt was sheer, flowing, and jagged.

Tynae was pleased with O'leana's selection. "This should do nicely. What does the top look like?"

The top had thin straps. A long piece of sheer material was attached to the straps and ran across her back, almost like a cape. Today's jewelry was mainly sapphires. In Tynae's hair they placed a small fan of peacock plumes resembling a crown. Once she was dressed, Tynae looked in the mirror.

"Perfect." Although her voice remained flat, it was no longer harsh.

Once her maids had finished, Tynae wanted to be left alone until Béo returned.

"Thank you once again for your assistance. Now if you would, please bring in breakfast then show yourselves out and close the door behind you," Tynae said impatiently, her bad mood still clearly intact.

"Enjoy the game today, My Lady."

"Thank you, Sireeon," Tynae replied, her back to the door.

Hearing the door shut, Tynae turned around. Gasping, her heart about leapt out of her chest when she saw Béo standing there.

Once she was able to dislodge her heart from her throat and begin breathing again, she ran into Béo's arms. The warmth and security she felt when he held her was so comforting. She wanted him to hold her for all eternity, never letting her go.

"Good morning, love." Béo kissed her forehead. "What's the matter?"

Tynae closed her eyes, inhaling his distinct scent. "Nothing," she exhaled. "I just missed you." Tynae had never been one to burden others with her issues and she was not about to start now. Besides, she had dealt with the problem. As far as she was concerned, it was now a matter of the past.

Looking up into Béo's soothing blue eyes, Tynae couldn't help but move forward.

Lips fused, Béo slid his tongue between Tynae's lips.

This was more than she could handle at the moment. "Mmm," she sighed, gently pulling away.

Béo laughed lightly. "What?"
"I'm still feeling the amazing sensations from last night and that's dangerous right now. If we don't leave this room in the next hour people will truly be talking." She chuckled, "Not that they aren't already...let's eat."

"Sounds good to me, I'm starving."

Now that Béo was back, Tynae quickly returned to her cheerful self.

They were in the middle of their meal when a knock came at the door.

"Enter," Tynae called.
It was O'leana. "My Lady, I just wanted to see if you needed anything."
Tynae raised a brow. "No...Thank you."
Bowing, O'leana departed without another word.
Béo looked at Tynae perplexed. "I've never heard you speak to anyone in such a bitter tone."
"I think she's suspicious of us," Tynae informed then took a drink of juice.
"Why do you say that?" Béo asked, serving himself a second helping of breakfast.
She sighed, "Because she was in the room this morning, spying on us. You were still asleep." Tynae's tone did not depict

the true anger she felt over the situation. "I had a few words with her."

"Would you like me to say something, or have her replaced?" Béo took a bite of food.

Tynae shook her head. "No, she may just be following your father's orders," she said patiently. "We'll just have to be careful with our actions when others are around, that's all. We already knew that was the way it was going to be." Nibbling on some fruit, she gave Béo a half smile.

Béo took a bite of his eggs. "You're a tolerant woman."

"Right," Tynae said derisively. "I don't think O'leana would agree with you on that matter."

"So, about last night..." Tynae grinned taking a bite of her own eggs. "Ordinarily I never ask about age, but you are far more than just a friend so I must ask. Exactly how old is your father and more importantly, how old are you?" she asked wearing an amused smile.

Chapter 36
Heartache and Loss…Happiness Found

"The greatest griefs are those we cause ourselves."
~Sophocles

While Béo explained, Tynae ate her meal.

"Well, for our people we are both considered rather young. My father is 430 and I'm 157. My father was the youngest person to ever be elected Chief in the history of the Greer. He was only 177. I guess that would equate to someone in their late 30's in your world. We are fully mature by the time we reach the age of 20, but we live for so long that our elders do not consider us the least bit 'wise' until we reach 150. I have no idea how they came up with that number." Taking a bite off his fork, Béo grinned at Tynae's bemused expression.

"That's…wow." Tynae set her cup down. "Are you immortal?"

"No, and yes. We don't die from old age, but we can be killed."

"Do you only marry other Greer?" Tynae probed.

Béo grinned. "No, as you now know we are able to transfer some of our abilities to others and long life is one capability we can share with another. Although it's not something we do often." Béo helped himself to yet another serving of food. "Would you like some more?" Béo held up a bowl of fruit.

"Please. What happened to your mother?"

Béo sighed, "She died when I was 34. She took me to Pallor to meet…" Béo's brows knitted together. "You know, I'm not really sure who they were. They spoke a different language so I didn't understand a word they said. Pass the juice please."

Tynae held out the pitcher. "Here you go."

"Thank you. Anyway on the way home my mother fell. Under normal circumstances something like a fall would never have been an issue, but for this particular trip she'd insisted that none of her Archimagi travel with us. When she fell she hit her head on the edge of a jagged rock. Though I was only a few months away from my 35ᵗʰ birthday, my magic had not yet manifested itself. Unable to heal her, I carried her back to Calai as fast as I could. But it was too late," Béo said sadly.

"I'm so sorry." Tynae reached out touching Béo's hand. "Would it have made a difference if you had been 35?"

"I keep forgetting, you don't know a lot about us. Yes, it would have made all the difference in the world. We, the Greer that is, don't come into our powers until we're 35."

"What sort of powers do you receive at that time?

"Well we all have the same abilities to start with. We can heal, fight, and manipulate feelings to some extent, read minds, control the elements, you name it. Yet as my father said, we generally excel in a particular area." Béo took a bite of eggs. "The thing is, even though we specialize in one area, we can still use our magic for anything we choose; healing, fighting, it just won't be as strong as our specific skill," Béo explained.

"Understandable," Tynae nodded. "But why didn't your mother heal herself?" she asked with a confused look.

Smiling, Béo shook his head. "You really don't miss a thing do you? She was a Gridel. While they have many strong powers of their own, healing is not one of them. They age much slower than humans, but their life span is not quite as long as ours. My mother was only 149, which once again is quite young, relatively speaking. It was because of this that my father had not yet *made* her a Greer. Ideally the transition would have occurred the next year when she turned 150."

The obvious question was weighing on Tynae's mind, *how exactly does one get* made *into a Greer?* She chose to save that question for another time.

"So your father, he never remarried?"

"No, not yet, and I don't know that he ever will. To this day he has not forgiven himself for my mother's death."

Tynae cast an inquiring glance at Béo. "Why? He didn't kill her."

"No he didn't," Béo said gloomily. "But he still blames himself. I hope that someday he will allow himself to fall in love once more. Forever is a long time to go without a soul mate." Béo sounded heartbroken.

The mere thought of such a life made Tynae's soul ache. Staring at the table, she asked her next question. "So what about you? There are many beautiful women in Calai. Do none of them interest you?" Tynae was terrified of what Béo's answer might be. Nevertheless she needed to know exactly where she stood with him.

Béo laughed. "You don't get it," he said. "As far as the Greer are concerned I've only recently come of age. And yes there is a stunningly gorgeous woman in Calai I've been in love with for many years." Béo placed his hands on Tynae's cheeks, "You."

He stroked her face, his gaze piercing her soul. Their connection was undeniable.

"You are the first woman I have ever been interested in and the only one I ever want to be with," he explained lovingly.

Tynae froze, "Are you telling me…I mean…was last night…was I your...?"

Béo blushed slightly, "One and *only* as far as I'm concerned. I would gladly spend eternity with you and you alone." Béo hunched his shoulders meekly. "Had you…you know…was I?" Béo couldn't get his words out either.

Reassuringly, Tynae placed her hand on Béo's leg, looking directly into his beautiful eyes. "Only you, Béo," she lovingly confessed, smiling. It was all she could do. Tynae knew she wanted to spend the rest of her life with the man sitting beside her.

Plate now empty, Tynae stretched. "Mmm, I'm full. How about you?"

Béo pushed his chair back. "I've had more than my share," he said patting his stomach. "Are you ready for your first vorbix match?" He grinned, getting up.

"Yes!" Tynae beamed. "I can hardly wait," she said excitedly, standing. Tynae glanced at Béo as they walked toward the door. "Do you think we'll have time for you to show me more of the city today?"

Béo stopped just shy of the door. "I doubt it. The game normally lasts several hours then afterwards the two teams dine together. You know, good sportsmanship and all. I suspect we'll be out late, but day after next definitely. After you meet with Demric we'll have loads of free time." Looking at Tynae affectionately, Béo stepped closer to her. He kissed her tenderly on the lips.

Tynae's heart leapt as Béo slid his fingers over her bare shoulders.

The pair unwillingly parted.
"Ready for me to take you to father's?"
Tynae swallowed the butterflies that suddenly erupted. "Yes."

Arriving at Kerszon's door, Béo gave Tynae a quick kiss. Walking inside, they saw Kerszon emerge from a door on the opposite side of the room.

"My two favorite people," Kerszon said with a huge grin. "I was wondering when you were going to arrive."

"Hello," Tynae said slightly nervous.

"I need to get going," Béo leaned forward hugging Tynae. "I'll see you in a bit, my angel," he whispered in her ear. "You're in great company," Béo said walking to the door. "Father has the best seats in Calai."

"Good luck today, Son, not that you need it."

Béo turned back, "Thank you, Father." Winking at Tynae Béo left to join his teammates.

Tynae looked around the room. It seemed quite empty compared to the prior eve.

"Tynae?" Kerszon called.

Tynae turned. Kerszon had just been right beside her. He was gone.

"Up here," he called. Looking up, Tynae saw Kerszon standing above her on a balcony. *How odd, I didn't see that second floor last night.*

Smiling he waived for her to come up. "Why don't you join me?"

"Okay." She looked around for a staircase. *Where are the bloody stairs?*

Kerszon leaned over the railing. With a wave of his hand a dark panel on the wall faded, revealing stone stairs.

Tynae shook her head. "I should have known," she muttered, climbing the circular staircase. At the top was the most elaborate library Tynae had ever seen.

"We have an hour before the game, so I thought I'd show you around," Kerszon told her.

The library consisted of multiple levels. Walls lined with bookshelves, each jam-packed. The level they were on appeared to house maps, charts, log books, and other various writings. Trinkets, from what Tynae could only assume were from around the world, covered numerous tables. A handsome claw foot desk stood resolute in the center of the room.

Spotting a huge telescope on a mezzanine Tynae smiled.

"What?" Kerszon asked.

"That telescope. It's magnificent, but you can't possibly get much use of it down here."

The chief admired his star gazer. "Oh contraire, my dear," he smiled. "The pages of the sky will be open tonight and the moon full. Would you care to join me?"

Tynae was thrilled by his invitation. "Absolutely, but what do you mean *the pages of the sky* will be open?"

Kerszon turned to Tynae. "Have you ever read the stars?"

Tynae was confused. "I don't believe so."

"Then you should really enjoy this. The stars can be read nightly, but there are particular nights that are more auspicious than others. I'll let Béo know. You'll need to arrive shortly before midnight. Will you be able to stay up that late?" Kerszon teased.

Clearly he'd heard about her late night with Béo and his team. It was then that Tynae realized there was nothing that happened in Calai that escaped the chief. "Not a problem."

Tynae's mind wandered to Ryedin and his mention of stargazing. "Does Béo read the stars with you often?"

"Quite, and he rarely misses a full moon."

"That explains it," she muttered softly, now understanding why Ryedin a.k.a. Béo had said something about stargazing.

"What was that?"

"Nothing...I can't wait. I've never looked through a telescope." Tynae turned to Kerszon with an expectant expression. "Can you teach me how to read the stars?"

"Not in one night," Kerszon chuckled. "But I can certainly teach you over time if that's what you desire."

Tynae lit up. "I do."

"I love your zeal." Kerszon grinned. "Then teach you I shall. I need to get changed then we can be on our way. Feel free to look around," he said, walking out of the room.

Tynae was fascinated by all the books. Wandering about the different levels of the library, she found a particular book she absolutely loved. Sitting down she flipped through the pages. The book contained hundreds of sketches of Béo during various stages of his life. Several of the pictures in the first part of the book included a lovely woman, which Tynae assumed was Béo's mother.

"Ah, I see you found my boy's picture book."
Tynae jumped slightly.
"I'm sorry, I didn't mean to startle you."

"It's okay." Tynae closed the book. "He was adorable...Well he still is of course." Suddenly nervous, Tynae ran her hand over the book in her lap. "But you know what I mean," she grinned.

"I do..." Kerszon smiled back. "You look lovely by the way. That color suites you, but I think you could wear a flour sack and make it look good."

Tynae blushed. "Thank you, you look rather dashing yourself."

The chief wore a fawn-colored loin cloth, red cloak, and sandals. A few leather straps adorned his body.

"It's always nice when I can dress casually." Kerszon extended his hand to Tynae.

Tynae set the picture book on a table. Accepting Kerszon's hand, she stood.

"My son is a very lucky man." Kerszon's tone was unfamiliar.

Tynae felt something from the chief's words, but couldn't place it. Perhaps it was sadness or maybe pride. Either way, she let it go.

"Let's be on our way," Kerszon said enthusiastically. "We wouldn't want to miss the pre-game events."

Looking back as they left, Tynae observed the second floor fade from view.

The tunnels were beginning to look familiar to Tynae. At first they'd all looked alike, but she was now noticing small, yet distinct differences.

Walking with Kerszon was an experience all its own. People not only stopped to bow, they completely stepped aside.

Reaching the heart of the city, Tynae and Kerszon headed for the huge double doors carved into the mountainside. Passing the two lakes on either side of the doors, Tynae spotted seven beautiful white swans swimming elegantly. Dozens of water lilies along with hundreds of tiny candles floated atop each glimmering lake.

When they entered the stadium, Tynae expected to go up to the seats as she had the last time she was here. Instead, Kerszon led her down the corridor the players use. Two large guards stood in front of a thick brass door that was divided into four equal parts. Each mascot representing a team was embossed on a quadrant of the door and in the center was a mighty dragon.

The guards opened the door, which led to a small foyer with two additional doors.

Tynae followed Kerszon through the doorway on their left. They where now in a room filled with roses and a white topless carriage sitting upon what appeared to Tynae to be a track made of stone.

Two additional guards stood beside the pristinely white vehicle.

"Pick a color, sunshine," Kerszon gestured to the many pots holding what must have been thousands of flowers.

Spotting a container of purple roses, Tynae's mind flashed back to her last day in Nombin when Xantara had bestowed her with such a rose. "Purple, I should think." Tynae pointed to a bucket in the corner.

"Very well." Kerszon waved his hand and every rose in the room turned purple.

One of the guards opened a small door on the side of the carriage. "After you, My Lady," Kerszon said standing by a short set of stairs leading up to the cart.

Walking up the stairs, Tynae realize the carriage contained a curved seating area that followed the shape of the cart. Huge pillows provided extreme comfort. The vehicle could easily sit ten large warriors. Tynae got comfortable, but didn't understand how they'd be able to watch the game from this enclosed room.

The chief followed, once seated the two guards laid several bunches of roses on the open seats.

"Hang on," Kerszon advised.

"What," Tynae asked.

Kerszon needn't repeat himself—their seat began to move and she grabbed on to the edge.

Tynae remembered seeing a railing that ran around the full length of the stadium. *This must be what runs on that.*

Their cart pushed forward toward a red velvet curtain creating a light breeze, blowing Tynae's hair back.

Kerszon leaned toward Tynae. "Be sure to toss the roses into the crowd."

"Okay." Tynae fastened on a smile as their cart emerged onto the field.

Thousands of people cheered, waving small colorful flags representing the team they supported. Children jumped up and down excitedly, waving at Tynae and Chief Kerszon as they passed. Little boys brandished wooden swords high in the air, while young girls clutched their dollies. Tynae could have sworn the dolls were miniature versions of her, but quickly dismissed that notion.

Picking up an armful of flowers, fortunately thorn free, Tynae began tossing them and waving to the crowd.

Their cart steadily made its way around the amphitheater. It looked nothing like it had when Tynae watched Béo's practice. Mascots representing each team were now on the field, hovering in the appropriate cardinal direction. Tynae tried to see what the mascots were made from. Every one of them was bigger than an elephant and more colorful then a court jester, yet somehow as sheer as a ghost. Each hovered effortlessly above the emerald grass. To the north was a glittering white orb that must have been three meters in diameter. To the south was an extremely colorful gnome. To the east was a huge blazing salamander. Pacing back and forth it occasionally opened its mouth, revealing what looked like a tongue made of lava. To the west was a breathtaking, iridescent undine. And in the center of it all was an enormous golden dragon.

Bright banners covered the arena, basically dividing it into quadrants. One would sit in the section representing the team for which they rooted.

Tynae could not believe the transformation or the innumerable amount of people filling the stadium.

Having made one full revolution around the arena, their cart now slowed.

Kerszon stood up as the vehicle stopped. He opened the little door that had enabled them to get into the carriage, it faced the field.

Tynae could not understand why he would open a door that led at least thirty meters down. *Does he know how to walk on air, too?*

Kerszon looked at Tynae. "I'll be right back, sunshine," he grinned.

Tynae started to say something, but all that came out was a muffled shriek.

The golden dragon from the center the field now hovered beside their cart. It had grown more then twenty times its original size.

Kerszon stepped out of their carriage and onto the dragons back with surprising grace for a man his size.

The enormous dragon flapped its wings, taking flight. Flying above the stadium, the spectators erupted with excitement. Flapping its wings the dragon flew higher, letting out a mighty roar accompanied by an inferno of flames. The crowd hollered for more as the flames transformed into fiery droplets. Falling toward the crowd the shower of fire transformed yet again into golden flowers, raining over the people. After a few flights around the arena the dragon came to rest in the center of the field.

Kerszon waited for the crowd to quiet, which they did without coaxing.

Tynae sat in awe.

The spectators were now quiet as church mice.

Kerszon touched his hand to his throat and the dragon opened its mouth slightly. "Good afternoon." Kerszon's voice echoed as it projected boisterously through the dragon. "And welcome to Calai's sixteen hundred and twenty third vorbix match. The winners of today's match will be moving on to the semifinals."

The crowd cheered, then became quiet once more.

"Today's game is between the Lacertusféuer Salamanders!"

The Salamander fans screamed and clapped for their team. Their mascot pounded around the field, bright red and gold flames flaring up from its body.

"And the Kejanpa' Islithra Dragons!"

The golden dragon Kerszon sat atop opened its mouth wide, letting out an earth shaking roar, blasting an icy blue ball of flame high into the stadium. The ball exploded, showering silver sparks over the entire arena.

Tynae was fairly sure Kerszon's last words were, "Let the game begin." But the crowd was so loud, she couldn't be certain.

Chapter 37
A Fan is Born

"The strength of the group is the strength of the leaders."
~Vince Lombardi

The golden dragon returned the chief to his cart. Shutting the small door, Kerszon took his seat. Tynae watched the dragon resume its previous size.

"Wow!" Tynae turned to the chief, "That was impressive!" she praised, smiling from ear to ear.

Kerszon bowed his head slightly. "Thank you, sunshine, all in a days work." Kerszon pointed to the field. "Here come the warriors...now the real fun begins."

Advancing toward the center of the field were at least one hundred men.

Those aren't the players.

They wore the same uniforms as the guards of Calai, but instead of spears, they carried staves. Each stave was made from what appeared to be clear crystal. The warriors marched in synchronized step, maneuvering around the field until they formed two long rows creating a giant 'X'. In a rhythmic fashion, the men began to pound their staves on the ground. Their crystal staves began to glow, radiating different colors. Maintaining their flawless precision, each man started to spin and toss his stave. The illumination in the stadium dimmed and the 'X' began to move. With each step the men took, the motion of their staves created magnificent waves of color. The 'X' appeared to pulsate in the darkened stadium. Each warrior moved in exact time with one another.

Tynae was mesmerized; she had never seen such accuracy.

The spectators, too, watched in amazement as the perfectly choreographed dance continued.

The finale was breathtaking. The men broke apart, moving until they formed three large interlocking circles. Their staves spun so rapidly they were little more than a blur. With one final and precise movement; the warriors shouted, lunged forward, and pointed their staves toward the center of their circle. A blazing fire erupted from the center of each ring. The men raised their staves, tips ignited, until they pointed skyward again. Blue, white and red fire now ran along the top of each formation. The warriors, each holding his flame high, began moving once more. Looking like organized ants as they moved, their flames sent up dazzling sparks. Each man took his appropriate place in a new formation. Extending their staves in front of them, each warrior added his flame to the man's beside him. The flames grew higher and brighter. When the last man stepped into place he completed a large circle. Adding his stave to the blaze the united flames grew even higher, engulfing the center of the field in an orange inferno. Thunderous bangs began to ring out from unseen drums in the darkness. The flames grew brighter with each beat of the drum until they reached bluish-white. Pulsating, the flames kept rhythm with the beat…beat…beat…of the drums. Drums growing louder, the flames continued getting brighter and higher. At last there came a bright flash…a mighty phoenix, created from the blue flames, rose out of the fire.

The crowd went crazy, applauding and yelling boisterously.

Taking flight, the beautiful creature soared through the stadium while the warriors uniformly pounded their staves on the ground. As the last boom rang out, the fiery phoenix exploded into thousands of flickering butterflies.

The fans hollered and clapped as the warriors departed and the lights came back up.

The stadium had just begun to calm down when it erupted in thunderous applause and earsplitting shouts.

Looking down on the field, Tynae saw players emerging from the tunnel.

Her heart skipped a beat when she spotted Béo leading his team.

Both teams wore flowing black capes.

Béo and his teammates had a golden dragon emblazoned on the back of theirs, and the opposing team's capes had a gleaming red salamander.

Tynae watched the salamanders walk to the goal their mascot guarded. It was then Tynae realized the Dragons, representing center earth and space, had no official goal. She wondered where they would go. Her silent question was quickly answered as Béo's team and their mascot joined the Garder'erdeu Gnomes at the north end of the field, opposite the Salamanders. Tynae was utterly engrossed in every action occurring on the field.

The players removed their capes.

With each team was a little boy. The players handed their capes to the lads. With great pride, the children carried the capes off the field.

All the players wore dark loin cloths that were bare on the sides, soft leather boots and brightly colored sleeveless tunics. Scarlet red was the color for the Salamanders and vivid yellow for the Dragons. Numbers distinguished one player from the other, a black numeral seven was displayed on Béo's back and Jubryi sported the number four. Across their upper chest and over their shoulders, every player wore padding as they had during practice.

Tynae sat riveted to her seat watching the newest members of the game come onto the field.

Two men wearing black britches and milky white tunics were followed closely by two black and white striped animals. Resembling horses, the creatures had wings. One had black wings, the other white. Each had a small silver horn in the middle of its head.

Tynae looked at Kerszon with a bewildered expression. "What are those?" she asked, pointing to the field.

Kerszon chuckled, "The man or the animal?"

Tynae laughed. "Both!"

"Those beautiful creatures, my dear, are equnus'. We have the only existing herd on the planet," Kerszon informed proudly.

"That I know of, anyway. And the men are called zevros. Their job is to insure the game is played fairly by all parties."

"You'll have to tell me about the equnus' some time. They're marvelous creatures."

"Any time you'd like, sunshine, you need only to ask."

Tynae turned her attention back to the players.

The captains, accompanied by two teammates each, walked to the middle of the field where both zevros waited. One zevro spoke to the men. When finished, the captains shook hands and the players returned to their goals.

The zevros, remaining in the center of the field, stood several feet apart facing one another. With arms extended out, the two men began walking in a large circle. Soon a great hole opened in the ground between them.

Tynae's eyes grew wide. *The vortex.*

The zevros walked around the circle a total of three times; this appeared to conclude their ceremony.

Over the top of the gaping hole hovered the ghostly image of the golden dragon—no wait it changed. It was the salamander—no, it changed again. The image over the vortex alternated between the different mascots.

"Chief, why does the image change?" Tynae's gaze remained on the field.

"When and if you go down the vortex, the mascot which is visible at that time determines what penalty you'll receive. If you go down as the image is changing you get a double whammy!" Kerszon laughed heartily.

Tynae turned. "Neither Béo nor Jubryi ever got into detail about that part. What happens exactly?"

"Well each of the mascots has its own special 'power', if you will. You're subjected to that particular element when sucked into the vortex."

Tynae's brows rose. "How so?"

"Let's see." Kerszon thought for a moment. "If you get pulled down when Undines are visible, you will be sucked through a gurge. A gurge is a swirling vortex of water. The gnome is thick mud. Fire…" Kerszon glanced toward the red mascot, "is clearly for the salamander. If the image is a white cloudy haze, it's the Lijfbreeth Sylphs. This represents a hurricane and that, in and of itself, is a double whammy because it's comprised of gale force winds mixed with torrential rain. Last, but certainly not least, is the dragon. It is represented by lightning." Kerszon smiled broadly at Tynae, patting her shoulder. "The rest you just have to see to understand, sunshine. You'll love it."

Tynae turned when the crowd erupted with loud shouts.

The zevros were on their equnus'. One planted firmly on the ground, the other flying low over the field.

All the team members had taken their positions. The wards were by the goals, the bläkers stood in the area in front of the goals, and the rest of the players formed two lines facing each other near the center of the field.

The mascots on the field all took flight, each flying to their respective place among the spectators. There they perched high above the stands. When the zevro on the ground tossed the rucx between the players, the cart Tynae and Kerszon were in began to move.

Tynae cast Kerszon a wary glance.

"It follows the rucx!" He shouted over the crowd, pointing to the field. "This way I never miss a thing!"

Smiling, Tynae nodded with understanding.

The rucx landed on the ground between the two teams. The Salamanders took control of the ball, moving it away from the middle of the field quickly. From out of nowhere hundreds of little gold and silver balls, about the size of walnuts, flew onto the playing field.

Tynae watched Béo move swiftly, repelling the assaulting barbuls and overtaking the player with the rucx.

An announcer, which Tynae had not noticed until he began giving a play by play, shouted out every move the players made.

Tynae had no idea where this person was, but he apparently had a bird's eye view as well.

The crowd screamed wildly as Béo stole the ball. "And it's Lord Béo with the rucx, no surprise there, he's heading for the goal. Ooh watch out for the holes, they're sneaky little buggers, he just missed that one! Lord Béo moves right and blocks Dekarr. Nice try, Dekarr. The barbuls are out in full force today!"

"Oooh," the crowd moaned in unison.

"Ouch, that looked painful. Syler took a speeding barbul to the back of the head...Looks like he'll be frozen in that block of ice for a bit."

Tynae gawked at the frozen man, the announcer brought her attention back to the game.

"Lord Béo just narrowly escaped Fadree thanks to his bläkers. The bläkers are doing a fine job today, but can Lord Béo make the goal? He's lining it up. Looks like he's going for the big points. Ahh! He had to divert. Eoin, the Salamander's mobile wall, almost stole the rucx. Lord Béo's going back in, looks like all the Dragons have formed a protective barrier and eww three of them just got taken out by barbuls. Edvard may need to take a break after that last one, that lightning strike got him right in the...OH! hold on, Lord Béo still has command of the rucx, he's going in, he shoots. HE SCORES!!!"

Tynae danced around excitedly, waving her hands in the air.

The fans went crazy, their hollers and foot stomping was almost deafening.

Tynae was so caught up in the moment that she flinched when the golden dragon let out a roar, soaring once around the stadium.

"100 points to the Golden Dragons, that makes the score 231 to 331, Dragon's. Don't forget, those of you joining us for the first time, the objective is to get the score down to zero. And whichever team wins today goes on to the semifinals to compete against the Sylphs.

"The zevro releases the rucx. Heath of the Dragons manages to take it, but will he be able to hold on to it? He's letting it get too close to the center of the field, he needs to be careful! If the vortex doesn't get him, Fadree will. Heath moves left, passes to Jubryi, Jubryi takes the rucx, ahh a barbul got him, but it was fire."

The crowd roared as fire encircled Jubryi.

"Jubryi is headed for the goal with Lord Béo right beside him. Vecenté and Matteo are right there keeping the...AHHHH!!! Can you believe it! A small vortex opened up and swiped the ball from Jubryi! It's always the little ones that take the ball. But where will it come out? That's the big question here. There it is, holy cricket! It just popped out right in front of Jubryi. What are the chances? Did you see that?! Jubryi regains control of the ball and they're headed back for the goal and Ohh...Eoin steals the rucx, he passes it to Marek who takes it in for the goal, but Pe'er is hot on his tail! Will he get it back? Marek looks like he might take the shot, he shoots and HE SCORES!!!"

Tynae clearly heard the Dragon fans groan as the Salamander fans roared with cheers and applause. Their mascot zoomed over head leaving a trail of golden sparks.

"Marek shot from the double score line earning the Salamanders 108, which makes the score 223 to231, Salamanders take the lead!!!"

There was so much going on, Tynae didn't know which way to look. Men were moving in fast forward motion, slow motion, and freezing in their tracks as they got pelted by barbuls. It was all so exciting, but Béo was where she chose to keep her attention most of the time. Jubryi had been correct in saying that Béo was an excellent player.

The rucx was back in play.

"And it's Dekarr with the ball again! He's moving fast, but looks like he's losing control of the ball. He's getting too close to the vortex, can he recover? NO!!! He's down and it looks like he went down between the sylphs and the golden dragon, you know what that means! Lightning bolts, violent winds and pelting rain…ouch!"

The zevro on the ground produced another rucx, literally out of thin air. The game continued on for several plays before Dekarr resurfaced.

"Here comes Dekarr."
From a large opening in the wall beside a set of goal posts, Tynae watched the player slide back onto the field. He was drenched, but the wind must have dried his hair partially because it was tousled or maybe that was a side effect of the lightning. A small clump of hair atop Dekarr's head stood straight up and was on fire.

Dekarr looked up irritably. Wetting his fingers he extinguished the flame.

The Salamander fans applauded the return of their player.

Tynae turned to Kerszon. "Is he okay?"

Kerszon chuckled jubilantly. "He's fine, sunshine, don't worry. He is a Greer after all."

Smiling, Tynae turned back to the field.

Dekarr had already rejoined his team. He was easy to spot since he was still smoldering. The game resumed.

"Welcome back, Dekarr. You look like you had an *en-lightning* experience." Dekarr looked smugly toward the stands, nodding his head in an 'I'll see you later' manner.

Tynae thought she saw the announcer, but wasn't certain.

The game resumed and where the commentator sat held the least of her interests.

"And it's Eoin of the Salamanders with the rucx, look at him go! The barbuls have him in their sights, Ohh! And the bläker's do their job unbelievably well; those sinking barbuls are nasty little sods! Syler and Fadree will be up to their loincloths in mud for a bit. It looks like Adish and Jalil of the dragons are trying to double team Eoin.

"An Eoin runs to the right, managing to deflect a barbul directly at Adish and Adish gets hit.

That may have worked against Eoin. Adish is now moving with super speed and swipes the ball from Eoin! Adish passes it to Ebrem, Ebrem takes it down the field passing it to Edvard, Edvard was ready for that! But the Salamanders are gaining ground. Edvard passes it to Jubryi, who runs it to Lord Béo, who's waiting by the goal. He's only got a second to get it lined up before the entire salamander team is on him. Can he do it?"

"GO!!!" Tynae screamed at the top of her lungs, "GO, GO, GO!!!" Waving her arms, she leaned out of the cart.

"Can the ward keep them from scoring?!? NOOO he cannot! Lord Béo scores from the double point line!!! 200 points to the dragons, that makes the score 31 to 223, the Dragons are back in the lead. Can you believe it?!"

Bouncing up and down, arms flailing, Tynae shouted at the top of her lungs along with the rest of the fans.

The Dragon mascot shot out blasts of fire as it darted around the amphitheater roaring.

The zevro once again took the rucx near the center of the field. Tossing it back into play, he quickly moved aside.

"Did you see that? The Salamanders had the rucx before it hit the ground. Can the Salamanders catch up? Never count them out. I've seen them do miraculous things at the last possible instant. Dekarr kicks it to Eoin and ohhhh he almost takes Eoin's head off. Keep it low Dekarr. The Salamanders manage to hold on to the rucx and…oh a small vortex pilfers the rucx from Marek and the ball resurfaces…? At the other end of the field! This game could go either way folks. Who will get to the ball first? Ulric and Fadree are neck and neck with their teammate's right behind them…annnnd it's Fadree! Fadree gets to the rucx first. The salamanders take possession of the ball once more, but can they hold on to it? The Salamanders are covering Fadree like fur on an ickel! They are not letting anyone get near him. But the Dragons are moving in, they're going to try and steal the rucx! The Dragons split up, and the barbuls are trying to pelt the players every chance they get! Looks like the Dragons are using this to their advantage, deflecting barbuls at the Salamanders…and it works!!!

"Willoughby pilfers the ball from Fadree, passing it to Jubryi, but Jubryi's too close to the vortex, him and the ball are going to get sucked in and there they, WAIT!!! That was amazing! Jubryi managed to kick the ball to Lord Béo just before he got sucked down. Lord Béo takes the ball and his chacier's surround him! I don't think I've ever seen a team move so seamlessly."

The fierceness of the game was at an all time high. Tynae was absolutely enthralled.

"They're going for the goal, but the barbuls are picking off the players one by one. There are just three players left to guard Lord Béo. Can they do it?!

"Remember they're down to 31 points, he has to make the score from the single line, anything else will be considered a foul and the Salamanders will get a free shot. There goes Ebrem and oh, now Ulric is down, that just leaves Lord Béo and Willoughby! And here comes the entire Salamander team, they look like they're out for blood. Lord Béo lines up, ohh! Willoughby is hit by a freezing barbul, but he's in the perfect position, all the other barbuls are being deflected by his frozen body. Lord Béo avoids the bläkers he shoots, and, and HE SCORES!!! The game is over. The Dragons win!!!"

The golden dragon soared, roaring its way around the coliseum as thunderous screaming erupted from the crowd. Their shouting, clapping and stomping actually shook the stadium.

Tynae jumped up and down hollering at the top of her lungs. She bounced around so much she almost bounced right out of the cart.

"And here comes one of the hero's of the hour," shouted the announcer.

Just then Jubryi flew out of the opening beside the goals, landing square on his arse. Soaking wet, he was covered in seaweed and had a fish sticking out of his mouth.

"Looks like you've got yourself supper, Jubryi," the announcer taunted. The entire arena burst out with laughter. Spitting the fish out, Jubryi shot the announcer an evil glare. "He doesn't look happy folks. Jubryi, thanks to you, your team won. You're going to the semifinals!" the announcer declared.

Jubryi looked at his teammates who were running over to him. Standing up, he grinned widely, pulling kelp off himself. When Jubryi's teammates got to him, they smacked him on the shoulder and shook his hand.

"Come on guys, the zevros and the Salamanders are waiting for us," Béo reminded everyone.

Tynae knew her new hearing had become acute, but she couldn't believe she could hear individual men down on the field over the shouting crowd.

Walking to meet the zevros with his team, Jubryi let out a yelp.
The entire team stopped, looking at Jubryi warily.
"What is it?" Heath asked.
Twisting around Jubryi lifted his loin cloth. "Bloody vortex!" Jubryi muttered, removing a small crab that had attached itself to his buttocks. Before any of his teammates had a chance to comment, Jubryi gave them a verbal warning. "NOT A WORD," Jubryi glared at his teammates, "FROM ANY OF YOU," he growled, wagging a finger. "OUCH!!!" Jubryi jerked his hand back when the little crab clamped itself firmly onto his finger, "Bleed'n little bastard."
The entire team roared with laughter, as did every spectator in the arena.
The team walked toward the center of the field, which was solid once more. Shaking his hand, Jubryi attempted to dislodge the crustacean. Every time he got it off one finger it latched onto another one.
Béo couldn't stop laughing. "Hold still!" Béo said, catching his breath. Béo waved his hand over the crab and it was gone.
"Thanks," Jubryi said, sticking his finger in his mouth.

Just as the team reached the center of the field, so did their mascot.

One of the zevros put his hand on the golden dragon and the dragon opened its mouth. Extending his arm toward Béo's team the zevro said, "I declare the winner of today's game; the Dragons." The zevro's voice echoed through the stadium and the crowd roared with cheers.

Waving their fists in victory the Dragons shouted, "Huzza!!!"

After the Salamanders congratulated the Dragons, the two teams left the field.

"So, what'd you think, lass?" Kerszon asked as their cart moved slowly down the track, heading back to the little room they'd started off in.

The people waved to Tynae and she waved back as she answered Kerszon. "It was fantastic!" she said, smiling at the crowd. "I've never seen anything like it." Tynae glanced at Kerszon. She was smiling from ear to ear. "It was so exciting! I can't wait until the next match."

Kerszon beamed, "Told you, you'd like it."

As the cart cleared the red velvet curtains, Tynae saw Béo standing in the room waiting for them. She almost leapt out of the cart.

Kerszon had the door open and was out of the cart before it had come to a complete stop. "Wonderful game, Son!" Kerszon pulled Béo into a bear hug.

"Thank you, Father."

"I'll give you two a moment," the Chief said, his eye falling on Tynae, "But don't be too long." With a wink, Kerszon left the room.

Tynae looked appalled. "Why did he say that to *me*? What have you told him?" she asked accusingly.

Béo put his hands up. "Don't look at me, I haven't told him anything."

A huge grin spread across Tynae's face. "Oh, who cares, you won!" she squeaked wrapping her arms around Béo's neck.

"Are you my prize?" he asked in a quiet voice.

Tynae took Béo's face in her hands. "Only if you want me to be," she whispered putting her forehead to his.

"Can I keep you?" he asked, pressing his lips to hers.

"Mmm, forever," she breathed.

"I love you," he whispered, pulling away gently. "I'm going to get cleaned up." Béo walked to the door. "I'll meet you in a few minutes. Just wait with father."

"Okay," Tynae sighed. "Béo…"

Béo turned back, his hand on the door knob. "Yes?"

"I love you, too."

Béo smiled. "I know. How did I get so lucky?" Blowing Tynae a kiss, he left.

Chapter 38
Camaraderie, Laughter, and Lust

"The wise man carries his possessions within him."
~Bias

Sitting in a comfortable chair in the small room, Tynae waited.

Béo poked his head in the door. "Ready?" He looked around the room, "Where's father?"

Tynae shrugged, "He said something about…umm I think the word he used was Ere or something like that. Does that mean anything to you?"

"Yes it does." Béo looked impressed. "Let's go. This'll be great," he said brightly. "And it's Erzé Danz'ers."

Tynae looked at Béo quizzically.

"Just trust me; you're going to love it. Have I ever lied to you?" Béo teased…but felt a twinge of guilt the second the words had left his mouth.

"Well..."

Béo stopped her, "Since you've been in Calai."

Tynae giggled. "I hope not. Where are we going?" She looked around, "We've never been through these tunnels before."

"Father has his own private dining hall for large events, Sadar Hall. It's on the tenth level of the city."

Tynae was taking in the new landscape when…

"Boo!"

Letting out a shrill shout Tynae spun around, punching Jubryi square on the shoulder. "Don't ever sneak up on me like that, you arse!" She tried to be serious, but was unable to conceal her grin.

"Damn, lass that's gonna leave a mark," Jubryi chuckled rubbing his arm.

"Good," Tynae snapped with a grin. "It will serve as a reminder not to sneak up on people. "You scared the…"

Jubryi interrupted her. "Tut, tut watch your language, missy," he warned wagging a finger.

Tynae narrowed her eyes. "Fine," she said snidely. "Frick, you scared the carp out of me."

Jubryi wore a huge smile. "That's better," he teased, bumping against Tynae, knocking her slightly off balance. "Besides, it's part of my job as a 'big brother' to torment and tease you, Jack." He nudged her again, this time knocking her into Béo. "And the way I see it, I have years of pranks to make up for. So you see my point here, I can't let any prime opportunities pass."

"So you're my big brother now?"

"If Béo's my little brother it only makes sense." Jubryi grinned.

Tynae glanced at Béo.

Chuckling, Béo just shrugged. "I learned a long time ago that Jubryi takes his 'job' as a big brother quite seriously. There's really no use in fighting it, love. Besides he grows on you." Béo glanced at Jubryi, "Like barnacles on a whales arse."

Béo and Tynae laughed boisterously.

Walking into Sadar Hall the trio was greeted with an ear splitting, "Huzza!!!"

Without skipping a beat, the three returned the greeting. Some men appeared surprised by Tynae's retort.

Sadar Hall was much different and larger than Quenby Hall. This hall, brightly lit with numerous torches, lanterns, and crystals, had long rectangular tables with benches for seats, instead of square tables with individual chairs. At the front of this hall was a large elevated platform with red velvet curtains running along the back.

The threesome made their way toward the table reserved for the Dragon team.

Béo watched Tynae as they walked. He knew it would only be a moment or two before she made the observation.

Tynae looked around at the many men seated at the elongated tables. "Béo," she whispered.
"Yes, love?"
"Umm, if this is something you normally do without women present, I would be more than willing to return to my room."
"Don't be silly," Béo said. "You'll do no such thing. The only reason there are no other women here is because there are no women on the teams, and there are no other visiting royals in Calai at the moment."

Tynae eyed Béo appraisingly, clearly trying to decipher if he was being honest or just trying to make her feel like she wasn't intruding.

"Don't look at me like that, I'm telling you the truth. If you don't believe me father is sitting right there," he pointed to Kerszon, who sat among his teammates. "Ask him yourself."

"He's telling the truth, lass," Jubryi interjected. "If this was a men's only function, I would be the first to object."

"If that isn't the truth, I don't know what is," Béo muttered.

Tynae took a long look around the room. "Who are all these men? There must be more than just the vorbix teams here."

"All four teams are here, plus the substitute players, and remember the warriors?"
Tynae looked at Béo perplexed, "Warriors?"
"The performers before the game." Béo clarified.
"Oh…how could I forget? They were amazing." Tynae looked around at the numerous men.

"Trust me, you're more than welcome here," he reassured.

Tynae smiled. "Fine, fine, but you two had better not leave my side. I feel like the last banana in a room full of hungry monkeys!" she joked.

Béo and Jubryi laughed.

"Lass, these boys know what's good for them, and most of them value their lives. Trust me, none of them would ever harm you," Jubryi said confidently. "If they did they would have me to answer to."

Kerszon walked up to the trio. "And more importantly, they would have *me* to answer to. Trust me, sunshine, no-one wants that," Kerszon said in an authoritative tone. "Do they boys?" He eyed Béo and Jubryi.

"No," they said in unison, both knowing from history past that Kerszon was not a man to be trifled with.

"Good evening, Sire," Jubryi said bowing slightly to Kerszon.
"Good evening, Jubryi. That was a spectacular save, Son." Kerszon clapped Jubryi on the back.
Grinning, Jubryi puffed out his chest. "Thank you."
"Why don't the three of you have a seat?" Kerszon motioned toward the bench. "Ale's on the table and food is on the way. I have duties to attend to. I'll be back soon."
"Make way for the queen." Jubryi pushed his way between Edvard and Pe'er.

"Jubryi really, do you have to be such a brut?" Tynae smacked him on the shoulder. "And since when are *you* a queen? Are you trying to tell us something?" she razzed.

The men at their table rolled with laughter.

Tynae grinned slyly. "I have my 'jobs', too, as a 'little sister'."
"Touché, lass." Jubryi slammed his fist on the table, "Let us have a round boys."
"Good evening Lady and Gentlemen," Kerszon's voice boomed.
Tynae turned to see Kerszon standing center stage.
"I must commend the two teams that played today on a job well done. They deserve a round of applause."
Everyone in the hall clapped.

"To a game well played!" Kerszon shouted, holding up his tankard.

Everyone in the hall held up their tankard and shouted, "Huzza!"

"I've arranged for a little treat this evening in honor of our special guest, but first I would like to introduce her to you. Lady Tynae, please join me." Kerszon looked at Tynae expectantly.

"No," she groaned quietly.

"Go on, just get it over with, there's just a few people here tonight, wait till he introduces you to all of Calai," Béo said impassively.

Tynae's head snapped around like it was on a swivel, gawking at Béo horrorstruck. "What?" she gasped.

"That'll be a riot won't it?" Jubryi laughed, elbowing Tynae.

She elbowed him right back, almost knocking him off his seat.

"Don't keep father waiting, love." Béo warned. "Just get up there and get it over with…like ripping off a bandage." Béo winked.

Tynae's mouth fell open slightly, but she didn't retort. Standing up, she made her way to the stage.

Jubryi leaned toward Béo. "Crikey she's strong."

"You don't know the half of it," Béo said more seriously than he had intended. "You better watch yourself or she'll kick your arse…again!" he added, laughing heartily.

"Gentlemen allow me to introduce you to the newest resident of Calai, Lady Tynae." Every person in the room stood up clapping and hollering.

Tynae curtsied.

Kerszon turned to Tynae. "I don't know if you're aware of it, but the people of Calai have dubbed you, 'Lady Nadaya,'" he told her in front of everyone.

Tynae stared at Kerszon blankly. "Thank you," she said graciously. She turned to the men, "and thank you."

Everyone clapped.

"Thank *you,* My Lady." Kerszon gave her a bow.

With a simple curtsy Tynae hastily exited, stage right.

Looking out at the audience, Kerszon beamed. "Tonight we have a rare treat, the Erzé Danz'ers have joined us, so please put your hands together and help me welcome them."

As Kerszon walked off the stage drums began to pound and the red velvet curtains lifted.

Two by two, men and women took center stage, forming one long line. Their feet clacked on the stage, keeping perfect time with the pulsing drums.

Tynae turned in her seat, resting her back against the table. "What does the name Nadaya mean?" she asked Béo.

Moving closer to Tynae, Béo discreetly caressed her hand, "It means hope."

Tynae's focus moved to the performers.

Béo watched Tynae, who was clearly fascinated by the Danz'ers. Their movements, the rhythm, and the speed at which their feet moved never failed to mesmerize.

The next hour was spent eating, drinking, and being entertained.

A standing ovation and a deafening round of applause signaled the end of the Erzé Danz'ers splendid performance.

Halfway through the evening Kerszon excused himself. "Son, Tynae," he said bending between the two, "I shall see you in a few hours." Kerszon stood to leave. "Tynae, O'leana will have your attire prepared for you." Tynae looked puzzled. "Béo will explain. Enjoy your evening, sunshine." Patting Béo on the shoulder, Kerszon departed.

Once Kerszon was gone the atmosphere lightened up slightly. Kerszon was not an uptight man, nor was he overly *proper,* but he was the 'Chief' after all, and that alone caused many to behave differently around him.

At some point throughout the night every man in the hall came to the Dragons' table to congratulate them, but it was evident to Béo that their true objective was to meet Lady Tynae.

Most of the players had grown up with Béo and were used to his nonchalant demeanor, but meeting another royal as carefree as their future chief seemed to take most of them by surprise. Although Tynae's beauty alone would have caused a riot, it was her charming personality and 'just one of the boys' attitude that made her completely irresistible.

Leaning toward Tynae so only she could hear him, Béo whispered, "It's getting late, darling we should head back to Vu'tella so you can get changed."

"Okay." Getting up, Tynae walked over to Jubryi, giving him a hug and a kiss on the cheek.

After bidding the other Dragon's farewell, the couple made their way through the hall, waiving to the rest of the attendees on their way out.

"You've got quite a few admirers, angel," Béo teased as they walked to Vu'tella.

"Please, they know nothing of me to admire," Tynae replied. "They see a crown, riches, and status. They do not see me, they do not know who I am, nor do they care."

"You're right," Béo sighed.

"I know." She grinned, intentionally bumping into Béo.

"What is it like?" he asked.

Confused, Tynae looked at Béo. "What is what like?"

"Having people fall all over you, wanting to please you, marry you?"

"Why would you ask such a question? Besides, you know exactly what it's like. Are you going to stand there and tell me women do not throw themselves at you on a daily basis? I've seen how they look at you and glare at me."

"I don't know what you're seeing, but women have no interest in me," Béo refuted.

Tynae waved her hand in front of Béo's face.

"What are you doing?" he asked.

"Just checking, I thought maybe you were blind." She chuckled. "How can you not know that women desire you?"

"Me or my title?" he asked plainly.

"There!" She pointed at him. "You see, you do know they look at you!" Tynae stated with a smirk.

"It's not the same as when men look at you," Béo insisted.

"It's not?" Tynae looked at him with raised brows. "Isn't it? They do not see *me*. They do not care what my hopes and dreams are. They do not care that I have a brain or opinions. And they certainly do not care that I am my own person. They would rather see me as their subservient bitch, than the strong independent woman I truly am!" Tynae said defiantly.

Béo glanced at Tynae from the corner of his eye, but did not interrupt.

"I am no-one's *pet,*" she hissed. "And if I'm a bitch that makes him a dog. I'll be damned if I would ever be married to any man that is humping and screwing his way across the countryside and possibly the world." Tynae paused for a moment then resumed her tirade. "Why is it that men want their woman pure and virginal?" Tynae held her hands out in front of her daintily, rolling her eyes. "And if we have a lover prior to or during our marriage we are whores, yet men can fornicate with every woman they are attracted to, whether or not they're married, and this makes them more masculine and manly," she said in a throaty voice. Tynae stopped in the middle of the corridor. "And do you know what the proviso to all this is?" Tynae raised an irritated finger.

"No?" Béo said quietly, unsure if the question was rhetorical.

"We as women are to remain 'pure' until we are married so that we may give ourselves to our husband and our husband alone; but if a man's eye falls upon us, specifically a man who holds a title; we are expected to bed him. We are 'ruined' for other men, even though we never wanted to be with the filthy dog in the first place. Why can't they just hump the willing whores who gladly spread their legs for them and leave all the others alone?"

Béo's mouth fell open slightly. "Not all men are like that, they can't be," he insisted.

"Come here," she said softly, grabbing Béo's hand and pulling him toward her. Looking him in the eyes, she ran her hand lightly over his cheek. "You're a good man, Béo, but you are an exception, or maybe it's different among the Greer. Most men, human men anyway, want nothing more than an ornament to hang on their arm," she said bitterly.

They resumed walking.

"Well you are a rare beauty," Béo admitted then quickly recanted. "But I know there is much more to you than looks," he added, hoping too not offend.

Tynae glanced over at him. "And if I was not attractive would you still..."

Béo cut her off. "Don't you dare," he said sternly. It was he who stopped this time. Gripping Tynae's arm firmly, Béo took care not to hurt her. "I love you, *you!* I would not have you submit to me, nor would I dare to control you." Béo took a step closer. "I love that you're smart and funny." He took another step closer. "And I admire your back bone. You are like no other person I have ever met, man or woman." Béo's body now pressed lightly against Tynae's. He didn't bother to check the corridors to see if anyone was watching, he didn't care. Leaning forward Béo pressed his lips to Tynae's. Having longed all day to feel her lips against his, he wrapped his arms around her waist. He became lost in her energy as their tongues seductively danced together.

Stepping back Béo was breathless and hungry. Hungry for the body of the woman he loved more than life itself. Béo shook his head. "I'm sorry I shouldn't have done that."

"It takes two, my love, and you don't hear me complaining." Tynae brushed her hand over his arm.

"Let's go before someone shows up, this would not look good for either of us," Béo said in his rare 'Chief' tone.

When they opened the door to Vu'tella O'leana was there to greet them. "Good evening My Lord, My Lady."

"Good evening," the couple unintentionally said together. Both chuckled.

"I have your clothes ready, My Lady. And Ezro dropped off your attire, My Lord." O'leana pointed to a small pile of clothes sitting on a table.

"Thank you," Béo said grabbing his clothing. "I'll use the lavatory."

"Okay, I will get changed, too." Tynae walked to her dressing area, O'leana followed.

"My Lady, I do apologize, but this is what Chief Kerszon sent." O'leana held up a petite pair of suede trousers.

Tynae smiled, walking over to where the rest of her clothes lie. "It's rather nice actually." Tynae ran her hand over the matching suede corset.

O'leana sighed with relief. She did not want to upset her mistress, yet again on this day. She went to work dressing Tynae. She laced the princess' trousers, which laced up the sides. Next she slipped a custom made beige tunic over Tynae's head. She then fastened Tynae's snug corset over the top of her tunic. Last O'leana helped Tynae pull on a pair of long boots that reached over her knees.

Tynae attempted to fill her lungs with air, but fell short. "Ahh, now I remember why I like your clothing so much more than ours," Tynae chuckled.

"But you look exquisite," O'leana said honestly. "Even in Calai women do not wear trousers such as those." Looking Tynae over, O'leana smiled. "Perhaps it's your perfect figure, but it seems that you can make anything look attractive. You wear trousers well, My Lady," O'leana said admirably. "Oh, here," the maid picked up a thick black floor length cloak, handing it to Tynae. "You'll need this, too, but you won't want to put it on until your ready to head out. Lord Béo can help you with it."

Tynae laid the cloak over her arm. "Thank you, O'leana. I know the hour is late. You may retire for the night." Tynae walked out of her bedchamber. "I do not necessitate your assistance tomorrow, take the day for yourself and let the others know, too," Tynae turned, looking at O'leana.

"That's not..." O'leana stopped mid sentence, perceiving the look on Tynae's face. She did not dare to cross Tynae at this point. She knew better and she wanted to keep her job. "Thank you, Your Majesty. I will indeed let the others know. We shall see you at sunrise the day after?"

"That would be lovely," Tynae said with a pleasant grin. With a curtsy O'leana retired to her room.

Béo looked at Tynae curiously. "What was…?"

Tynae put her hand up. "I don't want to talk about it," she said. "It's been dealt with and so is over."

Béo nodded.

"Wow!" Tynae looked Béo up and down.

He wore black suede trousers, a green tunic, a thick brown belt, and black boots that went just below his knees. He too carried a thick black cloak.

"Why do we need these?" Tynae inquired, holding up her cape.

"You'll see," Béo teased. "Let's get going, father does not like to be kept waiting."

Due to the late hour the corridors where empty, allowing the playful pair to tease and chase each other through the halls.

Béo glance at Tynae as they walked. "Tynae?"

"Yes?"

"Can I ask you a question?" His tone was serious.

"Always."

Béo grinned at her. "What do you want from a man?"

Tynae smiled thoughtfully. "Man as a friend, or as a husband?"

"Husband," he clarified. "You must have had a hundred suitors if you've had one. Why have you not settled down with any of them? They can't all have been flawed." Béo smirked, "Not that I'm complaining," he added with a wide grin.

Tynae shook her head, smiling her bright, enchanting smile. "I want to know who I'm marrying. I want him to first and foremost be my friend, my best friend. I want to be in love with him and he must be in love with *me*, not my title, not my material possessions, me, exactly the way I am flaws and all."

"What flaws!" Béo blurted out.

Chuckling Tynae continued. "We all have flaws, my love, even if you're not aware of it. Many people do not accept others for who they are, and when they marry they do so with the intention of changing the other individual into the person they want them to be." Tynae paused to think for a moment. "It's like watching a wild horse run. Have you ever done that?"

"Yes."

"Don't you think they're majestic, almost magical?" she said with wonder.

"Incredibly so," Béo mused. "They have a magnificent spirit and pride about them."

"Exactly," Tynae said. "We see that and we want it. We want to ride atop the magnificent beast so we too may feel the freeness and openness 'it' feels. So what do we do? We go out, capture it, make it ours and in doing so we must break it. We drive the very spirit and pride that we thought was so amazing right out of it," Tynae explained in a saddened voice.

Béo looked at Tynae as if she'd just revealed to him some deep dark secret he'd been trying to uncover for centuries.

"I'm not saying that marriage is a bad thing. I'm not saying that owning a horse is a bad thing. But if what you love about the horse is its spirit, let it run in open pastures. Do not lock it in a stable. Let it be the animal nature intended it to be. When you're not using it to pull a cart or whatever you use it for, let it run and make sure that you allow it to frolic with its own kind. Do not lock it away with rabbits and squirrels or bears and lions. When you captured it in the wild it ran with a heard of horses, it did not live a life of solitude. Horses are a social animal by nature and need to socialize with their own kind. And one should never lock their horse away, only to take it out for show. If you take care of it properly you could leave the gates of the barn wide open and the horse would never leave, not even to return to the wild. Why would it, when it has everything it could ever desire by staying with you? Open space, an abundance of food, friends, and the most important thing of all, your love."

Béo stared at Tynae so intently he almost walked into a statue. Tynae pulled him toward her just in time.

"Béo, I'm not against marriage. Please don't get me wrong. But people, both men and women, marry with the secret intent of changing the other person into the person they expect them to be. People become miserable and unhappy. They lose themselves trying to please their spouse and in the end they resent the other person horribly. I want a man who is his own man, and allows me to be who I am at the same time. We will remain faithful to each other because it's what we both want. We will stand beside each other. The only time I will stand behind my husband is figuratively, never literally. And we will stand by one another through the good times and the bad." Tynae thought for a moment then nodded her head. "Yes, I believe that is everything. Can you see now why I have not found the proper man for me yet?" Tynae grinned timidly at Béo.

Béo shook his head. "I don't think that you're asking too much, my love, it sounds exactly like what I'm looking for."

Tynae smiled sweetly. "Like I said before, you are not like most men." Grabbing Béo's arm, Tynae stopped walking and pulled him toward her. "This is why I love you so much," she whispered.

Standing there, Béo became lost as he stared thoughtfully into Tynae's soul-warming eyes.

Tynae pressed her warm lips to his for a brief moment. "Come on. *We mustn't keep father waiting,*" she repeated his words teasingly, pulling him by the hand.

Chapter 39
Guidelines, Not Commands

"Silently, one by one, in the infinite meadows of heaven,
blossomed the lovely stars, the forget-me-nots of the angels."
~Henry Wadsworth Longfellow

Once again Béo waved his hand in front of the statues guarding the entrance to Kerszon's residence, and the two entered.

"Son, Tynae, wow look at you two!" Kerszon cheerfully gestured to their attire. "What do you think, Tynae? I can't imagine you wear trousers too very often."

"I don't, but I do like them. It's a bit warm here in Calai to wear them on a daily basis, but on land it would be wonderful."

Kerszon glanced at an over sized hourglass standing in the corner of the room. "It's getting late, shall we?"

Béo nodded.

"Oh, I almost forgot! Excuse me for a moment while I go grab my cloak." Kerszon walked away. He, too, wore long pants, a long sleeve tunic and boots similar to Béo's.

Béo threw his cape over his shoulders, fastening it. Reaching for Tynae's cloak, he wrapped it around her shoulders and fastened a silver clasp across her chest.

Lost in each others eyes, the pair jumped slightly when Kerszon re-entered the room.
"Ready to go up and out?" Kerszon asked.
"Up?" Tynae repeated, "Out?"
"We sure are!" Béo said, giving Tynae a wink.
The three walked over to the large telescope. A rail standing waist high ran along three sides of the platform the huge scope stood upon.

"Okay, stand over here and hold on," Béo said, escorting Tynae to the railing on the left of the platform. "I'll be right here," Béo assured in hushed tones, "standing directly behind you."

Tynae looked up at him over her shoulder. She suddenly felt very nervous.

"Son, why don't you hold her against your chest? It might make her feel a little more secure," Kerszon suggested.

Taking a step forward, Béo pressed his chest against Tynae's back, and wrapped one arm around her waist. With his other hand he held tight to the railing.

"Ready?" Kerszon asked, walking to the front of the star gazer.

"Yes," Béo told his father. Leaning forward he whispered in Tynae's ear. "Hold on and don't be frightened. I'm right here. I would never let anything happen to you."

Tynae's heart began to pound wildly and her breath came quickly.

"Relax, take a deep breath. It's okay, Tynae," Béo assured.

Glancing at the couple over his shoulder, Kerszon gave them a wink. Turning back, he raised his hands into the air.

Tynae watched as a wall of glass encased the whole of the platform, encapsulating them and the telescope in a cube. Once the cube was complete, they began to rise. The jerk of the first movement startled Tynae, her knees buckling slightly.

"What the…" She held onto the railing as tight as she could.

"Turn around, angel," Béo whispered.

Tynae couldn't move her body, she was paralyzed with fear. Her hands and feet seemed to be welded into place.

Tynae's body shook with terror as their glass box ascended skyward through the oceans depths.

Béo unlatched her white-knuckled fingers from the railing, helping her turn.

She quickly attached herself to his chest, wrapping her arms around his waist.

"Tynae," Béo's words wheezed out. "Loosen your grip a little, I can't breathe."

Looking up Tynae saw Béo turning bright red. She loosened her arms slightly. "Sorry," she whispered.

Béo inhaled deeply. "It's fine," he chuckled. "Look." Béo pointed out into the sea surrounding their box. Fish and other sea creatures were out in abundance. It must have been feeding time.

Tynae's head remained against Béo's chest. She kept her eyes open, despite the urge to shut them tight.

Their glass box continued to climb.

Looking up Tynae could see the surface of the water slowly approaching. Once they had broken the surface they kept going up…up…up. When they finally stopped they must have been a good two or three kilometers above the water.

With a wave of Kerszon's hand, the glass box began to disintegrate.

Tynae's eyes got huge and she began to hyperventilate.

"Father," Béo said lightly.

When Kerszon turned Béo gestured toward the panicking Tynae. "I'll just lower the walls slightly, not remove them. Will that make you feel better, sunshine?"

Tynae nodded anxiously.

"Relax," Béo insisted. "The air is much thinner up here. You'll pass out if you don't calm down."

When Kerszon finished, the walls were a bit above waist high.

Looking through the eye piece of the telescope Kerszon adjusted it, aiming it toward the moon. Stepping back the chief looked at Tynae. "Sunshine, would you like to take a peek?"

Tynae swallowed, realizing for the first time that her mouth was as dry as a desert in the middle of a seven year drought. Smiling weakly, she looked at Béo with distressed eyes. "I can't move my arms," Tynae admitted softly. Embarrassment coated her words.

"Give us a moment, Father."

Kerszon peered through the eyepiece, giving the couple as much privacy as the small cube would allow.

Béo took Tynae's face gently in his hands. "Tynae...angel, I know this is intimidating. But I've been up here hundreds of times. It doesn't get any safer. Neither my father nor I would ever let anything happen to you, ever," he promised softly.

Tynae smiled nervously. "I believe you, really, and I want to look at the stars." Tynae glanced at her paralyzed arms wrapped around Béo's waist. "I just can't get my body to cooperate. I feel so stupid."

"There's nothing to feel stupid about," Béo said lovingly. "Come on, try to relax." Putting his hands behind him, Béo pulled Tynae's hands apart.

The second her hands were free she grabbed onto the rail, but kept one hand on Béo's waist.

"I can carry you, if you'd like."

"No!" Tynae snapped. "I'm sorry, but please let me keep my feet on what little ground there is," she pleaded.

"Okay." Béo grinned. "Do I need to unlash your fingers again or can you do it?" he glanced at her hand that was once again bonded to the railing like a vice grip.

Tynae looked at her hand as if it belonged to someone else. Concentrating, she willed her fingers to move. Tynae considered using her other hand to assist, but was unwilling to let go of Béo, even for an instant. One by one her fingers dislodged themselves from the metal railing.

Béo took her hand.

With one arm around Béo's waist and her other hand in his, Tynae allowed him to lead her over to the telescope.

Grinning, Kerszon held his hand out. "You're going to have to let go of him, sunshine, if you want to look through here."

Removing her hand from around Béo's waist, Tynae placed her hand into Kerszon's. She squeezed tight as Béo loosened his grip on her other hand. Looking down through the floor, which too was made of glass, Tynae's knees buckled slightly. The thought of lying on the floor became quite appealing.

"You okay, sunshine?" Kerszon asked.

"Fine…Just give me a few seconds." Tynae was determined to find her strength, even if it killed her. *You are safe. Béo would never put you in harms way. Neither would Kerszon. Look at where you are. It's amazing. This is an experience of a lifetime so pull yourself together.* Her inner dialog was working. Taking a deep breath, Tynae let Béo's hand go and stood at Kerszon's side.

"Are we good now?" Kerszon asked.

Tynae nodded. "I think so."

"Sunshine, I need my hand." Kerszon looked at his hand Tynae was clutching. "Besides I think you've cut off all my circulation," he chuckled.

Tynae dropped Kerszon's hand like it was a red hot cattle prod. "I'm so sorry."

"No need to apologize, but you've got quite a grip there." Kerszon massaged his hand.

Tynae blushed. "I'm really sorry," she apologized again.

"Relax, Tynae," Kerszon insisted, "and have a look." He gestured toward the telescope.

Tynae looked through the eyepiece then took her eye off to look at the moon with her naked eye. She resumed looking through the lens of the scope. "This is amazing," she breathed. Once she had looked through the telescope all of Tynae's fear dissipated. Now able to move her limbs freely, she realized why they needed the cloaks. Tynae pulled her hood over her head as freezing winds blew. "Chief, you mentioned something about reading the stars. How does that work exactly?"

"Well, I will give you the brief version, and if you'd like to learn more, I will personally teach you." Kerszon waved his hand and three chairs appeared out of thin air. "Have a seat," he said, "Where to start? Do you understand and accept that even though we are made of flesh and bone, we have a spirit that lives on long after our flesh dies?" Kerszon asked.

Tynae nodded. "I do, though I don't completely understand it," she admitted, fidgeting with her bracelet.

"Not many do, sunshine. In order for me to explain how the stars are read, you must have a basic knowledge of the soul that resides within your body. That soul, spirit, or whatever you want to call it is made of energy. The world we live in is made from that very same energy. Everything from other beings and animals, even the mountains and streams, are connected to one another."

Tynae was a little confused. She'd never heard anyone talk of such things.

Kerszon thought for a moment. "Have you ever walked into a room where someone was sitting and known immediately what kind of mood they were in, without them ever opening their mouth or even looking at you?"

Rolling her bracelet through her fingers, Tynae considered the question. "I believe so."

Kerszon grinned. "Okay. Have you ever been upset or sad and someone who was in a good mood came around and all of a sudden your mood changed?"

Rubbing her and Béo's tiny entwined wolves between her fingers, Tynae thought about it again. "Yes," she nodded. "I suppose I have."

"That's because energy is contagious, good and bad," Kerszon explained, "this is why events that happen on the other side of the world affect everyone. The energy may not be as strong as it originally was by the time it reaches us, but it still gets to us nonetheless, and affects all of us."

"Okay."

"Well the stars have energy, too, and their energy affects us here. We are not sure how the energy of the stars works, but it can, and often does have a profound influence on our mood, disposition, and even our outlook."

Tynae gazed up at the stars.

"The stars tell us when to plant crops, when is a good time to hunt, and when to watch for our foe. They even tell us when one is likely to be born that will bring renewed hope and light to our world," Kerszon said thoughtfully.

"So they tell the future?" Tynae asked, continuing to fiddle with her bracelet.

"They don't foretell the future so much. It is more like they influence people's attitudes and drive. What is written in the heavens is not written in stone, we do have free will. We make our own choices. If we know a time is approaching that will bring mass depression or violent anger we can plan for it, taking the appropriate steps to counteract the affects of the star's energy on us and our world."

"How so?" Tynae asked, intrigued.

"There are many plants that have calming affects on our bodies. Some even induce happiness."

"Like the plants Chenoa tends to?"

"Exactly," Kerszon smiled. "We make elixirs and potions out of them. Never anything too extreme, just enough to balance the negative energy coming from the heavens, other countries, or even other people."

"That's amazing."

"Some even believe that how the stars and planets are arranged at the precise moment one is born, will influence their entire life."

Tynae pondered this for a moment, rolling her tiny sword and wings between her fingers. "Do you believe that?"

"I believe that they can influence people at any time. I do not believe that the placement of a star or planet in the sky determines whether you become a king or a peasant. You can be born into poverty or wealth, yet become whatever you choose. A peasant can work hard, and earn his way into a king's court. He may never become king, but he does not have to stay a peasant. A king may be born into royalty, but that does not mean he will be a good king or that he will run his country nobly." Kerszon gazed at Tynae intently. "What determines if a person is born into a peasant family or a wealthy family?" he asked. "Who says that a boy, born unto peasants, must remain a poor country pauper all his life? Does he have to be so if he chooses not to?" Kerszon gave Tynae a moment to contemplate his words. "And if a king is a noble king it is because of his choices— personal choices. Neither the stars nor anyone around him can make those choices for him. Only the individual can determine what path he or she elects to follow." Kerszon paused. "Look at it this way; these bodies that we wear," Kerszon patted his chest, "they are merely costumes. We choose the roles that we play and in doing so we project an image to the world at large and this is what they see. If we choose to be the victim, then that's what we will be and that is what people will see." Kerszon shrugged, "And if we choose to be something more, then that's what others will see as well. Not the costume we were born with, but who we truly are inside. Reality is merely an illusion we choose to believe is factual. Everything is an illusion and everything is reality," Kerszon stated matter-of-factly. "Stars inclinate, they do not dictate," Kerszon finished with a grin.

Tynae smiled broadly. "So you believe one can create his or her own destiny? You believe we can change our stars?"

"Absolutely," Kerszon nodded. "We can do anything we set our minds to," Kerszon said with confidence. "Look at where you're standing, Tynae. Do you honestly believe anything is impossible?"

Looking around, Tynae shook her head. "Not any more!" She laughed. "I would definitely like to learn more about the stars."

"Done! I will have a look at my schedule and see what days I have available. I'll let you know next week when I take you to meet Zandore."

Tynae lit up. "Perfect."

The next several hours were spent looking up at the stars. Both Kerszon and Béo pointed out constellations, explaining what they meant.

When it was time to return, Kerszon handed Tynae a vial containing a clear liquid.

Tynae looked quizzically at the glass tube. "What's this?"

"I believe Béo gave you this very thing when you went out in the versaire the other day."

Understanding registered on Tynae's face and she drank the liquid. "Why didn't you give this to me before?"

"I didn't know how you would react; not many people do well with heights. If you vomited it would be out of your system and you would not be able to see anything anyway. This way the initial shock is gone and hopefully you can enjoy the ride back," Kerszon stated. The chief waved his hands and the glass walls once again surrounded their platform.

Béo took his place with Tynae, wrapping his arms around her. She insisted on being as close to him as possible. Acceptance of the situation or not, traveling in a glass box—God knows how many kilometers above the water—and through the ocean, was a bit nerve racking.

Submerged beneath the water, Tynae saw the lights of the city approaching, they twinkled like stars. If she hadn't known any better, she would have sworn she was looking up at the sky. "This must be what it looks like to the angels when they look down from the heavens," she said softly.

Almost back in Calai, Kerszon remained standing in front of the telescope guiding their cubed chariot through the water. Poking his head around the mountain of metal, Kerszon looked at Tynae. "By the way, I spoke with Demric and he's expecting you in three days time." The chief spoke loudly so Tynae could hear him over the noise of the water rushing past them.

"Demric? Is that the man who will be teaching me hand-to-hand?" she shouted back, never loosening her grip on Béo.

343

Kerszon grinned. "Precisely," he said in a normal tone, walking around the telescope as their flying room came to a cushioned halt.

"Wonderful," she chirped.

Tynae thanked Kerszon for the extraordinary experience then she and Béo headed back to Vu'tella.

"Did you enjoy that?" Béo asked as they walked.

"It was remarkable."

"I'm really sorry you were so frightened, but the next time should be a snap, right?" Béo asked playfully, intentionally bumping into her.

Tynae laughed. "It will take some getting used to, but it's worth the momentary lapse of terror. After all, those who live in fear never truly live. They simply exist."

"Too right you are, my love."

The pair entered Vu'tella and before Tynae could run off to the lavatory to change, Béo pulled her to him. "I really do like these clothes on you." He ran his hands over the curves of her bum.

Tynae giggled, returning the favor.

With a wave of his hand, the music box he had given Tynae began to play its enchanting tune. The couple danced, becoming lost in each others eyes. No-one in the world existed at that moment except for them. Neither was sure how long it had been when they realized the music no longer played. They chuckled knowing it had been some time, yet they still swayed in each others arms.

"I should get dressed for bed." Tynae jutted her thumb toward the loo.

"Why don't I help you with that?" Béo suggested, pulling on the lacings of her corset.

They spent that night like they had every night since the eve of Kerszon's supper, entwined in each others bodies.

The glistening mist delivered Tynae to the warm shores of her and Ryedin's private beach paradise. Ryedin was a fair way up the beach when he saw Tynae. Spotting her, a bright smile shone on his face and he quickly joined her, holding her tight in his arms.

"You act as though you've not seen me in a fortnight. Is something the matter?" Tynae asked with concern.

Ryedin touched her face lovingly. "It feels as though it has been a lifetime since I've last seen you, my love." Staring at Tynae intently, Ryedin shook his head. "Several lifetimes actually," he murmured.

Tynae cradled his face in her hands. "I am always with you, my love, as you are always with me," she said softly.

Ryedin closed his eyes, committing to memory the way her fingers felt as they gently touched his skin. The way her hair smelled like sweet honeysuckle as the wind blew through it, and the angelic tone her voice carried when she spoke. It was the most loving, most comforting sound he had ever heard.

"Why do you look so sad, my angel?" she asked.

Ryedin shook his head passively. "Because I want nothing more than to make you my wife and I cannot have you."

"You have me. I am yours, forever. That will never change," she asserted firmly.

Ryedin perked up. "You're right, I'm being foolish." He shook his head. "This will all work itself out somehow. Come on, we have training to do."

"I love archery," Tynae said, "and I love the fact that you are teaching me."

Ryedin had taught Tynae how to shoot long bows and short bows. Now he was teaching her how to shoot while riding Tarak. Next would be shooting at a moving target while riding.

"Do you know anything about reading stars, Ryedin?" Tynae asked as they walked their steeds to a fresh spring.

"I do. What did you think of tonight's little astrology lesson?" Ryedin asked, although he already knew the answer.

Tynae lit up. "It was like nothing I've ever experienced and I want to know more!" Tynae said spiritedly.

Ryedin laughed." Of course you do. I can teach you what I know. We can add it to your lessons, but tonight I need to give you something to take back with you." He glanced up at the sky. "Twilight is fast approaching," he sighed.

Taking Tynae by the hand, Ryedin led her over to a stone bench while their stallions drank.

"Here," he said holding out a leather satchel. "Inside you will find three packages, they are not for you," he warned, "They are for Chenoa."

"Chenoa? Are you joking?"

"This is no joke, my love. They are for Chenoa and Chenoa alone."

"Why can't you give them to her?"

"This is not the time for explanations. Give them to her along with this." Ryedin held up a tightly bound scroll then placed it, too, into the bag. "This is what you must tell Chenoa before you hand her the satchel. Tell her that you have a job to offer her and that the job is being offered by he who is known by many names. She will know what this means." Ryedin chuckled at the confused look on Tynae's face. "Don't worry. You will remember all this," he assured. "If she accepts she will say, 'I accept the bag and the blood oath that it carries.' If she does not, keep the bag in Vu'tella with you. Tuck it back where you found it. If that is the case I will find someone else to help us." Ryedin knew his riddles confused Tynae, but this was how it had to be. "Can you do this for me?"

"Of course," Tynae took the bag, hanging it over her shoulder. Leaning forward she pressed her sweet lips to his.

He could feel the love she felt for him wash over his entire being.

Tynae did not let go of Ryedin. Pressing herself to him, she clearly wanted more. "Please, Ryedin."

He did not push her away, but he did not let things progress any further. "Tynae," he said breathlessly, "You must go, angel."

Tynae sat back, flushed yet radiant. "Why can't…"

Ryedin placed his finger over her lips. "In this world I am king. Yes, you are my queen, but in this world there are certain rules I will not break." He pressed his lips firmly to hers once more. "Tomorrow, my angel, I will see you tomorrow. One last thing, the bag will be tucked under a lose floor board in the far right-hand corner of your sleeping chamber, the corner nearest the stained glass window."

Tynae gave Ryedin a quizzical yet cheerful smile. "Okay." Her loving eyes pierced his soul, "I love you."

"And I you—more than you could ever imagine."

Chapter 40
Time to Leave

"Fortune and Love Favor the Brave."
~Ovid

"What are you doing, Vinard?"

Vinard grabbed several articles of clothing from his chest of drawers. "I know you're getting on in years, Enessa, but surely you recognize packing when you see it."

Walking into Vinard's room Enessa shut the door behind her. "I can see that you're packing. The question is 'why'? Where are you going?"

"I need to find Tynae. I can't sit around here any longer doing nothing. I need to know what happened." Vinard ran his fingers through his hair irritably. "Did we send her to her doom?"

Enessa walked over to the bed, standing beside Vinard. "We did what we thought was best. Would you change it?"

Vinard thought about it. "No, no I wouldn't. I stand by what we did, but…" Vinard sat on the edge of his bed. "I can't function anymore, Enessa. I can't eat. I don't sleep. Every noise I hear, I think it's her. And if I actually manage to fall asleep, my dreams are consumed by her." Standing up he gathered more of his belongings. "I need to know what happened." Vinard neatly placed his clothes into his pack. "Other than you, I don't know who I can trust. So the only thing I can do is set out on my own, and pray that I find answers."

"What are you going to tell the king? Your regiment was assigned to Pathrow. Yurgon said he wants you to stay close to home."

Vinard continued grabbing items from around his room. "I can't explain it, Enessa. I need to leave. I feel like I'm being pulled." Vinard stopped, staring at a trinket he'd pulled out of a drawer.

"What if..." Enessa hesitated, "she's dead?"

Visions of Tynae's beautiful and very alive face flooded Vinard's mind as he turned the object over in his hand. "I can't even think about that."

"Yurgon is not going to let you go."

Tucking the trinket into his pocket, Vinard resumed packing. "He won't have a choice. I'm not going to tell him."

"Vinard, if her body is found and you're gone, you will be accused."

"Stop it, Enessa. Her body won't be found because she's *not dead*."

"Fine, let say she's not dead, wha..."

"Damn it, Enessa, she is NOT dead!"

"Fine, she's out there somewhere, and she's alive. But going out on your own may just get *you* killed."

Walking over to Enessa, Vinard looked her directly in the eyes. "I would rather be dead than not know what happened to Tynae. What if she's hurt and needs help? What if someone's holding her captive? I...I just need to do something." Vinard put his hands on Enessa's shoulders. "Are you really okay with not knowing?"

Enessa raised a brow. "Of course I'm not *okay* with not knowing. It might be entirely my fault she's dead." Enessa gestured to her face. "Do you see these bags under my eyes? I can't sleep either. Every night I relive the last moments we shared with her, but it doesn't end there. I see Gwillim chasing her and...killing her." A tear ran down Enessa's cheek. "I am terrified to shut my eyes." Enessa broke down in sobs. "Why, Vinard? Why did this happen?"

Vinard held Enessa. "I don't know, but I plan on getting to the bottom of it."

Enessa collected herself. "Should we tell Yurgon what we know?"

Vinard went back to packing. "What if he's the one who ordered Tynae's execution? We'd be next."

"Do you really think...I mean...I don't think he could possibly do anything like that."

Vinard shrugged. "I never thought he could, and I don't want to believe that he did, but I don't know what to think at this point. Did Gwillim act on his own accord or was he following orders? If Yurgon didn't issue the orders, who else would Gwillim take orders from?" Vinard sighed. "I just don't know anymore. I keep trying to make some sort of sense out of all this shite, but I can't. What could possibly be gained from Tynae's death?" Vinard looked at Enessa. "Why would anyone want her dead?" Grabbing an object off a nearby table Vinard threw it across the room. "I want to KILL Gwillim every time I see that bastard!" he growled, "I can't keep playing these ludicrous games." Stuffing the last of his possessions into his pack, Vinard irritably tied it up.

Enessa looked at Vinard thoughtfully. "I want to come with you."

"No."

"Why not? Are you really going to leave me here alone to go stir crazy?"

"Enessa, I have no idea where I'm going, or what dangers I may run into."

"I don't care, I want to come and I won't take no for an answer."

"Enessa, there's a very good chance I may never return to Pathrow."

"I don't care. Without Tynae here what point is there for me to stay?"

Vinard chuckled. "I can't talk you out of this, can I?"

Enessa smiled. "No."

Vinard smiled back. "We leave under the cover of darkness. Meet me in the stables shortly after the witching hour has passed and we will be on our way."

Chapter 41
Alone at Last

"A single rose can be my garden...single friend, my world."
~Leo Buscaglia

When the couple awoke the next morning they decided to spend the day in. When playtime was over and they finally decided to get out of bed, Tynae went to bathe while Béo made breakfast.

Unable to find anything in her closet that appealed to her, Tynae slipped into one of Béo's tunics. Walking out of her room into the living area, she saw Béo and started laughing hysterically. He was standing in the cooking area holding a half plucked chicken in one hand and a spoon in the other. Wearing nothing but an apron around his waist, he was cooking over an open flame.

Finally getting her laughter under control, Tynae walked over to Béo. "Do you think this wise, lover?" she asked stepping behind him. "We wouldn't want any of your appendages getting burnt," she teased, running her hand over his apron.

Tynae peered into the pan. "Mmm, that actually smells really good."

Béo faked a scathing glare. "What? Because I am a *man* I should not know how to cook?" he asked sarcastically.

Tynae shook her head. "Not at all, it's rather refreshing to see a man cooking. So what are we having?" Tynae eyed the half naked bird in Béo's hand. "Are we all supposed to go al' fresco?" she joked. "Shall I remove my covering as well?"

"Mmm," Béo considered the offer for a moment. "As tempting as that is I don't think it to be wise," he said. "Could you imagine the look on O'leana's face if she were to walk in?"

They both started laughing.

351

Tynae stood beside Béo as he cooked. "So what is it that we're having and why do you have a half plucked chicken in your hand? Did it get confused during molting season and couldn't make up its mind?"

Chuckling Béo shook his head. "This is to be our supper," he said, holding up the bare breasted bird. "I was killing two birds with one stone," he joked. "Or maybe it was more like ten birds since I cracked nine eggs in here." Béo pointed to the pan he was stirring.

Tynae rolled her eyes.

"I was getting the plucking done," yanking out a few feathers Béo tossed them in a rubbish pail, "while cooking," he stirred the eggs in the pan, "the liquid version of this." He held out the half-naked chicken, which swung pathetically.

"Eww." Tynae chuckled, wrinkling her nose, "That is disgusting."

Béo nodded his head with a look of repulsion. "It is, isn't it?" He laughed.

Taking the pan off the fire, Béo dismissed himself briefly. "I'll be right back." He disappeared into Tynae's room, when he re-emerged he had on a pair of trousers.

Tynae looked at him curiously.

He shrugged. "I don't like sticking to the chairs," he said in a serious tone.

Looking him up and down, Tynae started laughing.

Together they ate their meal. All the while laughing, chatting and enjoying each other's company.

After breakfast, which by the time they ate was really dinner; they spent the rest of the day in Vu'tella's mini forest. Béo pointed out many new sea creatures, explained how they lived and what their place was in the food chain. Time flew by.

Béo fixed supper then the pair got ready for bed.

"Are you ready for tomorrow?" Béo asked, pulling back the covers.

It took Tynae a minute then she lit up. "Demric? Yes," she said disappearing behind the screen in her changing area.

Béo laughed, shaking his head. "You are an odd bird, love, how could anyone not adore you?"

Béo sat on the edge of the bed watching Tynae's silhouette as she changed.

"Easy. I don't conform to their standards and 'poof' they don't like me," she said frankly.

"Why is everything so black and white with you?" Béo asked.

"It's not. I live in a world that is decorated with all the colors of the rainbow and many of them meld together, but black and white is the way most people see things, or me, to be more specific. I'm an open minded person, I just know better than to think others are like me. The world's been trying to get me to be something that I am not since the day I was born," she said sadly, stepping out from behind the screen.

"How so?"

"Well I was not born to royalty, yet I am expected to be the queen, which I will gladly do. It is my duty and I accept it happily, if at this point in my life it is still a part of my destiny." Tynae sat beside Béo on the bed. "I like to wield swords and fight, but the world wants me to carry flowers and skip about merrily." Tynae laughed heartily. "Could you imagine *me* prancing around with daisies, blowing kisses and spending my time in court batting my eyes pretending to be interested in the countless suitors who are only interested in my possessions and in possessing me?" They both laughed. "I can be a dainty girl, but it is not my preference. They expect me to marry the swarthy rich prince who's ego is bigger than the oversized pretentious land he presides over, and I want to marry who ever the bloody hell I want." Tynae shook her head as she thought. "People just don't know how to think for themselves. They're so used to being whom and what everyone else expects them to be that they don't know how to be who they truly are. And they certainly don't know what to make of someone like me!" she said wistfully. "A woman with her own mind and her own set of standards she is not willing to compromise…a woman who can do things a man can do, just as well as a man and sometimes better." Tynae exhaled loudly. "I don't care what they think. I play their game because I have to, but I've found a way to play that allows me to be happy even if it causes them to get their knickers in a bunch, and I don't rightly care." Tynae winked at Béo who stared at her in awe. Getting up, Tynae walked over to her side of the bed. "Let's get some rest, love." She crawled under the covers.

"You make it look so easy," Béo said climbing into his side of the bed.

"There's nothing easy about it, but in all reality I've got…or at least I *had* it good. My father allowed me to be who I am, or was, as long as I played my role as princess to a certain extent. I love helping people. There's nothing pretend about that. Don't get me wrong, I love my life. I just don't like having other people's rules and boundaries forced down my throat." Tynae rolled onto her side. "Besides, *you* certainly don't play by *'the rules'*. Seems to me that you have a fairly normal life, considering you're the future Chief of Calai." Tynae pointed out.

"I guess, but you still make life look easy despite any obstacles that get in your way," he observed.

"I don't see anything as an obstacle. Everything is just a part of life. We must deal with it, learn from it, and move on. When all is said and done, we are much stronger people because of what we've experienced in our life time; good, bad, and indifferent…it all balances itself out." Tynae thought about her last statement. "Well it only balances out if you learn from it. If not, it will keep repeating over and over until you actually 'get it'." Tynae sighed, snuggling into Béo's arms. "I'm not telling you anything you don't already know. I love you," she said drifting off to sleep.

Béo lay there, thinking of Tynae's words. They made sense, but she really did make her life look easy... even prior to coming to Calai. Every time he had seen her in Pathrow she was radiant and happy. He had no idea how many demands had been imposed upon her. *She truly is extraordinary.*

He kissed her forehead lightly then with a wave of his hand all became dark.

"My angel, I cannot stay long tonight," Ryedin said, taking Tynae in his arms.

"Why?" she asked disappointed.

Ryedin looked at her lovingly. "I cannot say. Please forgive me."

"You never have to ask for my forgiveness, my love." Tynae looked into his eyes. "I am grateful for even just a moment with you."

A horn blew from somewhere in the distance. "I must go, but I wanted to tell you that when the time is right for you to deliver the bag to Chenoa she will find you." Ryedin pressed his lips passionately to Tynae's. "I love you. We will spend much more time together when next we meet. I promise."

Ryedin's words faded as he did and Tynae was left with an emptiness she had never felt before.

Chapter 42
Grumpy Old Man

"We are young only once,
after that we need some other excuse."
~Author Unknown

Reaching the entrance to the city, Tynae was once again overwhelmed by its splendor.

"I just can't get over how beautiful this place is," she said looking around. "Where's Demric? Oh! I told O'leana I wanted special clothing made so I can move properly when I fight. Do many of the Greer women learn hand to hand?"

"No. You're the first. I'm not sure how Demric is going to feel about training you. Of course he'll do it. He has to follow father's orders, but that doesn't mean he has to like it." Béo's tone conveyed a touch of concern.

"If no other women learn to fight, why me?"

"I think it's because father knows how exceptional you are with a sword. Trust me, no women among the Greer sword fight either. Anyway, I'm sure father understands how much you'd really like to expand your abilities. You're unique, love, that's all there is to it. And Demric is located over there," he pointed, "near the sword arena."

Tynae lit up.

When they arrived at the fighting arena, Demric was busy sharpening a mace.

Béo attempted to greet him. "Morning, Demric."

Béo waited for Demric to respond, but he did not.

It appeared that Béo was right. Demric seemed disgruntled and they had only just arrived. Or maybe he was always cranky.

He appear to be older, but Tynae was learning fast that her perception of age and how the Greer matured did not coincide.

Béo looked at Tynae apologetically. "Sorry," he whispered.

Demric's rudeness was evidently wearing on Béo. "Did Chief Kerszon tell you of your new pupil?"

Demric's response was more of a grunt. "Ay."

"Very well then, Demric, this is Lady Tynae. Lady Tynae, Demric."

Demric finally looked up from the sharpening stone. Eyeing Tynae with a resentful glare, he looked her up and down as if she were a disease infested creature. Standing up, he threw the mace at a block of wood where it stuck. Turning his back on Tynae, he walked into the arena.

Anger flashed in Béo's eyes. His hands balled into fists.
"Relax, it's okay," Tynae said softly.
"No, it is not. I will not tolerate Demric's attitude or his blatant disrespect toward you." Béo started to walk after Demric, but Tynae grabbed him by the arm, shaking her head.

"I'll earn his respect…be patient, please," she requested in a whisper.

Tynae had dealt with men like Demric before. She wanted him to know that she comprehended his displeasure. "I understand you are not happy about having to teach a *woman,* but I will be one of the best students you've ever trained," she assured.

Demric spat at the ground.

Tynae saw Béo out of the corner of her eye. He was getting ready to launch himself at Demric. Before he could, Tynae looked at him with pleading eyes and shook her head slightly. "Please," she mouthed silently.
"Demric, like it or not, you're stuck with me. So let's get started," Tynae said plainly.
"Do you really think you could ever hold your own with a man…*My Lady?*" Demric asked arrogantly.

"Yes, I do actually, and I'll make you a deal…train me for thirty days. Then allow me to fight a man of equal training." Tynae's presence was strong. "If I lose, you will never have to teach me again. But if I win, you will train me for as long as I desire and you will *never* complain, ever again," Tynae explained flatly.

Demric, clearly intrigued by her offer, started to open his mouth. Before he could get a single word out Tynae held up a halting finger. "Let me make one thing perfectly clear before we agree on anything. The training you give me during those thirty days must be the same training you would give any *man*. Now, do we have a deal?" she asked with a biting tone.

After thinking it over, Demric stuck out his hand. "Deal," he grunted.

Tynae extended her hand and they shook on it.

Leaning back against the arena wall, Béo crossed his arms over his chest. He was plainly agitated by the way Demric was treating Tynae. "I'll be watching you, Demric!" Béo growled. "You are walking on thin ice."

Looking at Béo, Demric waved him off like an irritating bug.

Tynae smiled at Béo and winked.

Shaking his head, Béo chuckled and winked back.

Tynae stood in the middle of the arena, Demric sizing her up. Without warning he took a swing at her.

She blocked him with lightning speed. "So that's how it is? I'm not exactly inexperienced, Demric," Tynae warned.

"I need to see what your skill level is...*My Lady*." Demric's explanation was full of mockery and loathing. He came at her several more times, clearly not holding back. He was determined to put this *lady* in her place.

Tynae blocked every strike, upper cut, right hook, and jab. "Am I allowed to strike you or are you just *assessing* my ability to block?" Tynae tried to disguise her irritation. Unfortunately there was no hiding the iciness in her glare.

"If you think you can strike me, please do so," Demric challenged.

The old man's disrespect and cockiness was infuriating Tynae. It was at this point she decided to put this *man* in *his* place.

With an arch of a brow and the nod of her head, Tynae crouched into her fighting stance.

Béo covered his mouth with his hand.

Tynae could tell he was smiling from ear to ear. Of course he knew what was coming next.

Demric shook his head in disbelief, "Stupid girl," he muttered.

"Excuse me?" Tynae bit back.

"I didn't say anything."

Tynae waved Demric on, taunting him. Her face was hard and her voice arrogant. "Come on gramps, you know you're dying to land one."

Tynae caught Béo out of the corner of her eye. He was biting his lip, trying desperately not to laugh. Tynae wondered what he was thinking. Up until that moment he hadn't known Tynae knew hand-to-hand.

Demric came at Tynae again.

She quickly stepped out of the way avoiding his fist, getting in a solid punch to Demric's side as he stepped past.

The impact knocked the wind out of Demric causing him to stumble. The old man glowered at Tynae.

Grinning, she just shrugged her shoulders.

"Ah, come on, Demric. You're not going to let a little *girl* beat you, are you?" Béo taunted.

Tynae resumed her stance. Demric tried coming at her from the side this time. Planting her feet firmly Tynae grabbed Demric's arm, throwing him to the ground, flat on his back. Before Demric had time to figure out what was happening, Tynae's knee was buried in his chest and her dagger was at his throat.

Béo clapped loudly as Tynae stepped off Demric's chest.

Looking over at Béo, she gave him a small curtsy. Turning her attention back to Demric, Tynae offered him a hand up.

Demric pushed her hand aside. Back on his feet he shot Tynae a scathing glare.

Tynae let out a derisive laugh. "Such gallantry," she said sarcastically rolling her eyes. Turning her back to Demric she walked to the middle of the ring. "Demric, I was told you are the best at what you do. As you can plainly see, I already know a fair bit about fighting. I would like to learn more. Will you be able to teach me techniques I do not already know?" she questioned coldly.

Demric was so furious Tynae almost expected to see smoke come out of his ears. "You tricked me," he spat.

"No. You assumed that because I am female I would *not* know how to fight. Did you ask me if I had any previous training? No, you did not." Tynae reminded him. "So I ask you again, are you able to teach me beyond my current skill level?" Tynae fixed an innocent smile on her lips, waiting patiently for Demric's response.

"Ay, I can teach you…My…*Lady*," he spoke slowly, each word coated with vile venom.

Tynae couldn't help herself. *Two can play at this game,* she thought. Fixing a huge grin on her face and with the most annoyingly, bouncy and chipper voice she could summon, Tynae responded. "Great, Béo and I will go grab some food and we'll be back in a bit."

As Tynae walked away Demric tried to get in one last blow, coming at her from behind. Raising her elbow she caught him in the ribs. Demric flew into the air landing flat on his arse with an audible thud.

Not looking back Tynae walked on.

Béo did look. With a guffaw he shook his head.

"Very impressive, my love, but you never mentioned you knew hand-to-hand." Béo narrowed his eyes.

Tynae giggled. "Ah well…" She wrinkled her nose. "A girl's got to have at least one little secret," she teased.

"What other secrets do you have?"

"Well if I told you, they wouldn't be secrets would they?"

Béo looked at Tynae suspiciously. "Fine. How are you feeling about the lessons?"

"It's difficult to say." Tynae sighed. "Do you think he'll be able to advance my current level? I really do want to learn more."

"I don't know that he can teach you much you don't already know. You could probably teach him a thing or two." Béo chuckled. "Actually, I think you did. He's barely surviving as your sparring partner." Béo laughed so loud that everyone around them turned. "You're just too good," Béo said amused.

"There has to be someone better and faster than me in Calai. I need to train with that person." Tynae thought for moment, "I know!" she blurted out, "I never learned how to fight multiple opponents. That's something I really do need to learn."

"I do not like that idea. Let me think about it and maybe talk to father."

Tynae raised a brow. "It's not really up to *you*, is it?" she said in a matter-of-fact tone, dismissing Béo's disapproval entirely. "It's the training I'm lacking," she mused. "Yes, I will let Demric know when we return."

"I…"

"Béo, please remember, I was being groomed to be the Queen of many nations. Following other people's orders is not something I will yield to." Tynae leaned up on her tip toes to whisper in Béo's ear. "I love you." There was an apologetic tone in her words. "But I will not apologize for being my own woman."

Rolling his eyes, Béo shook his head and laughed. "What am I going to do with you?" he teased.

Tynae bit her lip, raising her eyebrows. "I have a few ideas," she purred.

Béo shuddered as goose bumps erupted from his head to his toes. "It really should be illegal to look that sensual outside of the bedchamber," he muttered to himself, trying to calm his thudding heart. Swallowing hard, Béo pretended Tynae hadn't said anything of the sort. "What would you like to eat, angel?"

The tender smile on Tynae's face made her look positively angelic. "Surprise me. I'd like to try something I've never had before."

Béo studied his choices..."Have you ever had laris?"

"No."

"Okay, I'll be right back. If you want, you can get us a place to sit over there," Béo pointed to a grassy area with lots of wooden tables.

Tynae picked the table furthest from the rest.

Back in no time, Béo set down two plates. A server brought two mugs and a pitcher of ale.

"Thank you."

With a bow, the server quickly departed.

Tynae looked at the ale then at Béo and started to laugh. "Do you really think it wise to be serving *me* ale?" she joked.

Béo looked at Tynae with innocent eyes..."Should I get something else? I wasn't thinking. It's just what I normally get," he said apologetically.

"It's fine." She giggled. "I just don't drink ale very often, that's all."

"I'll get you something else. I'll be right back..." Béo was gone before Tynae could stop him.

When he returned, he had a pitcher of juice.

"You didn't have to do that."

"I can't have you running around Calai intoxicated. My father would have me flogged."

They both chuckled.

Tynae looked at her plate. "So, what are we eating?"

"Well the meat is pheasant and the pink squares there are laris. It's a fruit that is both sweet and sour. Over here," Béo pointed, "these green and yellow long beans are tuvar. Even though they're vegetables, they have a sweet taste; and of course there's bread."

Picking up his fork, Béo stabbed a piece of pheasant and a piece of laris. He carefully fed it to Tynae. "It's always best if you get a little meat and laris in each bite," he explained, while watching her lips daintily remove the bite from his fork.

"Mmm, that is really good," she said.

Béo just nodded, rubbing his hand over his face trying to get a grip on himself.

"What?" Tynae was flummoxed by his reaction.

"Do you do anything that isn't totally...*seductive*?" he whispered the last word.

Tynae snickered. "I'm sure that not *everything* I do is..." she rolled her eyes and laughed. "Be patient, my love, we have all night."

The pair dug into their meals.

Tynae watched the goings on around them as they ate.

"What are you looking at?" Béo asked.

"The people," Tynae answered. "The energy coming from everyone here is so peaceful and welcoming—unlike most cities, which are generally chaotic and distressed."

"You can feel energy?"

"I can. It's something I've always been able to do."

Béo took a drink of ale, "Interesting."

Tynae looked at Béo. "Did you say that Chenoa is Demric's wife?"

Béo smiled. "She most certainly is."

"Wow, they certainly make an interesting pair."

"I suppose in their case the saying 'opposites attract' holds true."

After finishing their meal, the pair sat for a spell. "Will we have time to explore today? Tynae asked.

Béo nodded. "We should. Where would you like to go?"

Tynae thought about it. "You had mentioned something about an icy place..." Tynae snapped her fingers, trying to remember.

"The ice forest?" Béo chuckled.

"Yes," Tynae laughed. "That place."

"Then the ice forest it shall be." Picking up his stein, Béo drank the last of his ale. "Are you ready to go back and face Demric?" He grinned.

Tynae took a deep breath. "I am."

Chapter 43
Respect Earned

"Nature says to a woman: 'Be beautiful if you can,
wise if you want to, but be respected, that is essential."
~Pierre Beaumarchais

Returning to the training area, the couple saw two men speaking with Demric. When Demric saw Tynae and Béo approaching, the old man stopped talking and jerked his head toward Tynae.

Tynae glanced at Béo out of the corner of her eye. "Bit of a sore loser, is he?"

Béo chuckled. "Well, I don't think knocking the stuffing out of him is going to make him warm up to you, darling. Not that I didn't thoroughly enjoy it," he laughed. "Watch out for those two. They're worse than Demric, if that's possible."

"Noted."

Tynae smiled as they strolled up to the men. "Will we be continuing with my lessons, Demric?" Tynae asked using her sing-song voice.

"Absolutely, and I have enlisted the help of two of my finest warriors to assist us," Demric proclaimed triumphantly.

"Have you now? You don't intend to have me fight both of them without properly training me first, do you?" Tynae accused.

"Of course not...*My Lady*," Demric assured innocently. "You will fight them individually and I will watch. This way I can see where your weaknesses lie. Then we can focus on strengthening those areas."

Tynae pursed her lips. "Right then, let's get this thing moving, shall we? Who will I be fighting first?" she asked, looking at the two huge men.

Demric's smugness had returned with a vengeance. "I think Jax will do just fine."

Of course he picks the one as big as an oak tree.

Jax towered over Tynae. He was a hulking man standing at least 2 meters and built like a stone wall. He had dark hair, dark eyes, olive skin, and like most men in this city his body was very well chiseled.

"Lady Tynae, may I have a word?" Béo asked with an official tone.

"Yes, Lord Béo."

Tynae walked to where Béo stood.

"I am *not* comfortable with this situation..." Béo glanced at Jax, "at all."

Tynae looked over her shoulder. "I cannot learn if I don't fight them. Besides, I have speed on my side." Her face twisted into a sly smile as her confidence returned.

"This is true. You may be tiny, but you move like the wind, and you're stronger than I ever could have imagined." Béo huffed. "Go then."

Tynae blew Béo a kiss seen only by him then returned to the ring. It was time to face the grizzly bear waiting for her.

"Hello, Tingy." Tynae was elated to see her adorable admirer. "Are you here to work your magic?"

"Yes, My Lady." Tingy's voice was unusually serious.

The little Nanic put protective spells around both fighters.

"Tingy, don't look so worried. I'll be fine," Tynae assured.

Looking around Tingy gestured for Tynae to come closer. "You should not be fighting Jax, Mistress." Tingy's voice quivered. "He's three times your size."

Tynae leaned closer, ensuring Tingy was the only one who could hear her. "It just means he'll leave a bigger indent in the ground," she whispered, "relax." Standing up, Tynae winked at Tingy and shot Béo a bright smile. Turning, she faced Jax.

"Any rules, Demric?" she asked flatly.

Demric was looking rather pompous. "No. First one to deliver a death blow wins," he declared loudly.

Tynae nodded.

Jax and Tynae stood approximately a meter apart. Tynae was the first to move. She began prowling around Jax.

Measuring her every movement, Jax turned on the spot where he stood.

Tynae was feeling a bit smug, having regained her self-confidence. "Jax, you don't have to be a gentleman here, feel free to make the first move. Or are you afraid of little ol me?" she taunted.

Tingy was sitting on the wall next to Béo. The little guy still looked terrified.

Béo looked a bit nervous himself, but it was evident he was waiting for the fight to really begin before he allowed his fear to get the better of him.

Tynae knew once Béo saw she could take care of herself, he would relax.

Jax finally made a move, taking a step toward Tynae.

She stopped dead in her tracks.

Jax lunged, attempting to hit her with a left hook.

Grabbing his arm, Tynae twisted it behind him, jumped up on his back and locked her knees at his waist. "If I wanted to end this right now, I could put my dagger to your throat. But that would be much too simple!" Tynae said in his ear. Sliding her finger across his throat, she punctuated her point. Jumping off Jax's back, Tynae let his arm go and was on the move before he had time to wheel around and face her. Finally getting close enough to throw another blow, Tynae struck; left, right, face, stomach…she was astonished at her own speed. She'd never moved like this before.

Jax couldn't land a single punch.

Leaping forward Tynae struck Jax square in the face, causing him to stumble backward.

Tynae knew he was seeing stars.

Nose bleeding and off balance, Jax shook his head trying to regain himself. Once steady on his feet, he quickly went after Tynae throwing a punch at her face.

With lightning speed she sidestepped the blow. Turning, she struck him in the kidney with everything she had, dropping him to his knees. Stepping behind the warrior Tynae grabbed a hand full of hair, pulling his head back. "You're making this way too easy, Jax!" she taunted, running her finger across his throat again. "Come on; show me what you're really made of big boy."

Once he could breathe again, Jax stood up. His ego was taking a beating and he was fuming.

Tynae was ready to end this. She wanted to see the ice forest. Jax tried getting behind her.

Tynae was not going to let that happen. Jumping up, she spun in the air, kicking Jax square in the jaw then landed neatly on the ground. Lurching forward, Tynae punched Jax twice in his stomach. When he went to swing at her, she dropped down to a squat and spun around with her leg out.

Jax hit the ground so hard it shook.

He was on his back and this time Tynae was not going to let him up. In a flash she was on his chest, pinning him with her knee, dagger at his throat. Stepping nimbly off Jax, she offered him a hand.

He glared up at her. Grimacing, he accepted her assistance.

Once Jax was on his feet Tynae turned around to find not only an audience watching; but Chief Kerszon standing front and center, Béo at his side.

The crowd cheered and clapped.

Sheathing her dagger, Tynae walked over to Kerszon and Béo. "Chief," Tynae greeted, inclining her head.

"Lady Tynae, you were quite impressive."

"Thank you, but I wasn't trying to impress. I just didn't want to get hit."

The small crowd laughed.

Tynae leaned over. "Tingy, you can breathe now." Poor thing was more pale than normal. "And could you please remove the shield spell from me."

Tingy exhaled, breathing easy. "Of course, My Lady…You are fascinating to watch, I've never seen anything like it."

"Thank you, Tingy." Tynae looked at Béo who gestured with his head to something behind her.

Turning, Tynae saw Demric walking to her. "So, Demric, how did I do?" she asked coolly.

Bowing his head in defeat, Demric no longer treated Tynae as an inferior subordinate. "I would be lying if I said you were anything less than the best I've ever seen," he admitted.

Smiling, Tynae shook her head. "I promise you, I am not the best. I'm confident there are many others out there better than I."

Kerszon roared with laughter. "If there are, they are few and far between."

Tynae became sheepish. "Thank you, Chief."

"Demric, I would like to learn how to fight multiple opponents and I'd like to start tomorrow.

This is indeed an area I need to improve upon. Are you willing to train me?" she asked sincerely.

"Ay, M'Lady. I would consider it a great honor to assist you in advancing your skills," he said with a bow.

Tynae's smile was genuine. "Thank you, Demric. We will see you tomorrow." She turned to Jax. "Join us for a pint?"

Jax hesitated. "Do I have to fight you for it?" he asked wearily.

Their audience howled with laughter.

Feeling a twinge of guilt, Tynae's face flushed. Hunching her shoulders, she couldn't help but chuckle. "No. It's a peace offering."

Jax smiled, "Then I accept."

Tynae turned to Kerszon. "Care to join us?"

"I would love to take you up on that offer, but perhaps another time. There are matters that need tending to." Kerszon excused himself. "Lady Tynae, Béo."

Béo, Tynae, and Jax set off to the market place.

"Where did you learn to fight like that, Lady Tynae?" Jax asked intrigued.

Tynae snickered. "I think my father wanted a son. He started teaching me how to fight the moment I was able to walk. I liked it, and the better I did the happier my father was. After a while he added swords, daggers, you name it. Old Man Hern, a retired soldier from my army, even taught me a trick or two that not many know. When it got to a point that few could defeat me, my father requested that I personally train with the leaders of our army," she explained. "The fact that my strength and speed has dramatically increased since I've come to Calai certainly doesn't hurt."

"You mean to say, that the entire army of Pathrow fights as you do?" Jax asked, clearly stunned.

"In a manner of speaking, yes," Tynae shrugged. "A fair amount of them do anyway, and I can say with the utmost of confidence there are many among them that are much better fighters than I."

Jax considered Tynae's words.

Reaching the marketplace Tynae looked at Béo and grinned. "My Lord, would you please get two pints? I'd like to have some and between the two of you one pint will not suffice," she chuckled.

"Yes, My Lady." Béo winked at Tynae, "Two pints coming up. I'll be right back."

Tynae and Jax went to sit at a table.

Returning with two pints and three steins, Béo sat beside Tynae.

Glancing at Tynae, Béo grinned. "If it's any conciliation, Jax, she's beaten me twice. Well three times really, twice with the sword and once in a foot race."

Jax almost choked on his ale, he looked at Béo completely bewildered. "She beat *you* in a foot race?" he asked incredulously.

Picking up his tankard Béo took a swig. "She certainly did," he grinned.

Jax raised his stein. "To Lady Tynae, a most astonishing woman."

Béo conceded, "Here, here."

"Thank you," Tynae said modestly.

"Cheers," they said in unison.

"Would you be willing to work with our army, My Lady?" Jax asked.

Tynae nodded, "Certainly. The way things are going, it couldn't hurt."

Jax was delighted with Tynae's response. "Great! I will talk to Demric and he can speak with Chief Kerszon."

"Thank you both for the drink, I need to tend to a few matters of my own." Finishing off his ale, Jax stood. "See you back at the arena tomorrow?"

Béo nodded. "We'll be there."

They were finally alone and Béo was beaming.

Tynae looked around then back at Béo. "What are you thinking?" she asked with a devilish grin.

"You did it." There was excitement in Béo's voice.

Tynae looked disconcerted. "Did what?"

Béo smiled hugely. "You earned the respect of some of the toughest warriors in Calai. I had my doubts, I must admit, but you did it. I'm so proud of you."

Tynae blushed. "Thank you. I learned a long time ago that I have to stand up for myself from the start or I'll get walked on. I am not about to be anybody's patsy."

"You are a lot of things, my love, but patsy is certainly not among them," he said earnestly. "Are you ready to go explore?"

"Sure am," Tynae said elated. "Let's go."

Leaving their table, Tynae spotted one of her maids passing by. "Koralie," Tynae called.

The maid walked over. "Yes, My Lady."

"Please tell O'leana we'll be dining in my quarters tonight. She may choose the menu and let her know that all of you may return to your own quarters. There is no longer a need for you to stay with me."

Koralie looked a bit surprised, but knew better than to question Tynae. "Yes, My Lady. Will there be anything else?"

Tynae smiled. "No, thank you."

With a curtsy and a nod, Koralie departed.

Béo stood there, staring at Tynae.

"What?" she asked innocently.

"You don't think people will find it odd that I remain in your sleeping chambers?"

Looking around, Tynae ensured no-one was within ear shot then beckoned Béo closer. Getting up on her tip toes she whispered very quietly in his ear. "I have a plan." She stepped back.

Laughing, Béo flashed his perfect smile, "Never a dull moment when I'm with you. You add enchantment to my every day," he chuckled. "Come on let's stop at Lore's and grab a bite to take with us," he said, walking toward the market place.

"Good day, My Lord, My Lady," Lore greeted.

"Good day, Lore. We just wanted a little nosh," Béo said.

"Not a problem." Lore quickly loaded Béo's pack.

"Here you go, My Lord."

Taking his pack from Lore, Béo slung it over his shoulder and turned to Tynae. "We're all set. Let's get out of here."

Chapter 44
Hidden Kingdoms

*"In the right light, at the right time,
everything is extraordinary."*
~Aaron Rose

Béo grinned at Tynae. "So when are you going to let me in on your little scheme?"

Tynae glanced at Béo with a clever smile, giving him a wink. "Later..." she teased, "So how far do we need to travel?"

"Not too far. Once we get to the tunnel we'll have to walk to the other side, which is a fair distance, but we have all day. Want to run?" Béo asked playfully.

Tynae grinned, "Of course. Which tunnel are we headed to?"

Béo pointed. "See the blue crystal beyond that far pond?"
Neither waited for Tynae's response, the two took off like a shot. Both wore huge smiles. They ran past several small children who giggled and clapped as the royal couple zoomed past.
Dashing across the city, Tynae was in the lead once again. Realization began to dawn on her. It seemed the more time that passed, the stronger her body felt. Just how much was she going to change?
When they reached the tunnel the pair called a truce, but Tynae had definitely won. Walking through the tunnel Tynae resumed her never ending list of questions. Not wanting to appear smug she made it a point not to bring up the race, besides she had much more weighing things on her mind. It's not every day one is thrown into a world of never-ending fairy tales. She still didn't know what to expect from one moment to the next.

"Was Tingy scared earlier?" Tynae inquired. "He looked petrified."

"That's an understatement!" Béo laughed. "He was begging me to stop you. I told him you'd be fine." Béo reached into his bag. "Want some fruit?" He held out an apple.

Tynae took it. "Thank you. Were you really that confident?" she asked skeptically, eyeing Béo. "You looked nervous, too." Tynae took a bite of apple. "Mmm, juicy."

"I'm reasonably confident you would never intentionally put yourself in a situation you weren't fairly certain you could control. Although, I will admit, it's going to be difficult to watch when you're in a position in which you don't have the upper hand, *but...*" he spoke quickly when Tynae turned to cut him off. "I know it's the only way to learn a new skill. I will do my best to master the urge to step in and defend you every time I feel like you're about to get the stuffing knocked out of you." He chuckled.

Tynae appreciated his consideration. "Thank you. I really do need this particular training."

"I know," Béo acknowledged warily.

"See that white light down there?" Béo asked, pointing to a speck directly in front of them.

"Yes."

"That's where we're going. Race you!" Béo was gone before Tynae had time to respond.

"Hey! That's not fair!!!" she hollered.

Tynae was not about to get beat like this. Taking off, she drew on every ounce of energy she possessed. Running faster than she ever had in her entire life, it was only a matter of seconds before she overtook Béo, zooming past him.

Arriving at the wooden door with the white light above it, she wasn't even winded. Waiting for Béo, Tynae tried to wrap her mind around the speed at which she was now able to move.

Béo looked astonished when he reached her. "Wow! What was that?" he asked slightly winded.

Tynae looked equally astonished by her new ability. "I have no idea. I've never run like that, ever."

"I might as well give up trying to win right here and now. I'll never top that," Béo admitted earnestly.

Tynae felt a twinge of guilt. "I'm sorry," she said timidly.

"Don't be sorry. It's great." Béo had true enthusiasm in his voice.
"Really?"
"Really." He clearly meant it. "Are you ready to go in? I'm dying to share this place with you."
"Absolutely," Tynae said gleefully.
"Close your eyes and keep them shut until I tell you. Okay?" Béo's tone was a bit mischievous.
Tynae considered him thoughtfully. "Okay."
"Promise?" Béo teased.
"I promise." Tynae danced on her toes with anticipation. "Let's go!" she demanded shutting her eyes.

Tynae heard the large wooden door creak open. She kept her eyes closed as Béo led her by the hand.
"Okay, open your eyes," he whispered.
Opening her eyes, Tynae gasped when she saw where they were standing. "This is the most incredible place I've ever seen." With a huge grin on her face and a look of sheer wonderment, she turned to Béo. "This is...it's…wow…" she breathed. "This place, it's glorious, far beyond imagination. Is it magic?" she asked wide-eyed.
Béo grinned, shaking his head. "No," he said simply.

"This is the most mesmerizing place I've ever seen. I can't believe that it's actually possible for anything like this to exist."

Tynae stood at the edge of a glorious forest. Slowly she turned where she stood, making a full circle. Everything was made of ice.

"The dome," she said quietly not looking at Béo. "It's visible all the way around not just at the top, there's no rock or mountains in here."

"Technically this is outside the boundary of Calai," Béo clarified.

"Amazing," she continued to look around, walking over to a waterfall cascading down from the ice forest. The water was a shade of green she'd never seen, shimmering green-blue mist floating above it. There were a myriad of lush ferns and flora growing beside the fascinating waterfall. Although each and every little thing was made of ice, the entire forest was full of dazzling color. Walking to the waters edge, Tynae touched several of the plants expecting them to be cold and hard like ice...they weren't. To her surprise they were merely cool to the touch, and every petal soft, like normal plants.

Béo watched Tynae as she explored.

Kneeling down Tynae gazed into the pool of water at the base of the fall. Reaching out she touched the liquid, expecting it to be bitterly cold as it appeared to flow over ice after all. The unexpected sensation the water evoked caused her to giggle. She turned to Béo. "It's warm...and bubbly," she snickered "How is that?"

Béo shrugged, "We don't know."

Walking over to Tynae, Béo knelt beside her. "Look," he said, cradling her hand in his. Together they scooped up a handful of water.

Tynae examined the water captured in their hands, it sparkled like a diamond. She was once again in total awe. With her free hand she touched the fluid. The color changed from green to purple.

"It's never done that before," Béo said surprised. "Touch it again," he encouraged.

She did, this time it turned red.

"Maybe we should take some of this water back to your room and let you experiment with it," Béo suggested.

"Could we?" Tynae asked joyfully.

Béo chuckled. "Yes. We'll get some before we leave."

Letting the water pour back into the pool, it resumed its original color.

Standing up, Tynae looked around. Overly zealous, she couldn't figure out which way to go next. Tynae pointed, "Where does that path lead?"

"What path?" Béo turned to see where she was pointing.

Béo's brow wrinkled with confusion. "I...I don't know...I've never seen it before."

"Can we follow it?" Tynae bounced on her toes like a child pleading for a new toy.

Béo hesitated. "Umm, sure."

They walked to the head of the trail. Like everything else in this forest, the bricks lining the path were made from ice. Before stepping onto the path, Tynae tested the bricks by sliding her foot back and forth over the glassy gray rectangles. They weren't slippery in the slightest. As they followed the path, Tynae looked up at the humongous trees. Their trunks were as big as ten large men put together. Walking over, she touched the trunk of one of the trees. It, too, was cool to the touch; but wasn't rocklike the way true ice is. The forest had her spellbound. There were countless trees of all shapes and sizes...And the colors were so dynamic it was like being awake inside of a dream. Ice willows created an archway through the forest and frozen wild flowers lined the edge of the path, while ice foliage covered the forest floor.

Walking backwards Tynae looked up at the forest canopy. Mesmerized by her surroundings, more than once she nearly smacked into a tree. Fortunately Béo always guided her back onto the path.

In the distance Tynae could hear water, but it wasn't a waterfall or a river. She wasn't sure what it was. "What's up ahead?" she asked.

Béo shrugged. "I'm not sure, why?"

"I can hear water."

"Maybe it's the top of the falls."

Tynae shook her head, "No." She listened intently, "It's different."

Walking together, Tynae was a bit more taken with her surroundings than Béo, but they both stopped dead in their tracks when *it* came into view.

Before them stood the most majestic castle that had ever been created. It too was made of ice. The grounds were covered with perfectly manicured gardens, and in the center of it all sat a fountain shooting water up in thirteen perfect arches. Ice shrubs situated throughout the grounds were sculpted into various shapes. Some were simple like a cylinder and others cut into precise circles with hollow centers. Some created hedges, enclosing multitudes of ice flowers. Others were intricate in their design.

One piece in particular stood out to Tynae. It looked like two hearts intertwined, similar to the stained glass wall in her room. One of the ice hearts was covered with dark red flowers and the other with silvery white flora.

There were millions of frozen blossoms growing throughout the garden. Each one looking as if it had diamond dust covering it and the smell...it was simply captivating.

Tynae looked around as if searching for something, then turned to Béo with a curious look.
"Can you feel that?" she whispered.
"Feel what?" Béo asked warily.
"The energy, everything, the plants, the trees, the grass, it's so...ALIVE," she said with astonishment. "I feel like they are a part of me."

Béo's eyes narrowed. "You can feel their life force?"

Tynae shrugged. "I hadn't thought of it like that, but yes, I guess I can. It's so strong...yet incredibly..."

The feeling was distinct, yet Tynae had difficulty finding the right word to describe it. Closing her eyes, Tynae focused on the energy. Drawing in a deep breath, she was flooded with a sensation of intense tranquility. "Harmonious...that's what it is...," she breathed. "It's like nothing I've ever felt before." The feeling continued to wash over her. Opening her eyes, Tynae turned to Béo, her smile bright. "It's amazing. You can't feel it?"

"No," Béo said lightly.
"That's too bad." Tynae continued examining her surroundings. "Who's the caretaker of all this?" She leaned forward smelling a blossom.
"No-one?" Béo shrugged, "I honestly do not know."

Tynae thought Béo was pulling her leg. "Surely someone maintains all of this. It can't possibly tend to itself."

Looking very confused, Béo shook his head. "Maybe it does. I really have no idea how all this is maintained, or even where it came from." Béo's voice carried an uneasy tone. "I've never seen any of this before today," he said, looking around.

Seeing movement in one of the shrubs, Tynae walked over to see what it was. As she approached the frozen bush a dazzling ice butterfly flew out. Its wings looked like a miniature rainbow. After circling Tynae once, it landed on her shoulder.

Tynae placed her opposite hand up to her shoulder and the butterfly eagerly climbed onto her finger. "It's so exquisite. Are there many of them here?"

Béo hadn't said very much since they'd arrived at the ice castle estate and now he appeared to be troubled. "Tynae, I don't know what's happening, but none of this," he gestured to their surroundings, "has ever been here before."

"Maybe you just missed it," Tynae said, walking around. "This place seems to be huge."

"You don't understand. I've spent more time here than you can imagine. I know...or at least, I thought I knew this place better than Calai." Looking around Béo shook his head. "None of this has ever been here before today. And I have never seen any living creatures at any point or at any place in the ice forest. That butterfly, I...just don't know." Béo shrugged, "I have no idea what is happening or what else may be here."

"Can we go to the castle?" Tynae implored with her childlike innocence, she knew Béo couldn't resist.

"I don't know, Tynae...if something were to happen to you...I couldn't live with myself." Discomfort was evident in Béo's every word.

Shaking her head, Tynae rolled her eyes. "Come on, Béo you're being a bit overly dramatic. This place has always existed. You just missed it somehow."

Béo looked at Tynae with utter confusion. "You say that like you know it as a fact."

"It is..." Tynae stated spontaneously. Brows furrowed she turned to Béo, "I don't know why I just said that, but somehow I do *know* that this place has always been here."

She looked around. "I also know there's nothing here to fear. It's an exceptionally safe place... Please, I really want to go inside the castle," she begged, her eyes now pleading.

Drawing in a deep breath Béo let it out slowly. "Okay, but if anything feels amiss we leave immediately. Agreed?"

"Yea!" Tynae nodded once, "Agreed...Now let's go!" Tynae was so excited she could have done cartwheels, but being the tom-boy that she was, she had never learned how. Setting the butterfly back on her shoulder, Tynae made a bee line for the castle. The walkway leading to the door had several ice statues lining it. They seemed to actually be guarding the entrance way, not just decorating it. They were angels and warriors. Walking in a circle around one of the angel statues, Tynae touched its wing. It was soft—not like anything she had ever felt before—not stone, bronze, marble or even ice, but perhaps almost like air with substance, if she knew what that felt like. "Have you ever seen such perfection?" Tynae murmured with admiration.

"Only once," Béo answered.
Tynae looked at him with surprise. "Really, where?"
Béo swept his hand along her cheek, "Here."
Blood rushed to Tynae's face.
Béo laughed softly. "You're so modest. You have no idea how beautiful you truly are, do you?"

"Thank you, but stop it." Tynae ran her hand lovingly over the angel's face. "I could never compare to *this*," she told him simply.

"Think what you want, but you are a million times more beautiful than that piece of ice ever could be."

Tynae rolled her eyes and giggled. "Come on." Grabbing Béo by the hand, she led him to the castle door. "Here goes nothing," she grinned, knocking.

No-one answered.

"Hmmm," Tynae turned to Béo. "What do you think we should do?"

Before he had a chance to answer, the butterfly flitted off Tynae's shoulder landing gracefully on the door. The door opened and the butterfly blissfully floated back to Tynae, resuming its perch atop her shoulder.

The couple looked at each other with disbelief.
Pulling Béo into the castle, Tynae beamed.

Chapter 45
Untold Stories

"All the art of living lies in a fine mingling
of letting go and holding on."
~Henry Ellis

The beauty of the castle was overwhelming. While the castle itself appeared to be made of ice, the furnishings were not.

Entering a sitting area, Tynae and Béo were greeted by a blazing fire crackling in a huge hearth that was plenty big enough for a man of two meters to stand in and not knock his head.

The furnishings were made from a dark wood Béo did not recognize. Some of the pieces of furniture were covered with white silk and others with royal blue velvet.

Tynae ran her hand along the back of a chair as she walked past. "Hello?" she called out. No-one answered. Turning to Béo she shrugged. "I had to try."

"Ellow," echoed a small voice.

The pair looked around to see where the voice had come from.

Hiding behind a large marble pillar was a small figure.

All they could see were small trembling fingers on either side of the column.

"Hello. I am Lady Tynae and this is Lord Béo," Tynae said softly.

The tiny creature poked its head out cautiously, eyeing the couple. Slowly it stepped into view, bowing respectfully. "Greetings, My Lord, My Lady. I iz Azmina."

Azmina was unmistakably a Nanic and was definitely female. She wore a simple dress as white as freshly fallen snow.

"Do you live here, Azmina?" Tynae asked her voice as light as mist.

"Ay, My Lady, I iz the Watcher," she said in a soft childlike voice.

"Watcher?" Tynae questioned.

"Yes, Watcher, My Lady. I iz the Watcher over..." Azmina looked around, "Everytingz you sees ma'am, tiz my job it is. I'z to *watch* until'z the rightful master returns, I am."

"And who is the master?" Tynae inquired.

Azmina shook her little head. "I'z iz not knowing, My Lady. And even if I'z did, I couldz not be saying."

"How long have you been here?" Tynae asked.

"Long, long'z time, Lady Tynae. As long as I'z can'z rememberz."

Tynae smiled at Azmina. "Are there others here with you?"

Azmina shook her head. "No'z others, My Lady, only onez may'z be here until'z such time az the rightful master returnz and choosez how'z he'z...or she'z wantz this...realm to be governed. I'z is the only one." Azmina glanced around. "But I'z does have a pet. If she showz herself I'z will gladly introducez youz," Azmina told Tynae happily.

Azmina was quite petite. Standing only about two thirds of a meter tall, her skin was a delicate pink tone and her eyes bright green. Her eyes differed from Tingy's in that they were slightly angular like a cat's. Her ears too were different. They were smaller and more rounded. Standing there wearing a shy little smile, she was the most innocent being Béo had ever seen.

"May I'z show'z you around, Majestiez?"

Tynae looked at Béo, clearly hoping to gain approval. Seeing the excitement in her face, he nodded.

Tynae beamed, "That would be lovely, Azmina."

Azmina showed them many of the rooms on the main floor. While doing so, Tynae took notice of several paintings of exceptionally beautiful men and woman. "Are any of these your master?" Tynae asked, gazing at the paintings.

"No'z, My Lady, those are masters and mistress' of time long since past. The new master'z painting has yet to be created." Azmina bowed to Tynae, "My Lady, there iz far too many roomz and floorz for me'z to be show'in you all'z of them in one day. Perhaps you'z and Lord Béo would like'z to return from time'z to time. I'z will'z gladly show'z you every bit of…" Azmina hesitated for a second. "Well I'z will show'z you whatever you'z wish'z to see, My Lady."

"Thank you, Azmina we will most certainly return."

Azmina smiled brightly. "I'z have one last room me'z would like to be showing to you'z and then you'z must be on your way, tiz getting late," Azmina said with concerned sentiment.

The couple followed Azmina down a long hall where she opened the door to an extravagant library.

Bookshelves covered more than half the room. Running from floor to ceiling, every inch of shelving was occupied with a multitude of books. A handsome arched desk made from the same beautiful dark wood as the furniture in the first room they'd entered, sat in the right-hand corner of the library where it was surrounded by windows. The chair behind the desk was covered with deep reddish brown leather. The windows looked out onto more ice gardens that must have been behind the castle.

Béo could tell that the visible gardens were not the ones he'd seen when they entered.

There were couches and chairs situated throughout the room. They too were covered in the same reddish brown leather.

Béo's attention was drawn to the many books throughout the expansive library.

There where many paintings suspended upon the walls, but Tynae seemed to gravitate to one specific portrait. It was that of an extraordinarily beautiful woman. Even Béo noticed there was something entrancing about her.

"Who is this, Azmina?" Tynae asked, staring at the portrait.

"That, My Lady, is Mistress Serafina, the Bearer of Harmony." Azmina's voice carried a proud tone.

Tynae's head tilted. "Odd…I feel as if I know her," she mused. "Oh, well." Shrugging it off, Tynae continued to wander around the enormous room, fiddling with her bracelet all the while.

The butterfly on Tynae's shoulder flew over to Azmina who stood with Béo. It hovered in front of Azmina for a moment then landed on a book.
Azmina gave an almost imperceptible nod and the butterfly returned to Tynae's shoulder.
Carefully Azmina removed the book from the shelf, handing it to Béo. "Lord Béo, I'z believe you'z and Chief Kerszon may'z be finding this book of great interest," Azmina whispered.
The book was bound with plush leather and adorned with two gold plates, one on the front and one on the back. The front plate was deeply embossed with an angel kneeling over a fallen warrior. Several small images surrounded the outer edges, but Béo was uncertain as to what they represented. The center of the back plate was embossed with the image of a tree Béo did not recognize. The other four quadrants of the back cover were embossed as well, but Béo did not take the time to examine them. Turning the book on its side, Béo glanced at the insignia residing in the center of the red wax seal securing the book shut. He did not recognize this either. "I can take it with me?"

Azmina nodded. "Yes," she replied softly.
Béo was taken aback. "Thank you very much."
"Lord Béo, dair'z just one'z thing…" Azmina spoke in hushed tones.
"Yes?"
Azmina glanced at Tynae then back at Béo. "The book, it is for you'z and you'z father only, for now'z anyway." Azmina's voice remained barely above a whisper.

Béo's eyes flashed over to Tynae. "Understood," he said, sliding the book discreetly into his pack.

"My Lady, I'z believe'z that Serry has taken a liking'z to you. May she accompany you'z back to Calai?"

Tynae looked incredibly befuddled.

Azmina grinned. "The butterfly on you'z shoulder, her'z name iz Serry," she explained.

"Oh!" Tynae giggled. "Will she survive outside of…" Tynae's brows knitted together as she looked around. "Does this place have a name, Azmina?"

"Yes, My Lady, this be'z Tergalia and Serry can survivez aanny'z where she desirez."

Tynae looked at Béo. "Do you think it would be alright?" she asked hopefully.

Béo contemplated for a moment. "Sure, I don't see why not."

Tynae almost squeaked with excitement, "Thank you."

Béo looked at Azmina, "What does she eat?"

"You'z need'z not worry'z about her, My Lord, Serry is very capable'z of taking good's care of herself, she iz. And she'z may return's to Tergalia any'z time she'z needz."

Béo smiled at the tiny Nanic. "Thank you for your hospitality, Azmina, we will return soon."

Azmina glanced at Tynae to see where her attention lied.

The princess had drifted back to the painting of Mistress Serafina once more. Transfixed, Tynae stood fidgeting with her bracelet staring up at the painting. Her winged friend still perched upon her shoulder.

Discreetly Azmina motioned for Béo to bend down to her level. "My Lord, you'z wills not'z be'z able to'z return'z to diz place if Lady Tynae is not'z wiff you'z." Azmina's voice was barely above a whisper now. "Read'z the book and you'z will understand'z."

Standing up, Béo nodded his head slightly in comprehension.

"Lady Tynae, are you ready?" Béo asked. "It is getting late."

"Yes, My Lord," she turned sharply, walking to Béo's side. "Thank you so much, Azmina. We will be back as soon as we can," Tynae said gratefully.

Walking the couple to the foyer, Azmina smiled sweetly, "I'z look'z forward to it, My Lady."

Azmina reached into a decorative box sitting on a table in the entry way. "Here'z," the little Nanic handed Tynae a large blue glowing crystal. "You'z may'z be need'nz this, it'z will light'z yourz way."

Both Béo and Tynae smiled at Azmina. "Thank you again."

Stepping out of the castle the pair realized it was noticeably darker. The sun was setting and very little light penetrated the glass dome.

"We need to get out of here as quickly as possible, so no stopping. Okay?" Béo urged.

"Okay, but why?"

"It's getting late and I don't want to have to explain to O'leana, or anyone else for that matter, where we've been. Not yet anyway."

"Okay. Do you want to run?" Tynae asked.

Béo shook his head. "No, a steady pace should do fine."

They did need to use the crystal Azmina had given Tynae, once they'd traveled further into the ice forest. The denseness of the trees prevented what little light remained from shining through.

Walking quickly, the pair were back in Calai before the sun finished setting. Emerging from the tunnel that led to the heart of the city, there were still a few people shopping and eating.

Tynae turned toward her shoulder. "Welcome to Calai, Serry."

The butterfly waved her wings in what seemed like an acknowledgment to Tynae's salutation.

Now that Serry was out of Tergalia she was even more beautiful. The part of her that was ice now glittered like liquid diamonds.

"I hope O'leana has supper ready," Tynae said eagerly. "I'm famished."

"Me, too."

Chapter 46
Evolution

"To will is to select a goal, determine a course of action
that will bring one to that goal,
and then hold to that action till the goal is reached.
The key is action."
~Michael Hanson

Glancing briefly at the couple as they walked through the door of Vu'tella, O'leana greeted them. She and Koralie were diligently preparing their meal. "Good evening, Majesties, your fare shall be ready momentarily."

When O'leana finally looked at Tynae properly, she visibly jumped back. "Mm, Mm, My Lady," she stuttered pointing to Tynae's shoulder with a trembling finger. "There's...there's something on you."

Tynae chuckled. "Relax, O'leana, this is Serry. Have you never seen a butterfly before?" Tynae tried to keep a straight face.

"Of course I have, but not like...*that*."

"Get used to her, O'leana, she's staying with me. And speaking of which, before you leave would you please prepare the couch in my room for Lord Béo? He will be sleeping there from now on." Tynae gave the order casually.

Turning away from O'leana, Tynae winked at Béo.

"Yes, My Lady," O'leana bowed.

"I'm going to wash up. I'll be right back. Serry, this is my dwelling," Tynae said, walking into her sleeping chambers. "Please, make yourself at home."

Serry flew off, presumably to explore. Tynae wasn't sure why, but she was fairly certain Serry could understand every word she spoke.

After cleaning up, Tynae went back into the dining area.

The table was set and their supper served.

"This looks wonderful," Tynae complimented.

O'leana went to ready the couch for Béo. With her task complete she practically sprinted out of the room, Serry fluttered out merrily after her.

Looking down at her plate, Tynae struggled to conceal her giggle.

"Will there be anything else, My Lady?" O'leana asked apprehensively.

Continuing to look at her plate, Tynae fought to hold back the laughter aching to get out. "No, O'leana, all of you have a wonderful evening. We'll see you an hour after day break tomorrow."

For once O'leana seemed eager to leave. The instant the door shut, Tynae and Béo both burst out with boisterous laughter.

"Serry, you did that on purpose, didn't you?" Tynae questioned between giggles.

Dancing in the air for a moment Serry flew off continuing the exploration of her new surroundings.

Béo shook his head, looking at Tynae he smiled smoothly.

Instantly Tynae forgot all about O'leana. Standing up, she walked to Béo, climbing on his lap.

He wrapped his arms tight around her waist.

Tynae ran her finger down his chest. "I want to tell you a secret," she said softly.

Béo raised his brows, "Really? What is that, my love?"

Leaning down, Tynae kissed Béo's warm soft lips. She had been longing for this moment all day. Everything in the entire world, except for them, slipped away into nothingness.

Delicately they separated from each other.

"Mmm, I like the way you tell secrets."

"Good, because I have lots and lots of secrets I want to share with you," Tynae purred.

Béo reluctantly let go of Tynae as she stood up.

She brushed her hand lightly over his muscular shoulders as she stepped away and took her seat. Tynae looked at Béo serenely. "I've wanted to do that all day. I just couldn't wait any longer."

Béo grinned. "You won't hear any complaints from me, love."

Tynae smiled back. "Did O'leana say what this was?" she asked, poking at her food with a fork.

"Duck," Béo replied. "And I'd venture to say that it's probably a right sight better than my chicken," he joked.

"Yum, smells great." Tynae cut into her meat. "And your chicken was rather good. Better than anything I can cook, that's for certain." Tynae took a bite of food.

Béo smiled a crafty smile. "So you shocked a lot of people today," he said, taking a bite.

Tynae looked at him with poise, "I may have earned a little respect, too."

"Indeed, you did. Like I said before, I am very proud of you. Demric is not an easy bloke to sway," Béo said delighted.

"I don't think I *swayed* him so much. It was more like I knocked him flat on his arse."

Béo let out a jovial laugh. "That scene is forever burned into my memory. I will never forget the look on the ol' codger's face," Béo mused.

"I really had no intention of being that mean, but he was so rude. He needed to be taught some manners," Tynae explained with a hint of guilty pleasure. "Tomorrow should be interesting. I hope we're all on the same side now," she said, reflecting on the day's events.

"I think you've more than earned your place today." Béo ran his hand softly over hers.

"I hope so." Tynae smiled. "Thank you for taking me to the ice forest today. It was amazing." She took a swig of cider. "Why didn't you know it was called Tergalia? May I have some bread please?"

"Of course, here you go." Béo handed Tynae the bread basket. "Well it's a long story, would you like me to tell you how we came to be here…under the sea?"

Tynae lit up. "Yes, please."

"I guess it was about 917,743 years ago if you want to get into exact numbers. Back then we were not Greer, we were actually Gridel, and Chief Nuval was the leader."

Tynae stopped mid-chew, looking at Béo.

"And where we now sit used to be above water. As a matter of fact, the nearest sea was over 11,000 leagues away." Béo grinned at his captivated audience.

Smiling back, Tynae resumed eating.

Serry floated over, landing fixedly on Tynae's shoulder.

Béo continued, "Osmond, who was the leader and most powerful of all the Archimagi in all our history, foresaw a great storm coming that would cross our land. He said it would rain for many seasons and that Calai would be claimed by the sea. Calai stood alone in an endless valley. We had already been here for many centuries. *Most* of our people did not want to leave their homes. So Osmond, Chief Nuval, the dragons, members of the council, and several Archimagi, all worked together to try and ascertain a solution to the inevitable destruction of Calai. Would you like some cider, *my lady*?" Béo asked with a mischievous smile.

Tynae grinned. "Please." Holding out her mug, she stared at Béo provocatively.

He almost spilled the drink.

"Umm, where was I?" Béo took a sip of his cider. "Oh, yes, the meetings. The meetings went on for several months. The first thought was to move the mountains and valley. Though do-able, it was far too vast. The only logical solution was to shield Calai. So they set out to master the conundrum. After experimenting with many different theories and ideas, they figured out how to use fragments of diamonds and crystals to create a *cover,* if you will. The next problem would be how to make it big enough and strong enough to shield an entire nation which included our vast mountain ranges. And the *cover* would have to last an eternity. Easy as pie, right?" Béo chuckled, taking a bite of meat. "The goal was to make this a permanent and immovable fortress. They did not want to rely upon magic too much. Most magic only lasts as long as the person who cast it, though there is some magic that is permanent. Whatever solution they settled upon, it needed to be an unyielding, impenetrable, steadfast structure. They could not and would not take any chances. They had to be one hundred and ten percent positive the dome would *never* fail. Once Osmond figured out what the dimensions of the dome needed to be, the miners went to work collecting an adequate amount of diamond and crystal fragments. There were two other issues to deal with, one much easier to solve than the other." Béo took another bite of his meal. "The first issue was regarding those who did not wish to live underwater. They needed to find new homes. The second issue was truly a matter of life and death. The fact that we were human meant that we would have no way of getting in and out of Calai without putting our lives at risk every time we entered the water, if we could withstand the pressure at all. No being that we knew of had the ability to hold their breath for more than a few minutes. We needed to figure out how to become more powerful, how to breathe while under water, and how to become incredibly strong swimmers.

"Finding new land was simple. Few others inhabited the surrounding countryside at that point in time. Those who wanted to relocate just needed to make sure the new sight they chose was high enough to escape the cataclysm heading our way. Scouts from the tribes who had decided to stay above ground went in search of prime region, while those who wished to remain in Calai searched for ways to become both air and water breathers. We *had* to evolve. There was no two ways about it. Evolve or die trying, is the way it's always been explained to me." Béo grinned, "More cider?"

"Please." Tynae was spellbound by Béo's words. His tale was one that was almost unimaginable, yet here they were.

"We are still closely related to the Gridel, but we are now called Heah-Gesceapu, are you familiar with what that is?" Béo asked, using the opportunity to take a few bites of food.

Tynae shook her head. "No, everything that lay beyond the borders of Montronvarr was off limits to me, unless I was traveling on royal dealings. I have traveled to nearly every corner of the world, but have admittedly not seen much. Heck I thought you, the Greer, were a mere myth. Honestly, I've been wondering lately just how many myths are actually real," she confessed with fascination.

Béo chuckled. "That's a whole 'nother story, love. We'll discuss that later. Heah-Gesceapu means shape-shifters. We needed to go beyond this though, as a human and even more specifically as a mammal; we could only shape-shift into another creature that breathed air on land. An air breathing organism could not change its entire genetic make-up in an instant and become an aquatic creature, but that's exactly what we needed to do. We required the ability to breathe both above and below water. A passing traveler shared an account of creatures that looked human in appearance, but lived underwater. We had no way to confirm their existence and time was starting to run short. Chief Nuval, Osmond, and Zandore decided that our only hope was to seek out these underwater humans if they truly did exist. But even if they did exist, and if we did somehow manage to find them, there was no guarantee they would even consider helping us.

"Riding atop Zandore the three set off. Flying as many hours each day as they could, they slept only when absolutely necessary. Despite their efforts, it still took a fortnight just to reach the water's edge. Unclear on how to find the water dwellers, Osmond began searching the ocean with his magic. To make a long story short, he eventually felt something in the depths that did not come across as customary sea life.

"It took a few days, but Enako the Chief of the Aldernen—that's what the water dwellers are called—became curious and approached the trio. Fortunately the Aldernen spoke a broken version of our language. Once they understood what the three travelers needed, Enako requested a day or two to speak with his high council. Enako and his people decided to help us. They placed a temporary spell upon Osmond, Nuval, and Zandore that allowed them to breathe underwater, so they could get to Mongari. That's their city."

Tynae served herself a bit more meat.

"May I have another slice, too?"

"Of course," Tynae set a thick slice of duck on Béo's empty plate.

After taking a few bites Béo continued. "You see, their city is truly underwater. They may look like humans at first glance, but they're more fish than human. Osmond had brought cut crystals with him from Calai. We had already discovered the crystals could be infused with energy from outside sources, and if the spell was done properly, it would remain in the crystal for all eternity. Only the Aldernen knew the spell that would allow a human to breathe underwater, but there was a distinct difference between us and them. We did not want to be permanent water dwellers as they were. So Osmond and Ugradar, the Aldernen's most powerful magus, began working together to create the proper spell. The wording had to be perfect as there was no room or time for error. This spell would be incredibly difficult and had to be precise." Béo took a bite of food and swig of cider. "Chief Nuval would be the first to have the spell cast upon him. Carefully Osmond and Ugradar infused the crystals with the magic intended to save our lives. Everyone knew if these two magi could not do it, no-one could. To this day they remain the two most powerful magi that have ever lived. After the incantation was complete and securely sealed within the crystals, a single crystal was placed in each of Nuval's palms and thus began what we now call the Elanprana Vetal Ritual. During the ceremony the crystals dissolve into ones body. After Nuval had absorbed the crystals, they removed the temporary spell allowing him to breathe underwater to test his new ability. It worked wonderfully. They thanked the Aldernen and were on their way."

"Why do you call it the Elanprana Vetal Ritual?" Tynae asked, eating her salad.

"Because, in order to breathe underwater this ritual must still be performed. It means 'essential breath for life.' Without it we would die. This is why we are also called the Elanprana Vitally," Béo explained.

Tynae nodded and Béo continued.

"To this day only the Chief and his highest Archimagus know exactly how this transformation is accomplished. We are still born as humans, well as Heah Gesceapu and Gridel technically. Our elders place temporary spells on us so that we may travel in and out of Calai safely. Once we turn thirty-five and our indacaté has appeared, we go through the rite and become full fledged Greer...hopefully," he added with a shrug.

Tynae's brow furrowed, "Hopefully?" She pushed her empty plate aside.

"The Chief maintains the right to banish any person he feels is of a questionable nature," Béo raised a brow. "In other words, if someone is considered dangerous or is causing severe problems, either above or below the sea; they will have their powers stripped, their memory altered, and be sent to live on land. They are given enough provisions to get them started, but they're on their own after that. To the Greer it's as if they never existed. To the one cast out, they will know not from where they came or who their true family is…or more accurately, was. They become orphans," Béo said in a flat tone.

Tynae stared at Béo, her mouth slightly open. This was a lot to take in. She had dozens of questions swimming around in her head. "Do many people get sent into exile?" she asked, looking distressed.

Béo shook his head. "It's rare, but it has happened. Never in my time, though."

Tynae contemplated her next question. "What's an indacaté?" she asked, hoping to say it correctly.

"It's a mark that appears on each of us that indicates what our life's work will be. You know how we *specialize* in different jobs?" Béo asked.

She nodded, "Yes."

"Well this is how we know what we'll excel at," Béo said with his matter-of-fact tone.

Tynae stared, feeling as if her head might explode from having so much crammed into it in one sitting. "Oh, okay...what's your indacaté?" she asked cheerfully.

"I'm a warrior," Béo replied proudly.

Tynae thought about everything she had just heard.

With a flutter Serry flew off, leaving the couple alone.

A few moments passed before Tynae asked any more questions. "Where does the indacaté appear on a person?"

Béo smiled at her. "For the men, it generally appears on the inside of their right wrist. Occasionally it will show up on the left wrist, but that's extremely rare," he clarified.

Intrigued, Tynae smiled. "Which wrist is yours on?"

Removing the leather strap from his wrist, Béo extended his left arm toward Tynae. There directly in the center of his wrist etched upon his skin was a distinctive mark.

Taking Béo's hand in hers, Tynae absentmindedly traced the marking with her finger. "Where do the women's show up?"

"I'll show you."

Standing, Béo walked behind Tynae. Gently brushing her long hair to one side he leaned down, kissing the nape of her neck. "Right here," he breathed against her bare skin.

Tynae closed her eyes. His hot breath sent a jolt of lightning through Tynae's entire body. Her heart began to hammer so hard it felt like it might just pound right through her chest. The multitude of questions Tynae had buzzing around in her head evaporated like wisps of smoke in a breeze the second Béo touched her. Tynae's breath caught as his scorching lips prowled hungrily over her neck.

Stepping in front of Tynae he offered his hand.

She stood.

Pulling her tight to him he slowly kissed along her jaw line. Longingly his lips drifted lightly across Tynae's anticipating mouth; kissing her one...single...delicious kiss at a time.

Reaching out, Tynae touched Béo's sweltering chest, her hands slid like satin over his tight body. Delicately her hands floated up his neck until her fingers entwined in his lustrous hair, pulling Béo tight to her. Her kiss was ravenous yet their tongues danced sensually.

Béo waved his hand extinguishing the lights in the room then bent down picking up Tynae. Cradling her in his strong arms Béo carried Tynae to the bedchamber, closing the door behind them. It was a night of passion neither would ever forget.

For the first time ever, they were able to truly fall asleep in each others arms. Warm bodies pressed tight against each other not worrying about who might walk past her room.

Tynae had dismissed her entire staff to their own dwellings. They would no longer reside in Vu'tella with her.

Blissful and content, they couple slept soundly without fear of being discovered.

Chapter 47
A New View

"That is what learning is.
You suddenly understand something you've
understood all your life, but in a new way."
~Doris Lessing

Tynae walked onto the picturesque beach of her dream world. Looking at her attire, she was pleasantly surprised to find she wore trousers again. Searching for Ryedin she spotted him standing near a cove.

Glimpsing Tynae, Ryedin ran to meet her. "Hello, my love," he pressed his lips to hers.

Gently pulling apart Tynae noticed the contented smile Ryedin wore on his handsome face.

"So you're going to be learning to fight multiple opponents?" He continued to smile.

"Yes." The fact that Ryedin knew everything about her never fazed Tynae. *How could he not know everything, we spend almost every waking and sleeping moment together.*

"I was thinking we could alternate your training between archery, hand-to-hand, and stars. If you decide you'd like help with something else we will add that as well. How's that sound?"

"Sounds perfect!" Tynae smiled wide.

"Wonderful. Asria will be here in a moment. She will take us to where I will train you in hand-to-hand."

Tynae's eyes opened wide. "You mean we're going to fly somewhere?"

Ryedin chuckled. "Yes, my love, relax." Pulling Tynae tight to him, he stroked her hair. "Before you know it, you will love the freedom of flying. To get to that point though, you must consistently face your fear. Soon your fear will no longer exist. It may even become a passion."

Tynae wished she was as certain as Ryedin. Either way, she'd never been one to run away from a challenge and wasn't about to start now. Tynae looked at Ryedin. "Can I ask you something?"

"Anything...Well almost anything," he grinned.

"How is it that when I am here I am attired in clothing I have never seen before?" She had been wondering this since the first night she'd arrived in their dream world.

"Would you prefer to be naked? I can arrange that if you'd like," he said slyly.

Tynae flushed bright red. "No that's quite alright," she giggled. "It's just that they fit so perfectly, like they were made specifically for me."

"They were." Ryedin smiled at her. "The clothing you wear is yours. You picked it out. It belongs to you." Ryedin's brow furrowed. "That's probably more than I should have said. Look," he pointed to the sky, "here comes Asria."

"I won't ask any more," Tynae assured.
"Thank you."
The two walked hand in hand up the beach to meet Asria.

"You really did do great with Demric today."

Thinking back on the day's events with Demric caused Tynae to blush slightly. "Thank you."

Ryedin helped Tynae onto Asria's back.

The take-off wasn't quite so scary this time and after a few minutes Tynae truly was enjoying the ride. Soaring through the clouds, wind in her face. It was delightful.

Nearing their destination Tynae was a little surprised to see they were flying to the top of the forest. Dismounting from Asria, Tarak and Gideon joined the couple.

"Okay let's get today's lesson started." Ryedin walked into a clearing. "I have to start by telling you that you are much stronger than you realize, angel. Your speed will nearly always protect you," he assured. "Remember when you were in Tergalia, how you could feel the energy of your surroundings?"

Tynae was a little perplexed by his question. "Yes?"

"You have the ability do that all the time, with anyone and anything. Personally, I find that it is generally easier to feel with my energy than judge with my eyes. If you learn to perfect this skill, you will be virtually untouchable," he grinned. "We'll work on it during your lessons."

"Anything that will help me avoid getting too bloodied up is always welcome," Tynae said with a chuckle. "Teach me, oh, wise one," she teased.

The two sat at the base of a lush willow tree. "Are you comfortable?" Ryedin asked.
"Yes."
"Good, now close your eyes and reach out to the world around you with your energy. Feel what's here."
Tynae did as she was told. There was much around her she could feel. The energies were mingled, vibrating as one.

Ryedin showed Tynae how to pull the energies apart so she could identify the being or object it belonged to.

She could sense everything, from tiny birds tucked away in nests high above the ground and baby bunnies hidden deep in their burrows, to bumble bees humming merrily through the air. Even the essence of the trees and flowers had its own personal signature. The balanced energy from the world around her was intoxicating—one might even say contagious. She loved the serenity this special place held. Tynae was truly enjoying her lessons. She wondered why Béo didn't do this when they were awake, but she was learning there were a lot of things that just didn't make sense in this new world and let it go.

After several hours of energy work, the pair took a break. Ryedin held out his hand. "Come on. I want to show you something."

Tynae took his hand and they walked a ways up a trail. When they reached their destination, she could clearly see why he had brought her up here.

They stood at the top of a mountain overlooking the ocean. The sky looked like it had been painted by hand. Golden rays from the setting sun mingled with the majestic purple sky and pink gossamer clouds coating the heavens. The breath taking scene reflected in the shimmering aqua-blue waters below. Ryedin stood behind Tynae, his arms wrapped tight around her waist. She rested her hands atop his. Together they stood, taking in the glorious view.

Ryedin did not insist she leave at twilight on this day. Leaning forward, he whispered in her ear. "I have a place for us to lay if you'd care to star gaze for a bit."

His warm breath slid smoothly over her exposed skin, sending shivers, like fingers of lightning through her body. "Mmm," was all she managed to get out.

Keeping one arm around Tynae's waist, Ryedin led her to a plush blanket. Big feathery pillows welcomed them. Tynae knew they were in a forest, but it appeared more like a faultless painting. Everywhere she looked, there was lush green vegetation. Not a thing was out of place. Each individual leaf on every bush looked as if it had been polished by hand, and the flowers that grew throughout the vast forest were bright and incredibly fragrant. Even the ancient trees appeared unblemished. A faint wind blew, bringing with it the refreshing mist from the ocean. Taking a deep breath, Tynae drew in the crisp clean smell of the salty sea air. She was finding it more and more difficult to believe this was only a dream. Together the two lay on the blanket. Snuggled close with one another, they watched as the night sky slowly revealed her twinkling gems. Below them, Tynae could hear the soothing serenade of the ocean as its waters washed over the shoreline and retreated over and over.

Ryedin pointed out the stars, planets, and constellations above them. He explained what they were believed to mean. After the astrology lesson, the couple sat up. "You will need to learn how to quiet yourself in order to feel the energy of every living thing in the universe, big and small. Once you have mastered this we will be able to move on to the next lesson," he

402

explained. "Fair warning though, this will take a bit of time. When you have learned to quiet yourself while in the heart of a torrential storm, you will be ready to move on to the second part of your lesson." Leaning forward, Ryedin kissed Tynae tenderly on the cheek. "It's getting late, love, you need to return soon."

Tynae drew a breath deep into her lungs. "I don't want to." She sighed, smiling gently. "But I know that I must."

The pair stood up.

Ryedin took Tynae in his arms, holding her tight.

Leaning back slightly, Tynae looked into his eyes.

He lovingly placed his hands on her cheeks.

Tynae shut her eyes, savoring the feeling of his strong hands against her skin. Gently she nuzzled her face against his hands, committing to memory the amazing sensations she felt in just a single touch; warmth, tenderness, and undying love.

"I love you, Tynae. I promise I will take care of you for all eternity," Ryedin assured.

"I know…I will see you tomorrow, my love."

Ryedin smiled tenderly. "I will be counting the seconds."

The couple kissed good-bye. It was a long, deep, passionate kiss that made Tynae's heart hammer uncontrollably for the second time this night.

"Sleep well, my love," Ryedin said.

"Good night, *my* angel," Tynae whispered, their world dissolving into darkness.

Béo woke an hour before dawn the next morning. Getting out of bed, he was careful not to wake Tynae. Retrieving his bag from the outer room, he brought it back into the bedchamber. Sitting in a chair across from the bed, he lit a lantern. Withdrawing the book Azmina had given him from his pack,

Béo carefully studied the picture on the front. Tracing the embossed images on the cover with his finger, he couldn't help but notice how much the angel leaning over the warrior resembled Tynae.

Not wanting to destroy the seal holding the book shut, Béo carefully removed it. It bore an unusual insignia Béo did not recognize, but he thought his father might be able to identify it. Opening the book to the first page, Béo started to read...The book began with the history of Tergalia and how it came to be, which was quite interesting. Then it told of the connection between the Greer and the Clair'letté. Clair'letté is what the people of Tergalia were called. Béo read enough to know that Tynae was correct. The path had always been there in the ice forest...invisible to *his* eyes. Béo's gaze drifted over to Tynae as she slept. Her purpose here on earth was more important than any of them had ever realized. He loved her so much. He couldn't imagine his life without her in it. Béo decided that when he dropped the book off to his father, he would speak to Kerszon about the relationship between himself and Tynae.

Dawn quickly approached. The maids would arrive in an hour's time.

After putting the book back into his bag, Béo briefly climbed into the couch ruffling it a bit.

Returning to Tynae's bed, he mindfully climbed in, snuggling up tight to her warm body. He was never going to let her go.

Tynae rolled onto her side.

They were now face to face. Béo noticed the glow of Tynae's skin was brighter than normal. Without thinking, he pressed his lips to hers.

She woke instantly. Wrapping her arms around Béo's neck, Tynae hitched her leg over his hip.

Slowly, steadily, Béo allowed his hand to flow along Tynae's side. When he reached the curve of her hip; he slid his hand to the small of her back, firmly pulling Tynae tight against him. He could feel her heart pounding. Béo's lips moved gently to the hollow at the base of Tynae's neck. Slowly his lips and tongue playfully teased their way up her throat. Tynae's breathing uneven and chest heaving, he knew he was driving her crazy.

In one smooth movement Tynae pushed Béo onto his back and was on top of him.

Béo twined his fingers in her hair, pulling her down to him, pressing his lips fervently to hers.

Gently Tynae bit Béo's lower lip as his tongue lightly brushed hers.

Béo's breaths were coming in short fast huffs. His body was on fire. "I love you so much, Tynae," he breathed.

"I love you, too."

Béo's heart was hammering so hard it was almost painful. Sighing he ran his hand through Tynae's long hair. "I'm sorry, love, your maids will be arriving soon. I'm afraid if we keep going we'll never leave your room."

Smiling her crafty smile, Tynae leaned down pressing her lips to his once more. "I don't see a problem with that," she purred.

Béo shook his head and laughed. "Come on, get ready, please."

"Oh, fine," Tynae conceded with a smile.

Climbing out of bed, the two dressed in their appropriate sleeping attire.

"After we eat breakfast I'm going to speak with my father." Béo informed her.

Climbing back into bed, he laid on his side, enjoying the 'show' as Tynae's silhouette flowed elegantly behind her changing curtain.

"About what?" she asked.

"Us."

Tynae stepped out from behind the curtain, her face lit up the entire room. "Really?"

Béo's stomach did somersaults when he saw her reaction. "You approve then?"

"Of course I do. Have I not made my feelings for you completely clear?" Tynae jumped onto the bed playfully like a child. "What do you think he'll say?"

"Honestly," Béo shrugged, "I have no idea. But I can't see how he would be against us being together. I don't really care what he says though, you know that, right?" Béo clarified, pulling her to him.

"I know," she said, placing her hand on his cheek. "I love you, Béo, no matter what your father, or anyone else, says."

Béo pressed his cheek against the heel of Tynae's tender hand. "My world would fall apart without you in it, Tynae. You are *my* everything," he said solemnly.

Tynae looked lovingly into Béo's eyes. "And mine without you. Let's never find out if we can survive without each other, okay?" Tynae suggested with a peaceful smile.

"Sounds perfect to me."

Chapter 48
Unexpected Guests

"The only thing that makes life possible is permanent,
intolerable uncertainty; not knowing what comes next."
~Ursula K. LeGuin

Right on time, O'leana and the others arrived. Koralie and Sireeon prepared Tynae's bath, while O'leana prepared breakfast.

"Breck will be here shortly, My Lady, he's picking up your new clothing," O'leana informed.

"Already? That's great," Tynae said, pleased.

Serry floated down to greet Tynae. She'd spent the night in the miniature forest.

"Good morning, Serry." Tynae beamed.

After a quick flutter against Tynae's nose she flew off.

Tynae giggled. "I think she just kissed me."

While eating breakfast, Béo and Tynae discussed what Demric might have in store for her.

Finishing his meal in record time, Béo excused himself from the table. Grabbing his bag he was ready to head out the door.

"Hang on." Tynae stopped him. "I'm going to wait for you to get back," she told him, sounding as nervous as he felt.

"Okay, I'll be as quick as I can. I love you, my angel." Béo gave Tynae a quick kiss on the forehead then set out for Kerszon's chambers. One of the advantages of being the Chief's son was you never had to make an appointment to see him.

Tynae's heart raced as she sat by herself finishing breakfast, which she now had no desire to eat. Fiddling with her bracelet, thoughts pinged around her mind like fireflies in a jar. *I wonder what Kerszon will say. Will he try and keep Béo and me apart if he doesn't approve? What if there is someone else Kerszon would prefer Béo to be with? After all, I am not from their world...*

"My Lady?"

"What?" Tynae turned. "What is it, O'leana?"

"I was just letting you know your bath is ready."

"Thank you, I'll be right there."

Grateful for the interruption, Tynae did her best to push her nerve-racking thoughts as far out of her mind as possible. Stepping into the warm water, Tynae's mind lingered on Béo and nothing else. She'd forgotten all about her new clothes, which were sitting on the neatly made bed when she emerged from the lavatory.

"What color would you like?" Koralie asked.

Tynae had an entire rainbow of outfits to choose from. Looking at the piles of colorful garments she pointed, "I think I'll wear black today."

"Black it shall be." Koralie extracted a matching outfit.

Once Tynae was ready, she examined herself in the mirror. The skirt was short and straight, covering only a few inches of her thigh. The built-in britches were snug and basically undetectable. The top covered more than any of the others had, but her midriff was still exposed.

"I like that, My Lady," Sireeon said.

Koralie nodded, "Me, too."

"I do, too," Tynae agreed. "What do you think, O'leana?"

"As I said before, I think you could wear practically anything and make it look good." O'leana looked Tynae over. "I will admit I had my doubts, but I really do like this."

"Well, we are done here ladies," Tynae told her maids. "You are free to go."

"Yes, My Lady." O'leana bowed.

Béo reached Kerszon's study in record time. Gareth, the guard outside Kerszon's study, announced Béo's arrival. Entering the office, Béo found Kerszon behind his desk in his overstuffed chair. Béo took a seat in front of his father. Looking around, the office was once more the way Béo was used to seeing it. Not barren as it had been on the night he brought Tynae to Calai.

"To what do I owe this unexpected visit, Son? I didn't think you could tear yourself away from Tynae for more than the necessities," Kerszon joked.

Béo smiled at his fathers comment. Clearly Kerszon already had a fairly good idea of how Béo felt about Tynae. Setting his leather pack atop his legs, Béo extracted the book Azmina had given him. "Tynae and I went to the ice forest yesterday and it turns out that much more is there than we ever realized." After recounting what had happened, Béo handed Kerszon the book.

After Kerszon Skimmed the first few pages he looked up at Béo, smiling broadly. "Seems that Lady Tynae is quite a remarkable woman," Kerszon mused.

"Ay, Father, she is amazing."

Kerszon smiled at his son. "Something tells me you didn't come here just to deliver this book. I've seen the way the two of you look at each other. I may be getting older, but I am not blind, and I certainly have not forgotten what it's like to be in love," Kerszon said with an air of admiration.

Béo's face flushed. "Then you are okay with Tynae and I...I mean, I can court her and not hide it?" Béo attempted to keep his exhilaration to a minimum.

Kerszon gazed at Béo. "You've become a fine man," the chief said proudly. "Please remember you are my son first and foremost. Your happiness is very important to me. But if I may, I would like to make a couple of suggestions."

"Of course, Father."

"Slow down just a bit. She's not going anywhere, Son. There is much she has to learn over the next few years and I expect you to be by her side through all of it. Second, don't flaunt your relationship too much. I'm not asking you to keep it secret. I don't think that's even possible. All someone has to do is look at the two of you, and they can see how much you love each other. Just keep it modest, please." Kerszon's fatherly words were truly heartfelt.

Béo was about to burst with excitement. His father approved of his relationship with Tynae and they no longer had to hide their love for one another. He wanted to get back to Tynae as fast as possible to share the exciting news. Sitting on the edge of his chair, Béo was ready to sprint out of the office. "I understand, Father. Thank you."

"Now that that's settled, there are two things I would like to discuss with you, since I have you here," Kerszon said in a serious tone.

Béo's brow furrowed. "Okay, what is it?" he asked, settling back into the chair.

Kerszon took a deep breath. "I'm not so sure we should be keeping secrets from Tynae. She has asked a lot of questions, questions that if answered truthfully, we would have to tell her everything we know." Kerszon drummed his fingers on his desk lightly, lost in thought for a moment. You know I don't believe in accidents, Son, and I feel that if Tynae herself provides us with an opportunity to tell her the truth, we should probably do just that. I'm going to speak with Ge'annã and Zandore about this matter. If they agree we will tell Tynae as much as we know." Kerszon slapped his hand lightly on the desk, "That reminds me, Zandore has agreed to meet with Tynae eight days from now." The chief opened a drawer in his desk, extracting a rolled piece of parchment. "Here's a map."

Béo took the scroll.

"If you could have her there shortly after dinner, that would be perfect," Kerszon said cheerfully.

Béo nodded. "I can do that. And, Father, I think telling Tynae the truth would be a good thing. I'm confident she can handle it, if that's what you are concerned about."

"It was, but after getting to spend some time with her, I'm no longer worried," Kerszon admitted then paused.

"Was there something else, Father?"

"I was going to ask you to come back in the next few days to discuss the book after I've read it, but if we end up telling Tynae everything there will be no need for you and me to meet in private."

"Not a problem," Béo said, gathering up his bag. As he did, something fell out, "Oh yeah." He picked the item up. "The book was sealed with this." He handed Kerszon the wax seal.
"Father?"
"Yes, Béo?"
Béo grinned at Kerszon. "When will you explain to me the magic Zandore performed on Tynae?"

Kerszon thought for a moment. "Be patient, Son. In due time you and Tynae will know *everything.*"

This satisfied Béo. His father always kept his word.
"Thank you, Father, for everything. Tynae is waiting for me and I really want to get back to her."
Kerszon chuckled.
"What?" Béo asked.
"I wish you could see yourself right now. I am certain your smile could light up the entire city."

Béo felt himself blush. He stood to leave and Kerszon rose as well.

Walking around his desk, Kerszon pulled Béo into a fatherly bear hug. "I am truly happy for you, Son." Kerszon patted Béo heartily on the back.

Béo couldn't stop smiling. "Thank you, Father, thank you."
"Give Tynae a kiss for me."
"I'll do that. Good day, Father," Béo said, walking out of the office.
"Good day, Son."
Once Béo was in the tunnel outside Kerszon's study he jumped up, hitting the ceiling with his hand and let out a roar,

"YEAH!!!" Béo really was in a hurry to get back to Tynae, but he had a few things to do before he went back to Vu'tella....

The knock on the door made the butterflies in Tynae's stomach lurch. Running to the door, Tynae flung it open. Anticipating seeing Béo, her face fell when she saw Chenoa.

"I could come back later, My Lady, if this is not a good time," her unexpected guest offered.

Realizing how she must have appeared, Tynae shook her head. "No, no, I'm sorry." She gestured for the woman to enter, "Come in, I was just expecting…" Tynae's words were cut short as Serry fluttered in the door behind Chenoa.

"You were saying?" Chenoa asked.

Tynae's attention came back to her guest, "Oh, someone else." Tynae closed the door. "I must admit this is a surprise. Is this a social visit?"

Chenoa shrugged. "You tell me, child, you're the one who summoned me," she informed in her matter-of-fact tone.

Tynae's brows furrowed in confusion, "I did? But I didn't. That's odd. Who said I sent for you?"

The old woman smiled. "I don't recall, but they did say something about a….package?"

"That's right!" Tynae remembered the satchel Ryedin had given to her. "But…" Tynae shook her head, waving her hand as if shooing a bug. She was not going to try and figure out what was going on. There were far too many inexplicable things that happened here in Calai, besides Ryedin had told her Chenoa would come to her when the time was right.

"Give me just a moment." Tynae went into her room, she hadn't checked to see if the bag was where Ryedin said it would be. *Let's see, he said it would be in the left, no right side of the room under the floor board.* Getting on her knees, Tynae pushed on the boards until she found the loose one. Lifting it up she found Ryedin's bag. *Wow.*

Tynae walked back out to were Chenoa waited. "Okay. I'm supposed to tell you something before I hand this to you. Give me just one second; I want to make sure I repeat it perfectly. "I have a job for you. It has been offered by…" Tynae thought the words through carefully in her head. "He who is known by many names, that's it. Do you accept this offer?"

Chenoa smiled at Tynae. "I accept the bag and the blood oath that it carries."

Tynae held out the bag to the woman. Chenoa went to grab it with her right hand then stopped, reaching out with her left hand instead. Taking a deep breath, Chenoa took the satchel into her hand and let out a gasp.

Tynae's eyes grew wide. "Are you okay? What happened?"

Her guest shook her head. "You do not know how a blood oath works do you, girl?"

Tynae shook her head. "No."

Chenoa switched the bag from her left hand to her right. Holding out her left hand, palm up she showed Tynae.

Tynae gasped. There was a raw patch of flesh on Chenoa's palm where a symbol of some sort had been burned into her flesh.

Chenoa chuckled. "I knew I would be…branded, I suppose is the best way to put it. I accepted this willingly and wholeheartedly. I consider it a great honor and privilege," Chenoa explained as she transferred the packages and scroll from the leather satchel into her own bag. "Please tell no-one of my mark, not even Lord Béo. It will fade in a matter of hours and resurface only when necessary." The old woman handed Ryedin's bag back to Tynae. "Will there be anything else, My Lady? I have work I must tend to." She patted her bag.

Chenoa's lack of confusion mystified Tynae. To the contrary, Chenoa seemed to know exactly what was going on and what was expected of her.

"There's nothing else." Tynae's gaze wandered to Chenoa's scorched hand then she looked up suddenly. "Actually, there is something."

"Spit it out, child. I don't have all day here. I'm not getting any younger, you know."

"Right, I understand that the name Nadaya means hope. Is that correct?" Tynae asked.

"You learn fast, child," Chenoa grinned. "It does indeed mean 'hope'. Why do you ask?"

"Well…I've been told it is what the people of Calai call me, but I don't understand why. Do you?"

"Perhaps Chief Kerszon can shed some light on this particular quandary of yours. Will there be anything else?" Chenoa asked smoothly.

"No. Thank you."

"By the way," Chenoa said, her hand on the door knob, "That outfit of yours is quite becoming on you. It should serve you well. Good day, My Lady."

Before Tynae had a chance to say thank you, Chenoa was gone.

Once out the door Chenoa went down a few corridors and stopped. Pulling the scroll from her pack she anxiously opened it, revealing her tasks.

> *By accepting these packages you have sworn your blood oath.*
>
> *Your silence and loyalty, of your secrets you may not boast.*
>
> *There are now six tasks set before you on this day.*
> *The first two items will keep the enemy at bay.*
> *The first shall be small, sturdy and feather light.*
> *The second will end the long and dreary fight.*
> *Neither will break, rust nor will they bend for that hidden within them strikes fear into men.*
>
> *The next two shall be for her to feast upon, death to those who do her wrong.*

Next a potion in a bottle that's pure, lives it will save, time it will endure.

There is now one left upon her body she shall wear, it will reveal to her when evil is in the air.

Go forth now and recruit two more.
The mark you share will bring them to your door.
Together unite and stand as one.
We will all need one another once the battle has begun.

Your silence will be rewarded, your patience repaid, for in your heart the light has remained.

Above all else you must remember this;
Evil will always triumph when good men turn a blind eye...Light may only prevail where there is hope. Hope, like the mighty phoenix, shall emerge from the ashes of death with the promise of new life. With hope all things are possible...with hope comes light even in the darkest of times.

All are one,

He who is known by many names

Rolling up the scroll, Chenoa placed it into her bag and set off. With an exuberant smile and a spring in her step, Chenoa was ready to begin her numerous tasks.

415

Chapter 49
Approval Gained

*"I have found the best way to give advice to your children
is to find out what they want and then advise them to do it."*
~Henley S. Truman

Tynae had dismissed everyone, and her unexpected guest had long since left. She now waited, somewhat patiently, in her chaise lounge beside the glass wall in her forest. Serry sat nearby on a large yellow flower.

"What do you think Kerszon will say, Serry? I really do love Béo. I hope he approves," Tynae rambled nervously.

Serry fluttered her wings.

"I wish you could talk to me," Tynae said.

"*I can,*" said a delicate voice.

Tynae jumped. She glanced around the room then looked at Serry with a bewildered expression. "Did you just say something to me, Serry?" Tynae asked cautiously.

"*Yes, Mistress,*" came the feathery soft voice, yet again.

Tynae's eyes got huge. She could hear Serry speaking to her inside her head.

Tynae laughed lightly. "Why didn't you say something before now?"

"*I am required to wait until asked.*"

"Wow, so you *could* understand everything I said to you. I knew it!"

"*As to your previous question, I think Chief Kerszon will give you and Lord Béo his blessing.*"

"You really think so?" Tynae fidgeted with her bracelet. "I'm so worried." Her foot nervously bounced up and down. Staring at the picturesque view beyond her window, deep in thought, something suddenly occurred to Tynae. "Can you hear my thoughts?" she asked tensely.

"*I can only hear that which you direct specifically at me,*" Serry explained, setting Tynae's mind at ease.

Someone reading your every thought. Tynae pondered this for a split second. *Now there's a terrifying predicament.* Letting her shoulders relax, Tynae let out a silent sigh of relief. *"I've never talked to someone without opening my mouth, this is quite different."* Tynae giggled.

"I'm sure there are many new things you will be learning over time, Mistress."

Tynae turned. "Was that the door?" she asked anxiously.
"Tynae?"
Her heart skipped a beat, *He's back.*
"Tynae, are you here?" Béo called out.
"In the forest! I'll be right there!"
"No, stay there. I'll come to you."
"Okay," she squeaked. Her heart beat frantically. She couldn't tell by his tone if he was happy or upset.

When Béo came into view Tynae fixed her gaze on him. He was beaming.
"Father gave us his blessing."
"Ahhhh!!!" Tynae ran, jumping into Béo's arms.
Holding her tight, Béo spun around.
"Really!?"
Béo set Tynae back on her feet. "Really. And he said to give you this." Béo kissed Tynae lightly on the cheek. "And this is from me." Béo lovingly pressed his warm lips to Tynae's mouth.
The two walked over to the chaise. Béo sat, leaning back. He placed one leg off the chair with his foot in the sand and the other leg was stretched out on the long seat.

Tynae sat sideways on the edge of the chair between Béo's legs, her toes buried in the warm sand.

"I want to give you something," Béo said his voice full of emotion.
His tone confused Tynae slightly. "Okay."
Béo pulled a small red velvet pouch out from his leather bag that hung at his side, handing it to Tynae.
Tynae stared at the gift.

Gently taking her hand, Béo placed the pouch in her palm. "Go on, open it," he urged.

"You didn't have to get me anything."

"I know I didn't. I wanted to. Open it," Béo pressed.

Loosening the draw string, Tynae reached inside the velvet sack. Clutching its bounty, she withdrew her hand. When she realized what she was holding, her eyes filled with tears.

"Do you like it?" Béo asked softly.

Tynae held in her hands the exquisite seven carratus heart and key pendant she had admired on her first day in Calai. Wiping the tears away, she looked at Béo thoughtfully. "Yes, I love it, but you really shouldn't have."

"My heart has always belonged to you, Tynae. This will just serve as a daily reminder." Béo took the token out of Tynae's hands, carefully fastening it around her neck. Once it was on, he thoughtfully touched the pink heart then looked deep into Tynae's eyes. "Consider this to be my very heart. It is yours forever. You're the only person who has ever made me feel like I'm completely out of my element. My world spins in slow motion when I'm with you. You have literally touched my soul, Tynae. I could never live without you."

The light in Béo's eyes was more than soul piercing. It was soul shattering. *I never knew I could love another so much.* The love Tynae felt for Béo made her heart ache with adoration. "I love you, Béo, more than you will ever know. I would give my life for you." She meant what she said and clearly Béo knew it.

His face fell slightly. "Tynae, promise me that you will never do that, please. I could not survive a day without you by my side. Promise me," he pleaded.

She shook her head. "I'm sorry, that is a promise I cannot make...I will promise you this though," she ran her hand over his cheek tenderly. "I will do everything in my power to stay alive. Is that a fair compromise?" she asked. "You can not tell me you wouldn't do the exact same thing." She knew she was right.

Béo smiled. "That sounds fair enough and yes, I would do the same," he admitted.

Serry gracefully floated by, landing on a rose bush near the couple. *"Congratulations, Mistress."*

Tynae looked at Serry. "Thank you." Tynae spoke aloud out of habit.

Leaning back, Béo looked at Tynae. "Are you talking to me or Serry?"

"OH!" She giggled. "I forgot to tell you, she can talk. I can hear her," Tynae said excitedly.

Béo looked highly confused. "What do you mean, 'you can hear her'?"

"Well, I was sitting here waiting for you to come back. I was so nervous I was ready to crawl right out of my skin, so I just started talking to her. Honestly, Béo, had she not been here I would have talked to the trees. Anyway, I said 'I wish you could talk to me' and she did. She said she was required to wait for me to ask her directly before she could let me know that she's able to communicate."

Béo looked over at Serry. She fluttered her wings at him. "Hello, Serry, can you speak to everyone or only certain people?"

"I can speak to whomever I choose, Lord Béo." When Serry spoke both Béo and Tynae could hear her.

"See," Tynae said earnestly.

Béo grinned. "Please call me Béo, Serry. I consider you a friend," he said cheerfully, speaking aloud.

"Thank you, My Lord. Congratulations to you both."

"Thank you, Serry. It will be nice not to have to hide my feelings for Tynae from the world any longer." He looked at Tynae as he spoke.

She beamed.

Serry flew off, giving the couple their privacy.

Tynae laid her head against Béo's shoulder, nuzzling her nose against his neck. Inhaling deeply, she took in his scent, slowly exhaling. "I don't want to move from this spot today," she said softly.

Béo leaned back so he could see Tynae's face. Tenderly he brushed her hair aside. "You don't have to do anything you don't want to do, my love. Demric can wait until tomorrow."

Sitting up slightly, Tynae considered Béo's words then smiled. "Thank you, but I am expected. Let's just sit here a bit longer."

"Very well then, we'll leave shortly." Nuzzling back into his arms, Tynae rested her head on Béo's warm chest, listening to the calm rhythmic beat of his heart. Her hand wandered to the heart that now hung around her neck. She lovingly closed her fingers around it.

After a short while had passed Tynae decided she was as ready as she was ever going to be. She didn't want to go, but she had given her word…Sighing Tynae sat up.

Béo looked at her. Taking her face in his warm hands, he tenderly pressed his mouth to her lips. Slowly, gently, passionately, they melted together.

After only three heartbeats they pulled apart as if in slow motion.

"I love you," Béo whispered.

"I love you."

They stood up, but weren't getting very far. Standing still they held on to one another for a few more heartbeats.

Tynae laughed softly. "Let's get out of here, or we're never going to leave."

Looking around for Serry, Tynae didn't see her. "Serry," she called, "will you be joining us today?"

"Absolutely, My Lady, now that I can speak with you I will be able to help you."

"Spectacular," Tynae said brightly.

Serry took her place on the princess' shoulder and the three left the sanctuary of Vu'tella's forest.

"Oh, hang on!" Tynae blurted out running into her room. When she came back out she was strapping her dagger to her thigh. With this outfit there was no hiding it.

"Wouldn't want you to forget that, love," Béo jested.

"Me either," Tynae winked

"I like your new attire. It's different."

"Look," Tynae lifted her skirt. "It has built in britches. Now I can move in any direction and not worry about it. I think I'm going to have some more long trousers made, too."

Béo lifted an eye brow, "Really?"

Tynae laughed. "Does that bother you?"

"No, you're free to wear whatever your precious heart desires, angel," Béo said with a crafty smile as they walked out the door. "I told you the other night I liked them on you."

Béo grabbed Tynae's hand as they walked to the heart of the city. "We can do this now," he beamed. "Are you nervous?"

"A little," she admitted.

"You know you'll do great. Even if it's difficult at first, you'll have it mastered in no time."

Tynae smiled brightly, "Thank you for having so much faith in me."

"It's not a difficult thing to do, my love," Béo said sincerely. "You still look nervous. What's bothering you?"

"I just don't know how Demric's really going to feel about working with me. After all, Calai is my new home and I really don't need any enemies."

"Hmm, I like the sound of that."

Tynae looked at him disbelievingly. "You *like* the sound of me having enemies?"

Béo chuckled, "No, silly. The part about Calai being your home."

"Ahh," she sighed with an understanding smile, "me, too."

Walking into the city for the first time, hand-in-hand as a couple, they notice several passersby staring.

Tynae bit her lip, a little embarrassed by the attention. She'd just gotten to the point that people didn't gawk at her when she came into the city. Now all eyes were upon her again.

Béo must have felt Tynae tense up. "Relax, poppet, we are their future leaders, they're just curious. Perhaps it's actually a complement that they care. Besides, I would think that a woman as beautiful as you would be used to people looking at her constantly." Béo chuckled.

Tynae rolled her eyes. "Say what you will. I don't think I will ever get used to the stares. It was bad enough being the new spectacle in Calai. It will be even worse now that I've won your heart. I'm sure there are many women who will detest me." Tynae sighed. "But that is something I'm willing to tolerate. It just comes with the territory," she said resolutely.

It was Béo who rolled his eyes this time. "Who and why would anyone in Calai hate *you*?"

"Are you serious? You are joking, right?" she asked incredulously. "Well let's see...First of all, I am an outsider. Second, I am not like most women on many, many different levels; which we've already gone over, and that alone makes both men and woman uncomfortable around me. You saw that first hand, yesterday. At least in Pathrow everyone knew me. They had either watched me grow up or they grew up with me. Third, not only are you an incredibly handsome man, you are their future leader. I'm certain lots of women had their eye on you," Tynae explained patiently. Stopping she looked directly at Béo. "They can stare all they want. I'm here to stay, dirty looks or not. You are *my* treasure, *my* life, and *my* future." Tynae gazed into Béo's eyes. "*You* are my happily ever after..." Tynae's grin became wicked. "And you are all *mine*," Tynae proclaimed with a cocky attitude.

"You know it, *my* lady," Béo crooned reinforcing her disposition. Leaning forward he kissed Tynae gently on the lips then they resumed walking.

When they reached their destination Demric and his two warriors were waiting.

The couple was a little surprised to find Demric looking rather pleasant.

"Good day, M'Lady, Lord Béo," Demric nodded. "Lady Tynae, your attire is outstanding."

Tynae and Béo shot each other bemused glances, stunned by Demric's 180 degree turn about.

Both struggled to conceal their grins.

Walking over to the couple, Demric looked down noticing their clutched hands. He then glanced at Tynae's new necklace. Throwing his head back, Demric let out an exuberant laugh. "I should have known," he barked heartily.

"Is there a problem, Demric?" Béo asked smoothly.

"Not at all, My Lord. Lady Tynae is a lovely woman," Demric said earnestly. "And she'd make a mighty fine bride as well, if I might be so bold to say." Demric winked at Tynae.

"Ay, she would, wouldn't she?" Béo grinned at Tynae, who had turned about thirty shades of red.

"Lady Tynae, I owe you an apology for my poor behavior yesterday. Most men are not accustomed to a woman such as your self. I am ashamed of my ignorance. You have proven to me that women are capable of things I never thought possible. Clearly they can be and *are* just as strong as some of the strongest men I have ever known. Please accept my humble apology. I will never underestimate or disrespect you again." To punctuate his sincerity Demric bowed deeply.

"It's all water under the bridge now, Demric. I thank you and happily accept your apology," Tynae said frankly, returning his gesture.

Demric examined Tynae with curiosity. "I have to ask, M'Lady…the butterfly on your shoulder. Wherever did it come from? I've not seen anything like it in all my years."

Tynae had all but forgotten about Serry. "Oh, I'm sorry. Demric this is Serry, she is from…"

Tynae paused, *"May I tell him, Serry?"*

"You may tell him that I came to you in the ice forest. There is no need to mention Tergalia."

Tynae smiled, "The ice forest."

"Well color me confounded and slap me thrice. I had no idea there were living creatures in that forest. I always thought it was just plant life. You know, green stuff; trees, shrubs, and such."

Tynae admired Serry, but it was Béo who spoke. "I believe she is rather rare, maybe even one of a kind. Either way, she is apparently quite taken with Lady Tynae."

"Who isn't?" Demric pointed out with a chuckle.

"Too true," Béo agreed, grinning at Tynae. "Anyway, Serry is welcome to stay with us for as long as she so chooses," Béo said warmly, eyeing Serry who fluttered at him.

"Very well…" Demric turned to Tynae. "M'Lady, are you ready to begin?"

Tynae took a deep breath. "Ready as I'll ever be."

"Are you nervous?"

Tynae nodded, "Mm-hum, a little."

"We're going to take this slow, I promise."

"Thank you, Demric," Béo said appreciatively.

Demric gave Béo a slight nod.

"Come on." Demric and Tynae walked to the center of the fighting arena. "I have no concerns about your competency, M'Lady. I would, with the utmost of confidence, select *you* to fight by my side in battle right this second."

Demric looked over at his two champion warriors. "No offense, men."

"None taken," Ander said lightheartedly.

"We'd make the same choice," Jax chortled.

"Thank you, all of you." Tynae blushed. "Let's get started. Shall we? Serry, my sweet, you need to go sit with Béo."

"Yes, Mistress, good luck."

"Thank you." Tynae turned her attention to a new arrival. "Afternoon, Tingy," Tynae said warmly.

Tingy bowed. "Good afternoon, My Lady." Tingy looked at Béo, "My Lord."

"Tingy." Béo nodded back.

"Please work your wonderful magic," Tynae requested.

"With pleasure." Tingy raised his hands in the air, "*Transmornah*." The words rushed out of Tingy's mouth in hushed tones whirling around Tynae's body. This was the first time she'd ever heard Tingy speak actual words when casting a spell, and the first time she ever felt the spell touch her body. "Tingy, I know this works against actual penetration of the flesh so you can't get stabbed. I believe that I will still feel the full impact of a punch when I get struck, am I correct?" Tynae dreaded his response, but was fairly certain she knew the answer.

"Indeed, you are correct, My Lady," Tingy replied in a monotone voice, clearly concerned for Tynae's well being once again.

"Just checking." Tynae touched the Nanic's shoulder lightly, "Tingy, please relax. I'll be fine." Tynae wasn't sure who she was trying to convince more, Tingy or herself.

Tynae could see apprehension in the men's faces as well. They needed a smidge of encouragement. "Gentlemen, I appreciate that I've earned your respect and I thank you for giving it freely. It's because of that respect you will inevitably treat me different. Please, do not hold back because I am a woman. They won't hold back on the battlefield. I must learn properly. My life, or more importantly yours, may depend upon it someday. Bruises and cuts will heal."

The men looked from one to the other.

"Shall we?" Tynae asked, stepping into the middle of the arena.

"We are going to start you with basic blocks," Demric explained. "Your job is to see, or maybe a better word is to *feel,* your opponents coming at you from different angles. You're used to looking at your adversary and watching the moves they make." Demric shook his head. "No more. I'm going to come at you from the front, Jax stand behind her to the left.

"Okay, let's take this slow. Block me with your right and push your left arm back stopping Jax. You can look at both of us, but there is always going to be a moment you'll have to take your eyes off one or more of your attackers."

Tynae did as she was told.

They all moved in slow motion.

"Okay, again, faster this time. Jax, actually raise your arm so she has something to block," Demric instructed.

This went on for a while. Next Demric wanted to try a mock fight. "Let's go boys and girl," he said.

Béo stood up. He had been sitting on the wall of the arena. When Tynae looked at him he gave her wink.

Demric came at her from the front, Jax stayed to her side. She hated competitors to come at her from the side as this was a vulnerable area. Tynae blocked both men fairly well at first, but when she turned toward Demric she lost sight of Jax. It was only a split second, but that was all it took. The next thing she knew she was on her arse with the wind knocked out of her. Standing up, Tynae shook it off. She gave Béo a reassuring nod, knowing this was difficult for him. Regaining her footing, and breath, they tried again, this time she got it from both sides. Jax caught her in the stomach at the same time Demric landed a left hook to her cheek. She was thrown a good meter into the air, landing flat on her back.

Béo stood frozen, eyes wide.

Once able to breathe, Tynae got up. Looking at Béo, she gave him a wink and a smile. "I'm fine," she insisted.

"I am so sorry, Lady Tynae," Jax apologized profusely.

Tynae put her hands up. "Jax, it's okay. I'm fine. It's the only way I'm going to learn. We all knew I was going to get hurt," Tynae reiterated. "Do you think I came out of my mother's womb with a tiny sword, knowing how to use it?" She chuckled at the thought. "No," she said sternly, shaking her head. "I've taken my fair share of blows and I know there are many more to come."

"Yeah, but…"

"Stop," Tynae said lightly. "Jax, *it's the only way I am going to learn*, it's okay."

Demric hadn't said anything. He seemed to be lost in thought. Scratching the stubble on his chin, Demric surveyed Tynae carefully. "I'd like to try something new. Lady Tynae, stand here in the middle of the ring," he pointed to where he wanted her.

Tynae moved to where he instructed.

"Okay, I'm just working on a hunch here, but it's worth a try. I heard your senses have become heightened, is this correct?"

There are no such things as secrets in this city, she thought. "Yes," Tynae replied.

"So let's give this a try. If it works, you'll be learning two new skills," Demric said. "I want you to close your eyes and reach out with your mind and your energy. Find and identify the energy surrounding you," he challenged.

Tynae eyed Demric suspiciously.

Snickering, Demric shook his head. "We won't strike you. You don't have to worry about being blindsided. For now, I just want you to tell me where the people are that are surrounding you."

Closing her eyes, Tynae could still hear their footsteps. Though they walked on soft dirt, each step was crisp and distinctive. Tynae took her time, concentrating intently. "There is someone in front of me, slightly to the left, and…there is someone directly to my right, but standing further back than the other two." She had to focus all her attention to find the last one. "Okay, the third is behind me, to my left." Tynae felt around carefully once more. "That's everyone. May I open my eyes?"

"You may," Demric said.

Opening her eyes, Tynae was a bit surprised to see everyone standing precisely where she'd felt them. She beamed.

"Impressive." Demric commended. "We're going to do it again, but this time you will not know how many I'm going to have surrounding you. Close your eye's."

Once again, Tynae did as she was told.

Focusing all her attention on her task, Tynae could feel the presence of more bodies. "There's someone to my right, slightly back." She extended her hand, pointing.

"That would be Tingy." Demric confirmed.

"And…there's someone to my right front, further out than the rest again." She pointed to that person as well."

"Dead on."

"There are two to my left, one directly adjacent to my arm."

"Perfect."

"And the other…further behind me."

"Your accuracy is uncanny, that's Ander."

"There is one more." Pausing, a wide grin slowly spread across Tynae's face, she touched her necklace lightly. "My future stands directly before me. May I open my eyes?"

"By all means," Demric replied.

Tynae didn't really care who stood where, she just wanted to see Béo. When she opened her eyes, he was smiling broadly at her.

"Hmm, do I get a prize?" she teased, talking to Béo and Béo alone.

Walking forward, Béo put his hands on Tynae's shoulders. Leaning in, he ensured only she could hear him. "And what would you like, *my lady*?" he purred in her ear.

Leaning back so he could look at her he saw the intensity flair in her eyes. Leaning forward again he brushed his lips lightly against hers. "Please try and behave yourself, my love. I am *yours* forever."

"Sorry, sometimes…wow." Blushing, Tynae regained her self control.

Béo touched Tynae's cheek lightly where Demric had landed his punch. "Does it hurt?"

"A little. How bad does it look?"

"It definitely left a mark. It's a bit purple."

"We've been at this for a while. Would you like to take a break?" Demric asked once the couple stepped apart.

Tynae thought about it. "No, can we work a little longer then call it a day?"

Demric nodded. "As you wish, M'Lady. Do you feel like you have a good grip on sensing the energy around you now?"

Tynae contemplated her answer. "Fairly well," she nodded. "I think I know what I'm feeling for now."

"That'll do," Demric said, cheerfully walking up to the couple. "My Lord, may I borrow one of those leather straps," he gestured to Béo's midsection.

Béo looked down at his waist. "Sure."

"Thank you. Please tie it around Lady Tynae's eyes," Demric instructed. "M'Lady, you will only be working with me for the time being. I will be standing directly in front of you. Once again we will start slow. You're going to block my blows."

Tynae's face went blank. "Blindfolded?" she stammered.

"How is this different from closing your eyes?" Demric asked.

"You're going to be taking swings at me to start with." Tynae shrugged, "I don't know. Somehow it just seems more daunting."

"You can do this, I know it," Béo whispered, tying his leather strap over her eyes. "Hmmm, you know this gives me an idea," he whispered slyly.

"And what would that be?" she whispered provocatively in return.

"Never mind," he chuckled.

Tynae giggled. "I'm certain we're both thinking the same thing…" she whispered. "And *I'm* supposed to behave!"

"Later then, *my* love...good luck." Giving her shoulders a slight squeeze Béo returned to his place against the wall.

Demric took his place in front of Tynae. "Ready?"

Tynae took a deep breath. "Ay," she said pulling herself tall.

True to his word Demric began slowly, but Tynae was better at this then anyone had anticipated. "This is too easy for you, M'Lady. I have to change things up a bit. I need to move around.

For now I will not go beyond your side," Demric reassured. Mixing things up he went back and forth, coming at her with left and right jabs. It took a while, but he got another good hit in, directly opposite from his previous punch.

Great, I'm going to look like a raccoon by the time we're done, Tynae thought.

Tynae improved quickly; blocking everything else Demric threw at her.

"I'm getting tired and the sun is beginning to set. I think that's enough for one day, M'Lady."

Béo came over taking the cover off Tynae's eyes. "You did wonderfully."

Tynae sighed. "Thank you, love..."

Once the strap was off Tynae turned to Demric. "Would you like me to bring a veil with me tomorrow?"

"No, I want you to bring something of your beloved's...beloved" Demric chuckled heartily. "Sorry," Demric clapped Béo on the shoulder. "I've known this one since he was a wee lad; it doesn't seem possible that he's old enough to be courting. He's still that little boy who used to drive me crazy asking millions of questions, *every day,*" Demric mused. "The reason I want you to use something of his, preferably an item strong with his scent, is because it will take more effort for you to concentrate. He seems to distract you easily."

Turning bright red Tynae looked away, pretending not to hear his last. "Okay, well, we'll see all of you tomorrow then," she said in a cheery voice

Tynae walked to Tingy, who stood with his ickel beside the wall where Béo had been sitting.

"Tingy, if you would, please."

"Of course, My Lady," the little Nanic bowed.

"Thank you; Tingy...As usual it has been a pleasure seeing you, have a wonderful night."

"You, as well, My Lady."

Serry danced through the air, floating to Tynae's shoulder.

Chapter 50
Trails Forged

"Whoever has trusted a woman has trusted deceivers."
~Hesiod

Arona stood looking out the window of King Yurgon's study.

"Sire," addressed a soldier entering the room. "We can locate neither Vinard nor Enessa."

The king set down his quill. "Where have you looked?"

"Throughout the castle and the grounds of Darvah."

Rubbing his chin, Yurgon sighed. "Continue looking. Send soldiers into Pathrow as well as the forest of Nombin."

"Yes, Majesty. Will there be anything else."

"No."

Arona walked over to the king. "My Lord, the princess' disappearance plagues me. I just cannot stop thinking of what a great loss this is for all of us, but to you most especially. I've thought of this extensively and I believe I may have a theory as to what may have happened. I'd like to share this with you, if I might?"

"Of course, my dear."

Sitting down across from Yurgon, Arona glanced at the parchment on which he'd been writing then looked at the king thoughtfully. "I know how much you value Vinard and Enessa, Sire, but don't you find it rather curious that they too have disappeared only a matter of moons since Tynae went missing?"

"It is a bit unsettling, but I will not jump to conclusions."

Arona was not about to let this opportunity slip through her fingers. Intricately she began spinning her web. "Do you have any thoughts as to why or where they may have gone?" Arona asked.

"Not particularly." Yurgon drummed his fingers on the desk. "I am certain there is a reasonable explanation, no doubt."

"My, Lord," Arona smiled gently. "You are always so trusting. But I fear your confidence may be misplaced this time. The indications do not bode well for Vinard and Enessa."

Yurgon looked at Arona somberly. "What feasible reason would either one of them have for harming or taking my daughter?"

"Prince Kaleal was to announce his plan to court Princess Tynae on the eve of the ball. Was he not?"

Yurgon nodded. "He was. But what could that possibly have to do with Vinard and Enessa taking Tynae?"

"Everything, My Lord," Arona said. "Don't you see? Vinard was in love with the princess. It was evident in the way he looked at her."

The king thought for a moment. "I suppose I could understand why you might think that, but Vinard grew up with Tynae. I am certain he loved her as a brother would a sister. I do not believe he was *in love* with her."

Arona looked at her king sympathetically. "Sire, perhaps you did not see them when they where together, but I did. I know the look of a man in love, trust me. Vinard was most definitely in love with your daughter."

The king settled back in his chair, clearly considering Arona's words.

"Okay," Yurgon said, "Let's say that Vinard was in love with Tynae, for argument sake. Why would he harm her?"

Like a lamb to the slaughter.

"Try to put yourself in Vinard's shoes, My Lord. Can you imagine how heart broken he must have been? He's been in love with Lady Tynae, probably ever since they where children. I'm sure he secretly imagined that she would someday be his. But on the night of the masque, you announced that Prince Kaleal was to make a declaration. Vinard and the princess where very good friends, that is certainly no secret. I'm sure he asked her what the announcement was to be, assuming she hadn't told him already."

The king looked at Arona perplexed. "I still don't understand. Even if any of this where vaguely true, what does it have to do with Tynae's disappearance?"

"Vinard must have become fearful that he was going to lose Tynae to the prince, so he decided to take her away."

Yurgon let out a guffaw. "That is absurd, Arona. Where would he take her? How would he keep her from returning home?"

"Perhaps he believes he can make Lady Tynae love him, or maybe he has enlisted the services of a sorcerer. It is rumored that there is a magic so strong that when administered even your worst enemy will fall madly in love with you."

"Where do you hear such things, Arona?"

"People talk. Who knows, maybe he or Enessa have even dabbled in the art of black magic themselves. Enessa has always been fascinated with the world of spirits."

Yurgon shook his head. "It is true that magic was once real, but those who wielded such powers no longer exist," Yurgon clarified.

Arona shrugged. "Believe what you will. But your beloved daughter is gone and the people who could most easily persuade her to leave are now gone as well."

"Why would Enessa participate in such an impractical scheme?"

Arona shrugged. "Perhaps Vinard convinced her that he and Lady Tynae should be together. After all, the three of them have been together every single day for how many years now? Maybe she just didn't want to be left alone, so she chose to go along with whatever Vinard proposed. Or maybe she went because she believed she could keep Lady Tynae safe."

The king shook his head. "I just don't know. It all sounds so incredibly far fetched."

"Desperate men do desperate things, My Lord," Arona said smoothly.

Yurgon sat quietly for several long moments. Finally he shouted, "Guards!"

Three of the guards positioned outside his study came in. "Yes, Sire?"

"I want all of Montronvarr searched until Vinard and Enessa are found. Place notices in every town across the nation. The second you have them in custody, I want them brought directly to me."

"Yes, Your Majesty. Will there be anything else?"

"No."

The guards departed immediately.

Arona stood up. "I shall let you get back to your affairs, My Lord. Good night."

With a satisfied grin the baroness excused herself. *My work here is done.*

"Enessa, you need to keep up with me. I understand you don't care much for horses, but we won't be traveling by carriage any time soon. You will have to get used to it."

"I'm trying, Vinard, this beast just won't cooperate."

"You better become real friendly with that *beast*. The two of you are going to be spending a lot of time together."

"I'm trying." Enessa did her best to catch up to Vinard. "Where are we headed anyway?"

Vinard slowed his horse. "To one of the few places I know we will be safe for the time being."

The two had been riding for a fortnight. Finding caves to hide in, they slept during the day and traveled only at night.

"We'll be there soon, Enessa. Tonight we will have proper beds and real pillows."

"Sounds lovely, using rocks for pillows is starting to take its toll." Enessa moved her head around in an attempt to relax her muscles. "I don't know if my neck will ever move properly again."

"I know what you mean," Vinard stretched. "I think I chipped a tooth last night when I rolled over. There it is." Vinard pointed toward an ominous looking forest.

"We're supposed to travel into *that* forest?" Enessa asked, clearly alarmed.

"Don't worry; I know this wood the way Tynae knows Nombin."

Enessa grudgingly followed Vinard through the formidable forest. Eventually they reached a clearing, in the center of it stood the dilapidated ruins of a once-elegant castle.

Enessa looked around. "Are we in the forest of Tynan the Cruel?"

"Indeed, we are in the forest of the dark one."

Unblinking, Enessa stared at the castle. "Then that is the castle of Samara."

"It is."

"These woods…" Enessa jumped halfway out of her seat as an owl swooped overhead. "Vinard, these woods are rumored to be haunted."

"That they are, and because of that very reason not many venture here."

"We're supposed to sleep here?"

"Do you have a better idea?"

Looking petrified Enessa shook her head.

"Let's get inside. We need a place to rest and this is the safest place I could think of. No-one will bother us here. In the days to come, we can come up with some sort of plan on how to find Tynae. At the very least, maybe we can figure out what's happened to her. I didn't want to discuss it while we were in Pathrow as you never know who might be listening."

"Right, can we just get inside." Enessa looked over her shoulder. "I feel like the woods are watching us."

Vinard led the way to the far side of the castle. Jumping off his horse, he motioned for Enessa to do the same. "We have to lead the horses from here. We need to cross that bridge," he pointed.

Enessa looked to where Vinard was pointing. "Are you mad?! It's falling apart! It must be at least a hundred years old."

Vinard laughed. "I'll go first, you follow. Either you trust me, or you don't. It's the only way across."

Enessa looked around and as far as she could see, it was the only way to get to the castle. Once across the bridge, they led their horses through a gate and into a covered courtyard with plenty of grass for the horses to eat and lie upon. There had clearly been no grounds keeper here for a number of years, perhaps decades.

"I'll bring them some water and remove their saddles once we're settled." Vinard grabbed his saddle bag. "Follow me, and watch your step."

Vinard walked back through the gate which they had led the horses through. Closing it behind them, he latched it.

"Are you sure the horses won't get out?" Enessa asked.

"I'm sure, there's only one way in and you just saw me lock it."

"Have you been here before?"

"I have. Come on, it will be daylight soon and I don't want to be caught dawdling about. If you see any sticks or small bits of wood along the way, gather it up."

Vinard led the way along a path through an overgrown garden. Eventually they reached a large wooden door that was rotting and falling off its hinges. Once through the doorway, Vinard turned to his right. This passageway led to a cooking area. Several dirty windows running along one wall, some broken and some still intact, allowed moonlight to stream in. Walking over to a large cooking pit made of bricks, Vinard placed the tinder he'd gathered in the center of it.

Enessa did the same.

Setting down his saddle bag, Vinard pulled a flint from it and used it to light the wood.

"What about smoke?" Enessa asked. "If there's anyone around, they'll see it."

Vinard shook his head. "The cooking pits we will use are unlike most. The duct that pulls the smoke out goes down into the ground and comes out many kilometers away near a lake. If someone were to see it, they would believe it to be fog, not smoke, if they see it at all." Looking around, Vinard found a few candlesticks that held partially burned candles. He lit them with the fire in the pit.

"I don't understand," Enessa said. "How are we going to get a good night sleep here?"

Vinard grinned. "Patience, dear one, patience. Let's heat up our food then we'll get some sleep. I will go hunting later and get us some fresh meat. If you could take care of the cooking, I will go relieve the horses of their saddles. While I am at it, I will get them some water and bring some back for us, too."

Back inside, Enessa served Vinard a helping of leftover porridge.

Exhausted and famished, they ate in silence.

Once finished with their meal Vinard stood, handing Enessa a candlestick. After dowsing the fire in the pit with some water, he picked up a candle of his own, and blew out the remaining flames.

"Be careful, there are a lot of loose bricks throughout this place," Vinard warned as he led her deeper into the castle.

"How do you know all this?"

"Tomorrow," Vinard smiled. "Right now we need to sleep."

Cobwebs hung like curtains from the ceiling, and mouse droppings littered the floor.

Climbing several levels of stairs, they finally reached a room that had only three walls. The entire back wall, which should have sealed it from the outside elements, had completely deteriorated. Because they were so high up, the missing wall allowed them to see a great distance out. Unexpected visitors would be easily seen long before they arrived.

Vinard walked over to one of the standing walls. Feeling around, he located the loose stone he was searching for. With a turn and a twist, a portion of the wall slid open. This opening exposed a previously concealed area.

Enessa stood awestruck. "How did…never mind. It looks so different from everything else. It's fully in tact and…clean."

Vinard smiled, "I can't be certain, but I think this may have been a secret chamber for the previous occupants in case of an attack. Clearly it has not been affected the way the rest of the dwelling has, so I suppose it has served its purpose. It may not be a full size castle, but it is fully equipped with everything we might need for the time being. There is a living area, a loo, and there's even a small cooking area, in case we become truly trapped. It's not ideal, but it will do in a pinch. Come on, I'll show you where the bedchambers are, they all have a warm cozy bed in them."

After shutting the secret door, Vinard led Enessa to the sleeping chambers. "Which one would you like?"

Enessa looked at her choice of rooms. "I will take the one on the right."

"It's yours. Good night," he said.

"Sleep well."

When Vinard woke several hours later he was starving. Not wanting to wake Enessa he left her a note.

Going out to hunt.

If you want to build a fire, do so only in the fire pit in the center of the living area.

To open the passageway, pull the lever to the left of the fireplace.

Back soon,

Vinard

Grabbing his pack, bow, and quiver; Vinard headed out the concealed door.

Once outside, Vinard looked up at the sky. He estimated it was late afternoon. After a quick check on the horses, he ventured deeper into the forest on foot.

Vinard had always been an exceptional tracker. Walking quietly through the wood, he watched the ground as he went. It wasn't long before Vinard spotted deer tracks. Kneeling down, he examined the imprints. *They're fresh and it's a good size animal.*

Traveling east for several kilometers, Vinard finally caught up to his prey as the sun began to set. *Very good size, fifteen points.* Quietly withdrawing a bolt from his quiver, Vinard took aim. He could already taste the venison. Taking a deep breath, he drew back his bow. With his exhale, he let the bolt fly. True to its mark, it brought the animal down.

Walking over to his prize, Vinard set down his bow and pack. Opening his pack he extracted a rope. Looking around, he spotted the perfect tree growing on a fair incline. Setting his hand on the deer's side, Vinard issued a silent expression of gratitude. *Thank you for your sacrifice. Your death shall sustain life for many. Peace be with you brother.*

Wrapping the rope securely around the animal's hind legs, Vinard threw the cord over a large Branch. Pulling hard, he hoisted the deer up. Fastening the loose end of the rope around another branch, Vinard was ready to begin.

Removing the knife from his belt, Vinard quickly skinned his kill. Removing the hide from the animal, he laid it flat on the ground slightly uphill a few meters away from the buck he was about to cut open. Tossing his pack next to the hide, he was ready to begin.

A prickle on his neck told him that he had an audience. Glancing up, Vinard discovered glowing eyes watching him from the tall grass.

"Tynae would absolutely love you." Looking skyward he sighed. "Where are you, Tynae? Do you gaze upon the same stars as I?" Vinard looked at the wolves in the grass. "Several of your mates had befriended her. They loved her…as most do."

Grabbing hold of the deer, Vinard cut into it, removing its organs. Next he began quartering and cutting the meat. His guests in the grass crept on their bellies trying to get closer. Soon Vinard could see their beautiful faces. "Give me just a bit longer you three. Tonight you too will have a marvelous meal."

Continuing to slice meat from the carcass, he laid the cuts on the hide. Thanks to the incline the tree grew upon, the blood ran neatly downhill. Once finished, Vinard wrapped the hide around the meat and tucked it all neatly into his pack. Loosening the rope, Vinard brought down what remained of the buck. Removing the rope from its hind legs, he set the remains at the base of the tree.

Replacing the rope into his pack, he closed it up and slung it over his shoulder. Picking up his bow, he set off. "Enjoy your meal."

When Vinard arrived back at the castle, Enessa had a large fire going in the cooking pit in the kitchen.

"Enessa, I'm back. Where are you?"

Enessa came around the corner carrying a small basket. "Did you get anything?" she asked hopefully.

"It's me you're talking to. Have you ever known me to come back empty handed?" he joked.

"What did you get, hare, pheasant?"

"Venison."

Enessa's eyes lit up. "I figured you would get something, so I gathered herbs from out in the garden." She set down the basket. "I even found some potatoes."

"Perfect." Vinard pulled the hide containing the meat out of his pack. "Here you go. You get started on this, and I will fetch more wood and water. I'd like to take a hot bath tonight."

By the time Vinard had finished bringing in many buckets of water and several pieces of wood, supper was ready.

"It smells and looks marvelous, Enessa," Vinard complimented, sitting down at the table.

"Thank you."

"I have a little treat," Vinard said, presenting a bottle of wine.

"Where did you get that?"

He smiled mischievously, "I have my ways."

Enessa laughed, holding out her goblet. "Are you going to tell me how you know this place so well?"

"I am," Vinard served himself a large slab of meat. "When I was a young boy, my father used to bring me here. This is where he and his friends would meet. They belonged to an elite group, or brotherhood, as father liked to say. Unfortunately the group no longer exists, all the men have passed."

"Were you part of the brotherhood?"

"I was supposed to be, but my father died before I was inducted."

"What were they called?"

"The Son's of Shamira. They were a select few. All were soldiers sworn to protect the 'Chosen One', if and when he or she ever made an appearance." Vinard took a bite of food. "Are you familiar with the prophecies?"

Enessa swallowed her bite. "Very."

"Do you believe?"

Enessa shrugged, "I don't know. It's been so long. It is said that the 'Chosen One' will bring peace where there is chaos; but there is no chaos, so perhaps the 'Chosen One' is no longer needed." Enessa took a bite of food.

"I don't know about that, things certainly seem to be getting a bit chaotic...too chaotic for my liking."

"True." Enessa took a sip of wine. "What exactly was the duty of The Son's of Shamira?"

Vinard tilted his head. "They had their own prophecies. One foretold that a Son of Shamira would personally protect the 'Chosen One'. Another said that when the time was right, the protector of the 'Chosen One' would deliver him or her into the hands of the Chief of Calai. The people of Calai would protect the 'Chosen One' until the time came that he or she was needed." Vinard took a bite of food. "I guess one would have to believe that Calai actually existed, to believe any of the fables."

"Do you not believe in Calai?" Enessa asked.

"I don't know. My father certainly did."

"How was the 'Chosen One' to be delivered to the Chief of Calai?"

Vinard shrugged, "My father never told me that part of the prophecy."

Enessa took a few bites of food. "What did the Son's of Shamira do, or discuss, when they gathered together?"

"I have no idea, I was always sent off to play. That's why I know this place so well."

Enessa smiled. "That makes sense. How did you know about the hidden room?"

"There are many things hidden here." Vinard smiled, holding up his goblet of wine. "All of which my father showed me. He told me that if ever I sought shelter from an enemy, this would be the safest place."

"Do you believe we are in danger?"

"I don't know. I certainly never believed Tynae was in danger. All I know is that the snows will be coming soon and we need to come up with a plan. Tomorrow I am going into town to see what I can find out."

Once finished with their meal, the pair went back up to their hidden sanctuary.

"Are you going to take a bath?" Vinard asked.

"Yes, but I'd like to read for a bit."

Vinard got the fire pit in the center of their hidden chamber going.

Enessa used the fire to light many candles. Because the rooms where windowless, there was no fear of the light being seen.

After his bath, Vinard retired to his bed.

The next day Vinard showed Enessa around the grounds. He waited until twilight before heading into town. "I would prefer that once I am gone that you stay in the concealed chamber," Vinard said seriously.

"Then that's what I shall do."

"Thank you."

"Please be careful," Enessa said.

Vinard smiled, "I always am."

Donning a black cloak, Vinard saddled his horse and departed. Vinard knew the best place to get information would be at the local tavern. Drunken men equal loose tongues. Dismounting his horse, Vinard pulled his cloak over his head concealing his face. Taking a seat in the corner, he positioned himself so that he could watch the door and hear many conversations. Vinard then ordered a stein of ale.

The chatter was nothing out of the ordinary; work, wenches, and wine, generally in that order. Vinard was getting ready to leave when a soldier from Montronvarr entered. Vinard recognized his brother in arms. Sinking deeper into the darkness of the corner in which he sat, Vinard became virtually invisible. He watched the soldier nail up several notices.

Once the soldier had left Vinard stood, departing unnoticed. When Vinard had arrived, he thought ahead, tying his horse a fair distance away from the tavern. Walking back to his steed there were several notices posted. Glancing about to make sure no-one was around he pulled one down, tucking it under his cloak. Quickly mounting his horse, Vinard made his way out of the city limits as fast as possible.

Keeping a weather eye, he did his damndest to ensure that no-one followed him. Stopping, turning, and even backtracking, he did his best to confuse anyone who might try. When he returned to Samara, he found Enessa reading in the living area.

"Did you find out anything?" she asked.

Vinard removed his cloak. "Ay." He handed Enessa the notice.

Enessa looked horror-struck as she read.

"We are wanted by the king?!"

"Looks to be that way."

"We knew the possibility of that happening, I suppose." Enessa set the paper on a table. "What now?"

Vinard sat in a chair across from Enessa. "I have no idea," he said rubbing his forehead. "I believe we are safe here. When we do leave, we will have to leave this nation all together. I don't want to think about it anymore tonight. We will discuss it tomorrow." Vinard stood up, "Good night."

"Good night."

Chapter 51
Follow Your Heart

"As soon as you trust yourself, you will know how to live."
~Johann Wolfgang von Goethe

Walking back to Vu'tella, Béo wrapped his arm tight around Tynae's waist. "I love you so much," he said.

She smiled brightly. "I love you, too."

"You did really great today."

"Thank you," Tynae said bashfully. "Do I look like a raccoon? Be honest."

"No, you look ravishing as usual. I noticed that you heal extremely fast, ever since…*'that night'*. I think you'll be fully recovered by tomorrow. You had much worse when I rescued you, and there was not a trace of a scratch or bruise the next morning."

"*'That night'* is that what we're calling the night I plummeted to my death?" She laughed.

It was easy for Tynae to joke about that night. She never had to see her broken body.

"How about we just call it the night of your *rebirth*," Béo suggested.

Tynae glanced at Béo. "Okay, rebirth it is." She continued to stare at Béo.

"What?"

She smiled her magical smile. "We'll talk when we get back to Vu'tella."

"Okay." Leaning over, Béo kissed the top of her head.

"Good evening, My Lord and Lady," O'leana greeted with a bow as the pair walked in, "Serry."

"Ladies," Tynae nodded.

"Supper will be ready soon."

"Wonderful, I'm starving," Tynae said.

"Me too," Béo agreed.

"It smells amazing, O'leana," Tynae commended. "What is it?"

"It's ox, My Lady, with cream sauce and wild mushrooms. I also prepared purple potatoes and tuvar."

"Sounds as good as it smells. I think I could eat an entire ox right now. I can't wait to try it!"

"If you'd like to go wash up, it should be ready when you come back," O'leana suggested.

"We'll be back momentarily." Tynae motioned for Béo to follow her. "Serry, would you please excuse us."

Serry flew into the miniature forest and Béo followed Tynae into her bedchamber.

The second he shut the door, he grabbed Tynae around the waist, pulling her tight against him. "Hi," he whispered putting his forehead on hers.

"Hello," she cooed.

Tilting his head to one side, their lips melded together.

The two quickly became hopelessly lost in their impassioned kiss.

Tynae's hands flowed over Béo's chest, across his shoulders, and into his hair. Knotting her fingers in his long locks, she pulled Béo closer. Tongues dancing erotically, bodies ablaze, Tynae reached for the lacings of Béo's loincloth.

"Whoa…" Leaning back, Béo laughed. "What happened to 'I'm starving'?" he teased.

"Who needs food when I have you?" Tynae tried pulling him back to her.

"We need to get back. O'leana's waiting." Béo brushed his lips against Tynae's. "Let's get out there…" He kissed her one last time. "Before one of us bursts into flames," he chuckled.

After washing up, the couple re-entered the dining area, sitting at the table.

"Will there be anything else, My Lady?" O'leana asked, apparently getting use to Tynae's desire to be rid of the help as soon as possible.

"No," Tynae admired the scrumptious feast set before them. "It all looks perfect. We'll see you in the morning. Good night."

Sitting side by side, Béo smiled thoughtfully at Tynae. "So, I think tonight I should get to ask the questions. Would that be alright with you?"

"No, and yes," Tynae smiled. "I just have one thing I'd like to ask. Then you can ask me all the questions you'd like." Tynae took her plate from Béo. "I could have done that, thank you."

"Just one question?"

"Just one," Tynae confirmed.

Grinning, Béo pretended to ponder his response. "Hmm, I suppose I can live with that." He nibbled on a piece of bread. "What's your question, angel?"

"On our way back I mentioned, *that night.* It seemed to bother you...ale?"

"Please," he held out his stein.

Tynae continued with her train of thought. "Anyway, it was then that I realized that we've never talked about that night. Why is that?"

The mere mention of *that night* made Béo tense up. Lovingly, he put his hand on Tynae's cheek. "That was the worst...and best night of my entire life," he said lightly.

Considering Tynae thoughtfully for a moment, Béo took a deep breath then began. "I was hunting when I heard you fall into the water. I swam to you to see if I could help. I didn't even recognize you. When I realized that it was *you*...when I saw how *broken* you were. I knew you were dead and I wanted to die." Béo focused on his plate. "I just couldn't give up, I had to do something. That's why I brought your body back here. I don't think you understand how much I loved you prior to you ever coming to Calai. You haunted my dreams at night. I thought of you throughout my days. I wanted desperately to tell you how I felt. I just couldn't find the right words or the right time." Béo took a bite of his food. "I had decided that I was going to Pathrow that very eve and tell you exactly how I felt about you, point blank...consequences be damned. For once in my life, I was going to let the chips fall where they may..." Béo sighed.

"But I got cold feet. I vowed to myself that I would tell you exactly how I felt the next time I saw you. There would be plenty of time…right?" he mused, gazing at Tynae with sorrowful eyes. "The next time I saw you, you were dead. In that instant I was certain I had lost you…lost everything…forever. I felt responsible somehow for what had happened to you. I thought that maybe if I had gone I could have prevented or stopped whatever had caused the atrocities brought forth against you. Fortunately, for everyone, all the Archimagi were in Calai that night. When I laid your body on the table…" Béo winced at the thought. "I wanted desperately to kill whoever had hurt you. Black and blue bruises covered you from head to toe. The cuts covering your body still bled. Though the sea had cleared the blood away briefly, once you were out of the water it returned and your body…" Béo closed his eyes, wishing he could forget that horrifying image.

Tynae held his hand securely.

Looking up at her, his expression was rigid. "You can't even begin to imagine. I think every bone in your body was broken, *you,* were broken. I honestly didn't think you could be brought back. I was living in my own personal hell." Béo shook his head.

"All I could do was pray that somehow, someway, you would be saved. That was also the longest night of my life."

Leaning forward, Béo kissed Tynae on the forehead. "And here we are. You're alive and absolutely perfect. I did learn a valuable lesson that night," Béo said.

"What was that?" Tynae asked sweetly.

"Always follow your heart." Béo's expression softened. "I will NEVER allow anyone to take you from me ever again," Béo said with resolve. "When I went to speak with my father today, I had thought about what I might do if he was opposed to us being with each other. I decided that if he was against us, we could run away together." Béo touched Tynae's hand again. "I would do anything to be with you, Tynae."

"That's funny," Tynae's smile was dazzling. "I had toyed with the same idea," she admitted running her hand over his.

448

"Béo, I know this may sound a bit ludicrous, but I'm glad I died. If it hadn't happened the way that it did, we might not be here together. I would do it all again in a heartbeat. I would die a hundred deaths, a hundred times over, as long as I get to spend my eternity with you."

Béo grinned serenely. "I understand what you're saying, love, and I do agree. I just wish it hadn't required such extreme measures on your part." Béo took a bite of meat. "So that is the night of your rebirth. Not the night of your death or anything else. At least that's how I prefer to remember it. And I'd rather not talk or think about it unless I absolutely have to."

"I can live with that, but I hate how much it pains you. I wish I could remove the memory from your mind."

Béo sighed, "It is what it is. Enjoying your meal?"

"I am," Tynae looked at Béo. "I love you…Hey, I thought you were going to ask me questions tonight?" Tynae reminded him, flashing her perfect smile.

Béo exhaled. "You know, it really is impossible for me to be in a bad mood when I'm around you." He chuckled, taking a drink. "I don't know a lot about your family, tell me about them. Mom, Dad, you…"

Tynae hunched her shoulders. "I guess I'll start with my mother. I never knew her. She died when I was still an infant. My father met her on his travels. He said it was love at first sight…"

A cunning smile crossed Béo's face.

"What?"

Looking at Tynae innocently, Béo shrugged. "Seems your father and I have something in common. I never believed in love at first sight until I met you, but we are not talking about me tonight," he teased.

Tynae rolled her eyes. "Fine. I think maybe I should back up a little. You do know that Yurgon was not the true heir to the throne, correct? He was named to it."

Béo nodded. "I don't know the whole story behind that. But, yes, I am aware that he is an appointed king."

Tynae smiled. "It's an important fact. My father loved to travel the world. It was on one of his many expeditions that he met my mother, Aletta. He said she looked just like an angel." Tynae's smile grew.

"Hmm, something else we have in common," Béo mumbled with a grin.

Snickering, Tynae kept going. "I loved to hear him talk about her. To this day he's still madly in love with her. I can hear the passion and love in his voice whenever he speaks of their time together." Tynae sighed. "Though they'd only known each other for a few weeks, he says he knew without a doubt that she was the only one for him. So he asked her to marry him, and she said *yes.*"

"Mmhmm," Béo muttered. He found it very interesting how much King Yurgon and he had in common when it came to the woman they loved.

"Shortly after they wed, she became pregnant. Her pregnancy was normal for the most part, but I guess I made my appearance a few months early. No-one thought I would survive coming as early as I did, but I was healthy. A year or so after I was born, my mother went to my father, incredibly distressed. She told him she didn't believe she would be alive much longer. She said she'd taken ill and wanted to ensure that he could care for me on his own. Of course, my father sought out the best doctors. They ran tests, drew blood, yet found nothing wrong with her. Still she maintained that she was ill and would soon pass into the void. To my father's dismay, a few months later she died. He found her in their bed. She went in her sleep."

"How awful."

"My father was shattered. I think I'm the only reason he remained alive. He couldn't stay in Edelmira. It held too many memories of the time he'd spent with my mother, so he packed everything up and returned with me to Montronvarr. Pathrow is where he had grown up and still had many friends. Together the town raised me. I must have had five fathers if I had one," she mused cheerfully. "When I was four, King Nuhad, my father's oldest and dearest friend, passed away. Having no living relatives, he had named my father as his successor and went so far as to name me as my father's successor. That was odd, and I'm sure you know, unheard of. Anyway, life was good. My father was my best friend and I had many other friends as well. I went to school and Enessa, my handmaiden, took wonderful care of me. I wanted for nothing." Tynae took a swig of ale.

Béo used the brief pause to interrupt. "Do you miss her?"

"Enessa?" Tynae set her stein down.

"Yes," Béo replied, taking a swig from his own tankard.

"I do. She was the closest thing I ever had to a mother. She saved my life you know. Well her, Vinard and you; but she and Vinard were the first step, and you the second." Tynae smiled.

Béo's brow's knitted together, "How so?"

"It was she and Vinard that told me to run. Had they not, I would still have been in the castle when the soldiers arrived. If not for them, I probably would not be sitting here right now. I also owe Filipe much gratitude. He's the stable hand who told Enessa he had overheard some of the guards arguing in the stables. Enessa told Vinard and the two of them came to me straight away. Filipe told Enessa that soldiers had been arguing about their orders…" Pausing, Tynae looked at Béo sadly. "Which were to kill me," she sighed, "Apparently some of the men did not want to follow the command. Anyway, I guess that brings us to Baroness Arona. She came into our lives several years ago. I must have been about ten, so she was around nineteen. Her father and mine were quite close. When her father passed unexpectedly, she was left with no-one and nothing. My father offered to take her in, making her his ward." Tynae shrugged, "Overall my life has been fairly uneventful." Tynae laughed, "That is up until late. As of right now, I have no idea what's happened to my father. I don't know what Arona's planning to do next. And I haven't an inkling as to why she wanted me dead, but here I am. As it now stands, I know a fragment of diddly and a smidgen of squat. This means…I know a whole lot of diddly squat!" Tynae huffed, "It's rather frustrating." She took a long draw of her ale.

Béo ran his hand over Tynae's leg, "I am so sorry."

Tynae grinned, "It's not your fault, no reason for you to be sorry."

"I know but…" *There is reason to be sorry. I know precisely why Arona wants you dead and I can say nothing.*

Tynae continued to grin. "Any other questions? My life's pretty boring. No mystical creatures, magical dragons or talking butterflies." She laughed, "Well until now that is."

"Hmm, what's your heritage?" Béo asked.

Tynae took a bite of food. "Are you asking if I'm a specific race?"

"Mhmm." Béo nodded his mouth full of food.

Tynae shook her head. "Father and I never really discussed that sort of thing." She shrugged sadly. "I guess I'll never know now. I am human, I am from Montronvarr, and now, I am a woman without a family or a country." She pushed her empty plate aside.

"It doesn't matter," Béo assured her. "You're mine and that's all I really care about."

Tonight Béo cleared the dishes off the table.

"It's getting late, my love, let's go to bed." Béo offered his hand. "I'm sure I'll come up with lots more questions over time."

Tynae looked up at Béo. Standing, she wrapped her arms tight around him.

Holding her firmly, Béo knew just how much she needed him. He needed her equally.

"I love you so much, Béo," she said, looking deep into his eyes.

He kissed her forehead. "I love you, too, my angel, I love you, too. Come on, let's get some rest." Taking Tynae's hand he led her into their bedchamber.

Together they slept soundly, cradled in each other's arms.

Dreams came fast this night, and Ryedin stepped out of the sparkling mist as he did most every night since Tynae had come to Calai.

Tynae beamed. "Good evening."

"Ay, it is a good eve indeed." Ryedin used a seductive tone Tynae had never heard.

Walking up to Tynae, Ryedin pulled her tight to him, kissing her with a ravenous passion that took her breath away.

Wrapping her arms tight around his neck, Tynae ran her fingers through Ryedin's dark hair. Their passion grew into something much more as their souls entwined. Confident that tonight would be the night she finally got her way, Tynae pulled Ryedin's tunic over his head.

He did not fight her.

His well-chiseled, tight abdomen magnified his resemblance to a god. His skin was golden as if he spent many hours in the rays of the sun. Tynae ran her hand gently over Ryedin's bare skin.

He closed his eyes at her touch.

Kissing his chest tenderly, she allowed the connection of their flesh to burrow and burn its way into her soul. Sliding her hand down Ryedin's chest, she reached the top of his britches and began unlacing them.

Reaching down gently, Ryedin set his hand a top hers, simply saying, "No."

Tynae looked into his sky-blue eyes. "You can't be serious."

Ryedin looked at her, clearly contemplating his response. Taking a deep breath, he cradled Tynae's face in his hands. "I am, Tynae. When you and I finally make love I want *you* to be clear on why you have chosen to give yourself to *me*," he said seriously.

"I already know why, because I love you. I love you with all my heart, mind, body and soul, what more could there possibly be?" Tynae asked, teetering on the verge of tears without knowing why.

Ryedin stroked Tynae's cheeks with his thumbs. "There is still so much for you to learn, my love. I must ask you for patience. Please remember that in our dream world, a world only you and I share, there are rules. Whether or not we like them is beside the point. They must be followed." There was a distinct apology woven into his words.

Tynae took a deep breath, "Fine."

Picking his tunic up, Ryedin went to pull it back on.

Tynae stopped him. "If I promise to behave myself, will you leave it off?" she asked hopefully.

"You're incorrigible, you know that?" he chuckled.

Raising a brow Tynae shrugged her shoulders. "It's who I am, take it or leave it," she said simply. "Besides, I think it's a fair compromise."

Ryedin shook his head. "Okay, but you gave your word, so no trying to…" He narrowed his eyes, "You know," he said with a huge grin.

Nodding, Tynae accepted his condition. Finally looking around to see where her dream world had landed her this night Tynae saw that they stood in the middle of their private garden. She wore an off the shoulder, long, fitted, pale pink silk gown with a matching corset.

Taking Tynae by the hand, Ryedin walked over to their chaise lounge. "Your performance today was stupendous, love," he said, pulling her into the chair with him.

"Thank you," she said modestly, nuzzling against his bare chest. "It was all thanks to your training."

"Does that mean you're ready to begin today's lesson?"

"Already?" she asked, slightly disappointed. "I guess." She started to get up.

Ryedin pulled her back to him. "You're going to stay right here for today's lesson," he said mischievously. "Today we're going to work on honing your sensory skills. The next time you meet with Demric, you will be so competent no-one will be able to touch you," he said with smug certainty.

"I love lying here with you," Tynae said, running her hand over Ryedin's warm chest. "But won't your energy interfere with my abilities?"

"Precisely," he said slyly.

Tynae looked at Ryedin with an amused smile. "Okay, I'll bite, how shall we do this?"

"I will guide your thoughts and help you to reach beyond what is here. You must learn to see with your heart and feel with your soul, for your eyes will always deceive you," Ryedin said plainly. "Ready?"

"Yes."

"Close your eyes," he said softly, sliding his hand over her lids. "Because of our feelings for each other, our energies are merged as one. Find *your* energy, identify it from mine, and separate the two," he explained.

"How do I do that?" she asked, keeping her eyes closed.

"First locate our energies that dwell intermingled within your very being, within the true you."

Tynae searched within herself. She wasn't sure what she was feeling for. She only knew that when she was with Ryedin she felt a joy and peace she had never known, a completeness that made her whole. After about an hour of searching, she located it.

"That's it," he breathed. Lovingly, softly, intentionally, he kissed her neck and…poof, she lost it. Ryedin chuckled quietly. "Concentration is key, my love," he reminded her.

Tynae turned to him, wagging a finger. "You did that on purpose!" she accused, unable to conceal her smile.

"Ay. Blocking out loud noises is one thing, but blocking out feelings and emotions is something on an entirely different level. The concentration necessary to master this skill is somewhat, nay, *exceptionally* difficult to master. Though I am certain you will find it easier than most to accomplish this."

Tynae resumed her assignment. Now knowing what she was feeling for, finding and quickly separating their energies was easy. Except each time she did, Ryedin would nibble on her neck, kiss her bare shoulder, or whisper lovingly in her ear. Finally planting her intention firmly in her mind, Tynae was able to maintain the separation of their two energies despite Ryedin's incredibly distracting actions.

Ryedin's grin went from one ear to the other. "I told you that you'd master it in no time."

"How long does it normally take?"

Ryedin looked at her with a cunning smile. "Until this moment, the fastest anyone has ever been able to accomplish this particular type of separation with such distractions was a year and a half."

Tynae's face fell in disbelief then she started giggling. "Very funny," she said pushing his shoulder lightly. "How long, really?"

Ryedin looked at her, amused. "I'm telling you the truth. Your skills here," Ryedin gestured to their marvelous surroundings, "are not of *your* world…but you are able to take back with you that which you learn *here*," he clarified. "Now, on to step two, are you up for it?"

Tynae grinned, "Absolutely."

The sly grin was back on Ryedin's angelic face. "Somewhere, not far from here, is at least one large animal, reach out and find it…if you can." Ryedin gave her a wink.

Closing her eyes, Tynae settled back onto Ryedin's chest.

Again, it took Tynae about an hour. There were so many different energies within the forest it was difficult to discern one from the other. The multitude of animals alone was overwhelming and a bit confusing. Small birds fluttered and darted through the air, rabbits played leap frog in the thick undergrowth, and squirrels raced along the branches of the ancient trees. Then there were the trees themselves. Their energy was immense, almost overpowering.

When Tynae found what she was 'feeling' for, or so she thought, Ryedin let out a boisterous laugh. "Leave it up to you to find the only one around for ten kilometers. It's not the large animal I had intended on you finding, but I dare say it's actually more impressive. Care to see what you've stumbled upon?" he asked cheerfully. "This will allow you to work on another skill as well."

"Sure."

The pair stood.

"Close your eyes again," Ryedin insisted. "Now, I won't let you walk into anything, but I want you to do your best to feel your way without any help from me."

Finding this particular challenge intriguing, Tynae lit up.

Seeing Tynae's excitement, Ryedin beamed.

Walking through their garden and beyond, Tynae felt her way with her energy. This was an area she had never explored. Willing her invisible feelers to stretch out before her, Tynae found her way through what was now a lush forest. Locking onto the critters energy she was tracking, it felt as if the energy were guiding her directly to the animal. Weaving her way through the unfamiliar land became easier with each step, until finally she was comfortable enough to trust her senses entirely. Finally standing in front of whatever it was Tynae had sensed she anxiously awaited permission to open her eyes.

"You can look."

Upon opening her eyes, Tynae drew in a deep breath and dropped to her knees. A tiny black wolf pup loped over to her, followed closely by its mother. Tynae giggled as the excited little pup licked her face. She attempted to speak to Ryedin between the licks of the pup's gleefully lapping tongue. "Why was this little thing 'more impressive' than whatever it was you had anticipated me finding?" Tynae asked as the playful pup nipped at her nose. "I love puppy breath, but if you bite off my nose I won't be able to smell it," she giggled.

"Because it's smaller than what I had predicted you'd be able to find and track." Ryedin confessed. "This is Otsana," Ryedin patted the large she-wolf on the head. She had lain beside Tynae. "And this energetic little guy is Volrum." The rambunctious pup ran circles around Tynae, yapping and bouncing playfully.

Something occurred to Tynae and she suspiciously eyed Ryedin. "*Leave it up to me*, what did you mean by that?"

"I know how you love wolves and how they love you," Ryedin said, patting the pup on the head. "You're just naturally drawn to one another." Ryedin looked over Tynae's shoulder. "Ahh and right on cue, here come even more." Ryedin gestured toward a clearing.

Tynae turned.

Nine majestic wolves were leisurely making their way toward them.

Ryedin introduced each wolf to Tynae.

They seemed to be as enamored with Ryedin as they were with the princess.

Ryedin smiled, "Up for another challenge?" he asked, raising his brows as if daring her.

"I do like a good challenge. Is there anything at stake?" She eyed Ryedin's bare chest like a tasty treat, hoping he might offer himself up as her prize.

"Not a chance," he said playfully. "But I can offer you this," he pulled a small ring of what looked like tiny forget-me-knots from his pocket.

A wisp of wind blew the flowers' sweet fragrance toward Tynae. Closing her eyes, she inhaled the rich bouquet.

"They're fairy-knots," Ryedin said. "They're enchanted and when given to another, in friendship or love, the receiver will not forget the one who presented them. Hence how they got their name."

Tynae looked at him with an odd expression. "But they look like ordinary forget-me-nots."

Ryedin shrugged. "They're where forget-me-knots originated, but fairy-knots are magical. They never dry and will sustain their sweet smell for as long as you, the receiver, possess them. I just thought you might like to set them beside your bed."

Noticing Ryedin's slight blush; Tynae smiled, touching his cheek softly. "I'd like that, a lot. So what do you have in store for me now?"

Ryedin gave Tynae a charming smile. "I want you to find your way back to our garden, but this time with your eyes open. You'll recognize its energy. Of this I am certain, because *our* energy resides there."

Concentrating, Tynae located their garden then began to make her way back. She found this far more difficult than she would have imagined. Now that she was seeing with her eyes her senses were muddled. Her energy was telling her to go one way and her eyes another. This forced her to concentrate harder than ever. Finally her eyes agreed with her gut and soon they were back in their garden.

Turning to Ryedin, Tynae smiled. "That was really difficult," she admitted.

"But you managed, didn't you." He grinned, "Now you know how truly misleading your eyes can be."

"I do, and now I don't know that I'll ever believe my eyes again," she said uneasily.

"Always follow your heart. It will never deceive you, angel, unlike your eyes. Remember that, practice your skills as often as possible, and soon you will be unstoppable."

"I like the sound of that," Tynae admitted. "But I will never take any of my abilities for granted."

Pulling Tynae into a loving embrace, Ryedin gazed devotedly into her eyes.

Tynae returned his gaze and their souls danced as one. Their lips joined as did their hearts, and it was time to go.

"You did wonderfully today." Ryedin handed Tynae her prize.

Tynae inhaled the fragrance of her treasure. "Where shall I say I got it, if someone asks? People will think I've gone completely mental if I say I got them from a dream," she joked, tucking the small wreath of flowers under her corset.

"All you have to say is that it was lying beside you when you awoke. Calai holds many creatures you have yet to meet, all of which are fascinated with you. A gift from any one of them would not be unusual."

Tynae watched as blue and gray wisps of fog rolled in to take Ryedin away. "You tell me these things, knowing full well I can't ask you to elaborate. That's really unfair," Tynae grumbled with mock annoyance.

Shamefaced, Ryedin shrugged his shoulders, sliding his tunic back on. "Sorry, my love, I must go now. Tomorrow I will provide you with an exciting new challenge." Ryedin pressed his lips to hers one last time then walked toward the shimmering mist.

"What's the challenge?" Tynae called out.

"Learning to shoot a bow while on horse back. I know you're good, but that will take more than one day to master," he called back.

Tynae chuckled. "That does sound like a challenge. I look forward to it," she shouted.

Ryedin walked backwards. "I know you do. Until tomorrow, my love." He blew Tynae a kiss then turned and faded away.

Chapter 52
What does it all mean?

"Nothing is as simple as we hope it will be."
~Jim Horning

Waking briefly, Tynae snuggled deep into Béo's arms. Closing her eyes, she drifted back to sleep. Before she knew it the mystical fog was back. This had never happened before. She was going to get to see Ryedin twice in one night. Walking out of the mist wearing the same pink dress she'd had on previously, Tynae found herself in a dark and unfamiliar forest. She had never asked how it was exactly that she moved between dreams, but right now she was wishing she knew the secret. She wanted to get out of this place as quickly as possible.

A figure in the shadows moved toward her.

She didn't know if she should stay or run.

"Hello?" A male voice called.

Rooted to the spot on which she stood Tynae's heart skipped a beat.

The voice called again. "Hello?"

"Vinard?"

Vinard stepped out of the shadows.

"Tynae?"

"Dear God," Tynae breathed.

Vinard stared at her in disbelief.

"Vinard?" Tynae walked up to him, touching his cheek lightly. "Is it really you?"

"Are you a ghost?" Vinard asked.

Tynae laughed, "No silly. It's me."

"How?"

Tynae sighed, "I don't know where to begin." She looked around. "I wish there were someplace for us to sit and talk."

Vinard scanned the area. "There," he pointed.

Looking, Tynae saw a large fire pit with a roaring fire. "That wasn't there a second ago, but I've learned not to question too much in these dreams. It will do." She smiled.

Vinard stared at Tynae with absolute disbelief.

"Relax, Vinard," she laughed. "I am very real, not a ghost."

Sitting down side by side in front of the fire, Tynae looked at Vinard. "I'm not sure where to begin. I have spent time with another in my dreams, but only one other. This is the first time someone other than he has come to me."

Vinard huffed. "Well that gives you one up on me."

"Where would you like me to start?" Tynae asked.

Vinard thought. "What happened on the night you left Pathrow? You were supposed to hide then return...you never came back."

"Ah," Tynae sighed, "Of course. Well Gwillim and several of his men chased me relentlessly."

"Do you know why?"

"Not exactly, I know they where acting on Arona's orders."

"Arona?"

"Yes."

"Why?"

"That I do not know."

"How'd you get away?"

"I didn't."

Vinard's brows furrowed.

"I decided that if I had to die, it would be on my terms...so I jumped off the cliffs of Nombin."

Vinard's eyes widened in horror. "Then you must certainly be a ghost."

Tynae smiled softly. "There is more to the story...I promise I am real and very much alive," she assured, touching his hand gently. "A man from Calai rescued me." She had decided to keep Béo's true identity concealed.

"Calai? It exists?"

"It does. Many magi with incredibly powerful magic brought me back from beyond the veil."

Vinard stared, "Magic?"

"Turns out much of what we believed to be myths is very real," she grinned.

"Then where are you now?"

"I have remained in Calai."

"Come home," Vinard pleaded.

Tynae looked at him thoughtfully. "I wish I could, but I cannot. Arona must believe I am no longer alive."

"Why?"

"I don't know. I only know it is for my protection, as well as the protection of many nations."

With sadness in his eyes that made Tynae's soul ache, Vinard stared at Tynae. "Where are you?" she asked.

"In the forest of Tynan."

Tynae's eyes widened, "Why?"

"Enessa and I needed answers. Your father sent Gwillim and thousands of other soldiers to search for you across the lands. I was asked to stay in Pathrow. I couldn't take it any longer. Nothing made sense. I needed to seek out the truth."

Tynae smiled, "I may not be able to give you answers, but now that you know I'm alive you may return to Pathrow."

"No," Vinard shook his head. "We didn't know who we could trust, so we departed without telling anyone." Vinard shrugged. "We knew it would look suspicious, but we had no other choice. I went into a small town tonight and it seems that your father has put a price on our heads."

Tynae gasped, "He wouldn't."

"He did."

"What will you and Enessa do now?"

"We'll figure something out." Vinard gawked at Tynae. "You're really not a dream?"

"Ask me anything…something only I would know."

Vinard thought. "You gave me something when you were fifteen. What was it?"

Tynae smiled, "That's easy, a pink stone in the shape of a heart. I found it when we went to Boden." Tynae laughed. "Remember we weren't supposed to go, but we snuck off anyway?"

Vinard chuckled, "Yeah, how could I forget? Do you remember what you told me when you gave me the stone?"

"Of course I do." Tynae smiled softly, "I told you that my heart had always belonged to you and that I wanted you to court me." Tynae looked at the ground, rolling around a pebble with her finger. "I also remember you telling me that you did not think it was proper for us to be together and that we needed to remain only friends."

"Biggest mistake of my life," Vinard said. "I've regretted telling you that every second of every day since."

"Why did you say it then?"

Vinard shrugged. "I didn't have riches, land or a title. I guess I thought it was for the best." Looking at Tynae, Vinard moved closer. Gently putting his hands on her face, he whispered, "I love you, Tynae. I always have." Leaning forward, Vinard pressed his lips to hers.

Tynae knew she should protest, but she'd waited so long for this moment.

Slowly the two separated.

"I should have done that a long time ago," Vinard said.

"Yes, you should have." Tynae smiled. "So whatever happened to that rock?"

"It's right here." Vinard patted his hip pocket.

"I may have something for you." Tynae felt under her corset for the circlet of flowers Ryedin had given her. "Here." She pulled them out. "They're called fairy-knots, I was told they are magical and will never die." Tynae split her small wreath of flowers in half. "Now, when you awake you will know this was not all a dream."

Taking the flowers Vinard grinned. "How do I find you?"

Seeing the shimmering mist roll in, Tynae stood up. "I don't know and it's time for me to leave." She pointed, "That mist is what brought me here."

Vinard stood, too. "Will I be able to see you like this again?"

"I honestly don't know, Vinard. I certainly hope so."

"Tynae," Vinard took her in his arms, kissing her passionately. "I love you."

"I have to go, Vinard. Things are not as they once were. Much has changed, but I just don't have the time to explain it all to you right now…Please know that I love you, too. I always have and always will."

Not wanting to leave Vinard, Tynae slowly walked backward into the fog. "Give Enessa my love. Be safe, Vinard." Watching the vision of Vinard fade into darkness was one of the most difficult things Tynae had ever done. But she was overjoyed to have seen him.

Waking in the morning, Tynae felt exhilarated. She felt different, like something had changed within her. She felt strong, really, really strong. Looking at her bedside table, half her ring of fairy-knots lay in perfect condition along with a white rose. A perfect, fresh rose awaited her every morning when she awoke. Smiling Tynae leaned over kissing Béo softly on the lips to wake him.

"Mmm," he sighed. "I could get used to waking up like this."

The maids soon arrived and it was time for breakfast and baths.

Finished with breakfast, Tynae gave Béo a quick kiss when no-one was looking and he left for his own room to clean up.

The four women went into the lavatory to commence with their daily bathing ritual.

"O'leana, how many fighting outfits did you have made for me?"

"Several, My Lady. At least ten, all in different colors. Why do you ask?"

"I just wanted to make sure I have enough. I want long britches made for me as well, like the ones I wore the other night. Could you arrange for me to meet with the clothier please?"

"Of course." O'leana proceeded to scrub Tynae's back. "Lady Tynae, per chance are you part Greer?" O'leana asked.

Tynae shook her head, "No, why."

"Nothing, I just wondered." She paused thoughtfully. "You're so powerful. I thought maybe…I heard you did excellent yesterday with your training. Would it be agreeable with you if I watched you practice sometime?" O'leana asked.

"Absolutely."

Today they dressed Tynae in purple, with matching colored threads running through her hair. Her hair was in a long plait running down her back; it seemed to be the most convenient hair style for her daily activities.

Béo returned just as the maids were finishing up. His timing impeccable, as usual.

"Will there be anything else, My Lady?" O'leana asked.

"No, O'leana, we will see you this evening for supper."

O'leana bowed to Tynae. Opening the door to leave, O'leana addressed Béo, "Master Béo, I was wondering if I might have a word."

Béo looked at O'leana curiously, "Certainly."

Following the maid out of Vu'tella, Béo spoke quietly with her out in the corridor.

"What is it, O'leana?"

"It's about Lady Tynae." O'leana looked around before she finished. "Is she Greer?"

Béo shook his head. "Not that I am aware of. Why?"

"I noticed when bathing her today, what looks to be the start of indacaté," O'leana said quietly.

"Of indacaté?" he questioned. "Don't you mean *an* indacaté, as in one?" Béo corrected.

O'leana shook her head slowly, "No, My Liege." O'leana glanced around again. "The princess has three," she whispered holding up three fingers.

The lines in Béo's forehead deepened. *"Three?"* he repeated.

"Yes, My Lord, one on her neck and one on each wrist. I am fairly certain they are indacaté. They were not there when the princess first arrived, I would have noticed." O'leana dropped her head and her voice slightly. "I hope I'm not overstepping my boundaries, Lord Béo. It just seemed rather remarkable and I thought it required mentioning."

"You did the right thing, O'leana. If they are indeed indacaté, I will need to speak with my father right away." It was Béo who looked around this time. "O'leana, if you are correct, this is extraordinary. I must ask you to keep this information to yourself, tell no-one. Is that understood?" Béo said sternly. This was clearly a direct order.

"Understood, My Lord."

"Thank you, O'leana. We'll see you this evening."

Béo turned to go into Vu'tella then spun back around. "Oh, and bring some flowers and a new piece of jewelry for Lady Tynae, preferably earrings. Tell Ildrai to help you select something. Make sure the gifts are as exquisite as Tynae is, please." Béo guffawed. "Well as close as possible anyway, *nothing* is as exquisite as she."

"Yes, My Lord." O'leana bowed then departed.

Béo went back inside Vu'tella.

"What was that all about?" Tynae asked, walking out of her bedchamber.

With a wink, Béo walked over to her. "You'll just have to wait until this evening to find out, now won't you?" Grabbing both of Tynae's hands in his, Béo kissed each of them then turned her hands over and kissed each of her wrists. Letting her hands go, he admired her attire. "I really do like these outfits," he said as he walked around her. He moved slowly taking in every inch of her, conveniently pausing at her back. Moving Tynae's hair to one side, Béo lovingly kissed her neck once, twice…three times.

"I told you I asked O'leana to send the clothier so I could speak with her about making me long trousers, didn't I?" she said, clearly flustered by Béo's attention.

"Yes, you did, that should raise a few eyebrows." Béo laughed, walking back in front of Tynae.
"You know what I just realized?" Béo blurted out.
Tynae eyed Béo suspiciously. "What?"
"I have no idea when your birthday is."
"Oh," she laughed. "The 7th day of the time of the Rose Moon."
Béo eyed Tynae with a grin. "Let me guess your age."
"Go right ahead; but I warn you, no-one ever gets it right." Tynae chuckled.

"Lets see here, the snow moon is upon us, so you recently turned...thirty four, which means you'll be thirty five when next the rose moon returns. Am I correct?"

"You are. That was impressive."
Béo attempted to look innocent. "Naa, just a lucky guess."
Tynae snickered. "When's your birthday then?"
"I too was born during the rose moon, only on the 2nd."
"That's the same as my father, how convenient." Tynae laughed. "I can never forget it now."
"I do not care if you remember my birthday, as long as you forget-me-knot," Béo asserted.
"Now there's an impossibility." Tynae giggled lightly, putting her arms around Béo's neck. "How could I ever forget the man whose soul is *forever* entwined with mine?" Leaning forward, she pressed her lips to Béo's.

He wrapped his arms around Tynae's waist, pulling her tight to his bare chest. "Forever?" he whispered against her submissive lips.

"All eternity," she purred.

Slowly they pulled apart, neither wanting to let go of the other.

"Ready to go?" Béo asked.

"No really, but yes." Tynae looked around, "Serry, are you coming?" she called.

"*Always, Mistress.*" Serry flew to Tynae's shoulder, and the trio set out.

Hand in hand, the couple walked to the heart of the city. "I'm not going to be able to stay at Demric's all day, my angel. Father has requested a meeting with me."

"Oh, okay. What does he want to see you for?" Tynae looked at Béo. "I'm sorry. Perhaps I should not have asked that."

"It's okay." Béo shrugged, "I'm not sure what he wants, it's probably something simple. I shouldn't be long. I think I'll leave after we have dinner, is that okay with you?"

"You can leave whenever you want, love, you don't need to ask permission."

"I know I don't have to ask permission, but I don't want to leave if you're not comfortable."

"I think I can manage for a bit without you," Tynae teased.

"I'm sure you can," Béo chuckled. "But I hate being away from you," he admitted.

Tynae smiled. "I didn't say that I liked it, I said I could manage. If I had my way, we'd be together every second of the day; but that's not realistic." Tynae pulled their clasped hands to her lips, tenderly kissing Béo's hand. "I know that no matter where you go, you will always come back to me. That's all I need to know."

"You're perfect, you know that?" Béo said.

Tynae giggled. "I am so far from being perfect, but I'm glad that *you* see me that way. You're equally as perfect to me. What *we* think is all that matters, right?"

Smiling Béo shook his head. "Like I said, you are perfect...How did I get so lucky?"

"We are both lucky," Tynae smiled. "I expect we must have done something very right somewhere along the way."

Arriving at Demric's, the trio was greeted by Tingy. "Majesties," the Nanic said with a deep bow, his ickel hovering beside him making a chipper purring sound.

"Good morning, Tingy," Tynae said with her magical smile. "Morning, Demric."

"M'Lady, M'Lord," Demric said politely.

Ready to start, Tynae stepped in to the arena.

"Give me just one minute, Lady Tynae. My Lord, would you please cover her eyes," Demric instructed.

Walking over to Tynae, Béo removed the same strap from his waist he'd used the previous day, and tied it over Tynae's eyes. Keeping his hand on her shoulder so she'd know where he was, Béo walked in front of Tynae. "Does my smell really distract you?" he whispered in her ear.

Tynae bit her lip. "Do *you* really have to ask that?"

Béo snickered quietly. "I was just wondering. Good luck, angel," he breathed softly against her lips.

Tynae leaned in to kiss Béo, but found nothing but air and stumbled forward slightly. Pulling the cover off one eye, she shot Béo a scrutinizing look.

He was watching her over his shoulder as he walked away. He knew he'd be in trouble for that little maneuver later, but for now he enjoyed the moment. Trying not to laugh, he mouthed the word '*sorry*'.

Grinning, Tynae shook her head and replaced the cover over her eye.

Demric picked up where they left off the night before.

By the time dinner rolled around Tynae was blocking everything he threw at her. She could block from all sides, including the back.

"Let's take a break, M'Lady. After dinner we'll work on you striking me as well as blocking," Demric said.

Tynae pulled the strap off her eyes. "Sounds terrific, we'll see you in a bit then." Tying the leather strap around her waist, she walked over to Béo.

"It looks better on you than it does on me." Béo eyed her tiny waist.

Tynae laughed. "Thanks, I only put it on because you said you were leaving after dinner. I didn't want to have to use someone else's sweaty strap." She wrinkled her nose.

The two grabbed some food from ol' McDugle's then sat down to eat at what had become *their* table.

"Did you get a chance to ask Jubryi about supper tonight?" Tynae asked.

"I did, he will be at Vu'tella this evening. I told O'leana this morning before I left to make extra food."

When they were done eating, Béo walked Tynae back to the fighting arena.

"Serry, would you like to go with me, or stay here with Lady Tynae?" Béo asked.

"I will stay here, thank you, My Lord."

"I'll be back soon, my love."

"Okay," Tynae said with a soft smile.

Kissing the top of Tynae's head, Béo left for his 'meeting' with Kerszon.

Tynae watched Béo walk away until she could see him no longer. When she turned around Demric was staring at her.

"I'm sorry, Demric, you should have said you where ready."

Demric shook his head. "No, the more I understand you the more I can teach you. Please put the cover on your eyes. I want to see what you can really do." Demric said with a devilish grin.

Demric started slowly, but evidently had every intention of giving it all he had by days end....

Béo ran to Kerszon's chambers as fast as he could. He needed to tell him about Tynae as soon as possible.

Gareth, Kerszon's guard, greeted Béo with a bow. "Good day, My Lord. Chief Kerszon is in a meeting at the moment, he'll be finished momentarily.

Béo nodded. "Thank you." Too stressed to sit down, he impatiently paced around the sitting room.

The door opened. "You may go in now," Gareth said.

"Son, I didn't expect to see you back so soon. Is something the matter?" Kerszon asked with concern.

"I don't know if there's anything wrong, per se." Béo hunched his shoulders. "O'leana came to me this morning and told me she thought she'd seen indacaté on Tynae. I looked and sure enough, it looks like..." Béo paused. "Father, she has three, one on her neck and one on each wrist. We spoke last night about her family and she's not Greer, at least not that she is aware. Despite what she said, I suspect her mother was a Clair'letté."

Kerszon's brow furrowed. "Why do you say that?"

"Well the most obvious reason is the fact that we were able to get in to Tergalia. But last night she told me that her mothers name was Aletta, which means winged one. I don't think Yurgon knew what she was. Also, Tynae said she was born early and was healthy, I believe her mother was already pregnant when she met Yurgon," Béo explained.

Standing, Kerszon walked around his study. "This is all...hmm."

"Father, she will be turning thirty five in less than a year, I think we need to tell her everything. It's not like she's going to run off on some killing spree if she knows about her future. I think she deserves to know. Her indacaté are going to become very clear in the next few weeks." Béo shook his head. "I'm actually surprised she hasn't noticed them already, and *three*...Has any person ever had more than one?"

Kerszon shook his head, "No."

Slowly pacing around the room, Kerszon seemed to be lost in thought. Despite the movement, he was clearly listening to Béo.

Sitting with his face in his hands, Béo ran his fingers through his hair with frustration. "You do realize that when we tell her it is going to destroy her. In a single instant she will discover that the man she grew up believing was her father is not. We must tell her the entire truth or she may assume that the Greer side of her came from her mother, and I for one am fairly certain that that is not true. Although I cannot prove it as of yet," Béo sighed loudly. "The one thing I do know is that we can't keep lying to her, Father, it's just not right," Béo insisted.

Kerszon nodded. "You're correct, Son. Allow me a few days; you have given me a lot to think about. I've not had a chance to talk with Ge'annã or Zandore yet, but I will by the time you come to Zandore's."

Béo smiled softly, he knew he could always count on his father. "We will see you then. Good day, Father."

"Son."

Though Béo was relieved that his father was going to speak with Tynae, he remained concerned, unsure how she would take such life altering news. To learn of so much in one short night would change everything in her life, again.

Béo ran back to the city. He really did hate being away from Tynae. Not to mention he had a nagging feeling in the pit of his stomach that she would be taken away from him yet again. He knew it was silly to think like that, but he just couldn't shake it. He got back just in time to see Tynae send Demric flying through the air with a solid kick to the stomach.

Lifting the cover off one eye, Tynae grimaced. "Sorry," she said hunching her shoulders. "Are you alright?"

Demric lie on the ground trying to catch his breath.

"M'Lady, I think I would like to call it a day." Demric huffed, getting to his feet. "You have done wonderfully, once again," he said, panting.

"Thank you, Demric." Tynae removed her blindfold.

Turning, she saw Béo standing there and her face lit up.

"M'Lady, you may want to learn to hide your feelings," Demric warned. "The enemy likes to hurt us by hurting those we care about most."

Tynae smiled, "I'll work on that, Demric." She walked over to Tingy. "Tingy, if you please."

"Yes, My Lady," the little Nanic said with a deep bow. Once he'd removed the spell, Tingy handed Tynae a large stein full of cold water.

"Thank you, Tingy, very much," she took a drink. "Serry?" Tynae called looking around.

"I'll be back soon, Mistress, I will meet up with you in Vu'tella."

"Oh, okay." Tynae set down her mug. "See you tomorrow, Tingy, Demric," Tynae called, waving. Walking over to Béo, she gave him a big hug. "How long have you been back?" she asked.

"Long enough to see you kick Demric halfway across Calai," he laughed.

Tynae snickered. "I didn't mean to," she insisted, looking slightly guilty.

Béo just grinned. "Did Serry answer when you called for her?"

"Yes, she said she'd meet us back at home." Tynae smiled brightly at Béo. "So, what did your father want?"

"Oh, he just wanted to tell me Zandore's answer. He wants us to meet him at Zandore's in seven days time." Béo spoke in a low voice; ensuring no-one could overhear their conversation.

Tynae's eyes became bright. "Really?" she squeaked, quickly covering her mouth. "Oops, I can't wait."

474

Chapter 53
Decisions, Decisions

"In these matters the only certainty is that nothing is certain."
~Pliny the Elder

Between daily lessons with Demric, Béo's vorbix practice, which Tynae truly loved to watch, their constant exploration of Calai and her lessons with Ryedin by night; every second of Tynae's days seemed to be occupied. Trying to sneak alone time in with Béo proved to be almost impossible, and things were about to get much, much more complicated. The remainder of the week went by quickly and before Tynae knew it the day had come for her to meet Calai's dragon at last. Each and everyday since Tynae had arrived in Calai; she either met a fanciful creature from her childhood fairy tales, learned of creatures she never even knew existed, or found out about lost and unknown cities that were said to be purely myth.

Now she was about to come face to face with a real, living, breathing dragon. She was so nervous about meeting Zandore that she changed her outfit at least nine times. Béo reassured her that each one looked just as magnificent as the previous, but she had it in her mind that she must look as perfect as possible. After all, one does not meet a legend of lore every day. In Tynae's case, there did seem to be an exception.

"You might as well get comfortable," Tynae told Béo. "This could take a while. I just can't decide what to wear."

Béo laughed. "Take as long as you need. I'm going to go relax by the waterfall. Let me know when you're ready."

Béo left the room, leaving Tynae and her maids to carry on.

Kerszon, along with Ge'annã, met with Zandore.

"I don't think it's wise to keep lying to her," Kerszon said pacing the room. "She has given us too many opportunities to tell her the truth and none of us believe in coincidence." Kerszon continued walking in circles around Zandore's cavernous dwelling. "Who are we to decide when she discovers her fate? If we hadn't lied to her from the onset of this whole thing she'd already know." Kerszon muttered looking around the room. He seemed to be arguing more with himself than anyone else. He already knew Zandore and Ge'annã would go along with whatever he decided.

Kerszon's gaze drifted to Ge'annã. "Have you seen nothing in your visions?" he asked, already knowing the answer having asked her a hundred times before. His recent request made one hundred and one.

"I'm sorry, Chief, no," Ge'annã shook her head. "I have searched the heavens, read the bones, and drawn the cards. There are no definitive signs saying how or even when Lady Tynae's destiny is to be revealed to her."

Kerszon's frustration grew. He adored Tynae and feared that once she was told the truth any peace she had in her life would be stripped away once and for all.

Continuing to wear a groove in Zandore's stone floor, Kerszon reflected back to the day Lady Tynae's fate was revealed to him.

It had been thirty-four very long years earlier....

Kerszon was in his office sitting at the large meeting table with his high council. They were in the middle of a meeting when Ge'annã quietly interrupted them with urgent news.

"The one we have been waiting for has been born, they named her Tynae," Ge'annã told Kerszon. "But we are not the only ones who were anticipating this particular little bundle of joy," Ge'annã stated grimly. "The Dark Ones have long awaited the one born of light and have every intention of turning her to their side. For as long as they believe they have a chance at transforming her, they will see to it that she lives. Yet if they find that she is truly one of unwavering faith and light, they will seek to destroy her."

Having issued her stern warning, Ge'annã turned and vanished from the room as quietly as she had entered.

The council members sat silently after Ge'annã had left, waiting to either be dismissed or continue their meeting.

Distressed, Kerszon sat with his face in his hands. Looking up slowly, he drug his hands over his face letting out a loud sigh.

"I don't get it," he said in a monotone voice shaking his head. "I just don't get it!" he shouted, slamming his fists on the table. Standing up quickly, his chair fell over. Huffing, Kerszon ran his hands through his long hair and began to pace around the large table were his council members sat.

"I, for the life of me, cannot figure out these pestilent human beings," he growled with frustration through gritted teeth.

The high council sat quietly while Kerszon continued pacing around the room deep in thought.

"I try." Kerszon's voice began to elevate, "And I try to see things as they do, but I just cannot do it," he hissed.

Kerszon pointed to a council man who sat across the table from where he stood, the man had once been a true human. "Perhaps you," he barked, "could explain to me the inner workings of these self consumed deplorable...creatures," he spat bitterly, his brows furrowed in utter confusion.

The man just sat there, knowing full well this was a rhetorical statement.

"Why can they not see that what they do is wrong?" he asked with great sadness, shaking his head. "*Horribly, horribly* wrong," Kerszon's words faded into a whisper, his head hung in defeat.

Regaining his train of thought, Kerszon began to pace again.

"They lie, cheat, and steal from one another then justify it by saying that it hurts no-one," Kerszon snarled with disgust looking at his council members scornfully. "How can they say that?" he asked with disbelief. "It hurts EVERYONE!!!" he roared.

Shaking his head Kerszon resumed walking in circles. To everyone's surprise he began to chuckle, but this was not a happy laughter. It was dark, sarcastic, and scornful. "And those who run their governments, huh, they're the biggest buffoons of them all." His voice was full of distain as he shook his head with disgust. "Looking out for the *people's* best interest, my arse," he muttered to himself.

Kerszon turned sharply back towards his council. "As leaders are we not supposed to lead by example?!" Kerszon asked wandering off again. "I suppose the humans *are* doing exactly as they have been taught, are they not? Primate see, primate do," he said flatly.

"Do they not know the will of the one above?" Kerszon asks seriously. "Of course they do, I know they do. How could they not? But they are so blinded by selfishness, lust, pride, and greed that they cannot see the endless beauty and bounty of blessings surrounding them constantly," Kerszon said with true pity.

Staring intently at the floor, Kerszon continued to pace. "I hate that they force my hand," he growled in a low husky voice. "I hate it!" he shouted, slamming his fist on a table again. Kerszon unexpectedly grabbed hold of one of the council men's chairs, turning the man so that he now faced him. Kerszon put his hands on the table, leaning over until his face was mere centimeters from the man's. "Do you hear me?" Kerszon asked through gritted teeth.

The man nodded nervously.

Kerszon pushed himself roughly off the table and his feet carried him around the room yet again. "It's the decent people, the good, honest, and true people like Lady Tynae that will end up martyring themselves for the ungrateful, unworthy heathens and hypocrites of the human world. And to what end?" he asked bitterly.

Shaking his head, Kerszon threw his hands in the air. "Sure a few may change, some will even convert, and there may even be a few who become martyrs themselves."

Kerszon's face became as hard as stone. "But the rest," he growled, his words dripping with utter revulsion. "The dirty, vile, loathsome animals…That's all they are, wicked, filthy beasts. They'll slither away into their depraved holes like the cowardly snakes they truly are. And when they re-emerge they will begin spreading their lies and treachery like a plague once more." Kerszon began ringing his hands, "Slowly devouring the world's inhabitants like a python, twisting and turning, draining the life from its victims, squeezing until ever last ounce of exquisite life has been extracted." Kerszon was appalled by his revelation. "The blind fools," he barked. "They choose immorality and corruptness because it is *easier* than living piously and ethically acceptable lives," he huffed. "Why is it that the malevolent people thrive while the good people perish?" Sadness returned to Kerszon's face and he shook his head. "I do not understand this *backward* world of theirs in the least," he said in a defeated voice.

Kerszon was silent for a moment or two while he wandered, then a thought occurred to him. His expression changed. There was a glimmer of hope in his eyes now. "Perhaps, just perhaps, this time will be different. Perhaps this time humanity will learn from its wretched mistakes and the world will change for the good," he mused.

Kerszon liked this thought, a lot. "Is this possible?" he wondered aloud. "It has to be and I must find a way to insure this, I must see to it that Lady Tynae does not perish before she awakens to her true destiny."

Rolling his eyes, Kerszon shook his head with dismay. "Bah, who am I kidding? As if this is truly possible," Kerszon shook his head dislodging the negative thoughts that had attached themselves to his mind. "NO!" he said sternly. "I will not allow myself to think like that, like *them*, no. There is hope and where there is hope there is light…there *is* light," he reassured himself.

"I will find a way to give Lady Tynae every possible advantage, yes, YES." Kerszon held up a finger as if to say 'ah-ha', he had an epiphany and his words came fast. "This is exactly what I must do. She will change the world, I just KNOW it. She will help the lost souls that wonder around aimlessly in the dark to discover their *own* true light. Lady Tynae will help save the poor wretches from their own self inflicted destruction," he said simply.

Kerszon suddenly became enthusiastic. "I must go; there are plans to be made and lives to save. Thank you for your ear." Kerszon breezed out of his office leaving his council members dazed and bewildered.

Kerszon remembered that day like it was yesterday. He and Ge'annã had sat with Zandore, as they were at this very moment, trying to decide if and how they should proceed. Now here they sat thirty-four years later, once again pondering the exact same dilemma.

Ge'annã looked at Kerszon with a firm expression. "Honestly, Kerszon, I don't think it will hurt to tell her." Ge'annã held her hand up, preventing Kerszon from interrupting her. "Just hear me out. Yes I understand that she's lost everything over the past few weeks, but she's a strong woman, Kerszon, we all agreed on that long ago. What do you propose? Let her get comfortable for a year or two, then drop another world-crushing bolder on top of her?" Ge'annã shook her head as she shifted in her chair. "Personally I feel Lady Tynae has the right to know. That's how I vote. Anyway, the final decision is yours no matter what my opinion is," Ge'annã stated in her no nonsense tone.

Kerszon turned to Zandore. A white puff of smoke wafted from his nostrils. "*I agree with* Ge'annã, *Chief,*" Zandore said in his deep throaty voice. "*We all agreed in the beginning that she was an incredibly strong person and that is why she, of all beings on this planet, had been entrusted with the lives of all, humans and animals alike, as well as the overseeing of our planet.*"

Zandore moved closer to Kerszon. "*After all, it was not us who gave her this task. This was asked of her by the Creator above. Apparently she accepted the job, whether or not she* knows it. So who are we to determine what is right or wrong for her? We are but mere specks in the overall spectrum of things. Truth is what she deserves, not lies."*

Kerszon nodded. "As usual, you both make perfect sense. It's settled then, we tell her *almost* everything today," Kerszon said with relief.

O'leana looked at Kerszon incredulously.

"Wait." Holding one finger up, Kerszon explained, "I have not finished the book Béo brought to me, and I want to know what I am talking about before I go blurting out life-altering information."

"Do we not agree on this point?" Kerszon asked.

"Agreed," Ge'annã said with a nod.

A ribbon of smoke wafted from Zandore's nostrils, *"Agreed."*

"Is she ready?" Béo asked, coming back into the room.

Finally happy with her attire, Tynae stepped out from behind her dressing curtain.

Béo's jaw fell. "You look like an angel," he muttered, barely able to speak.

Tynae had finally decided on a gossamer white outfit and chose sparkling platinum jewelry accented with amethysts. She wore her hair up and in it a one-of-a-kind silver and amethyst circlet that rested atop her brow.

Tynae turned to her maids. "You may go, thank you ladies."

Walking over to Béo, Tynae grinned slyly.

Not much was different about Béo's attire today. He wore a tan loin cloth, as he did everyday, along with a suede vest that hung open. This meeting was about Tynae, he was merely her escort.

"I am far from an angel, my love," she purred, running her hand over Béo's chest.

"Who says how angels are supposed to behave?" Béo asked, wrapping his arms around Tynae's waist. "Your heart is the purest I've ever encountered and so are your intentions. I hardly think that being with someone physically that you are in love with is considered a sin," he said smoothly as he gazed into her eyes.

"We need to get going."

Gently gliding his fingers over his angel's back, Béo leaned forward tenderly kissing Tynae's inviting and very willing lips.

Smiling, Béo let go of Tynae. Looking down he withdrew the map his father had given him from the leather pouch that hung about his waist. Béo studied it briefly.

"What's that?" Tynae asked.

"This?" Béo held it up. "It's a map father gave me. I've never been to where Zandore resides. It is one of the secrets of Calai that up until today has been hidden from me," he explained.

Just before they headed out the door, Béo grabbed an unusual looking parasol from a stand in the corner.

"What is that?" Tynae asked.

"It's like a parasol, but the material from which it is made shields us from rain. We call it an ombra."

Tynae looked at Béo funny. "What in the world do we need that for?" she asked.

"It's supposed to rain today," Béo said simply.

Tynae snickered. "Rain, there's a dome over the city, how could it possibly rain?" she asked confused.

Béo chuckled. "You have noticed the clouds in the sky within the city correct?"

Tynae thought about it. "Yes, I suppose."

"They're not just there for looks. Calai is its own fully functioning world. We have seasons just like any other land. We need rain for the trees and grass to grow, sun and moon which you have seen, are necessary, not only for the plants, but us as well. We have growing seasons for our crops, even though we have learned how to bend the seasons to our will. We even have high and low tide. The people have subtle necessities and a change of seasons along with environment are among those needs," Béo told Tynae.

Tynae looked at Béo like he had gone completely mad.

Béo grinned. "I have not taken you to any of our beaches yet, I told you this place is huge. There is still much I have not shown you, but in time you will come to know all of the secrets of Calai." Béo shrugged, "At least most of them, anyway."

Béo held out a thick roll of parchment. "Here…it tells of news. Not only of that which happens in Calai, but what is occurring throughout the world. It also tells what the weather is going to be like. After all it is the Chief that decides when the seasons will change, when the rains will fall and how long they will last," Béo clarified.

Tynae glanced at the paper. "The Oracle," she read aloud. "I'd love to read it later. May I keep it?"

"Of course."

It was time to leave. Setting down the paper, Tynae looked around the room. "Serry?" she called out.

"*Here, Mistress*," Serry fluttered out of the forest.

Tynae smiled at her beautiful friend. "Will you be joining us today?"

"*If I may. Master Béo, do you think it would be acceptable for me to accompany you?*"

Both Béo and Tynae could hear Serry's words. Serry had informed them that she preferred to keep their conversations as traditional as possible.

Béo thought about it then nodded. "It should be fine, I'm sure they would all love to meet you."

Serry took her place on Tynae's left shoulder. Her tiny spider-like legs tickled against the princess' bare skin.

The trio set off.

Chapter 54
Beyond the Boundaries

"Nature does nothing uselessly."
~Aristotle

"Does everyone in Calai know how to read?" Tynae asked as they walked.

"Of course, we learn as children."

"Really?" Tynae sounded surprised. "Who teaches you?"

"Everyone in Calai goes to school. For some Greer 'teaching' is their profession. I know for humans it's different, but our people feel that education is important, and that we are all equally entitled to learn as much as we choose." Béo smiled, "personally, I love to read everything I can get my hands on."

"Me, too," Tynae agreed. "But in my world…my old world," she corrected. "Most who have power seek to keep those they feel are *beneath* them as powerless as possible. The ability to read gives us great knowledge and in turn great power. Therefore education of any type is frowned upon for those who are not of noble birth," Tynae explained. "And it is almost unheard of for women to be taught to read, with the exception of future queens. Even if you are born into a royal family, if there are male heirs to the throne, the females will intentionally be kept from learning the written language," Tynae said reprovingly.

"Who taught you?" Béo asked.

Tynae smiled, "Enessa. She was not only my Lady in Waiting, but my private tutor in the art of reading. Her father was a scholar. She told me that when she was a young child she would sneak his books just to look at the beautiful pictures. One day her father caught her and insisted that if any child of his was going to hold a book in their hands she would know how to read it." Tynae laughed lightly. "I don't think she's ever stopped reading."

Tynae's thoughts lingered on Enessa and Vinard. She hadn't told anyone about her dream. What could she possibly say?

484

Every night as she faded off to sleep, Tynae hoped to see Vinard once more. *Maybe it was nothing more than an ordinary dream. Either way, I just hope they're all right.*

Heading out of the city, Tynae noticed they were traveling in a direction they'd never gone before. "Where are we headed?"

"Into the wilderness," Béo said, taking her hand.

They walked through many new corridors and tunnels until they reached a huge wooden door guarded by two large warriors. Bowing, the two men opened the oversized door allowing the threesome access to the dense wilderness.

The forest teemed with colossal trees, lush shrubs and colorful flora. Tynae heard the storm stirring above them, but the thick trees were so numerous and packed so tightly that only a fine mist was able to make its way through the canopy.

Opening the ombra, Béo pulled Tynae close. "There's not much rain here, but once we leave the cover of the ancient trees, the storm will be fairly rough. It is winter after all," he reminded her.

Tynae had all but forgotten about the seasons and the weather they brought with them. Calai had been so tropical over the past few weeks that this was an easy thing to do. Suddenly Tynae felt home sick. Winter was one of her favorite times of the year. Even though most things died in the winter, Tynae felt like everything was being cleansed and life was renewing itself for the new year. The rain always seemed to settle the earth, taking with it the dust and debris of the year that was currently coming to a close. Tynae sighed.

"What is it?" Béo asked.

Tynae shook her head. "Nothing really, just thinking about home."

"What about it? Tell me…please? I love to hear about your life."

"Winter, the rain…" Tynae shrugged. "I just love the two. Enessa used to make me the best hot cacao and I would sit all wrapped up in a warm fuzzy blanket by my window and watch the rain for hours." Tynae giggled. "That's all, silly I know, but I am a girl after all. It does show every once in a while."

Béo pulled her tight to him as they walked. "I don't think it's silly," he said. "I think it sounds quite nice, actually."

Continuing on, Tynae took in their pristine surroundings and fresh air.

Béo had been correct, as usual. Once they were beyond the concentration of trees, the rain began falling in sheets. The drops sounded like hundreds of tiny pebbles falling on top of their ombra. Tynae was thankful the path they were on was paved with cobblestone and not dirt, or they'd be walking in mud.

Pulling the map from his pouch, Béo inspected it once again. "It's not much further," he shouted so Tynae could hear him over the thudding rain drops.

Tynae nodded in response.

It wasn't long before they reached a thicket of bramble that stood many meters high.

Béo walked forward scanning the ground carefully until he found what he had apparently been looking for. With a wave of his hands, the thorny vines rearranged themselves forming a wide archway. "Come on," Béo said, grabbing hold of Tynae's hand.

Once through the archway, they were able to tuck the ombra away. It turned out that the vines and leaves served as camouflage over a gargantuan structure.

Béo chuckled to himself.
"What?" Tynae asked.
"I just realized Zandore's lair has been right under my nose for decades."
Purple and white crystals, along with several large torches, lit the way. The stone walls were covered with intricate paintings telling a detailed story. Tynae wanted to look at each one carefully, but knew they didn't have time.
"On the way out if we can," Béo whispered.
"How'd you know that I wanted to stop?"

"I know you."

Tynae smiled. "Okay." She loved the way Béo seemed to read her mind. It was like they were connected.

The halls were at least thirty men wide, thirty very large men.

Seeing this, Tynae's heart began to pound erratically. The jumping jelly fish along with the quivering butterflies returned in droves. They apparently decided to turn Tynae's insides into a festival of jesters. Turning down the last corridor, Tynae heard voices.

"They're almost here." She heard a woman say.

Tynae swallowed hard, but it was completely in vain. Everyone knows that fear can't be swallowed, although that never stops one from trying over and over again.

"How do I look?" Tynae whispered anxiously.
"Stunning, my love, as always."
Shaking her head, Tynae rolled her eyes. "I could have a bear tap dancing on my head and you'd still say that, wouldn't you?"

Béo let out a bark of a laugh that echoed through the tunnels. "Only if you wanted him there," he teased. "Otherwise I would have to tell you that your hair piece was a wee bit gaudy."

Béo chuckled, lightly bumping into Tynae.
Tynae giggled, Béo's mere presence always made her feel better.
Reaching the door, Béo knocked lightly.
"Enter."
Tynae took a deep breath. Stepping through the doorway, her butterflies danced wildly.

There he was in all his splendid glory. The most magnificent, magical creature Tynae had ever seen. Stopping dead in her tracks, Tynae stared at Zandore. Realizing how rude she was being, Tynae attempted to walk further into the room, but her feet wouldn't move. She stood frozen, humiliatingly rooted to the floor.

"Help me," she whispered to Béo. "I can't move." Panic began to set in.

"Step away from her, Master Béo," Zandore said softly in everyone's heads.

Béo looked at Tynae apologetically. "You'll be fine," he whispered. Béo went to stand beside his father.

Zandore walked over to Tynae. His long heavy tail scraped along the rough brick floor. *"Good day, Your Majesty,"* Zandore said softly, lowering himself in a deep bow.

Unable to speak, Tynae's limbs trembled terribly. When she finally managed to locate her voice, her words trembled as well. "Your Highness," she lowered herself in an equally deep curtsey.

Kerszon walked over to the royal pair. "Your Majesty, may I introduce Emperor Zandore the Judicious," Kerszon said formally. "Your Highness, this is Princess Tynae Brimon Le'jonrey Du'Vonaire the Bringer of Joy of Montronvarr."

"It is a great honor, Sire," Tynae said.

Zandore puffed. *"The honor is all mine."*

By now Tynae was used to fantastic creatures speaking in her head, but even the deep rumble of Zandore's baritone voice demanded the utmost respect.

"You have no reason to be nervous, Princess. Come in and sit, please," Zandore said, walking to a large area covered with hay. Two small couches and several overstuffed chairs sat nearby.

Tynae and Béo took a couch to themselves, while Ge'annã and Kerszon sat in chairs.

"Relax, Mistress, he is as enamored with you as you are with him," Serry said to Tynae only.

"Really?" Tynae asked silently, then remembered Serry was new to this assembly.

Before she had a chance to introduce the butterfly, Zandore spoke. *"Who is the lovely little creature on your shoulder, Lady Tynae?"*

Tynae answered him verbally. "I am so sorry. Please forgive my lack of manners, Sire. This is Serry. She is from the ice forest."

Serry fluttered her wings. *"It is truly a grand honor, Your Grace."*

"Now that all the introductions are out of the way we can move on, but I do have one request of Lady Tynae. I wish for you to call me only Zandore."

Tynae smiled. "Thank you, Zandore. I would like to request the same, Tynae would be perfect."

Zandore's eyes twinkled. *"I was wondering if I might call you Kaida? I will explain why soon; just not right now, if that's okay with you?"*

"Okay," Tynae agreed, slightly befuddled.

"I'm sure you have several questions, please feel free to ask whatever you want to know," Zandore spoke in a soothing voice.

Tynae nodded, trying her hardest to swallow that darn fear that just wouldn't go away with a simple gulp. "I guess I'd like to know where you came from and what happened to the others of your kind."

Tynae's eyes grew huge when Zandore's entire body began to shake. For a moment she thought she had angered the gigantic beast then quickly realized that he was laughing.

A low grinding sound emanated from somewhere in Zandore's chest. *"You don't beat around any of those pesky bushes do you? I like that. Get comfortable,"* he told everyone. *"We, the dragons, have been here since the dawn of time. We had but one job and one job alone, and that was to guard this planet and all that lived upon it. Our task was simple in the beginning. The only other living creatures were plants and animals, but as time went on the Creator began to fashion other living beings. First there were gnomes and gargoyles. Then came goblins and other such beings. They served a similar purpose to ours, but did not have the aptitude or patience to carry it out. They were always running off and playing games instead of tending to their duties. We found that they made better ornaments than guardians."* Zandore's body shook with laughter once again. *"Just kidding. As time went on, the Creator kept advancing the intelligence of the new life-forms he created. Next came centaurs, fairies, and elves. Beings one might consider close cousins to the modern day human, but these individuals were blessed with powerful magic. A magic not as powerful as a dragon's, but powerful enough to be a formidable foe in the worst of times. This made our job difficult. How could we govern others if they opposed the laws of the land, if we were unable to punish them? No walls or bars could ever hold a fairy, and no chains could ever bind an elf. There had to be some sort of a compromise. Because I'm the ruler of rulers and emperor over all dragons, it was I who flew to the edge of heaven and spoke to the Creator."*

Tynae's mouth fell open slightly.

"Mistress, seal your lips," Serry insisted.

Tynae closed her mouth instantly.

"The Creator and I discussed the flaws with the beings he had asked us to watch over and humans were what he created next."

Tynae held her hand up the way she used to when she was a child in school.

"Yes, Kaida?"

"Ummm, do the other magical beings still exist and are you still their guardians?"

"You are astute. Yes, the Creator set down strict rules that one and all were to follow or be destroyed. In other words, he said 'play nice together or ALL will perish'. One has a tendency to listen intently when a being that can wipe you clean off the surface of the planet talks. There were a few in the beginning that doubted the Creator's seriousness and carried on as if no warning had ever been issued. Let us just say that when the gods above choose to make an example out of someone, no-one will ever forget the rules again.

"So peace ensued. This does not mean that the magical beings miraculously turned into saints. That would never be expected of anyone, but they did learn to control their maliciousness." With a huff, white smoke wafted from Zandore's nostrils. *"Then came the humans. Because they were only made of flesh and bone, had no magical powers, and only lived a short time; they were given only basic rules to follow. We lived among them, guarding them for many generations, but an illness came*

that destroyed hundreds of thousands of them. We stayed with the humans until the first dragon took ill. It was at that point we had to leave. We could not risk the destruction of our own kind. While humans breed like rabbits, dragons do not. We only have the ability to mate every few years. That is, if we are fortunate enough to find a mate. Once we have a youngling, we must care for it for the first few years of its life. Having more than one youngling would be suicide. Those little buggers will eat you out of house and home then come back for seconds.

"We did return to the humans, but by that time decades had passed. We needed to be certain that the disease had been eradicated. Most of the humans we had befriended were no more and the young ones that were now running their cities had never known us, therefore they feared us. That is where most of our troubles began. Most humans are very predictable. They fear that which they do not understand and they demand to have superior control over everyone and everything. Bottom line, they're greedy. If they cannot control a 'thing', profit from it, or humiliate it; they will find a way to destroy it.

"When we first made our re-appearance the humans feared us terribly. Once they realized we were not going to burn down their towns and eat them for snacks, they started looking at us in a much different light. The metallic luster of our scales was very intriguing to them. When they found out we possessed magic they wanted to make it theirs. Here is where the greed set in. When they killed the first of my kin, they soon discovered they could not possess our magic. Yet the Dark Ones among them found our bits and pieces rather potent in potions."

Tynae raised her finger.

Zandore nodded.

"When you say 'pieces'?" Tynae choked on the word, "Which ones would they use and why?"

"Everything about us is magical. Our power does not emanate from one specific body part. Our entire body is made of magic, even our essence, what you would call your soul." Zandore clarified. *"Our horns, claws, scales, you name it; not*

even bones where left when they got through dismantling our fallen brothers and sisters. The humans ground up whatever part they needed and used it in potions. They soon discovered that death awaited most that drank the tainted draught." Zandore repositioned himself in his sitting area.

"Needless to say that many of my 'living' brothers and sisters did not take to the humans actions very kindly and showed them exactly how a dragon could bring winged death from the heavens. I was able to rein most of the dragons back in, but there were a few loose cannons I could not settle down. The mighty one from above made shining examples out of them." Zandore huffed. *"The Creator did not want to wipe us from the planet, but we could clearly not co-exist with the humans. So there was a new compromise. We would remain here on earth, but we would be cloaked by an invisible veil human eyes cannot see through. And so it was, all things not of the 'human' world became hidden for all time."*

Tynae just sat there for a moment or two, trying to absorb everything. Then the questions started pouring in. "Are you the last of your kind?"

"No, we still exist. Only in much smaller numbers. Once we outnumbered humans two to one. Now we are only a small few, seventy-seven to date. We are hoping for a few new additions in the spring."

Tynae grinned. "Have you always lived in Calai and where do the other dragons live now?"

"I was born in Calai. I have always been dragon to the reigning Chief and will remain such until the day I pass, which like the Greer may be never. As for the others, they live in hiding as I do among the other eleven tribes of Guardians. Those who do not specifically guard a tribe live throughout the world, but the majority live in the Brantin Mountain range near the edge of heaven."

Much more relaxed, Tynae was letting the questions flow. "Do you have any offspring?"

"Can we come back to that one?"

Tynae shrugged. "Okay." It took her a minute to think of her next question. "How old did the Chief say you were? Don't answer that if its an inappropriate question," she added, not knowing if she was crossing any lines.

Zandore's body vibrated with laughter. *"You may ask anything of me, youngling. It is how one learns. I am nearly a million now, 996,334 to be exact,"* Zandore stated proudly.

Tynae did not know enough about dragons to know what types of questions to ask, so she thought hard about what to ask next.

"There is plenty of time for you to ask me questions. I'm not going anywhere and neither are you, at least not for the time being. You may come and see me anytime you would like," Zandore assured Tynae.

Tynae grinned. "I do have one more question, if I may?"

"By all means, please."

"The veil that conceals the magical creatures, can humans ever see beyond it?"

"Ahhh, very astute indeed. Yes, there are certain humans that can see beyond the veil at all times. Magic has chosen them, but it usually takes the magic of a fantastic creature like a fairy or hobgoblin to allow temporary sight. Fantastic creatures can also choose to reveal themselves to humans whenever they wish. This is why you can see me. The few humans that can see through the veil seldom reveal their special sight to another for fear of being locked away. Then there are the few that have had the veil permanently lifted. This can only be done by a dragon," Zandore explained.

Tynae nodded, but did not speak.

"Would you like for me to remove the veil from your eyes?"

Tynae's expression went blank. She hadn't thought of that. "You would do that for me?"

Serry flew to Béo's shoulder.

"Actually I think it is necessary. You have been here long enough to know that what your eyes see is not always real. Come to me."

Tynae's heart began pounding uncontrollably, yet again. She knew the dragon would never hurt her, but apparently her body didn't know this because it was trembling with fear. Tynae stood before the enormous creature and waited.

"Try and keep your eyes open," Zandore instructed.

"Okay," Tynae choked.

Zandore put his muzzle right up to Tynae's face; the warm air from his nostrils blowing her hair back.

Standing straight and tall like the warrior she was, Tynae did not move.

"Good," Zandore complimented opening his enormous mouth.

Tynae saw hundreds of razor sharp teeth lining his massive jaw and four huge fangs. His forked tongue twitched slightly then it happened. Flames shot out of his mouth, but they were not flames of fire nor were they flames of ice. They were flames made from his very essence. A cool feeling rushed over Tynae's entire body. It was exhilarating, refreshing, and absolutely terrifying. When it was all finished, Tynae blinked a few times then looked around the room.

Looking toward a corner, her eyes grew wide, seeing a tiny little man standing there.

"That's Nazeer, he's a gnome. He helps me with everything. I'd be lost without him."

Taking off his pointed green hat the gnome bowed to Tynae, revealing his shiny bald head.

Nazeer couldn't have been more than a meter tall. He was pudgy with a long white beard that almost touched the floor and rosy pink cheeks…He was quite adorable.

"You may sit now if you wish," Zandore told Tynae then turned toward Béo. *"I believe you are next, only if you want to of course."*

Béo hadn't said a word since they had arrived, and apparently he was now unable to speak at all.

Walking back to the couch, Serry flew to Tynae's shoulder. Smiling, Tynae stood in front of Béo holding her hands out.

Taking her hands willingly, he stood up.

"It doesn't hurt," she whispered. "It's rather exhilarating, actually." Kissing him on the cheek, she gave him a light nudge.

When Béo came back to their couch, he took Tynae's hand in his.

No-one spoke for a few moments.

"I believe you asked if I had any children. The answer is no, not until recently actually. The three of us…that is Kerszon, Ge'annã and I…have decided to fill you in on everything we know about your life; past, present, and future, and what happened on the night you came to Calai. Would you like to know all this?" Zandore paused. *"I will warn you, the picture is not always pretty, as we have established what we see with our eyes is very often not real."*

Tynae had not expected anything like this. She took Zandore's warning quite literally. *Do I really want to know everything at this very moment in time? Am I ready to hear the whole truth?* She wondered thinking back on her father's wise words. 'Once the ink is on the page it cannot be put back into the bottle, it will remain there for all eternity. Not even fire can erase the words that have been permanently etched upon the pages of one's mind.'

She thought back to her last night in Pathrow, standing in the doorway of Darvah, wind rushing past her. Her feelings from that night came hurtling back into her mind. 'I am ready for anything destiny has in store for me.'

She then thought about what Gwillim and the other soldiers. *What could possibly be worse than treachery, attempted murder, and death?*

Tynae looked at Zandore thoughtfully and nodded. "Yes, I want to know everything," she said softly.

Béo squeezed her hand and Zandore began.

Chapter 55
Too Much Information?

"Ye shall know the truth, and the truth shall make you free."
~Bible, John-8:32

"I have to say, first and foremost, that every one of us in this room loves you dearly. From the day you were born, we saw to it that you were looked after by one of our kind every second of every day. We also knew that one day Arona would try to have you killed. This is why for the last ten years the strongest of the Archimagi from around the world have resided in Calai. We knew that you would come to us, but we didn't know how or when."

Tynae looked at Béo.

"Master Béo was not privy to any of this information until late. Had he not been the one to bring you to us, he would probably still not know."

Tynae squeezed Béo's hand and with her free hand gently clasped the heart that hung around her neck, rubbing it between her fingers.

"Thirty-four years ago Kerszon came to me with a dilemma. A young lady had been born, the 'Chosen One', the one that we had been told would bring hope and love back into this backward world of ours…You had been born."

Tynae tensed.

Béo rubbed the back of her hand lightly with his thumb.

"The problem was that many wanted you dead, and we knew one would come very close to accomplishing this heinous deed. There were certain things we had to allow to happen and pray that with the proper preparations, perfect timing, and lots of faith, you would be saved. So we began putting our strategy together the very day you were born. We wanted to make you strong. We wanted to ensure that you would be stronger than any being, dragon, elf, or magus, had ever been. I suggested that we

put a piece of my soul star into you, but we had to KNOW that you would not turn on us. God help us if you ever did."

"Soul star?"

"Yes, you see, when a dragon is born, within its being, at its very core is a tiny crystal no bigger than a speck of sand. We call this our soul star. It holds not only the essence of a dragon, but its secrets and magic as well. This speck grows with the dragon. As it becomes larger it resembles a star, hence the name. Over time, we have learned how to share the power that resides within our star with other dragons. I wanted to share my soul star with you, but we had never shared our energy with a human.

"Ge'annã and I went to work on figuring out how to place the stone within you, and Kerszon set off around the world. You see, with each day that passes those who want to corrupt the world become stronger. Their stranglehold on society gets tighter and the lack of oxygen prevents the humans from seeing clearly. Kerszon traveled to the other eleven tribes, taking with him the fragment of my star that I had contributed. Each tribe infused it with their strongest bits of power. To shorten a fairly long story, you plummeted to your death."

When Béo flinched at Zandore's words, Tynae scooted closer to him.

"Young Master here found you and we were ready. The Archimagi brought you back from beyond the veil of death, and once you were stable enough, I hummed my star into your heart. You are now the most powerful being in the entire world. The only exception would be our Creator, but he is not of this world, so we do not count him."

Tynae let her necklace slide between her fingers as she touched her hand to the area over her heart. She hadn't noticed it before, but a distinct warmth radiated from her chest. She would have described it as an invisible, palpable glow.

"You asked if I had children, the answer is yes. Over the centuries my loyalties have always remained with the Chief of Calai and as such I was unable to find a suitable mate. I was one of the fortunate few who had the privilege of watching over you

as you matured, and I grew to love you. It wasn't difficult to do. I loved you as a proud father loves his only child. I could not imagine a more perfect daughter. This is why I willingly gave you a piece of my very soul." A single glistening tear fell from Zandore's huge purple eye.

Letting go of Béo's hand, Tynae walked over to Zandore. Wrapping her arms tight around his neck, she comforted him.

"You may be the size of a toothpick, and you may not have big shiny scales; but you have a heart ten times, nay a million times, bigger than any man, beast, or creature I have ever known...Kaida means 'little dragon'. May I call you by this name?" Zandore asked lovingly.

Tynae's eyes filled with tears. "I would be honored if you called me Kaida, and I would be even more honored if you were to truly consider me your daughter. After all it was *your* love that saved me that night wasn't it?"

All eyes in the room were on Tynae now.

"Astute could be the wrong word, genius may be more appropriate. Yes it was I that concealed you in the forest, deflected the artillery, and flew at your side once you had jumped. I could not let one that I loved so dearly end her life thinking she was all alone. The storm allowed me to disguise myself as a ball of lightning and together we flew. Unfortunately the Creator had forbidden me from doing any more than that, at least until you were in Calai. But here you are."

Tynae squeezed Zandore's neck even tighter. "Thank you," she whispered. "So what happens now?" Tynae asked, accepting a handkerchief from Nazeer.

"Training," Kerszon said brightly. "And then...more training. You will spend much time over the next few years with the different tribes. Each will show you how to perfect the gift they have bestowed upon you," he explained.

Tynae looked around the room, her gaze falling upon Béo. "So what gifts did I receive from the Greer?" she asked, never taking her eyes off Béo.

Kerszon chuckled. "Do not judge him too harshly, Tynae. Until this very moment, he had no idea what had been done that night. All he knew was that you were the 'Chosen One'. Plus, I may have made him swear an oath or two," Kerszon joked lightly. "As for the gift you have received from the Greer, there is more than one. The most powerful being the ability to control other living things."

Tynae's head swiveled around like an owl's.

Kerszon just smiled. "We will begin working on that soon enough. Until then we must continue your hand-to-hand, as well as other fighting skills. Chenoa will be teaching you herbology. Zandore and I will educate you in the fine art of star reading, and I believe Serry there has a few tricks up her...wing."

Tynae went back to sit with Béo.
"Here is where the picture takes a questionable turn, Kaida. We know a little about your mother, but nothing about your father. One of your parents was Greer and we don't believe it was your mother. Serry, could you elaborate on this?" Zandore asked.

Serry fluttered to Kerszon's shoulder. *"I can,"* Serry said to the room. *"Mistress, the man who has raised you is not your biological father, but he loves you as such and believes you to be his flesh and blood. Your mother was Clair'letté. She came from the Creator's right hand as you have. Just to set the record straight; until this very moment in time, no-one knew any of this."*

Tynae stared blankly at Kerszon's shoulder, listening to Serry with utter astonishment.

"Your mother fell in love with Raith, who is truly the most powerful Archimagus who has ever lived and still lives to this day. Astute as you are, I am certain you have surmised by now that he is Greer. Your parents were the two most powerful beings who ever walked this planet...until you, of course. Master Béo, Chief Kerszon, and Emperor Zandore will have to give you a crash course in what being Greer entails. But you are like no Greer that has been, nor will there ever be another like you. You

break all the rules, whether you want to or not. Your indacaté are coming in quite nicely, but you have them in all three places they are known to present themselves. If you were a typical Greer, then you would have only one on the back of your neck. No-one knows what this means, and so we shall all wait patiently to see how this development unfolds." Serry paused.

Tynae said nothing. She was in too much shock to even blink.

"Do not harbor ill feelings for your mother. She only wanted the best for you. She made two life-changing decisions. She allowed herself to fall in love with a man that was forbidden to her and she chose to give her life in order for yours to be spared. She did love Yurgon, never doubt that. Their love for each other was very real, but her true love was Raith. If at any point you decide you would like to meet him, please let me know and I will see to it."

Béo gently took Tynae's hands in his and turned them so her wrists were facing up.

Looking down Tynae noticed for the first time faint marks resembling veins beginning to form symbols. She looked at Béo with tear-filled eyes. The bottle of ink had just spilled onto the page and everything she had ever known was now washed away. None of it had been real. Her life in Pathrow had always been temporary. Her father was just a stand in, and the person she thought she was, was now no more. *Can I really do this?* She wondered. Why was I chosen? I just need *to understand all of this a bit better. My father…who's blood runs through my veins?*

"Are you alright, little one," Zandore asked.

Tynae nodded. "I'll be fine. This is just so much to take in and I know there is much left to be said…but I think I've heard enough for today, if that is alright with you?"

"Of course, my daughter, I understand," Zandore said compassionately.

Standing up, Tynae walked over to Kerszon. "Do not think I am upset with you. I just need to clear my head for a bit." She wrapped her arms around Kerszon, hugging him tight. Next she walked to Ge'annã. "You're always so quiet," she said smiling softly. "But I'm sure we will talk soon." Tynae touched Ge'annã's shoulder.

It was now Zandore's turn. Tynae stood before the mighty dragon and contemplated her words carefully. "I knew that today's visit would change my life, but I had no idea just how much.

"Know that I love you and you, too, are my father. I feel the love that you have for me coursing through my veins. I promise to spend as much time with you as I can, and I promise to make you proud to call me your daughter." Tynae wrapped her arms as far and as tight around the purple dragon's neck as she could. When she finally released him from her hug, she gave him a loving kiss on the nose. "I will be back, soon."

"Are you coming, Serry?" Tynae asked as she and Béo walked toward the door.

"*Yes, Mistress.*" Serry fluttered to her shoulder.

Béo grabbed their ombra and they were on their way.

Once they had turned down a few halls, Tynae stopped. "I only want to say this once so both of you listen to me very carefully, please. I am not mad, angry, or upset. I am, on the other hand, confused, overwhelmed, and a bit lost. I will talk to both of you about everything that was discussed here today, but I need time to let it all sink in. I don't know if it will be hours, days, or weeks; but I will come to you when I am ready to discuss this further. Can we leave it at that for now?" Tynae's voice was calm, almost too calm considering.

Béo kissed Tynae tenderly on the lips. "Take as much time as you need, my love."

"*I'm not going anywhere. When you're ready, I'll be right here.*"

"Thank you," Tynae said gratefully, and the trio set off once more.

"*Serry,*" Béo said inside his head.

"Yes, My Lord?"

"Would it be possible for you to give Tynae and me some time alone?"

Serry flapped her wings. *"Of course, I will excuse myself once we're outside."*

"Thank you."

Stepping out from the protection of Zandore's lair, the rain was still falling in sheets.

Taking a deep breath, Tynae seemed to welcome the refreshing coolness it brought with it.

Serry excused herself, and the couple found themselves alone.

"There's a place up there," Béo pointed to an overhang. "I'd really like to share it with you."

Tynae smiled softly, "I'd like that."

Béo returned her smile then hand-in-hand they set off.

"Béo?"

"Yes, my love?"

"Let's lose the ombra," Tynae said with a wide grin.

Béo looked up at the thin piece of material sheltering them from the rain and chuckled. Closing the ombra, he tossed it into the forest. "Done."

Closing her eyes, Tynae spun around in the cool shower.

Béo watched in awe as tiny silver droplets fell on Tynae's skin, glistening like moonbeams over the surface of the ocean. When Tynae stopped, she looked at Béo. "I love you so much." She wrapped her arms around him.

"I love you, Tynae. You're my entire world, the very air I breathe." Béo pressed his lips to hers. Standing there in the pouring rain, they kissed with a passion that only two truly in love could ever know. The rain washed over them taking with it the rest of the world. For a few blissful moments they were the only two people who ever existed.

Chapter 56
Reality Sets In

*"Family isn't about whose blood you have.
It's about who you care about."*
~Trey Parker and Matt Stone

Following a trail that was quickly turning to mud, Tynae and Béo reached a cave. Béo waved his hands. Several torches simultaneously lit, and a roaring fire in a pit in the middle of the cave flared to life.

Eyeing Béo, Tynae grinned brightly when she saw the cozy little dwelling. Béo had clearly used it for more than just a place to find refuge for a few hours. There were big overstuffed cushions on the ground, perfect for sitting or even sleeping on. A fluffy animal fur, that looked equally comfortable, covered a fair bit of the rock floor. "How do you keep it so clean?" Tynae asked. "I mean, why is the place not crawling with bugs?" Before Béo had a chance to answer, it dawned on her.

"Magic," they said together.

Béo walked to the far corner of the cave and came back with a few towels. He also brought a dry loin cloth for himself and one of his tunics for Tynae. Helping Tynae dry off, he took the towel from her and ran it gently over her wet body. It didn't seem to help, her dripping clothes clung to her form. Béo helped her out of her rain soaked attire then proceeded to run the towel over her nude flesh.

Dropping the towel, Béo's hands roamed freely over Tynae's skin. His mouth quickly found hers then happily began to wander. His lips slid down her neck, her head willingly moved to the side allowing him access to every inch of her flesh. His tongue danced savagely over her throat.

Tynae's body quickly became an inferno as Béo's strong hands fondled and caressed her scorching flesh.

Béo laid Tynae down tenderly on the plush animal fur. As the rain drops danced outside the cave, the couple made passionate love beside the warm fire and time stood still.

Needless to say, getting re-dressed didn't happen quickly. Lying securely in Béo's arms, Tynae's stomach grumbled. She giggled, putting her hand on top of her belly as if this would quiet it down.

"This cave is fully equipped, love. I do have food," Béo said, running his hand lovingly over her abdomen.

"Of course you do," Tynae chuckled. "That would be wonderful. I'm famished."

After dressing, Béo went to grab some food and Tynae tossed on his soft tunic. She enjoyed wearing his clothes and the fact that his signature aroma was infused in the fabric was an added bonus. Grabbing a fistful of material, Tynae held it up to her nose, inhaling Béo's sweet scent deep into her lungs.

Béo brought back a tray with cheese and crackers and a pitcher of cider.

The couple got comfortable on the pillows and ate.

"Is there anything you don't have in here?" Tynae asked, helping herself to some nosh.

A guilty grin emerged on Béo's handsome face. "I knew we were going to be out this way, so I brought up what I thought we might need," he confessed, taking a bite of cracker. "Just in case," he winked.

Tynae giggled. "I like it here," she said looking around. "Can we stay here locked away forever?" Her voice had suddenly grown sad.

"We can stay here for as long as you would like, my love," Béo comforted.

When they were done eating Béo cleaned up, insisting that Tynae just relax. Sitting with her back against the cool stone wall of the cave, Tynae hugged her knees, staring blankly into the hypnotic flames of the fire.

"I know I'm not supposed to say anything, but I'm out of my element here," Béo said. "I want to help. I can't even begin to imagine how it must feel to have everything you love so dearly ripped away from you in the course of one afternoon. Please tell me what to do."

Tynae smiled softly at Béo. "You're already doing it." She patted the pillow beside her. Asking twice was not necessary. Tynae leaned her head on Béo's strong shoulder. He was such an amazing comfort to her.

Béo held out his hand to Tynae.

When she went to take it she glanced at his indacaté, tracing it with her finger. Looking down at her own wrists, she could see the faint outline of what would soon be her own indacaté…her future. "What do you think they'll be?" she asked quietly.

Béo took one of Tynae's hands and traced the faint lines. "Love," he said simply.

The remaining pieces of Tynae's broken world had disintegrated this day, blowing into nothingness as the wind of her soul blew coldly through her heart.

With tear filled-eyes, Tynae looked at Béo. Words were unnecessary as the pain was clearly etched on her face.

Taking her in his arms, Béo cradled Tynae as she cried herself to sleep.

Chapter 57
Love is Thicker than Water

*"It is only hope which is real,
and reality is a bitterness and a deceit."*
~William Makepeace Thackeray

On this night when Ryedin made his appearance, he didn't say a word. Walking up to Tynae, he took her in his arms holding her tight.

Relief washed over Tynae as she melted into his embrace. In an instant all her anxiety, all her fears and doubts vanished. She was ready to talk. "I love you," she said, thankful for his presence in her life.

"I love you more." He lifted her head kissing her gently.

The pair were in their garden. A cool breeze sent the sweet fragrance of the blossoming flowers wafting through the air. Sitting in their over-stuffed chaise, Ryedin held Tynae tight in his arms.

Lying quietly with her head on his chest; Tynae listened to the hypnotic beat, beat, beat of his heart. Letting out a heavy sigh, she finally spoke. "Has my entire life been nothing but a giant lie?"

Ryedin kissed the top of her head. "No, my love. No-one ever wanted to hurt or deceive you, though I know it seems that way." Ryedin repositioned himself so he could see Tynae's face. "Would you like to know a bit more of the story?"

More. She thought. *I don't know how much more I can take.* Tynae inhaled, letting the breath out slowly. "Fine," she said forcing a smile.

Ryedin chuckled. "It's not as bad as you think. Nothing has changed, not really." Ryedin put his hand under Tynae's chin, lifting her head. "You're still you. You just have a better idea of who you are now." He kissed her forehead. "Do you remember the conversation about our world being nothing more than thoughts?"

Closing her eyes, Tynae lowered her head. She knew where this was going. "Yes," she sighed.

"Does the blood that runs through your veins determine who you love or who loves you?" Ryedin asked.

Continuing to look down, Tynae shook her head. "No, I suppose not."

"Tynae, look at me."

Tynae slowly lifted her head until her eyes met Ryedin's.

"Tell me what has honestly changed today. What has happened to make you love your father any less than you did yesterday?"

"Nothing," she retorted with a snap. "I don't love him any less, not today, not ever. He is my father. Nothing anyone says will ever change that."

Ryedin grinned.

"Why are you grinning?" she asked, miffed.

"Did you not hear what you just said? '*Nothing anyone says will ever change that...*'" he restated.

Tynae thought about it for a moment then smiled.

"So I ask you again, my love, what has changed on this day other than you finding out about your history and a bit about your future? Most would love to know what the future holds for them."

Tynae laid her head back on Ryedin's chest. Quietly she sat thinking. "Am I really the one they think I am?" She tucked herself tight against his warm body to repress a shiver.

"You are," he whispered.

"Maybe they're wrong. How can they be sure?"

Ryedin shook his head. "My love, your light is so bright and so unique that when you were born the entire world knew it. People may not have known why things felt strange or different on that day, or that it was you that caused the shift that they felt, but they felt something. And those who knew your arrival was imminent were always on the lookout. The second you were born all beings, those of light and darkness, knew you were here," Ryedin explained patiently.

Tynae didn't say anything.

"Nothing has changed. Your family just got a little bigger, that's all."

Sitting up, Tynae looked at Ryedin. "But everything *has* changed. I'm supposed to 'save the world' and I haven't got an inkling as to how I'm supposed to do that." She suppressed the distress flowing through her words.

"The same way you would have done it had you never been told what lies ahead."

Looking at Ryedin incredulously, Tynae waited for the magic answer.

Ryedin snickered. "With this," he placed his hand over her heart.

Tynae looked at him like he was a bit touched in the head.

"Okay, and with these, too." Ryedin wrapped his hands around her biceps.

Tynae couldn't help but laugh.

"There's my angel…your smile lights up my entire world." He gave her a light kiss. "It will all work out, you'll see."

Leaning forward Tynae put her arms around Ryedin's neck, returning the kiss. "I don't know what I'd do without you." Losing herself in his peaceful blue eyes, she felt their souls merge.

"Let's never find out," he whispered.
Before she could say okay, his lips were pressed to hers.
The two lay together in silence for some time.
"Ryedin?"
"Yes, my love."
"What if I can't do it?"
"What it takes to change the world resides within you. It always has and always will. You're the only one who doesn't seem to know it yet," he murmured gently.

Tynae saw the shimmering fog roll in. "Looks like it is time for us to part."

Ryedin smiled softly. "It is." He kissed her again. "Tomorrow, my angel."

The pair walked to the mist.

"Do you feel better?" Ryedin asked.

"I do," Tynae smiled.

"Just give it time, my love."

With a kiss, Ryedin stepped into the fog and Tynae's world turned to black.

Tynae woke the next morning to bright rays of light shining in through the doorway of the cave. Looking around for Béo, she saw him preparing breakfast.

"Good morning, beautiful," Béo said.

Tynae stretched. "Good morning."

The dawn of the new day gave Tynae a fresh perspective. Getting up, she walked over to Béo wrapping her arms around his waist as he cooked. Taking a deep breath she sighed, resting her head on his back.

"Feeling better?" Béo asked.

"Much."

Turning around, Béo wrapped his arms around Tynae. Giving her a quick kiss, he smiled. "Have a seat," he motioned toward a small table. "Our meal will be ready in just a second."

Tynae sat down.

After serving their food, Béo joined her.

"You really are an excellent cook," Tynae complemented after taking a few bites.

Béo smiled. "Thank you."

"So this whole 'Chosen One', prophesy thing. Who knows about it?" Tynae asked.

Béo shrugged. "A lot of people, guardians, fairies, mainly people who possess magic. There are several human groups that know of the prophesy as well, but humans generally dismiss it as a fairy tale, though."

Tynae pushed her food around her plate with her fork. "What is it exactly that this prophesy foretells?"

Béo set his fork down. "I don't know it word for word. Father keeps it locked away, but he does read it aloud once a year during one of our celebrations. What it basically says is that one will be born whose light and love shall be so great that it will unite the world, bringing every person together as one. By doing this, people will discover their own light. Together they will defeat those seeking to prey upon the world and its inhabitants. It is said the Dark Ones will repress the population of the world by spreading fear, taking lands, and controlling distribution of food and water."

"How could anyone do such things? It seems so far-fetched. It's no wonder people take no heed in the prophecy."

Béo shrugged. "It may seem far-fetched, but it is happening at this very moment and will continue. It is done so discreetly that most cannot detect the deception."

Tynae shook her head. "I can't imagine the monsters that would do such things are a rational, reasonable people."

Béo shook his head, "The Bringers of Darkness know nothing of peace or equality. They will stop at nothing to gain control over the human race. They've been known to go so far as to kill their own children if they believe that child may try to overthrow or oppose them."

Tynae stared at Béo for a moment. Grimacing, she shook her head. "So basically, I, along with many others, will probably die on this journey?"

Béo closed his eyes for a moment. "No, that is why you were given the many powers of the tribes. The world is counting on your survival."

"It's just so much to take in."

"I know. It will get easier and make more sense over time. Nothing is happening anytime soon." Béo put his hand on Tynae's. "There is much for you to learn and it cannot be rushed."

Tynae squeezed Béo's hand. "I'm ready."
"Are you sure?"

"Yes," Tynae nodded.

"You don't have to take any of this on. You know that, right?"

"I know. But I love this planet and all the people of the world." Tynae smirked. "I would never leave them as sitting ducks for those maniacal monsters."

"And that's precisely why *you* are 'The Chosen One.'" Béo sighed. "If I had my way, you would not be involved in any of this." He pulled Tynae's hand to his lips. "Since I cannot stop it, I will be by your side every step of the way."

Tynae smiled peacefully. "I'm counting on that. I may not have known about my future, or even my past, but with the truth finally revealed, I feel like I have been awakened. I am ready." Tynae looked at Béo, and simply said, "This is where my story truly begins."

*"In a decaying society, art, if it is truthful
must also reflect decay.
And unless it wants to break faith with its social function,
art must show the world as changeable. And help to change it."*
~Ernst Fisher